THE FAMILIAR

Also by Leigh Bardugo

The Ninth House Series

Ninth House

Hell Bent

The Shadow and Bone Trilogy

Shadow and Bone

Siege and Storm

Ruin and Rising

The Six of Crows Duology

Six of Crows

Crooked Kingdom

The King of Scars Duology

King of Scars

Rule of Wolves

Collections

The Language of Thorns

The Lives of Saints

THE
FAMILIAR

Leigh Bardugo

FLATIRON
BOOKS
NEW YORK

THE FAMILIAR. Copyright © 2024 by Leigh Bardugo. All rights reserved. Printed in the United States of America. For information, address Flatiron Books, 120 Broadway, New York, NY 10271.

www.flatironbooks.com

Designed by Donna Sinisgalli Noetzel

Endpaper illustration by Travis DeMello

Library of Congress Cataloging-in-Publication Data

Names: Bardugo, Leigh, author.
Title: The familiar / Leigh Bardugo.
Description: First U.S. edition. | New York, NY : Flatiron Books, 2024.
Identifiers: LCCN 2023044483 | ISBN 9781250884251 (hardcover) | ISBN 9781250357717 (international, sold outside the U.S., subject to rights availability) | ISBN 9781250884268 (ebook)
Subjects: LCGFT: Fantasy fiction. | Novels.
Classification: LCC PS3602.A775325 F36 2024 | DDC 813/.6—dc23/eng/20231020
LC record available at https://lccn.loc.gov/2023044483

Our books may be purchased in bulk for promotional, educational, or business use. Please contact your local bookseller or the Macmillan Corporate and Premium Sales Department at 1-800-221-7945, extension 5442, or by email at MacmillanSpecialMarkets@macmillan.com.

First U.S. Edition: 2024

First International Edition: 2024

10 9 8 7 6 5 4 3 2 1

For my family—converts, exiles, and ghosts.

A mi familia—conversos, exiliados, y fantasmas.

A mi famiya—konvertidos, surgunlis, i fantazmas.

THE FAMILIAR

Chapter 1

✦

I f the bread hadn't burned, this would be a very different story. If the cook's son hadn't come home late the night before, if the cook hadn't known he was hanging around that lady playwright, if she hadn't lain awake fretting for his immortal soul and weeping over the future fates of possible grandchildren, if she hadn't been so tired and distracted, then the bread would not have burned and the calamities that followed might have belonged to some other house than Casa Ordoño, on some other street than Calle de Dos Santos.

If, on that morning, Don Marius had bent to kiss his wife's cheek before he went about the day's business, this would be a happier story. If he had called her *my darling, my dove, my beauty*, if he had noted the blue lapis in her ears, or the flowers she had placed in the hall, if Don Marius hadn't ignored his wife so that he could ride out to Hernán Saravia's stables to look over horses he could never afford to buy, maybe Doña Valentina wouldn't have bothered going down to the kitchen, and all of the tragedy that was to follow would have poured out into the gutter and rolled down to the sea instead. Then no one would have had to suffer anything but a bowlful of melancholy clams.

Doña Valentina had been raised by two cold, distracted parents who felt little toward her beyond a vague sense of disappointment in her tepid beauty and the unlikelihood that she would make a good match. She hadn't. Don Marius Ordoño possessed a dwindling fortune, lands crowded with olive trees that failed to fruit, and a well-proportioned but unassuming house on one of the better streets in Madrid. He was the best that Valentina, with her unremarkable dowry and less remarkable face, could hope for. As for Marius, he'd been married once before to a redheaded heiress, who had stepped in front of a carriage and been trampled to death only days after their wedding, leaving him without children or a single coin of her parents' money.

On Valentina's wedding day, she wore a veil of golden lace and ivory combs in her hair. Don Marius, gazing at their reflection in the watery mirror propped against the wall in the front room of his home, had been surprised by the jolt of lust that overtook him, inspired perhaps by his bride's hopeful eyes, or the sight of himself in his wedding clothes. But it's more likely he was moved by the brandied cherries he'd been eating all morning, tucking them into his cheeks and chewing them slowly rather than making conversation with his new father-in-law. That night he fell upon his bride in a frenzy of passion, whispering poetry into her ears, but he had managed only a few awkward thrusts before vertigo overcame him and he vomited the plump half-chewed bodies of brandied cherries all over the nuptial linen that Valentina had embroidered with her own hands over a period of many weeks.

In the months and years to come, Valentina would look back almost wistfully on that night, as Marius's cherry-fueled ardor was the only sign of passion or even interest in her that he had ever shown. And while it was true that she'd simply gone from one loveless home to another, that didn't mean she didn't feel the absence of love. Doña Valentina had no acceptable name for the longing she felt, and no idea how to soothe it, so she filled her days irritating their few servants with constant correction and existing in a state of relentless dissatisfaction.

That was why she went down to the kitchen that morning—not once, but twice.

The cook had grown increasingly erratic as her son's obsession with the playwright Quiteria Escárcega became known, so Doña Valentina made sure to check on her every morning. That day, as she came down the stairs, feeling the heat rise around her, she was greeted by the unmistakable odor of burning bread and nearly swooned with the pleasure of something tangible to complain about.

But the cook wasn't there.

Valentina intended to remain, sweating in the heat from the fireplace, her anger rising to a furious boil, refining a long rant against wastefulness, negligence, and the cook's general character. But a knock at the door echoed above, and Valentina knew it might be someone who wished to speak to her husband about his olives. It might even be an invitation—unlikely, but just the hope was enough to make her move. There was no one else to answer the door at Casa Ordoño. Her husband had made it clear they could afford no additional servants and that she was lucky to have a cook and a scullion to help her around the house. There was nothing to do but set aside her rage and stomp back up the steps, dabbing at her moist face with her sleeve.

When she marched down the stairs again, a letter from her father stuffed unread into her sleeve, she heard the cook nattering about something to the squat lump of a scullion girl who smelled of damp and who was always stumbling about the house with her eyes on her graceless feet.

"Águeda," Valentina said as she burst into the kitchen, voice vibrating with the righteousness of a good scold, "can you tell me why you see fit to waste my husband's fortune and my time by once again burning the bread?"

The cook looked at her dully, sullen eyes red from crying over her foolish son, then turned her gaze to the table at the center of the kitchen, where the bread waited in its black pan.

Even before Valentina looked, she felt her body flush, the likelihood of her own humiliation coming on like a sudden storm. The bread sat, a little golden cushion in its iron bed, its top high, glossy, and golden brown, perfectly risen, perfectly baked.

Doña Valentina wanted to examine the bread, poke it with her finger, and declare it a liar. She had seen that same bread only minutes ago, blackened and ruined, its dome of crust collapsed by heat. And she knew, she *knew* it was not another loaf drawn from the fire to replace the first because she recognized that iron pan with its slightly dented corner.

It wasn't possible. She had been gone only a few minutes. They're playing a trick, Valentina thought, the stupid cook and the stupid kitchen girl are trying to goad me, to get a reaction and make me look a fool. She would not give them the satisfaction.

"You have burned the bread before," she said lightly, "and I have no doubt you will do it again. See to it that our midday meal is not late to table."

"Will Don Marius be home to dine, señora?"

Valentina considered slapping the cook's smug face. "I don't believe so," she said brightly. "But I will have two friends joining me. What are you preparing?"

"The pork, señora. Just as you asked."

"No," Valentina corrected. "It was the quail I requested. The pork is for tomorrow, of course."

Again the cook stared at her, her eyes hard as stubs of coal. "Of course, señora."

Valentina knew very well that she had requested the pork. She had planned the meals for the household a week prior as she always did. But let the cook remember that this was her home and she was never to be the butt of the joke.

After Doña Valentina left, Luzia plucked the quail and listened to the cook mutter angrily as she set aside the stewed pork, pots and pans clattering. She was making a fuss, but the pork could be kept for tomorrow with little trouble. It was Doña Valentina's manner that had further soured Águeda's miserable mood. Luzia was almost grateful. An angry Águeda was better company than a moping Águeda.

Still Doña Valentina's unhappiness bled into everything, and each time she came to the kitchen Luzia worried her bitterness might turn the milk or cause the vegetables to spoil. Her aunt had warned her long ago that some people brought misery with them like weather, and she'd told the story of Marta de San Carlos, who, jilted by her lover, had gone for a walk along the leafy paths by the Alcázar and wept so long and so hard the birds had joined in. For years after, anyone who entered the gardens and heard the birds sing was overcome by sadness. Or so Luzia's aunt said.

When Luzia had seen the burnt bread, she hadn't thought much about passing her hand over it and singing the words her aunt had taught her, "Aboltar cazal, aboltar mazal." *A change of scene, a change of fortune.* She sang them very softly. They were not quite Spanish, just as Luzia was not quite Spanish. But Doña Valentina would never have her in this house, even in the dark, hot, windowless kitchen, if she detected a whiff of Jew.

Luzia knew that she should be careful, but it was difficult not to do something the easy way when everything else was so hard. She slept every night on the cellar floor, on a roll of rags she'd sewn together, a sack of flour for her pillow. She woke before dawn and went out into the cold alley to relieve herself, then returned and stoked the fire before walking to the Plaza del Arrabal to fetch water from the fountain, where she saw other scullions and washerwomen and wives, said her good mornings, then filled her buckets and balanced them on her shoulders to make the trip back to Calle de Dos Santos. She set the water to boil, picked the bugs out of the millet, and began the day's bread if Águeda hadn't yet seen to it.

It was the cook's job to visit the market, but since her son had fallen in love with that dashing lady playwright, it was Luzia who took the little pouch of money and walked the stalls, trying to find the best price for lamb and heads of garlic and hazelnuts. She was bad at haggling, so sometimes on the way back to Casa Ordoño, if she found herself alone on an empty street, she would give her basket a shake and sing, "Onde iras, amigos toparas"—*wherever you go, may you find friends*—and where there had been six eggs, there would be a dozen.

When she was still alive, Luzia's mother had warned her that she wanted too much, and she claimed it was because Luzia had been born at the death of the king's third wife. When the queen died her courtiers threw themselves against the palace walls and their wailing was heard throughout the city. One was not supposed to mourn the dead; it was said to deny the miracle of resurrection. But the death of a queen was different. The city was meant to grieve her passing, and her funeral procession was a spectacle rivaled only by her stepson Carlos's death earlier that year. Luzia's first cries as she entered the world were mixed with the weeping of every madrileño for their lost queen. "It confused you," Blanca told her. "You thought they were crying for you, and it has given you too much ambition."

Once, though her aunt had warned against such things, Luzia had tried the same little song of friendship with the coins themselves. The pouch had jangled merrily, but when she reached inside, something bit her. Twelve copper spiders spilled out and skittered away. She'd had to sing over the cheese, the cabbage, and the almonds to make up for the lost money, and Águeda had still called her stupid and useless when she'd seen the meager contents of the shopping basket. That was where ambition got you.

Aunt Hualit had only laughed when Luzia told her. "If a little bit of magic could make us rich, your mother would have died in a palace full of books, and I wouldn't have had to fuck my way to this beautiful house. You're lucky all you got was a spider bite."

Her aunt had taught her the words, pulled from letters written in countries far across the sea, but the tune was always Luzia's. The songs just came into her head, the notes making a pleasant buzz on her tongue—to double the sugar when there was no money for more, to start the fire when the embers had gone cold, to fix the bread when the top had burned so badly. Small ways to avert small disasters, to make the long days of work a little more bearable.

She had no way of knowing that Doña Valentina had already visited the kitchen that morning, or that she had seen the burnt bread in its pan. Because while Luzia had been born with certain talents, far-seeing was not one of them. She wasn't prone to visions or trances. She saw no futures in the patterns of spilled salt. If she had, she would have known to leave the bread untouched, and that it was far better to endure the discomfort of Doña Valentina's anger than the peril of her interest.

Chapter 2

✦

Valentina had no handmaid, so it was left to the scullion to help her undress every night, to douse the candles, wipe down the windows and seal them tight, and set the chamber pots beneath the beds. Usually Valentina was able to ignore the girl. She was a good enough worker, appropriately drab in her linen and wool, not the type to attract notice. It was one of the reasons Valentina had hired her, though truth be told, she'd not had much choice. The wages she could afford to offer were low, and with so few hands to help, the work was hard.

But this night, as the girl unhooked the back of Valentina's gown and brushed it down to remove any dust, Valentina asked, "What's your name?" She must have known the scullion's name at some point, but had used it too rarely to commit it to memory.

"Luzia, señora," the girl said without looking up from her work.

"And do you have a suitor?"

Luzia shook her head. "No, señora."

"A shame."

Valentina expected a mumbled *yes, señora*. Instead, Luzia, folding the dress into its trunk, said, "There are worse things for a woman than being alone."

I was happier in my mother's house. The thought came unbidden to Valentina, the grief sudden and overwhelming. But of course there was no greater shame than an unmarried daughter, nothing more useless than a woman without husband and children. Was this girl happy? Valentina wondered, the question forming on her tongue. She clicked her teeth, biting back the words. What did it matter if a servant was happy as long as she did her job?

"You and the cook thought you'd have a laugh at my expense today, didn't you?"

"No, señora."

"I know what I saw, Luzia."

Now the girl looked up, and Valentina was startled to see her eyes were deep brown, nearly black.

"What did you see, señora?" she asked, her dark gaze like a slick river rock. Valentina had the uneasy sense of the two of them alone in this room, of the silence of the house, of her own weakness. She felt as if she'd opened up a cupboard and found a wolf.

"Nothing," Valentina managed, embarrassed by the catch in her voice. "I saw nothing." She stood and crossed the room, sense returning as she put distance between herself and the scullion. "Your gaze is very bold."

"Apologies, señora," Luzia said, eyes on the floor once again.

"Go," said Valentina with what she hoped was a careless wave.

But when Luzia had departed, Valentina bolted the door behind her.

Luzia didn't sleep that night and she took no chances the next day. She waited for the water to boil without singing a word to hasten it. She fetched wood for the fire without speaking a syllable to lighten it. She didn't breathe properly until she was hurrying down the street to San Ginés. Doña Valentina had been watching her closely since the incident with the bread. She wasn't looking for magic; Valentina thought Luzia and the cook were out to get her with some petty prank.

But on the streets, Valentina couldn't follow. No woman of her station could leave the house without her husband or father or priest to accompany her. Luzia had heard of rich ladies who broke bones toppling from their houses, and one who had even died when she had leaned out too far, trying to get a glimpse of something new. She sometimes played a game with herself when she was tired or her back was aching: Would she prefer to sit on a cushion and embroider all day but only see life bound by a casement? Or would she prefer to take another walk to the well? When the buckets were empty the answer was easy. Not so much when they were full.

As she passed in front of the house, she felt Doña Valentina's eyes on her from her high window, but Luzia refused to look up, and walked as fast as she could to San Ginés, the twists and turns of the dusty streets familiar, the mile vanishing beneath her feet.

Luzia's aunt had told her she must be seen at church every day. But when she entered the dark nave, it was her mother who she thought of, buried somewhere beneath her feet. Someone was always being buried at San Ginés, the stones lifted, resettled, and dislodged again, the bodies rearranged to make more space.

Blanca Cotado had died in a pauper's hospital, her corpse paraded through the streets with the other dead so the parish clergy could collect alms to put toward masses said for the departed. Luzia had been ten years old and she'd remembered her mother's words of instruction, of the true prayers she was meant to recite, a secret echo in her head. It was a game she and her mother had played, saying one thing and thinking another, the bits and pieces of Hebrew handed down like chipped plates. Luzia didn't know if God heard her when she prayed in the cool shadows of San Ginés or if He understood the language she spoke. Sometimes that worried her, but today she had other concerns.

She strolled out through the church's eastern door and into the neighboring garden with the statue of the Blessed Virgin nursing. *She might be Ruth*, her father had said, *she might be Esther*. But her mother came from a long line of learned men, and she whispered, *These statues aren't for us*. Luzia's feet carried her down a winding side street that led to Plaza de Las Descalzas and then on to a brick house with a grapevine carved over the door. Luzia visited every few weeks, though she would have come every day if she could. She always carried fresh linen in her market basket so she could pretend she was bringing it to one of Hualit's servants if for some reason she was questioned. But she never was. Luzia knew how to be invisible.

Once she had seen Hualit's patron, Víctor de Paredes, leaving her aunt's house. He'd worn black velvet and climbed into an even blacker coach, as if he were vanishing into a well of shadow, a piece of night that refused to budge in the afternoon sun. To avoid questions for her aunt, she had continued walking past Hualit's door, pretending she was on her way somewhere, but she hadn't been able to resist a peek inside the coach. She only glimpsed De Paredes's boots, and opposite him, bundled into the corner, a slender, sickly young man, his skin smooth and gleaming, his hair the cool white of a dove's breast, his eyes glittering like oyster shells. When she'd met his pale gaze, she'd had the odd sensation she was lifting out of her shoes, and she'd hurried on, only looping back when she could be certain the coach had gone. It was still winter, and she'd been surprised to see that the almond trees peeking over the walls on her aunt's street had burst into bloom, their branches thick with tufts of trembling white flowers.

Today there were no almond flowers, no inkblot coach sitting in front of the house, and Aunt Hualit opened the door herself, herding her inside with a smile.

Stiff lace and black velvet were the fashion now and Hualit wore them whenever she left the house, when she became Catalina de Castro de Oro, mistress to Víctor de Paredes. But at home, in the elegant courtyard with its burbling fountain, she wore robes of colored silk, her thick black hair snaking around her shoulders in waves scented with bee balm.

Luzia knew it was all for effect. A man like Víctor de Paredes had a taste for the exotic, and Hualit was even more exciting than the melegueta pepper that arrived in the bellies of his ships. De Paredes's ships never sank, no matter how rough the seas, and all over the capital people whispered it was a sign of God's favor. But in this courtyard he crooned that Catalina de Castro de Oro was his good luck charm, and Luzia often wondered if Hualit had managed some enchantment over her patron, for her fortunes were so bound up with his.

"Something's wrong," Hualit said once the door had closed. She grabbed Luzia's chin and stared into her face, her fingers like iron tongs.

"If you will let go of me, I can solve the mystery for you."

Hualit snorted. "You sound like anger but it's fear I smell."

She gestured for Luzia to join her on the low couch in the courtyard's corner, artfully arranged with embroidered cushions. None of it was strictly Moorish, but it was all decadent enough to give De Paredes the feeling of the forbidden. And the setting suited Hualit well. Everything about her was soft and lush, her honeyed skin, her luminous eyes. Luzia often wished she'd been born with a bare scrap of her aunt's good looks, but Hualit would only cluck her tongue and say, "You're not wise enough for beauty, Luzia. You'd spend it like coin."

Hualit's maid Ana set wine and a plate of olives and dates on the low table, and gave Luzia's shoulder a quick pat as if she were a favored pet. She was the only servant her aunt kept, a stout woman who wore her silver hair in three looping braids down her back. She loved playing cards and chewing anise seeds, and most important, she never gossiped.

"How do you know you can trust her?" Luzia asked when the maid had gone.

"She's had a thousand opportunities to betray me and never taken one. If she's biding her time, she may well be dead before she seizes her chance." Hualit poured wine into tiny jade cups and said, "Why ask after all this time? And why do you look so worried?

There's a divot between your brows like you took a spade to your forehead."

"Let me stay," Luzia said without meaning to. Autumn had begun and the leaves of the grapevines that twined around the courtyard's columns had turned a luminous orange, dropping away in places to reveal the twisting gray braids of the stalks, the fruit long since harvested for drying. "I can't bear to go back to that house." It was bad enough to fear and resent Doña Valentina, but pitying her, witnessing her lonely vigil at her window, waiting for a husband who was barely a husband, was unbearable.

"Your father would never forgive me for corrupting your virtue."

Luzia scowled. "I'll leave Casa Ordoño with my back ruined and my knees knobbled and my hands rough as sand, but at least my precious virtue will be intact."

Hualit only laughed. "Precisely."

Luzia was tempted to smash the jade cup on the tiles. But the wine tasted too good and the half hour spent eating dates and listening to Hualit's stories from court was too dear. When Luzia's mother had died and the wobble in their lives had become a quake, she'd hoped Hualit might let her work in her home, but her father's mind had still been orderly enough for him to forbid it. "If you work in a sinner's house it will be the end of your virtue. You will never have a husband or a home of your own."

Luzia was hard-pressed to know how she would make any kind of match when she spent all her hours toiling away at Casa Ordoño and seeing to Doña Valentina's demands. When she ventured out to the market, she found herself looking into the face of every young man—and the old ones too. But she'd gotten too good at being unseen. She walked unnoticed past the butchers and fishmongers and farmers. At well past twenty, she had never had a suitor, never so much as kissed someone, barring a drunk who had seized her at the market and tried to grind his stubbled face against hers before she planted a kick to his shin.

She had heard and seen plenty, men and women on their knees in narrow alleys, skirts up, trousers down; veiled beauties in their coaches at the Prado, fine ladies and whores indistinguishable in the darkness; the coarse talk that floated out of the stalls in the plaza. *What makes a good woman?* a priest had opined to a group of performers on their way into one of the mentideros. *She might have skill with a needle*, said a young actor, playing to the crowd. *Or a talent for conversation*, he went on. *Or she might be able to hold a man's cock inside her and squeeze until he sees God*, he shouted, and the crowd burst into laughter while the priest bellowed that they would all burn in hell.

When Don Marius's father had sickened, Luzia had been brought to the old man's house to help bathe him. They'd taken her to his bedchamber and she'd stood with her back against the closed door, clutching her basin full of water, the soap, the towel, whispering every prayer she knew, certain that they'd left her alone with a dead man. She'd watched his desiccated body until she'd seen his narrow chest rise and fall. But when she'd tried to bathe him, he'd seized her hand and clamped it to his cock. It felt like a mouse in her hand, soft-bodied and pulsing. He was strong, but she'd used her other hand to cover his nose and mouth, until he let her go. She kept her hand pressed to his face until his rheumy eyes started to bulge. "I am going to finish bathing you now, Don Esteban, and you will stay still or I will snap your sad little root off at the base." He'd been docile after that. He'd seemed almost pleased.

That was the extent of her experience with men's bodies.

"There must be more," she said, setting down her wine and closing her eyes. "Why teach me to read if I'm meant to live a life without books? Why teach me Latin when a parrot would have more opportunity to speak it?"

"Only God knows what we're meant for," Hualit said. "Now, have another date. They're good for sour stomachs and self-pity."

Chapter 3

✦

When the scullion girl went off to church, Doña Valentina took out her little silver fork. The gown in her lap was not her favorite. But it was one of only three she owned. The new styles were simple and austere. They were meant to emphasize a small waist—which she still had as she'd never borne children. They were also meant to be ornamented with strings of pearls and jewels—which she did not have. She used the two tines to catch at the thread and pulled, making a tear, right along the seam. Something easy to repair if she was wrong.

Valentina didn't really know why she did it, but she hadn't been able to stop thinking about the bread, the cook's blank face, the scullion shrinking away from the table. If it was a joke, they hadn't seemed amused by it. The cook had looked resentful and distracted as she always did. But the kitchen girl, Luzia, she had looked frightened.

Valentina had heard rumors of illusions and miracles at court. Lucrecia de León had dreams of the future, the disgraced prophet Piedrola claimed he spoke to angels, and the Mendozas were said to have a holy sage in their employ who could move objects with his mind. Of course, Valentina had never seen any of these things. She had never received an invitation to La Casilla, let alone the Alcázar, and she never would. *Unless.*

But her *unless* stank of desperation, and as she hunched over the seam of her skirt, tearing away threads like a bird picking at worms, she felt almost sick with disgust for herself. That shame was a shambling thing behind her, chasing her onward, driving her to do her worst.

As soon as Luzia returned from church, Valentina descended to the kitchen. She shouted at the cook and claimed there were weevils in the rice, which she spilled over the floor so that the scullion had to sweep it all up, crawling on her knees to find the stray grains. She demanded water for a bath when she'd had one only the day before, and when some of it sloshed on the floor, she slapped Luzia hard enough across the face to send her stumbling.

Valentina felt breathless, frightened, as if she'd slipped her reins, as if she'd gone suddenly mad. There was nothing she might not do.

"Bring me my gown," she snarled. "Be quick about it." She half expected to find fangs had burst through her gums, claws at the ends of her fingertips. In the glass of the window, she studied the pale moon of her face with wonder and almost forgot to watch Luzia, pulling the black velvet from the trunk, finding the tear, hesitating. Valentina watched her glance up, making sure Valentina's back was to her, and then she heard the faintest, softest humming noise.

Luzia shook out the skirt and brought it to her mistress. Valentina's hands were trembling as she took it.

The tear was gone.

Luzia knew she'd made a horrible mistake as soon as she looked into Doña Valentina's eyes. They were wild this evening, the unsteady blue of troubled waters.

She stood with her mistress in the quiet of the bedchamber, both of them holding on to the black gown, as if intending to fold it up, put it away, forget it.

"You will come to supper tonight," Valentina said. She licked her colorless lips. "When we serve the fruit, you will perform."

Luzia could think of nothing to say except "I cannot."

"You will," said Valentina, a smile beginning to form. "You must."

"I don't know what you want me to do."

Valentina seized her wrist. "Stop this," she hissed. "You mended my skirts. You fixed the bread. You will do this or I will set you out on the street tonight. Think of what it would mean to be a woman alone, without occupation, without protection. Think before you deny me again."

Luzia couldn't think, couldn't make sense of this moment. She could not do as Valentina asked. The magic was meaningless, a bit of fun, a trick of the eye, and in the hands of a poor but pious Christian woman, nothing to fear. But if anyone looked too closely, what would they see? If someone bothered to examine Luzia's lineage, to ask who her parents were, her grandparents? Her father's family was Portuguese. Maybe that would make her past harder to trace. But what of her mother's people? All of them dead and buried or burned, but as dangerous to her as if they stood praying in the street. *Say you are a simple girl, a stupid girl, who learned a few magic words, who was merely playing a game.* And when Doña Valentina demanded to know where she had learned these things, then what would she say?

Valentina must have seen some capitulation in her face because she released Luzia's wrist and patted her gently on the hand. "Put on a clean apron before you join us. And don't hunch like that, as if you're waiting for the next blow."

Luzia went about the rest of her duties that evening in a kind of trance. She helped the cook make the cold salads, and roll out the pie crust, and thinly slice the ox tongue. She filled little bowls with lavender and warm water for the guests to wash their hands. Aunt Hualit liked to describe the feasts at her rich friends' houses where hundreds of dishes were served, and jesters and dancers performed between courses. But fish pie and ox tongue and salad were the best the Ordoños could manage. Luzia carried the pies up the stairs and set them on the heavy table at the side of the dining room. Valentina would serve.

Up the stairs, down the stairs. The courses passed, one by one, faster than they should, an indication that the conversation was stalling and that the night would not be deemed a success. Luzia arranged the tongue on a plate, ladled sauce into a pitcher, listened to the cook mutter *Escárcega, Escárcega, Escárcega*, as if the playwright's name was a curse.

She thought of what Valentina had said about her posture and stood up straight, but it was difficult to lose the servant's shuffle she'd worked so hard to perfect. Best not to be seen. Best not to be noticed. All she wanted was to run to Hualit, but then she'd have to admit what a fool she'd been. What have I done? she asked herself, again and again. What might I do?

The answer of course had to be nothing. She would simply fail to do anything. She would stand at the head of the table looking foolish, maybe spill something on herself. She would endure a bit of humiliation and Doña Valentina would too. Maybe she'd kick Luzia into the street, but maybe she'd take pity, or maybe she wouldn't be able to find another girl miserable enough to accept her sorry wages. *Maybe the guests will go home before the fruit is served.* Luzia looked at the pears, red and swollen with wine, sitting in their pretty dish. She listened, hoping to hear the scrape of chairs as the diners above rose from the table, the front door opening and closing as they said their goodbyes. Instead, only Doña Valentina's voice came, her whisper descending the stairs like a curling finger of smoke. "Luzia."

The cook laughed when she saw Luzia tying a clean apron around her waist. "Putting on your best gown?"

"I hear Quiteria Escárcega has two lovers and lets them both take her at the same time," Luzia said, and savored the brief spiteful pleasure of the cook's mouth popping open. She picked up the pears in their silver dish.

I'll go to Aunt Hualit, she thought as she climbed the stairs. I'll walk to Toledo and start a new life. She'd become a beggar like her father had. Except even that wasn't safe work for a woman.

"Luzia will serve," Doña Valentina instructed when Luzia entered with the pears.

Candles blazed along the sideboard, the dining table, the mantel. This was expected in a nobleman's house, but Luzia knew they'd be eating bread and sardines for weeks to account for the expense. Don Marius slumped at the head of the table looking grim and bored.

Luzia made her slow way around the room, awkwardly supporting the dish of pears in the crook of her elbow, an unwieldy spoon in her other hand, conscious of the silence, the lack of chatter or laughter. She could feel Valentina's eager eyes upon her, the other guests deliberately ignoring her—just two tonight, Don Gustavo and his bejeweled wife.

When at last she slid the final pear from the dish, she turned, feet tangling as she lurched toward the door.

"Luzia!" Valentina said sharply.

Luzia stood frozen, the silver dish in her arms.

"Is there something wrong with her?" the woman whispered, her ropes of pearls gleaming like light on water.

"Put the dish down and come here," Valentina said, her voice high and bright. "Luzia has something to show us, a bit of entertainment for our guests."

At this, the woman leaned forward. "Does she sing? I love a villancico. You can hear them singing down at the market in the morning."

Don Marius shifted in his seat.

Doña Valentina took a burnt roll from her pocket and set it on the table. It looked like someone had thrown a rock through the window and it had landed among the precious glass goblets and old-fashioned metal trenchers.

Don Marius's laugh was unkind. "Have you gone mad?"

"Is it a trick?" asked Don Gustavo, stroking his beard. "I met a girl in Córdoba who could fit a whole orange inside her mouth."

Doña Valentina pursed her lips at the obscenity, but that was all she could do. "Luzia," she urged.

Some reckless part of Luzia wanted to reach for the roll, to correct it, make it a thing of appetite once more, but she kept her hands still at her sides. Would Valentina wait until morning or cast her into the street tonight? If she did, would Hualit take her in? Do nothing, she told herself. Be nothing. If she willed it, maybe she would vanish slowly into the stone walls.

"Well?" said Don Gustavo.

"Well?" repeated Don Marius.

Doña Valentina reached out and pinched her arm, hard. But Luzia didn't budge.

"Just send her back to the kitchen," Don Marius said. "It's late."

"It's not so late," Valentina protested.

Luzia didn't look up from the table, from the burnt bread and the candles, but she heard the misery in Valentina's voice. A party shouldn't end so early. It was a failure of the host and hostess if it did, and if word got out, there would be fewer invitations offered or accepted. Valentina would sit in her window, and she and Don Marius would dine alone. But that wasn't Luzia's problem to solve.

Don Gustavo heaved a sigh and pushed back from the table. "It's time we said our—"

"Luzia has something to show us," Valentina insisted.

"What is wrong with you?" growled Don Marius. "This is an embarrassment to me and this house."

"I only wanted—"

"There is no greater burden than a fool for a wife. I offer you my apologies, Don Gustavo, my friends."

"Please," Valentina said, "I . . . If you had seen—"

"And still she prattles on."

Don Gustavo laughed. "What is it the poets say? God gave women beauty to tempt man and speech to drive him mad."

Luzia didn't mean to look. She didn't want to see the shine of tears in Valentina's eyes, the smirk on the woman in pearls, Don

Marius and Don Gustavo smug and red-faced with wine. She had no intention of reaching for one of the goblets, Venetian glass, wedding gifts that Doña Valentina brought out only for special occasions, clear and perfect as drops of rain.

She smashed the glass against the table.

The room went silent. The guests were staring at her. The woman in pearls had covered her mouth with her hands.

Luzia felt as if she were floating up through the ceiling, over the roof, into the night sky, as if her arms had lost their shape, curving outward and becoming wings. Valentina would have recognized the emotion that spread through Luzia's blood, the wild and terrible potential, the same mad daring that had caused her to overturn the rice and slap Luzia's face. *There is nothing I might not do.*

Luzia clapped her hands together, hard and fast, hiding the words of the song she whispered, a quick, humming tune. She spread her palms over the shards of the ruined goblet and they drifted together, like petals caught in an invisible breeze, a trembling rose of broken pieces, and then in the barest breath, a drinking glass once more.

The guests gasped. Valentina released a happy sigh.

"Praise God," Don Gustavo cried.

"Maravilloso!" said his wife.

Don Marius's mouth hung open.

Luzia saw her reflection in the goblet, changed but unchanged, made perfect and ruined all the same.

Chapter 4

✦

Luzia couldn't sleep. She lay down on the dirt floor of the larder and stared up at the shelves, at the jars of preserves, at the dangling ropes of garlic, the hams hanging like disembodied limbs. She thought of lighting a candle and trying to read, but all she had was Alejo de Venegas's manual on dying well. Her aunt had passed it to her on their last visit and Luzia had hidden it behind a jar of pickled eggs that no one ever touched.

"Poetry next time," Luzia had pleaded.

Hualit only laughed. "Take what you get and be glad for it."

But Luzia doubted poetry would be any comfort now either. She didn't weep, though she wished she could. Instead, she looked into the darkness, unable to fathom what she had done. It was as if she were standing at the base of a wall, looking up and up. She had no way of knowing how tall the wall might be or how wide or what shape the building might have. Was she looking at a palace or a prison?

It's over, she told herself. It's done. Valentina is appeased. Morning will come, and you will wake and start the bread and walk to the market and that will be the end of it. She told herself this again and again, until at last she dozed off.

When dawn came, the air was cold and no one was on the street yet except the cats and the farmers and the fishermen calling to one another from somewhere near the plaza. She walked to the fountain and filled her buckets and tried not to think. Lorenzo Botas was in his chair by the fishmongers' stalls. He would sit there all day, making change and wrapping up mackerel, then falling off to sleep until his son slung him over his shoulders to carry him home.

"The garrucha," Águeda once told her. "They hung Lorenzo from the ceiling and put weights on his feet. Then they dropped him. I don't know how many times. His bones never fit right after."

"Why did the inquisitors take him?"

"A joke about the Virgin. A dirty one. He was always a filthy old man. Maybe if he'd confessed sooner he'd still be walking."

Luzia tried not to think of the old man's knees slipping from their sockets as she walked home. She was not the same girl who had stood in her clean apron at the table, moved by pity or anger or something equally pointless. The night had been a dream, the glass no glass at all but a soap bubble, born and burst in the same breath. If she could simply not think about it, then maybe it had never happened.

Luzia held this thought of nonthinking as if she cupped that soap bubble carefully in her hands. She considered only the flour and the water and the making of the bread, the heat of the cooking fire, the papery skin of the onions as they slid beneath her rough hands, the weeping fragrance of their flesh as they were cut. She noted Águeda's arrival at the kitchen door, the slam and rattle of the pots and pans as she set about the day's work. The cook's muttering was a comfort today. Luzia didn't think about the fact that Doña Valentina hadn't descended the stairs to nag at them this morning. She refused to listen when a knock sounded at the front door, echoing through the rooms above.

Visitors came rarely to Casa Ordoño and never this early.

Twenty minutes later, another knock came, a sudden drumbeat, like a clattering of hooves on the front step. Luzia hissed as the knife missed the garlic and sliced into her hand.

"Imbecile!" Águeda smacked Luzia's hand with her wooden spoon. "Stop bleeding into the vegetables."

Luzia wrapped a piece of cloth around her finger and continued her work. Águeda was singing now, as if the sacrifice of Luzia's blood had improved her mood.

The iron knocker sounded again and again. All morning long.

Águeda clucked her tongue against her teeth. "What's happening up there? Did someone die?"

Maybe, thought Luzia. Maybe.

"Luzia." Valentina's voice snaked into the kitchen. Her step was light this morning, as if she were dancing down the stairs, and her cheeks seemed to glow in the dim light. "Come with me."

Valentina led Luzia to her chambers on the second floor. She had never known the pleasure of anticipation. Marius's courtship of her had been solemn and brief, the preparations for her wedding businesslike. When she'd left her parents' home it had been with all the pomp of a wardrobe being moved to a different wall. But now she was buoyed, borne aloft. Though she'd never been drunk, this sensation was so new, so dizzying, she felt certain it must be the same.

"Look!" she said, her hand sweeping over her dressing table where folded bits of paper were scattered like a snowfall.

The scullion stared mutely at the bounty, a girl who had never tasted sugar presented with a banquet of cakes.

"They are invitations," Valentina explained.

"I know. How will you afford to feed them all?"

Valentina wanted to slap her. She supposed she could. But she was troubled to discover that didn't seem wise anymore. She wasn't afraid, she told herself. It was only that she wanted to be careful as one would be with an expensive bit of lace or a well-made brooch.

She could at least be rid of the sight of her. "Fine. Go back to the kitchen and enjoy your time by the spit."

Luzia went as if she wanted nothing more. Valentina wondered why she'd shown the dim-witted girl in the first place. Because she had never known the pleasure of excitement, she didn't understand the impulse to bring someone else into that glimmering state, the instinct to multiply her delight, to offer it up in a glass to be shared. Valentina began to collect the invitations, little white doves in her hands. She could almost feel their hearts beating with possibility. Muñoz. Aguilar. Llorens. Olmeda. Good names, if not great. Certainly better than hers. These people had only invited Valentina with the knowledge that she must invite them to her home in turn, so that they might catch a glimpse of the miraculous. She had no heavy silver candlesticks, no fine musicians to play for her guests. She could not serve pheasant or peaches in saffron. She had only Luzia, stubborn and sullen.

Stubborn and sullen, and smelling of damp, and dressed so shabbily it couldn't help but reflect on their household. She ran to her trunk. A fine lady would give Luzia one of her discarded dresses. But Valentina had no dresses she could afford to bestow. The rotten truth was that Luzia was right. Valentina didn't know how she would feed all these guests when she was forced to reciprocate their hospitality, and if she couldn't offer hospitality in turn, she couldn't accept a single invitation. All her precious doves would fly away.

"I will borrow." Marius stood in the doorway. She was so startled she dropped the trunk lid on her fingertips and had to swallow her yelp of pain. Valentina tucked her hands behind her back and realized she couldn't remember the last time she had seen her husband at her bedroom door. "We will have meat to serve our guests."

She bobbed a small curtsy.

"This is a good thing that has happened," he said.

She was torn between her joy at his praise and a desire to shout that this was not just a thing that had *happened*. It was not God's hand moving the stars or rain falling over the city. She, Valentina, had trusted her suspicions, trapped the girl into revealing her gift, maybe changed their fortunes. Was it blasphemous to think so? As a sin, pride was as unfamiliar to her as excitement.

"She is not bright," Valentina said.

"Or pretty," Marius replied. "But perhaps she doesn't have to be."

Valentina forced herself not to look at her reflection in the glass, the smudge of her ordinary face. She hoped that Marius was right, that it wasn't beauty life required, but will.

In the days and weeks that followed, Luzia never knew how Don Marius managed to pay for the candles that arrived with their wicks bound together like bushels of wheat, the lamb and pork and fish for Fridays, the sweet wines, and paper packets of spices. She went up the stairs and down the stairs, marveling at how quickly word had spread, grateful for the nights when Doña Valentina and Don Marius dined with friends instead of at home.

The whispers of the hidalgos were overheard by servants and became whispers in sculleries and markets. Doña Valentina had a girl who could work milagritos beneath her roof. Just how miraculous were these little miracles? Well, that was hard to say. It all might just be a bit of trickery—but good trickery. And wasn't the chance for such entertainment worth an evening of Don Marius drinking all of your wine and Doña Valentina's meager conversation? So they came to Casa Ordoño and ate whatever sad stew and scrap of meat Valentina served. They endured the tepid broth and equally tepid gossip, and then, when they'd suffered enough, Valentina would excuse herself and call the scullion.

Every night Luzia would serve the fruit and every night one of Valentina's guests would be offered a slender goblet, its rainbow glass gleaming in the candlelight. The chosen guest would take it giddily in her hands and then—sometimes with the nervous bravado of light blasphemy or the theatrical confidence of a player laying down a winning card—she would smash the goblet on the floor. The others would shriek and jump as if startled. But how could they be taken by surprise when the breaking was inevitable? Luzia wondered but didn't ask. Each night she clapped her hands or stomped her feet to hide her whispered words. The tune would fly from her lips like sparks caught on a draft. The pieces of glass whirled and reassembled, the goblet made whole again.

Each night the guests gasped and cheered.

"How is it done?" they demanded. "What is the trick?"

"Now, now," Don Marius would say, beaming at Luzia like a fond father, his finger ticking as if setting a rhythm to play by. "Her secrets are her own."

"Is she mute?" a woman asked one night. The pearls hanging from her ears were big as quail eggs.

"A servant who can't speak?" her husband said. "Dios, we should all be so blessed."

"Are you mute, Luzia?" Don Marius asked in that same warm way, a generous man always ready to grant a gift. It was the first time he'd ever spoken anything other than a command to her, certainly the first time he'd ever used her name.

Luzia didn't look up, but she could imagine Valentina's hands twisting her napkin in her lap, clutching the cloth as if squeezing Luzia's hand and urging her to speak, to keep her from embarrassment, to please Don Marius as nothing seemed to.

"No, señor," she said. "It is only that I have nothing to say." She had plenty to say. About the thin stew and those pearl earrings and the price of salt and about the unpleasant surprise that even magic could become drudgery. But it was nothing they wanted to hear.

"Never stopped me before!" boomed the husband, and everyone roared with laughter. Luzia thought, *If I could really work miracles you wouldn't laugh so easily.*

That night, she undid her mistress's hair, the braids bound so tightly that Valentina's face seemed to sag when they were released. Luzia brushed out the strands, that murky shade somewhere between blond and brown, a sluggish river in her hands.

"This cannot continue," she said, without breaking the rhythm of her stroke, surprised and pleased at the heavy quality of the words.

Valentina grabbed her hand. It was not quite a rich woman's hand. She had to turn it to far too many tasks for it to be properly smooth. "It will continue or I will throw you out in the street."

But Valentina's grip was like a woman clinging to a wet rope, afraid she'd lose hold and be plunged into the sea. She was watching a ship full of guests sail away, a lighted galleon full of gossip and delight.

Luzia met Valentina's eyes in the mirror. "I don't think you will."

"What do you want?"

"Money."

"I don't have money."

"Then I don't have miracles."

Valentina reached up and drew the lump of pearl from her left earlobe. It was nothing like the warm, glossy dollops that had hung from her guest's ears. But it was the only pearl Luzia had ever held.

It was useless, of course. If she tried to sell it, she'd be accused of theft. And yet still she clutched it in her palm as she fell asleep on the larder floor, a moon she'd plucked from the sky when such a thing shouldn't be possible, a treasure all her own.

Chapter 5

◆

Ten days passed before Luzia was allowed to go to mass. Doña Valentina had invented a thousand chores that needed doing to keep her from leaving the house.

"You can go to church next Sunday," she complained. "Surely that is enough."

Luzia studied the freshly cleaned game birds laid out for that night's supper. There was something accusatory in their nakedness, their pale, pimpled bodies. Her fingers were still cramped from the effort of removing their feathers.

"It is my soul we discuss," Luzia said, dropping her voice as if the devil himself might hear. "Surely *that* is enough."

Luzia knew Valentina would happily consign her to eternal damnation for the sake of a seat at the right table, but it would be a very bad thing if Luzia was not seen attending church, taking communion, making her confession. In the dim light of the kitchen, Luzia watched Valentina calculate the narrow difference between a little miracle and the crime of witchcraft.

"Águeda—" Valentina began.

"I go to mass at San Sebastián," said the cook.

"But—"

She was stopped short by Águeda's cleaver, cutting through the necks of each bird on the table in a series of decisive thuds that made her point clear: I am a cook and not a chaperone.

"Very well," Valentina said. "But no dawdling. I expect you back within the hour. I don't know how you can spend so much time confessing when you have nothing to confess."

I have many murderous thoughts, Luzia considered saying, but managed to restrain herself. She would never make it to Hualit's and back in the space of an hour, but she would go to church anyway. If she was kneeling in prayer, she would at least be off her feet.

Luzia was still puzzling over Valentina's determination to keep her housebound when she rounded the corner that led to San Ginés and a man dressed in velvet and fur appeared.

"Señorita?"

"Keep your coins, señor. I'm a woman of virtue," she shot back with as much force as she could, grateful for the people coming and going. When a rich man approached a servant, he could want only one thing.

"Señorita Cotado, I am employed at Casa Olmeda and my mistress bade me inquire if you might consider a change in position. She can offer you a far better wage and situation."

Luzia's steps slowed. "You're offering me a job?"

"My mistress is."

"It is a respectable house?"

"Most respectable."

"I will consider it," Luzia said, the words strange in her mouth when all she wanted to do was shout *yes*.

On the next street, she saw a wagon being loaded up with goods and furniture. Other pieces had been tossed into the street. Luzia wondered if someone had died and then saw the men emptying the house belonged to the Inquisition's alguacil. As they broke through the lid of a locked trunk with an axe, people hurried past, heads down, eager to be away from the tribunal's business.

"Books and papers," one of them said, and they lifted the trunk into the wagon, potential evidence for the trial.

Be thankful, she told herself as she sat and stood and knelt in the narrow pew at San Ginés. Think of Casa Olmeda. A new position with a wealthier family, better wages. Her hand curled around the pearl in her pocket. Maybe God had opened this path for her.

She thought of the books the alguacil's men had placed in the wagon. What would become of them? And what would become of the person who had collected them, who had laid them carefully in that chest, who might never return home? Torture, exile, a sentence of service on a galley or in a prison, banishment to a convent, death. All frightening. All possible. But there were plenty of bleak fates to be met in Madrid that had nothing to do with the Inquisition.

Blanca Cotado had taken a fall and died in a pauper's hospital before Luzia and her father could find or claim her. She didn't want to think of her mother now, to wonder who had washed her body, or if her spirit had rebelled at the prayers spoken over her corpse. *Leveyat hamet*, her father had whispered as he'd stumbled behind his beloved, as she was carried with the other paupers from the hospital to the church, wrapped in her linen mortaja, like a fly made ready by a spider.

Leveyat hamet. A mitzvah. A mitzvah. He had torn at his shirt, his voice growing louder, until in terror, Luzia had dragged him away. *Be silent*, she had begged him, berated him, unable to stop her tears. *Be silent or they'll take you too.* She'd been too young to really understand what was happening. She only knew that the priests had her mother's body and that if her father kept speaking someone would hear; the words would travel, a spreading stain, until they reached the ears of the inquisitors.

Luzia shook away the memory. The grief wasn't nearly as bad as the shame she felt remembering her father cowering against the wall, his eyes shining, his lips still muttering forbidden phrases. *I will not end that way.* Not like her mother, shoved beneath the stones of this church; not like her father, tossed into an unmarked grave. She reached for the thread of hope she'd had within reach only moments ago.

"Casa Olmeda," she whispered to herself as she made her way back toward the church door.

A hand slipped around her wrist, the grip hard enough to bruise. "I hope you're pleased with yourself, milagrera."

"Hualit?"

Her aunt hissed a warning and yanked her into one of the chapels that was usually locked behind an iron gate. A massive crucifix towered over the altar, the Virgin to the left, John the Baptist to the right, both of them surrounded by a gathering of saints and martyrs. Hualit was in her Catalina de Castro de Oro clothes, cocooned in a long black velvet cloak. A white ruff brushed her pointed chin, her face emerging like a luminous pearl above it, and her thick curly hair had somehow been bound up in a tidy pile.

"You're the talk of all the hidalgos and caballeros in Madrid," Hualit whispered furiously. "What madness has entered your body that you would play such a game?"

Luzia yanked her arm free of her aunt's grip. "I'm trying to make a little money, secure a better position for myself. That's all. The mistress of Casa Olmeda is offering me employment in her household."

Hualit snorted a laugh. "That humorless hag? You can do better for yourself than Vitoria Olmeda."

"Not sleeping on a dirt floor every night would be better, no?"

"If there is even a hint of heresy in your miracles, the inquisitors will snap you up and ship you off to Toledo for trial."

"How else am I to make my way in the world? You have remarked more than once that I am no beauty. I have no talents but this little bit of . . ."

Hualit seized on her hesitation. "What name will you give this, Luzia? Do you think to pretend the angels speak to you with your murky blood? Rome is already pushing for an end to the study of astrology and divination." She glanced at the altar as if the saints themselves might be listening. "The Church owns miracles. Not scullion girls and street prophets. You are no beata doing good works."

Luzia felt a kind of frantic anger that sat in the hollow of her throat, an ache that if she wasn't careful would turn to hot tears and make her look like a child. She took a long breath, trying to swallow the bitter mix of panic and rage and something nameless that had the shape of a bird, lost in the rafters of a building, searching for sky.

"I can't remain as I am," she managed. "My back is already twisting from the weight of water and washing and baskets full of apples. I'm growing old before I've had the chance to be young."

"There are worse things for us women."

Us women. As if they were the same. It was not just a difference in stature or comforts. She and Hualit were not a pampered hound with a silky coat set next to a stray dog scrounging for scraps in the rubbish. They weren't even the same class of creature. Luzia lived like a rat, and her only choice was to stay hidden or risk death. How many times had she complained to Hualit about the misery of her situation? But nothing had changed; there had been no pearls or offers from noble ladies until she'd dared to creep from the kitchen and let herself be seen.

"You say there are worse things, tía. But I say a quick death is better than a slow one."

Hualit rolled her eyes. "You are not in danger of dying from hard work. You think you know hardship, but men have a gift for finding new ways to make women suffer. If they don't charge you with witchcraft, you'll be branded a Judaizer. You are walking onto the pyre and whistling while you do it."

"A conversa is not the same as a Jew."

Now Hualit's jaw set. "It is to them. Never forget that. You think because we were dunked in water and whispered over by a priest, they consider us real Christians? We are poison to them. Something they've been forced to swallow that eats away at the very substance of who they are. You've shown off your little tricks. This must be the end of it."

"Is it me you fear for or yourself?"

"There is room in my large heart for us both."

"No one knows I'm your niece."

"How many questions will it take before you tell the inquisitors who I am, where I live? Before they learn you have the taint of the Jew in your blood? Do you not see where this is headed? Where is your own fear, Luzia?"

It was still there, alive and squirming, waking her in the night like a squalling newborn. Of course she was afraid. But she wasn't sorry. Not when she might carve some real luck from this moment. Her mother and father had vanished from the earth as if they'd been consumed, as if they'd never been here at all, uncelebrated, unsung, mourned by no one but Luzia and Hualit. Better to live in fear than in grinding discontent. Better to dare this new path than continue her slow, grim march down the road that had been chosen for her. At least the scenery would be different.

She reached into her pocket and held out Valentina's pearl. "Can you sell it for me?"

Hualit took the earring and held it up to the light. "You really do work for paupers, don't you? This is shit."

"So you can't sell it?"

"It's shit but it's still a pearl. You didn't steal it, did you? I won't sell stolen jewels. Even my friends have some standards."

"It was a gift."

"I think you mean a bribe."

"I suppose it depends who you're asking," Luzia countered.

"What do you intend to do with the money?"

"I don't know yet."

"Of course you don't."

"I'll buy a hat covered in ostrich feathers."

"You might as well throw your money in the river."

"Then the fish and I will be happy."

"For a time."

"Can any of us expect more?"

"How philosophical you've become in your new fame." Hualit

dropped the earring into her pocket. "I'll sell it and I'll get you a good price for it, but no more milagritos."

Luzia said nothing. She wasn't going to lie with the Virgin and all those saints staring down at her.

Hualit sighed. "Embrace me, Luzia. Quickly now, before anyone sees. And don't look so grim. That will age you before any amount of toil."

Luzia let herself be swept into her aunt's arms. Her hair smelled of almonds, and when she drew back, she expected to see Hualit smiling. But the look on her aunt's face was one Luzia couldn't quite make sense of. Her eyes were slightly narrowed, as if she were fretting over the household budget or dissatisfied with the cut of a gown.

"No more milagritos," Hualit repeated.

Only a few, Luzia bargained silently. Enough for another pearl, a chance to secure employment with Vitoria Olmeda. She was allowed to want more for herself. And even if she wasn't, she would find a way to get it.

Later Luzia would understand that when it came to anything worth having, there was no end to *more*. She would reflect on the path she'd seen before her and how wrong she'd been about where it would lead.

But on this day she only smiled at her aunt and said, "They will tire of my tricks eventually and then I will return to my sad servant life."

"If you're lucky," Hualit said. She gave Luzia a little shove through the gate. "And our family has never been lucky."

Chapter 6

✦

Back at the house, Luzia helped Águeda remove balls of lead from the game birds. She tucked cloves beneath their skin, stuffed their soft insides full of currants and bits of pork, tied their legs together with string, and slid them onto an iron spit, the rod so heavy she and Águeda had to lift it together. While Águeda strained a sticky syrup of pomegranates for the sauce, Luzia turned the spit slowly, high enough above the flames that the birds would cook without burning, her face pink and shiny from the heat. Soon she would baste them with honey and wine so that they might turn golden and become pleasing.

The birds didn't care if they were cooked or raw, their bodies soft and cold or charred and ready to burst with juices. They were past caring what the fire might do. She had heard of heretics and witches being burned alive alongside Jews and Muslims suspected of keeping to their laws after being baptized. Her own great-grandfather had ended that way, or so her father had told her. They too had been transformed by the fire, and their burning had transformed those who watched, the crowds who gathered to pray and be purified by the purging of dark forces from their midst. Luzia didn't want to end in misery, but as she contemplated her soot-stained hem and her feet rough as hooves, she had to admit she was well acquainted with ash and sorrow both.

Too much ambition, her mother had warned, telling the story of Luzia's birth and how the city had wept for a queen. *Too much wanting.* Luzia did long for things—a soft bed, fine clothes, a full belly, a chance to rest, and some things that were harder to name. When she was with Hualit, her mind felt different, as if a dam had burst and the mire of routine gave way, the water racing along, turning clear and lively, her tongue free to get her into trouble without really getting her into trouble. She wanted to live that way always.

When the roasted birds had been served on rosemary beds, tucked between split pomegranates, when the pears soaked in wine had been nibbled on in their bowls, Luzia climbed the stairs and watched the goblet shatter in the candlelit room. The happy gasps were like honey spread on her skin, turning her golden in the warmth from the fire.

Maybe these pleasures wouldn't last. Maybe her aunt was right to warn her. What had she really accomplished? She hadn't so much climbed a mountain as a low hill, but she might as well enjoy the view while she could. And if she was going to throw herself into the flames, why not do it with some decision?

She lifted her eyes from her shoes and met the gazes of the guests. "You all must clap."

"But you haven't yet performed," protested Don Marius, frowning.

"One feeds the goat before one takes the milk," she replied.

"How coarse!" the woman beside her shrieked happily. She nearly knocked her own goblet over as she struck up the clapping, and the others joined in. The laughter felt good this time, maybe because she was the one who made the joke.

Luzia ignored Valentina's worried expression and let the clapping mask her words as she sang her spell a bit more loudly, the magic leaping up to do her bidding, at play with her. It liked the rhythm of those clapping hands. *A change of scene. A change of fortune.*

When the glass came together it made a sweet *ping* as though someone had struck it gently. It filled the room and was then washed away by a tide of applause. But as the clapping tapered off, the man sitting in the corner, at Don Marius's right hand, leaned forward.

"And?" The word landed like a finger snuffing out a candle.

Valentina laughed nervously.

The man had a short beard that he'd used some kind of dye to burnish red. It made him look like he had blood on his chin. His eyes were heavy-lidded, as if the dullness of the evening's entertainment had lulled him into an early sleep.

"We have all heard about your little trick with the cup," he drawled. "What else can you do?"

It was as if Hualit had conjured this man to set her back on the proper path. Here was her opportunity to take her punishment, to slide down to the bottom of the hill and burrow beneath it once more.

Maybe if she'd been born on a different day, or even at a different hour, without the prayers for a queen's soul echoing in her ears, she might have done just that. But she could be no one but herself.

On that very first night, when she had repaired the cup, to save Valentina from her husband's contempt, to save herself from the tiresome weight of humility, she had felt herself rise into the night. She had seen Madrid from above, its crooked streets, the dark gap of the Prado. What might she see if she ventured higher? The old apartment where her mother had pushed a pen into her hand, the slums where her father once sold rags, the cursed bridge where he had died. Roads carved into the countryside, the torchlit walls of El Escorial far beyond, meadows and fields and farmland, and somewhere in the distance, the black nothingness of the sea, the faint glimmer of an island in the darkness, a hopeful lantern swaying from a ship's mast. How big might the world become?

Or she could remain here, in this room, in this house. She could return to her dirt floor and take root like some kind of turnip. She could shuffle her feet and play the oaf. Valentina would beat her.

Marius would join in. But they could all put their delusions aside and go back to what they'd been. All would be as it was, the goblet restored and placed back on the shelf to gather dust after its brief moment of incandescence.

"Well?" demanded the man with the red beard. "See how she stands there like a knob of rock. You expect me to believe God would place real power in the hands of such a creature?"

"God or the devil," murmured the woman who had laughed so heartily at Luzia's joke.

The man laughed. "Surely the devil would choose a more pleasing means of seduction."

"Clap your hands," Luzia said, surprised at the command in her voice. It had the snap of a whip over a horse's back.

The man's laugh died on his lips. Who was a peasant to command a person of his stature? And yet, in this room, on this night, he had asked for her to perform, and so her impudence must be permitted. Such was the temporary power of the singer, the actor, the fool.

"Clap your hands," she demanded, and they obliged.

Luzia felt the song, hot under her tongue like the seeds of a pepper. The noise cloaked her tune, a familiar song, one she used when the coals in the hearth had gone cold. Quien vende el sol, merca la candela. A warning. A chastisement. *He who sells the sun must buy candles.* Luzia could see Hualit's finger wagging, but in her mouth the words caught fire.

The candles on the table and the sideboard had been guttering in their wax pools, burned down to the nubs. But now the flames shot upward, gouts of yellow light that nearly reached the ceiling.

Don Marius gave a shriek as his sleeve caught fire. He banged his arm against the table, trying to quench the flames. Valentina hurled a pitcher of water at him.

Everyone pushed their chairs back. They were all talking at once.

Luzia knew she had done too much and yet she didn't want to stop.

En lo oskuro es todo uno.

The song took shape easily, as if it had been waiting for her; it sent a chill through her like a cloud passing over the sun.

There was no need for her to raise her arm, but she did, demanding the audience's attention. With a whoosh the candles were extinguished, leaving the room in darkness.

Now everyone was chattering and shouting.

"I shall faint!" the woman cried.

Valentina lit a candelabra. Her hands were trembling and she dropped the torch as it burned the tips of her fingers, but her wide eyes were full of happy wonder. The guests were laughing now, fanning themselves, their cheeks flushed with pleasure. Light had been restored, Luzia was once more just a serving girl who had done her best to entertain. The delicious illusion of danger had passed and they could all exclaim about it and marvel over Don Marius's scorched sleeve.

But not the man with the red beard. Only he stayed silent and seated. He didn't look sleepy any longer. He certainly didn't look pleased. He remained in his chair, staring at Luzia, still as a cat that has spotted its prey.

Chapter 7

◆

Huddled on the floor of the larder that night, Luzia kept her candle burning, though she knew she wouldn't be granted another for the week. She listened to the mice shuffling in their tunnels and thought of how quickly her time as a bird, even a land-bound bird, had ended. Rat or turnip, she'd been lucky to live beneath anyone's notice.

She didn't sleep that night. Instead she packed her basket: the end of a wheel of cheese, red sticks of spicy lomo embuchado that she'd helped Águeda make and that had been drying in the air above her as she slept for months. Some dried figs, a heel of stale bread, her second set of linen, and the few coins she'd managed to earn. It was all she owned. Hopefully Hualit could advance her a bit of money against the sale of Valentina's pearl.

She had no warm coat or traveling shoes, but she would have to make do. Maybe she should be grateful she didn't have much to carry, but she felt a jolt of anger at how little weight she had in this world, how little she had to keep her from being caught up in the wind and scattered like dust swept off the stoop.

She'd understood too late what the man with the red beard was, not just another bored nobleman but an informer. He would go to the inquisitors. He had probably been sent by them to discover the demonic nature of what was transpiring beneath the roof of Casa Ordoño. She would be thrown in a cell like Lucrecia de León, only she had no rich friends to advocate for her. She would be flogged and tortured, then burned as a heretic or a witch, or maybe they would decide she'd been possessed by a demon. Hualit had warned her: the Church owned miracles and their saints performed them, not scullion girls with muddy family names. She couldn't blame her mother's stubborn nature or her father's madness, or even some ancestor on her shadowy family tree. Maybe there really was a demon inside her. One that craved feather beds and fine food and applause.

She thought about leaving before sunrise, but she was afraid to travel the streets at night on her own and it was important she not look like she was running. So she waited.

At dawn, she wrapped her shawl around her shoulders and set out as if she were headed to the market, her basket swinging from her arm. Then she turned and made for San Ginés. She probably should have gone to confession or morning mass, but she was too afraid to stop moving. And what good would it do her?

It had been her mother's great-grandfather who had been dragged from his home in Sevilla and offered death or baptism, who had seen the Talmud burned and pissed on, his neighbors' houses ransacked for silver and silks. Once, her father had taken Luzia to a part of Madrid she didn't know. He'd pointed to six windows arrayed in a line beneath a roof. *Careful now*, he'd said, his eyes bright with excitement, *don't look too curious. This used to be a synagogue. You must remember. You must learn to see our secrets so that your name can be written in the book.*

None of it had quite made sense. After her mother's death her father saw signs and secrets everywhere. Luzia had asked Hualit about it and her aunt had flown into a rage. She'd slapped Afonso and cursed his name. But it had been Hualit who taught Luzia those precious, perilous scraps of language, that mix of Hebrew and Spanish and Turkish and Greek that arrived in letters carried over land and sea.

"What's the difference?" Luzia had asked when she was still a child. "My father gives me Hebrew. You give me . . . whatever the refranes are. Both are secrets to keep."

"Your father's Hebrew is as full of holes as his mind. Your mother was the educated one. And the difference, querida, is that my secrets may do you some good." Then she'd grinned and waved her hand over the wilted irises set on her dining table. "Quien no risica, no rosica."

A bit of nonsense, a little rhyme. But the curling edges of the iris petals had plumped and stretched, gently ironed by an invisible hand, smooth as if they'd just bloomed, their purple bright and new.

"You try, Luzia."

The words had tickled Luzia's tongue, gathering in her mouth as if they wanted to be said.

Whoever doesn't laugh, doesn't bloom. The words emerged in a singsong, and new buds burst into life on the iris stalks, their petals unfurling, their yellow mouths springing open, a chorus ready to join the song.

Hualit had seized her chin and there had been wonder in her eyes, but Luzia had seen fear there too. "Where did you learn that melody?" she demanded.

Luzia had no answer.

"Cuidado, querida," Hualit had said. "You must be careful."

Luzia didn't want to go to Hualit now, didn't want to admit she'd been a fool or risk painting her aunt's door with tainted blood. But Luzia had no father or husband to protect her, and if she had any hope of getting out of Madrid, she needed help. She had to laugh at the way she'd waved away Hualit's warnings. Had she thought fear made life interesting? Well, she hadn't really known fear, had she? She had tasted spice and found it pleasing. Now she was chewing the pepper, seeds and all.

She was sure that at any moment she'd see the man with the red beard, or one of the inquisitors, a priest, or an enforcer dressed in black, the white cross on his chest. Maybe a mob would form.

Maybe she'd die as her great-great-grandfather had, though now there was no Talmud to destroy alongside her. Maybe she would never see trial and simply be hauled into the street and beaten to death.

But tangled up with that fear was there a thread of anticipation too? Was there some small pleasure in the drama of whispering to herself, *This is the last time I will leave Calle de Dos Santos. This is the last time I will pass through the back door and along the streets that lead me to my aunt's house.* I will go to Pamplona. I will see a new city. I will survive by my wits. As her father had gotten older and his mind had slid away like a wet hillside, he'd told only the sad and terrible stories. But before that there had been tales of girls who bested kings, and orphans who lured djinn into rash bargains. Now she held tight to those stories. They would keep her alive, not the dread chasing her over the cobblestones.

Her aunt opened the door before Luzia could knock twice and swept her inside. Her dark eyes were so wide the whites seemed to glow.

"Just be silent and do as you're bid," Hualit whispered, gripping Luzia's arm. "You've fucked us now, querida."

In the courtyard, she could hear the voices of men and the heavy sounds of boots on stone.

I should have stopped to pray at San Ginés, Luzia thought, her fear eclipsing every tale and parable. *They're already here.*

Chapter 8

◆

B ut there were no soldiers standing in the courtyard beneath the cloudy autumn sky. Instead, Luzia saw a man she recognized, clad head to toe in darkest blue velvet, the sleeves slashed with cream satin, a fur-lined cloak tossed over his shoulder. This was Víctor de Paredes, Hualit's lover, the man whose money had bought this house and the very clothes on her aunt's back. His dark hair was short, his forehead high and white, his eyes cold, wet, and green as a mossy stone.

It was said Víctor de Paredes was the luckiest man in Madrid, maybe all of Spain. His ships passed through every storm unscathed. The men he sent looking for gold and silver always found it. Blight never struck his crops and his roof never leaked unless he was thirsty and in need of a drink. No one could account for the fact that he had achieved the rank of caballero and was accepted in the best circles—despite continuing to engage in trade. He had a scar shaped like a crescent moon on his cheekbone, the result of a piece of stray birdshot during a hunt, a testament to his good fortune. That bit of lead and iron would have taken the eye of a less lucky man. When people said his name, they tapped their own fingers to their cheekbones, as if the gesture might bring them luck too. But Luzia had to wonder, if he was so lucky, why the birdshot had hit him at all.

De Paredes had a tidy beard and close-cropped mustache.

Everything about him seemed precise and he stood at an angle, as if he were posing for a portrait. Luzia saw that he had removed his hat. Then he'd been here for a while, waiting.

"Go on," said Hualit. "Make your curtsy."

Luzia did her best, trying to remember her servant's stance of deference and to keep from staring at Don Víctor. But he didn't seem quite real to her. She had been visiting her aunt's house since she was a child, and she had only glimpsed Víctor de Paredes twice—first that time on the street and then once, when he'd arrived early, and Hualit had shooed Luzia into the kitchen with Ana, who hadn't looked up from the pot she was stirring. Luzia had waited for them to leave the courtyard and then scurried out to the street, doing her best to ignore the sounds of her aunt's sighs and laughter.

Now he had appeared like a man in costume, an actor in a play, but she had no idea what role he'd come to perform. She wondered where Ana was. Had Hualit sent her away, or was she hiding somewhere in the house? Was Víctor de Paredes here to warn them of the inquiry? Or—and Luzia knew not to hope it—had he come to offer some kind of rescue? For all her thoughts of brave orphans and wily queens, didn't they also have help from kindly mentors? Beneficent kings?

Don Víctor looked her up and down. A crease appeared between his brows and his long face lost its dignified stillness. He looked like an infant about to pass gas.

"When you described her . . ." His displeasure was obvious, a man who had ordered something at a high price only to be disappointed upon delivery.

"She is smart and obedient," said Hualit. "Far more valuable qualities in a young woman."

"But for what we intend . . ."

"Another challenge," conceded Hualit.

"A mighty one."

A woman could bear only so much. "If you wish to say I am plainer than expected, I ask only that you address your insult to me rather than talking around me as if I were a candelabra."

De Paredes stared at her as if she actually were a candlestick that had begun speaking.

Hualit laughed lightly but pinched Luzia's arm. "There, you see? A bit of spirit is just what's needed."

For what? Luzia wanted to ask, but Hualit's nails were digging into her arm through her sleeve, pressing her demand for silence into Luzia's skin.

"Has she any education?" Don Víctor asked.

"She's a quick study," said Hualit.

Even Luzia knew that wasn't an answer.

"Tell her what you want." This new voice seemed to come from nowhere, water without a source. It had the lifeless quality of ashes gone cold.

"Patience, Santángel," Don Víctor replied, with the barest glance over his shoulder.

Beside her, Luzia felt a shudder pass through her aunt's body.

Luzia peered into the shadowed alcove where she and Hualit usually sat to have their wine. A man was bundled into the corner, a black cloak drawn tight around him though there was no chill in the air. His hair was so fair it gleamed white, and his eyes glittered in the gloom, silvery nacre. He looked less like a man than a statue, an icon made from shells and stone, a sorry saint tucked into a niche in a neglected parish church.

"I have all the patience in the world," said the creature in the corner, the man Don Víctor had called Santángel. "But this is like watching a cat play with its supper. Let the mouse go or explain what meal you intend to make of her."

Don Víctor kept his eyes on Luzia. "I will see the trick you performed for Pérez's spy last night. Your milagrito."

So Luzia had been right. The red-bearded man had been a spy.

Was Pérez an inquisitor, then? A priest or a cardinal of some kind? And what was she meant to do now? Lie? Say that it had been some silly sleight of hand? She was afraid to look at Hualit for guidance.

"Go on," said Don Víctor as she stood there, motionless. "Pretend it is another of Doña Valentina's sad parties. Show me."

"There are no candles," she said, her voice reedy with fear.

"Show me something else."

Luzia whispered, "There is nothing else."

"No education, but she's learned how to lie."

"Don't be unkind, Víctor," Hualit scolded gently. "Luzia is a simple girl."

Simple, stupid, graceless. All the things she'd been warned she must be. Certainly she was fool enough to end up in this predicament. The crossroads was far behind her, all opportunity to make the prudent choice gone. Hualit had warned her, but Luzia hadn't listened. She'd liked the feeling of the refranes in her mouth too much, the music that belonged to her alone, a small thing, a nearly useless thing, but hers. Maybe the magic she used was demonic after all. She had wondered sometimes who answered when she sang her little songs. What if it was the devil who heard her whispered prayers?

"She's frightened," said Santángel. "And she's useless. Can you not see this is beyond her?" He stood beneath the arch now, like a bat emerging from its cave, still sheltered by the shade of the desiccated grapevines that grew over the colonnade. He was unusually tall, and the skin stretched tight over the sharp bones of his face. He looked at once beautiful and like he was dying, as if a sheet had been laid over a particularly handsome corpse. And he was lean enough that she wondered if he was a priest, or some kind of monk who would fast himself to dust to bring himself closer to Christ.

His eyes had a curious silver quality, glinting like coins, and it was only when she met his gaze that she realized she'd seen him before, that day on the street outside her aunt's house when the almond trees had bloomed. He'd been huddling in Víctor de Paredes's coach, and Luzia had experienced the same sensation that morning that she felt now, as if she were lifting straight out of her shoes. She gripped Hualit's arm more tightly, convinced for a moment that she might simply float away, or humiliate herself by vomiting on the courtyard stones.

"Perhaps some refreshment?" Hualit offered, lifting an elegant hand. "Good decisions are seldom made without a little wine."

Hualit's gesture was as graceful as ever, her voice steady and full of that warm tone that reminded Luzia of a sweet glass of jerez. Only Luzia knew her aunt too well. She was nervous. It was there in the tight corners of her smile, the tense angle of her head. Hualit was afraid—but not of Don Víctor. She was afraid of the pale stranger in the alcove, curled into his cloak like an autumn leaf. She was afraid of Santángel.

"I didn't come here for wine and conversation," said Don Víctor, an edge to his voice.

Hualit gave a brief nod and squeezed Luzia's arm again. "Show them."

Did she want Luzia to pretend to fail? Were they staging a play of their own? It would be easy enough. Don Víctor and his friend were already prepared to dismiss Luzia, to believe she was a fraud. He would be angry at Hualit for wasting his time, but no doubt she would find some way to console him.

Or did Hualit mean it? Luzia couldn't help but think of the look of assessment on her aunt's face the last time they had parted. How had Don Víctor come to be in this courtyard? How did he know of her association with Hualit unless her aunt had been the one to tell him? Calculation was a natural state of being for a woman who lived two lives, and looking around the courtyard, Luzia wondered: Had her aunt set this stage to her own liking?

Well, if Luzia had learned anything from Hualit it was the

value of powerful friends. She might snicker at Vitoria Olmeda trying to lure Luzia beneath her roof, but she couldn't sneer at Víctor de Paredes, her own patron. His servants dressed more finely than Don Marius himself. Luzia might burn. Or she might sprout wings after all—very fine wings of velvet and pearls.

Luzia stepped away from her aunt, forcing Hualit to release her arm. She curved her hand around her mouth, hiding her lips, and bent to the grapevine as if whispering some news to it. It was the first song she'd sung, the first magic she'd learned from Hualit. "Quien no risica, no rosica," she coaxed, words lifted from a letter written by an exiled hand. She would grow Don Víctor a splendid bunch of grapes and he would invite her to be a part of his staff. She could work in the kitchens or maybe be trained as a maid. She'd stuff her pockets with gold coins, and have more than one dress, and pay for masses to be said to help her parents' souls out of purgatory.

The vine unfurled as if eager to hear more of this glorious future, a green strand that emerged from the dead gray stalks, twisting and curling, reaching for purchase, hard green grapes bursting from its leaves in a swelling cluster, their taut skin flushing pink then red as garnets, sweet and round, begging to be burst between someone's teeth. She dared a glance up at Hualit, who stood with arms crossed, her hands cupping her elbows, at De Paredes leaning forward with his lips slightly parted, and at sickly Santángel, his disinterested eyes like opals, gray then green then gold. Again she felt herself rising out of her shoes.

The vines leapt, twining around the column, sprawling over the courtyard in an undulating carpet of curling shoots and velvety leaves. They exploded into thick bunches of red grapes, surging over the lip of the fountain, filling its basin. They climbed the walls, lunged up and over the roof. Hualit sprang back. De Paredes stumbled as the vines galloped over his shoes and twined around his ankles.

Luzia clapped her hand over her mouth, stifling her song. A few notes, a nothing, barely a milagrito, a scrap of tune she used to make a pot of herbs grow in the winter, a white rose bloom recklessly in the Prado to bring herself a little cheer, and once, when Águeda's daughter had wept on her wedding day, saying there were no flowers for her hair, a crown of sweet-smelling jasmine when it was most needed. It was the smallest magic, meager, slight.

So what had happened? Why were they now standing in a shaded bower of grape leaves, the sky barely visible, the vines creaking, water from the fountain splashing onto the fruit clogging its star-shaped basin and dribbling onto the courtyard tiles? Why did she feel the echo of that slender tune inside her lungs, a song desperate to be sung again, louder, the shape of it so large it might crack her ribs in its desire to be freed?

Víctor de Paredes's eyes were alight, his cheeks flushed. He looked like a man who had stumbled into a room full of treasure and didn't know what to seize first. Luzia could sense Santángel watching her from the deep shadows, but she was afraid to look at him again.

At last Don Víctor reached up and plucked a grape from the swollen mass beside his head. He popped it into his mouth, closed his eyes and chewed, swallowed, no sound in the courtyard but the click of his teeth and tongue and throat working, the sighing of the vines.

When his eyes opened, the greed was still there, but he'd lost his unruly air. He spread his cloak over his shoulders and settled his hat on his head. A man who knew what business had to be done.

"An invitation will come to you through your mistress and you will accept it," he said to Luzia. He gestured to Santángel to follow and strode past them to the door, crushing grapes beneath his black leather boots. "Turn your mind to making her presentable," he called to Hualit as he passed through the door to the street.

Santángel trailed him, his cloak gathered tight around his narrow shoulders. She could not make sense of the pity she glimpsed before he raised his hood to hide his face and those strange glimmering eyes.

Chapter 9

◆

"Presentable for what?" Luzia demanded when the door closed behind Santángel.

Hualit sagged as if her bones had gone soft, then marched to where the table was set with the small jade glasses and heaps of cheese and dates that no one had touched. She poured herself a cup of wine and gulped it down, then poured another and brought it to Luzia.

Luzia pushed it away. "What am I doing here? What does your patron want with me?"

Hualit downed the second cup. "Never refuse wine, Luzia. You don't know when you may be offered it again."

"Who was that man? The one with the white hair?"

This time, Hualit tried to pass off her shiver with a shake of her shoulders. "Guillén Santángel. He is . . . a member of the De Paredes household and has been for a very long time."

It was hardly an explanation, but Luzia had more pressing questions.

"Why did you do this? Why did you bring me here?"

"Your reputation demanded it. If I hadn't brought you to Víctor, someone else would have."

"Does he know I'm your niece?"

"Certainly not. I told him you're an orphan—which is true—and let him surmise the rest."

"So he thinks I'm a bastard raised at the Colegio de Doctrinos?"

"You gave me little choice." Hualit dropped onto the cushions and poured another glass of wine. She was one of the most beautiful women Luzia had ever met, but in this moment she looked only old and tired. "You need allies now. We both do. The man you met last night belongs to Antonio Pérez."

Antonio Pérez. "Not—"

"The king's former secretary, Luzia. He is the wiliest, most dangerous man in Spain, and now you have his notice. This is where your miracles have gotten you. You think Marius Ordoño can protect you from Antonio Pérez? You think that the king will simply watch you curtsy and bob your head stupidly and let you return to emptying chamber pots?"

"The king?" Luzia's voice frayed, cracking on the words. "But surely—"

"The king wants miracles and Pérez has promised to provide them. He is hosting a torneo at La Casilla to find a holy champion."

Luzia sank down beside Hualit. "I will have that wine now."

Hualit poured.

"Well," Luzia said when she'd finished her second cup. "I suppose I'm doomed."

"Don't be an idiot. You've been given an opportunity and I will help you seize it. For the both of us."

"Is the mouth of a shark an opportunity?"

"For the shark it is."

Luzia knew the price of fish and how to tell when an orange was at its sweetest. She knew how to get the stains out of linen and wipe the streaks from glass. She knew nothing of politics or influence. "These waters are too deep, Hualit."

"You must get used to calling me Catalina. Or better yet Señora de Castro de Oro."

Luzia gave an exaggerated bow. "My apologies, señora. But

changing your name doesn't change our circumstance. It can't shake the Jews from the boughs of our family tree."

"Let me see to that."

She had calculation in her eyes once again, and at last, Luzia understood.

"You knew," said Luzia. "You knew Don Víctor would take an interest. You told me to stop my milagritos because you were certain I would disobey you. Did you know Antonio Pérez's spy would be at Casa Ordoño?"

Hualit gave a small shrug. "It was for you to decide what disaster you might court."

Luzia rose and felt the wine pulling at her balance. Hualit had set the trap. She'd provoked her and it had been Luzia's own stubborn pride that she'd relied upon, her belief that her gifts must count for something.

"You know the same refranes," Luzia said. "You're the one who taught me the words. Why can't you be the one to court Pérez and the king?"

"You have no talent for politics. I have no talent for magic." Hualit said it lightly, but Luzia didn't think she imagined the bitterness in those words. How had she never grasped this? Hualit couldn't work the refranes, not the way Luzia did. She couldn't hear the music of them, or she gladly would have seized this opportunity for herself. "Think for a moment, Luzia. Consider what Víctor is offering you. How do you think I transformed myself into Catalina de Castro de Oro? Consider the cost of becoming a widow suitable for more than an hour's rutting from a man like Víctor de Paredes. You cannot imagine the degradation it required to make a new name and a new history for myself, to prune our family tree just so."

A stillness descended in the courtyard, as if something powerful might be listening. Fate or God, or more dangerous yet, a curious neighbor. The grapes Luzia had created hung heavy from the arbor, strange to her now, as if someone else had made them bloom and ripen. She had the uneasy sensation that if she held one of those grapes in her hand, she would feel it tremble in her palm, as if it were an egg, something waiting to be born beneath its thin red shell. What might it become? What might she? Could Víctor de Paredes rewrite her history so easily?

"He can give me a name?" A real name. An Old Christian name, free from doubt or taint or suspicion. She could seek employment in better households. She might marry and have children without fear. She might be free to speak, to read, to be seen.

"He must. If he is to present you to Pérez."

Impossible. Dangerous. They were all mad to consider it.

"Your ambition is clouding your judgment," Luzia said, angry at the hunger in her voice, the longing, the greedy thing inside her that couldn't turn away from this chance. "I can't play this game."

"You leave the game to me," said Hualit. "I can play with the best of them."

Not far from that quiet courtyard, Víctor de Paredes's coach clattered over the cobbles of one of the capital's newly paved streets, and Santángel watched the city slide past, the crooked mess of brick and sloping adobe walls, the occasional stone facade, all crowded together. He thought of the winding streets of Toledo, the hills of Granada. Madrid bored him. He was sick of the smell of horseshit and filth, the nattering of people. He was sick of everything.

"Are you listening, Santángel?"

He nodded, though he wasn't.

"It's late to secure an invitation to La Casilla," Víctor continued. "Pérez's little contest is only a few weeks away, but I will find a path."

"I have no doubt you'll try." Nothing was out of reach for Víctor de Paredes. There was no limit to his influence or his aspirations.

Or his good fortune, of course. "But Pérez's other hopefuls have been preparing for months. The girl will be at an impossible disadvantage."

"She will manage," Víctor said. "Or she won't."

His easy tone didn't fool Santángel. Certainly Víctor had hoped to build himself a menagerie before, a casa de fieras. His other prospects had proved too risky, and presenting an illiterate scullion to Antonio Pérez might prove more perilous still. If Víctor could have taken his family name out and polished it to a high shine every night, he would have. So if he really intended to back this girl in this very public endeavor, she'd have no choice but to succeed.

"You're so sure Pérez will allow it?" Santángel asked. "He doesn't like you." Bribes would be of no use. Pérez was the only man in Madrid with more money than Víctor de Paredes.

"He will. He's too desperate to regain the king's favor to bar the door to her potential."

"And what will he find when he opens that door?"

Víctor sighed. "I do wish she presented a more appealing candidate. But you saw what she can do."

"A bit of household magic."

"I know, I know. You've seen wonders. But try to remember that the court has not witnessed the miracles you have."

"You should remember that as well. What that sad, shuffling shadow of a girl managed has nothing to do with God or His angels."

"I am not concerned by that."

"More fool you. Is a title worth so much that you would risk your life and fortune?"

Víctor looked at him as if he were mad. "Of course. And when I'm done with her, that shadow of a girl will burn so bright with holy light the Pope will have to squint to look at her."

Santángel almost laughed. How human Víctor seemed, how at his ease, brimming with confidence and humor, happily blaspheming as if he and Santángel were old friends. Maybe they were. A master could never truly know a servant. But a servant must know his master well, and it was not hard to understand Víctor de Paredes. He was as ambitious as his father and grandfather had been before him. He was a caballero but he wished to rise higher, and for that he would need the ear of the king, something not even Santángel could provide. Since the loss of the armada, Philip had become even more of a recluse, hiding in El Escorial like some kind of wounded suitor, his gift of bloody war rebuffed by England's heretic queen.

It wasn't just the king who was sulking. It was as if all of Madrid, all of Castile, shared his dark mood. Their great navy in ruins. Their prayers unanswered. English pirates laying siege to the coast. The warnings of Piedrola and the dark prophecies of that stupid child Lucrecia de León had all been fulfilled. The filthy streets of the capital were as full of discontent as they were of piss and garbage. Who was this Austrian to squander their taxes and their sons in his endless wars? What if God had turned his back on Spain and her empire? Philip heard their muttering. It was why he'd sent the Inquisition after Lucrecia and her followers.

"You shouldn't be so eager to throw your lot in with Pérez," Santángel warned, even as he wondered why he bothered. Perhaps because after all these years he still wanted to save his own cursed neck, and his fortunes could not be untangled from Víctor and his kin. "The king has no love for him anymore."

"The king's mood will change when Pérez brings him a champion."

"Your champion."

"Precisely."

"A scullion."

"I am a beggar at the table and I must take what crumbs fall to me. Besides, the prospect of the Marquesa de Ardales is an olive farmer's son."

Now a small smile crept across Víctor's face, his scar crinkling slightly. If only that scrap of metal had pierced his eye and gone straight through his skull. Santángel had wondered about that moment too many times. Víctor had no sons. If he had died on that hunt, would Santángel have been free? Or would he have been doomed to sit in place, waiting until a De Paredes heir could be found to command him? "She surprised you," Víctor said. "Admit it."

Santángel would confess no such thing. At least not to Víctor. But to himself? He might as well admit he'd expected another fraud. He'd met countless supposed mystics and holy men in his long life. Monks who claimed they could levitate, seers whose hands bled when they were possessed by visions, dousers and diviners. But he couldn't deny what the girl had done in that courtyard or the way his blood had leapt at it. An unwelcome sensation. He had been asleep for so long. He didn't want to rouse himself to part the curtains and squint against the sunlight. Yet here was this sad servant pulling magic from the air and forcing him awake. And what a girl—shoulders hunched, eyes downcast, without dignity or beauty or fire. A sorry vessel for power.

His stomach growled. He was hungry for the first time in what felt like years.

"She has some talent," Santángel said grudgingly. "But that won't be enough. You expect that frightened, homely thing to survive among Pérez's vultures? If you wish to wreck your reputation and bring ruin upon your family, by all means, bring your scullion to La Casilla, and when she fails, I will enjoy your humiliation."

That much at least was true.

"She will not fail," said Víctor. "You will make certain of it. You saw the power in her."

Saw it? Santángel had felt his bones tremble with it. "What I saw was wild. Unpredictable. A child who has learned to start a fire is powerful too."

"She can be trained."

"How certain you are. And if something goes wrong? Will you see your family dragged to Toledo for trial? Yours is a grand fortune and one I'm sure Church and crown would love to pluck."

"*You* will keep my family from ruin, as you always have." Víctor tugged gently at his beard. "You will teach this girl. You will make sure she conquers the tests Pérez puts before her and that she wins his tournament. Pérez will have the king's favor and be made his secretary once more. The king will have his champion to best England's whore queen. And I will be a count. Perhaps a duke. In time a grandee."

"Everyone will be happy."

"Even you, Santángel."

"Now that truly would be a miracle."

"Of course you will be happy," Víctor said. "You will be free."

Santángel stilled the tapping of his gloved hand on his knee. He watched Víctor's face. Freedom was not something Víctor joked about, not something he ever spoke of. When he had been a boy he had made Santángel promises. That he would not be cruel like his father or his grandfather before him, that he did not wish for a slave. That had changed, as all things did. Santángel stayed silent, waiting.

"Train her well," Víctor said. "Secure her success as the king's favorite, and you will be released from my service."

He couldn't mean it. And yet . . . if this girl could win, if she could claim a place by the king's side, she might be both spy and servant for Víctor de Paredes, more valuable than Guillén Santángel had ever been.

Freedom. After hundreds of years. First hunger, now fear. And all in one afternoon. But they weren't such different things really. This was the fear of wanting something he had forced himself to believe would remain forever out of reach.

Was it even possible to make the scullion a success? He thought of her standing in the courtyard, her white cap clamped to her head, her ruddy cheeks, her rough, red hands balled into fists as the magic overtook her.

"This will end badly, Víctor."

Víctor de Paredes smiled. "For someone, perhaps. But not for me."

Chapter 10

◆

Luzia didn't have to wait long for revelation. The next morning, she returned from the market and had barely closed the door when Valentina careened into the kitchen, waving a letter in the air as if ringing a bell.

"La Casilla!" she screeched, the words like a spell she was casting, and perhaps there was magic in them. "We are to go to La Casilla!"

This was the invitation that De Paredes had said would come. But was it good news or bad? Was God speaking or the devil?

"A palace of sin," Águeda said with a sniff.

"Is it a very grand palace of sin?" Luzia asked, setting down her basket and unwrapping the shawl from her shoulders. She could see the broken wax seal of the letter and what looked like the impression of a horse standing in a labyrinth.

"Twenty-two rooms, works by the great Italian painters. It is said that Pérez had his bed . . ." Valentina giggled at her indiscretion. "He had his bed made as an exact copy of the king's!"

The cook slammed down the lid of the vinegar pot. "The pretense of the man."

"What a thing to get to see such a place," Luzia said carefully. "I imagine all of the women there dress very finely. They must have the most wonderful jewels."

Doña Valentina's fingers clenched around the paper, the

pleasure draining from her face. She looked around the kitchen, touched her hand to the front of her gown, as if just realizing what such an invitation entailed, what it would mean to enter a ballroom in her tired old velvet, with her sad yellow wedding pearls around her neck. How would she arrive with no private coach or horses?

"La Casilla," she said again, fighting for a smile, a bird who had been taught only one word. She turned and made a slow path up the stairs.

Luzia watched her fade upward into the gloom like a dying spark. Doña Valentina rarely looked happy, and Luzia had stolen that happiness from her. But better she take a knife to her hope and Valentina's, before it quickened and found form.

Wishes granted were rarely the gifts they seemed. Any goose who believed otherwise hadn't listened to a story all the way to its end. Víctor de Paredes could give Luzia a new life, scrub her antecedents clean, and he would control her as he did Hualit. Her powerful, beautiful aunt who laughed so easily and never doubted her own judgment, who took pleasure in all things and did as her mood suited. Luzia had always imagined her as some kind of sorceress, enchanting a powerful nobleman, keeping him in her thrall. But that wasn't what she'd seen in that courtyard. Hualit could claim she knew how to play this game, but it was Don Víctor who had issued commands and they had all jumped to do his bidding, even the strange Santángel, who had made Hualit quake with fear.

Don Víctor's whims weren't really what worried her. Luzia's days were already shaped and battered by Valentina's fits of temper. But last night she'd had to grapple with what a performance might require if she sought to climb higher. How was she meant to speak her refranes before Pérez or the king, let alone compete in the torneo? Her stomping and clapping were a feeble shield. What was Hualit's solution for that? And how was Luzia to explain to a man like Víctor de Paredes that she couldn't do as she was bid? Maybe the Ordoños' poverty would save her. They didn't have the means to visit La Casilla, no matter who issued the invitation.

Be glad, she told herself. Be grateful you can go no further down this path. But it was hard to claim victory at the thought of spending the rest of her days chopping cabbage and feeling her life drain into the dirt floor every night. Surely this bit of magic, this little scrap of power had to mean more.

Not so little, she thought as she rolled out dough for Águeda. Amid the grapevines, her magic hadn't seemed small. It had filled her like a well that would never run dry. It had nearly overwhelmed her. She had once ridden a horse with her father, when he was still doing business on the outskirts of the city. It had been a farmer's horse, old and flea-bitten, but Luzia had loved being up high, and she'd felt like someone else, a princess or a fine lady in a king's retinue, as the horse plodded through the dry hills outside the city walls. When they'd reached a gully, her father had said, "Hold on, Luzia," and kicked his heels into the horse's sides.

The animal had come to life beneath them, as if it were an entirely different beast, as if wings might sprout from its flanks. It leapt the trench, its muscles a coursing river beneath her. Less than a minute that horse had run, but Luzia's heart had run with it, exultant with the glimpse of another life for her, for the horse. That was what her magic had felt like in Hualit's courtyard, as the vines thundered into life around her, powerful and only barely within her control, a lunging, sinewy thing that might carry her anywhere. Or that might rear up and toss her from its back, leaving her in a broken heap on the riverbank.

Hualit had told her the refranes were nothing, a secret to be kept, small comfort for a small life. Why had Luzia been so ready to believe her?

High above someone rapped on the front door.

"Luzia." Her name floated down the stairs. It seemed the bird knew more words after all. "Come along."

Luzia wiped her hands and tromped up the stairs to find Valentina waiting, her face pale as candle wax, patting her hair as if for comfort. Would her mistress punish her now, for swiping away her delusions?

"Come along," Valentina repeated. But she didn't turn her feet toward the stairs.

Luzia followed her to the salon, the grandest room in the house, though it had no real view from its windows nor fine paintings on its walls. A fire was burning in the brazier and Luzia could tell it had been filled with coal instead of olive stones, despite the cost. Her steps faltered when she saw the man standing at the window, hands clasped behind his back. That was why the Ordoños were showing off. Víctor de Paredes. He hadn't wasted any time.

She was almost equally shocked to see Don Marius in the room. He was rarely home for the midday meal and spent most of his time in the house tucked away in his study. It was strange to see him in the light of day and she was surprised at how young he appeared. Because he's smiling, she realized. He looked pleased instead of sour and scowling because a rich and powerful man was in his home.

"I will leave you here," Valentina said with a quick curtsy.

Luzia wanted to call her back. As if Valentina could protect her from whatever was coming.

"Don Víctor, this is Luzia Cotado," Marius said.

If the sight of him in sunlight was strange, then the sound of him speaking her full name was utterly bizarre.

Luzia tried not to stare and performed her best curtsy, which was as bad as it had been the previous day. Of all the things she had imagined, Don Víctor in this room, in this moment, hadn't entered her mind.

Marius's chest swelled a little more. "Don Víctor has heard of your talents and has offered to become your patron."

Patron. In any other context, it would have been an obscene proposition. Hualit had told Luzia about the first time she met Víctor de Paredes, how he'd seen her carriage in the gardens of the

Prado and approached her, how she'd told him her name was Catalina de Castro de Oro instead of Hualit Cana, and that she was a
widow so that he would know she could be had without concern
for her virtue or at risk of angering some proud father. Neither the
name nor the dead husband were real, but they did the job of any
good story and opened the door to possibility. Mere days later he'd
arrived at her house with an emerald the size of a walnut and asked
to become her patron. Or at least that was the story Hualit told.
For the first time, Luzia wondered if it was true. If life could ever
be so easy, even for a woman as beautiful as Hualit.

Luzia wasn't sure if she was supposed to look surprised or happy
or fearful, so she stared dully at her shoes. Better they think her a
lump of clay, suitable for molding.

"Patron, señor?" she mumbled.

"He will see you educated and appropriately dressed for an audience with Antonio Pérez."

When Luzia stayed silent, Marius cleared his throat. "Say that
you are thankful and praise God for Don Víctor's generosity."

Luzia knew she should simply echo Marius, but the words on
her tongue somehow twisted themselves. "I thank God for the
generosity of selfless men."

"Very good," said Marius, relieved that she hadn't embarrassed
him. "You will begin your lessons today."

"Walk with me, dear Luzia," said Don Víctor.

He offered her his arm and as they set off down the hall, his
hand slid around her wrist.

"You will think carefully before you speak from now on, pre-
ciosa," he whispered. "I am not quite the fool Don Marius is, and
you are not quite the dullard you pretend to be. Let us both
remember."

His hand squeezed harder and she felt the small bones in her
wrist bend. Luzia sucked in a breath but didn't scream. Behind
them, she could hear Marius and Valentina whispering to each
other, trailing them like attendants.

Luzia nodded and stayed silent, as Don Víctor chattered on about the many rooms of La Casilla and the glory of the grounds and how they would need clothes for various meals and performances. Luzia's wrist throbbed but she ignored the pain. Yes, she would remember. She would be more careful. She had wished for a beneficent king, and if Víctor de Paredes wished to play the role then she would happily be the peasant girl he rescued. She would curb her tongue and master her curtsy and she would find a way to make a success of this. She would snatch this opportunity from the shark's mouth if she could only find a way.

Luzia looked back and saw Don Marius beaming. Valentina, walking two steps behind, merely looked nervous.

She felt as if she was being brought to some altar of sacrifice, but it was only the room on the house's second floor they used for storing linen. It was meant to be a nursery, but no children had ever come. Now the stacks of blankets and draperies were gone and the narrow bed on which they'd been placed had been made up. By whom? she wondered. Had Valentina beat the mattress? Aired the sheets? Smoothed the coverlet?

"Don Víctor asked to see your room," said Don Marius, staring hard at Luzia. "He is most concerned for your well-being."

So they didn't want the great man to know his milagrera slept in the larder.

"Perhaps she would be better served by private apartments in my home," Don Víctor said. "There is plenty of room, and there she might have her lessons without interruption or inconvenience."

Luzia did not like that thought. Just yesterday she would have jumped at the chance to be a servant in such a man's home, surrounded by wealth and plenty. But her wrist ached and she didn't want to imagine what might happen to her under Don Víctor's roof.

"We couldn't take advantage of your hospitality," Marius sputtered.

Valentina looped her arm through Luzia's elbow and Luzia

tried not to startle. "Don Víctor, you are too kind, but this is all so new for Luzia, and she has been in our household for years. It's best that she remain somewhere familiar, among people she knows."

Marius looked stunned at the way his wife had routed Don Víctor, and Luzia couldn't say she wasn't impressed. If the fear of losing me is enough to marshal Valentina's wit, Luzia marveled, I must be very valuable indeed.

Luzia waited, suspended, a wishbone caught between Don Víctor's arm and Valentina's elbow. The Ordoños weren't willing to relinquish her easily. She was *their* servant, their unexpected treasure, plunder from an unknown country. But if Víctor de Paredes wanted her in his household, Luzia had no doubt he would have his way. In fact, he could simply offer her more wages and she would walk out the door with him right now. Money was a wonderful tonic for fear.

Instead he smiled and dipped his chin the barest amount, the gracious loser. Luzia had the sense he hadn't lost at all. He wanted her here in this house, under the Ordoños' roof, not his own. Yet another mystery for her to try to unravel.

"Let us discuss terms," Don Víctor said to Marius. "We are at the start of a great adventure, my friend."

When Marius and Don Víctor had gone, Valentina said, "It is all very good fortune."

She had posed no question, but seemed to be waiting for a response, so Luzia simply said, "Yes."

"I have seen Don Víctor's palace. He had it built near the gardens of the Alcázar. It sits in such a way that one has a view of parks and meadows from nearly every window. One might forget one is in the city at all. Or so I've been told."

"Then he is very wealthy."

"Oh yes. And over many generations. The De Paredes family is well known for their good luck." She tapped her cheekbone, recalling that bit of birdshot that had done Don Víctor no real harm. "But this time it is our ship that has landed on the right shore."

There was ferocity in her eyes, a kind of fire Luzia had never seen there before. Don Víctor would buy them both gowns and perhaps provide the family with a carriage. Valentina must know there would be a price, just as Luzia did. But none of them could guess at it.

"Go on," Valentina said, gesturing to the empty room. Then, as if remembering herself, she added, "Just so you understand, your station hasn't changed. No matter where you rest your head at night."

Luzia didn't bother with a reply. They both knew it wasn't true.

Chapter 11

◆

Whenn Valentina had gone, Luzia let herself walk to the bed. She sat tentatively at its edge, afraid to place her full weight on it. She never came into this room except to gather quilts and bath sheets when they were needed, and to dust when Valentina reminded her to. Twice a year they took the heavy blankets and cloaks from the trunks and beat them in the alley to free them of spiders and vermin. Once they'd opened the trunk and discovered a massive rat lying on her side, nursing the squirming bodies of her babies. Valentina had screamed. Águeda had gathered them up without a word, taken the wriggling bundle of bedsheets down to the kitchen, and drowned them in a bucket of water. Luzia had felt bad for the rats, and then she'd felt bad for herself because she'd had to walk to the fountain a second time that day and lug two more pails full of water back with her.

This was to be *her* bed now. She looked out the window. On the street below she saw Don Víctor speaking with Don Marius. An enormous footman stood beside the glossy De Paredes coach, dressed in mustard-colored livery.

Across the street, she could see into the second-floor windows of a room with blue draperies where a woman stood beside a harp. She laid her hand on its wooden frame, as if taking its measure, and Luzia hoped she might play. The woman looked up, her gaze barely registering Luzia, and moved on to some other task. What was there to look at or take note of? Luzia was just a servant who had come in to straighten up the room.

I sleep here now, she wanted to shout. A roof over her head instead of an entire house weighing down on her. A window she could open at any time of day and hear the hooves of horses, the rattle of carriage wheels, birdsong if she was lucky. There might be more, said that hungry voice inside her, so much more. You might look from the windows of a palace. You might make the acquaintance of a king.

She walked to the basin. There was no water in the pitcher. In the mirror she saw her sallow face, her cap tight against her braided hair. Something moved behind her and she jumped.

A piece of shadow seemed to detach itself from the corner and Luzia had to bite back a shriek as Santángel emerged from the gloom. He wore the same dark clothes, his blond head bright as a cut jewel.

"How long have you been standing there?" she asked, trying to steady her voice. A man should not be in her room, but Guillén Santángel was somehow something other than a man. "You shouldn't be in here. With me. Alone. In my bedchamber."

She sounded like a hiccupping ninny.

"This is not your bedchamber."

"Of course it is, señor."

Santángel opened the wardrobe. "Not a single gown."

"This is my only dress, señor."

"Nor any clean linen."

"You've been looking through my trunk?"

"There is no trunk of clothes to look through." His pale brow lifted. "Not a single sign of occupation. No icon of your patron saint, no candle or dried flower or memento to be seen."

"I am a servant, señor. I have no use for such things."

"Even a servant is permitted a soul, Señorita Cotado."

"Can I be of service to you?" Luzia's cheeks pinked. She hadn't meant the words to sound vulgar, but they'd emerged that way.

Santángel studied her, his eyes glittering. "I highly doubt it," he said at last. His gaze traveled from the top of her covered head to her battered shoes. "You have a scullion's hands."

"Because I'm a scullion, señor."

"And there is dirt on your neck."

"Because I sleep in the dirt."

"So it is not your room."

"It is not," she admitted. Why did she care what he thought of her? Why protect Valentina and Marius? "I sleep on the floor in the larder. Like a common pig in the pen. If you don't wish for me to look like a common pig perhaps you will see to it that I have hot water and a bit of soap. Then I may at least look like a more worthy pig."

So much for curbing her tongue.

He frowned. "You cannot *be* this person, not if you hope to survive."

"And yet here I am." She should be careful with this creature who vanished into shadows and made her aunt tremble in terror. But keeping her mouth shut was proving harder than expected. Maybe it had only been easy when no one bothered to speak to her.

"The weed flourishes until it is yanked out by the root," said Santángel, grim as a priest. "The Torneo Secreto isn't just a game. It is not polite entertainment where your party tricks will impress. Pérez believes that he can regain the king's favor by bringing him a holy magic user. His life and his fortune are at stake."

"Some of us have no fortune to wager."

"And your life? Do you hold it in such low esteem?" Luzia couldn't help but feel he was asking her a different question, that if she could simply listen more closely she would hear his true meaning. He took a step toward her and she had to will herself not to back away. "Do you know why you're being allowed to join the tournament?"

"Because Pérez is desperate?"

At that, he paused and she knew she was right. "One of the competitors was killed," he said. "Good. I see you're listening now. A young monk from Huesca."

"He . . . did Don Víctor . . ."

Santángel's peculiar eyes narrowed. But he didn't exclaim, *Of course not* or *How could you think such a thing?* Instead he said, "No, the monk drowned over a week ago. Long before Víctor had heard of your gifts."

"An accident, then?"

"What a hopeful disposition you have. Men have been known to fall off of bridges. Or jump. Or be pushed."

"If not Don Víctor . . ." Luzia sat down. "There are other competitors in this torneo?"

"Three."

"So, one of these hopefuls had the monk killed?"

"More likely one of their patrons, but yes. Or maybe the monk was drunk on brandy and leaned over the bridge to get a better look at his reflection."

"I should go see to the soup."

"The soup," he repeated flatly.

"Águeda gets distracted and lets it cook too long. It will be too salty to eat."

It was all she could come up with to say. She needed time to think. She wanted money, a chance at a life that didn't end in a paupers' hospital or on a street where people would step over her body until someone had the courtesy to roll it out of the way. But she wasn't sure getting thrown into a river or poisoned by a rival sounded much better.

Santángel drew a velvet pouch from his pocket and upended it over the writing desk that sat beneath the window. It landed with a clatter.

"A bean?" she asked. "Do you wish for me to add it to the soup?"

"I wish for you to show me the talent you displayed in the courtyard."

She couldn't do that. Not in the quiet of this room. Not without some way to hide her words. "Then you're done trying to scare me?"

"If I wanted you frightened, you would be. I want you to recognize the danger you will face."

"Yes, señor. I understand. I will most likely be murdered in my bed."

"You may. But you may also see this through and win."

"Do you believe that?"

"I have lived long enough to believe all things are possible."

He didn't look very old. Ill and headed to an early grave, but not old.

"Possible," she said. "But unlikely."

"Very," he conceded. "My job is to prepare you and to make sure your miracles don't doom you."

"You can keep me from damnation?"

"I can at least try to ensure you don't bring it to your door."

"Or to Don Víctor's."

"Correct. There are certain places your miracles must not go. Resurrection, transformation. Only God in His glory can turn one thing into another."

"Like turning water into wine."

"Just so."

"But don't alchemists strive to turn lead into gold?"

"That is science, not a miracle."

"That makes no sense," Luzia protested, even as she told herself to stay silent. Be humble. Be grateful.

"Take it up with the Inquisition. Illusions belong to the devil. Miracles belong to God."

"And my milagritos?"

"Are the way God speaks through you. At least that is what you will say when asked."

"Why would God choose me?"

"Because God loves the wretched," he snapped. "I've answered enough of your questions, so here is one of mine: Have you heard of Lucrecia de León?"

"The girl who had visions."

"Prophetic dreams. Hundreds of them. She predicted the defeat of our king's armada."

"Then she was no liar."

"Maybe not, but now she dreams in a cell in Toledo, imprisoned by the Inquisition. She will be tried and found guilty of fraud and heresy, maybe witchcraft, maybe more."

"Will they burn her?" Luzia didn't want to show her fear.

"Another possibility. If she's fortunate she will be reconciled, whipped, and exiled. Did she predict the defeat of the armada, or did she somehow bring it about? There is a fine line between a saint and a witch, and I wonder if you are prepared to walk it."

"Have I been offered a choice?"

He seemed to consider this. "You could choose not to enter the torneo. It would spare us all the humiliation of defeat."

Here it was: a new invitation, a chance to choose wisdom over her own pride.

"And if I try to win?" she asked, unable to help herself.

"Then I will help you and we will strive to make the best of all our bad decisions. That means practicing, not spending your afternoon stirring the soup. Víctor de Paredes's commands must be followed."

Maybe so. But they'd reached the end of this dance. She could risk nothing before this stranger.

Luzia shrugged and took pleasure in turning her back to him. "And yet the soup must be stirred."

Chapter 12

✦

Had she really just turned her back on him? This lump of a servant who hung her head like a donkey but spoke as if she were bantering at the mentidero? She wasn't stupid, that much had been obvious in the way she had grasped Víctor's ruthlessness—no, his master hadn't sent someone to assassinate the monk on the bridge, but he could have.

"Why don't you want to show me your skill?" he asked. "Do you use some kind of heathen talisman? Are you afraid I'll recognize the language of your miracles? I saw you cover your mouth in that little pantomime yesterday."

Her shuffling steps halted and she peered back at him. She didn't seem to scare easily, another interesting quality, but this was fear she couldn't hide. If that was what it took to make her pay attention, so be it.

"What language are you using?" he persisted. "You needn't fear me. Not in this at least."

Still she said nothing. She wasn't as young as he'd thought, well past her first bloom if there'd been a bloom. Poor, unmarried, illiterate. Still, poor meant she was desperate. Unmarried meant there would be no fool husband to appease or eliminate. And if she couldn't read then she couldn't write and was at less risk of causing trouble. There was nothing more dangerous than a woman with a pen in her hand. "Arabic?" he asked. "Sanskrit? Hebrew?" It was like talking to a doll with glass eyes. "Whatever it is, you won't get away with it at the torneo. I can help you with that."

She kept her eyes on her feet, her shoulders still hunched, but he could see she was considering, her curiosity captured. "You can?"

"I can. The power is not in the speaking. You can learn to form the words in your mind as if you were about to speak. It isn't hard."

"Sing," she mumbled. "I sing the words."

A beginning. "I don't suppose you can read? It would be easier if you could."

"And easier still if I knew how to speak French and dance a pavane?"

There was that ready wit again, wit that shouldn't belong in this odd girl's mouth.

"Very well, since you cannot picture the words on the page, try to hear them in your head. Listen to them being spoken. Hear the song in the dark."

He took her hand and she flinched. Her palm was thickly calloused and there was dirt beneath her nails.

"Your skin is hot," she muttered.

"You see, I only look like a corpse."

Her brows jumped and her lips pressed together as if she were afraid to laugh.

"Close your eyes," he told her. She frowned. "I have no plans to assail your virtue."

She looked almost angry at that. Some vanity, then. An easy trait to leverage. "This will not work," she grumbled. But she took a deep breath and closed her eyes. Her lashes were black against her cheeks, heavily freckled by the sun.

"Let's hope for your sake that it does. I don't think your clapping and whispering will fool Antonio Pérez." The room was quiet. Her hand lay limp in his. "You are thinking how strange it is to be in this room, to stand this way together. Forget me and this house and this street and all of Madrid. Think only of the quiet, the stillness. All is empty as it was for God before He set about creation, before the first word was spoken. Now, let that word take shape, interrupting the silence. Hear it in your head, a song for you alone."

"The melody—"

"Hum the melody, or sing it. But keep the words to yourself."

Her chest rose as she breathed in, her head tilted back, her tongue touched her lips, then a soft hum emerged from her, the tune odd, a bounce from one note to the next. It made him think of people arriving at a party, one after another, the crowd growing boisterous.

Her hand tightened in his.

The bean on the desk hopped like it had been placed in a hot pan. Then there were two beans, three, ten. A flood of them. They cascaded over the edge, scattering onto the floor.

Her eyes popped open and she snatched her hand back from his, clutching it to her chest.

"There, now. You needn't be so stubborn. Víctor will be pleased."

"Does the king have a great appetite for beans?"

That startled a laugh from him, a dry bark that might have been mistaken for a shout. He was out of practice.

"How did you know I didn't need the words?" she asked. "Where did you learn this?"

He remembered Heidelberg, Al-Azhar, Khanbaliq, Granada. Late nights spent reading by candlelight, Arabic, Aramaic, the shapes of hieroglyphs, inscriptions wrought in bronze, the world opening beneath his fingertips.

"I will tell you if you tell me which language you sing in."

"Spanish," she lied.

"No great miracle has ever been worked in Castilian."

"And why is that?"

"Because it is a language that spends its power in command and conquest. But you were wrong when you said you didn't need the words. You do need them. Just as God did when He set this whole miserable clockwork running. Language creates possibility.

Sometimes by being used. Sometimes by being kept secret. I will see you again tomorrow, Luzia Cotado."

"What am I to do with all of these beans?"

"Add them to the soup," he said, and took some pleasure in being the one to turn his back on her.

Chapter 13

◆

The weather had finally begun to cool, and the walk through the city was a pleasant one. Santángel had known plenty of misery, but summer in the stench of Madrid was its own unique punishment. He turned his feet south to the rougher part of town. He could go far enough to manage his errand, but if he pushed much beyond the city walls, he knew he would feel the tether that bound him to De Paredes pulling him back. Santángel could ignore it, but not for long, not if he didn't wish to endure the consequences.

He didn't. Because he was a coward. He had always feared death more than he resented this unrelenting life.

His first lesson with the scullion had shown him two things: she had an agile mind and she was doing her best to hide it. Never a bad strategy for a servant, though he'd long since stopped bothering with such deception. Neither Víctor nor Antonio Pérez would be eager for a champion with thoughts of her own. She was stubborn, combative, secretive. But she wanted to learn and she was capable of it. He'd gleaned little else.

She might be a conversa or a morisca. Most of the magic that survived in Spain came from Morvedre or Zaragoza or Yepes. But who knew how long any of it would last, lost to exile and the Inquisition, magic bleeding away with the bodies of Jews and Muslims, their poetry silenced, their knowledge buried in the stones of synagogues made into churches, the arches of Mudéjar palaces. The tolerance for mysterious texts like the *Picatrix* would be stamped out by the Pope, and King Philip would follow.

He could already feel the effects of his brief time with her. His stride was surer, his lungs breathed more deeply. There was pleasure in shared magic, and danger too. It pricked the mind and the spirit. It filled the room with possibility.

Santángel cut down one of the crooked alleys, keeping Avapiés to his left, and hurried on to Garavito's workshop and kennels. This was the part of the city known as El Rastro, crowded with tanneries and coal burners and coopers, its slumping buildings snug against each other, its streets choked with mud and shit and blood from the slaughterhouse. No one saw him as he moved through the traffic of carts and wagons, men loaded down with cargo and goods. His gift for stealth served Víctor well, and so it had come easily to Santángel, but he wondered sometimes if, as he'd lost interest in the world, the world had taken less notice of him.

Garavito lived on the lower floor of a building with sweating plaster walls built around a courtyard where his landlord let him keep his cages. He came from a family of trappers, and though he'd tried his hand at becoming a furrier, he didn't have a talent for it. He sold lesser pelts to peasants and merchants for their bedding, but the martens and genet cats screeching and crying from the cramped wooden boxes in the courtyard would be sold to men with a greater gift for turning living things into fashionable fur-lined coats, felted hats, and scented gloves.

Santángel could have entered the house easily enough, but he knocked instead. A young man answered the door, hiding his face from the passersby on the street.

"Hello, Manuel," he said. "Is your father home?"

The boy nodded and stepped aside, turning away from Santángel. When Manuel had been only eight years old he'd accidentally released a fox in his father's care. Garavito had seized the hammer he used to nail and stretch skins, and smashed in the left side of

Manuel's head. The boy should have died, but he'd kept on living, his eye forever half-shut, the skin of his forehead healing over the crater in his skull. His mother was long gone, but whether she'd run away in the night or been murdered by Garavito depended on where you got your gossip.

Santángel set a stack of silver reales on the battered table. "Go from here. Find your uncles. Or set out on your own."

The boy kept his gaze on Santángel as if fearing a trick. "Are you going to kill him?"

Santángel didn't answer, only waited. There was a time when some sense of justice or righteousness would have made him want to kill a brute like Garavito, but now it was just a task to be done with.

Manuel snatched the coins from the table, holding them close to his chest.

"Go," Santángel repeated.

As he made his way through the courtyard, he caught the glint of panicked eyes and scrabbling claws through the holes in the cages. He hated this place and he was only glad that after today he wouldn't have to visit it again.

Garavito was seated on a bench, hunched over the body of a bloodied squirrel, his knife making messy work of separating the animal's limp body from its skin.

"Garavito," Santángel said softly.

The big man startled and lurched to his feet, knocking the bench backward. He had a thick head of black hair and a nose that had been broken so many times it lay nearly flat against his face.

"Shit," he blurted, registering Santángel. He stood with the mangled squirrel in one hand, his knife in the other, and bowed awkwardly. "Señor," he said. "I wasn't expecting you."

Again, Santángel held his tongue, letting silence fill the courtyard, the only sounds the mewls and hissing from the cages.

"I . . . I have no new information," Garavito said. "You can be sure I will send word when I do."

Garavito's brothers hunted and trapped far afield and spoke to other hunters and trappers. In the past, those contacts had provided Víctor with vital information and word of unusual happenings in the countryside.

Garavito shifted uneasily as the quiet stretched, then he tossed the squirrel's body onto the overturned bench. He wiped the blade of his knife on his breeches. His hands were still stained red.

"Well?" he demanded. "What do you want? I have work to do."

"Since you like to talk, I thought I'd let you talk."

Now Garavito's eyes skittered away. "Don Víctor knows I can be trusted."

"You were late bringing us word of the olive farmer."

"I explained all that. There were rumors, nothing more."

"Rumors of a milagrero. A milagrero who now belongs to Beatriz Hortolano."

Garavito spat. "If Don Víctor has a problem with—"

"It would be wise to stop saying his name. You've spoken it too freely already. He forgave the loss of Donadei, but he cannot tolerate being the subject of gossip. You've been talking about my inquiries into the olive farmer and our acquaintance in Toledo. You brought our employer's name into the conversation. So, no, he doesn't trust you, and that's a very bad thing."

Garavito lunged. Santángel knew he would. He'd seen the way the big man's stance shifted, the grip he adjusted on his knife. He stepped aside and let Garavito stumble past.

Garavito whirled and struck out again. Santángel could have dodged the blow, but his morning lesson with the scullion must have ruffled his mood. He let the strike land.

The knife lodged in Santángel's gut, its dirty handle jutting from his torso like a mysterious growth.

A surprised laugh burbled from Garavito's throat, as if he couldn't quite believe what he'd accomplished. "Don Víctor's scorpion doesn't have much of a sting!"

He sounded so proud, so triumphant. Santángel almost felt

guilty. Even so, he took some satisfaction in watching that triumph turn to bafflement when he yanked the knife from beneath his sternum.

He offered the hilt back to Garavito courteously. "Would you like to try again?"

Garavito stared at the knife in Santángel's hand with the same suspicion his son had shown the stack of coins. Then he grabbed the hilt and stabbed again and again and again, driving Santángel back against the wall.

Santángel let himself be shoved about. He knew he was being silly, theatrical. He should have crept into Garavito's house and slit his throat. Now he was bleeding and he'd probably have to suffer through some kind of fever tonight. Maybe he thought Garavito, who called his son *half-moon* and liked to skin the creatures in his keeping while they were still alive to feel it, didn't deserve a quick death. Maybe he was bored. His mind had moved ahead to the walk home and what he would choose for tomorrow's lesson.

Again he pulled the knife from his gut.

"Devil," Garavito said, backing away. He crossed himself, eyes locked on the blood seeping through Santángel's doublet. "God help me. Jesus save me."

"It does hurt," Santángel said. "If that makes you feel any better."

It was time to bring this scene to an end. He turned the knife on Garavito: quick jabs to the stomach—an echo of the attack he'd just endured, another bit of theater—one strike after another until his opponent crumpled, then a slash behind each knee to make sure he couldn't get up.

Santángel opened the cages, releasing coney, genet cats, weasels, ermines that had not yet sloughed off their brown coats for winter white, a single fox. Some fled. Others rose on back legs, scenting the blood on the air, their hunger making them bold.

He watched them creep tentatively toward where Garavito lay moaning, trying to cover the enticement of his wound. Maybe his neighbors would hear the screaming and come help him. Maybe they'd remember the shove he'd given them in the street or the clout across the face and they'd close their windows against the sound.

As Santángel passed through the cramped apartment, he saw Manuel hadn't left. He was lurking by the window, watching his father die.

"I needed to know," Manuel said. "Please don't kill me."

"Make sure you're gone before the authorities arrive," Santángel replied, and slipped back onto the street. Víctor would tell him to murder the boy too, but Víctor wasn't here.

It took him less than half an hour to traverse the city, his cloak drawn tight over his ruined clothing, the distraction of the crowded streets welcome as he made his way past the houses built over the old garrison walls. He hadn't lied to Garavito. His injuries were painful, but pain held no real interest for him. He knew it would stop. He knew death wasn't coming. Pain without fear was easy to bear. He would wash his hands and change his clothes, and forget Garavito's name the way he'd forgotten so many others.

Too soon he saw the Casa de los Estudios, the women calling to one another from the grocers' stalls in the Plaza del Arrabal, the acrobats performing in the square that fronted the Alcázar, and there, Víctor's new palace—a great slab of achievement. This was the third De Paredes palace Santángel had lived in. There had been rented rooms, then humble houses, then grand ones as the family's wealth grew. This palace had been built in the Italianate style, all stone instead of brick, a testimony to the De Paredes fortune. It was the newest of his many properties, built when rumors began that Philip would move his court to Madrid.

Víctor's massive bodyguard was outside his library. El Peñaco, he was called, a wrestler and fighter from somewhere near Sigüenza. Víctor always kept him near when Santángel wasn't in his presence.

"Garavito?" Víctor asked when he glimpsed Santángel in the doorway.

"Will gossip no longer."

"And the scullion? Is she hopeless?"

"Very much so."

"What a tragedy for you." Víctor did not look up from his writing.

Santángel had forgotten emotion long ago. He had no humors to balance, no bile, no spleen, no desire. And yet as he watched Víctor scratch away at his correspondence, he felt the old rage stir. Once he had craved revenge almost as much as freedom. It had driven him through the sameness of his days and given him purpose. But in time, even his fury had waned, extinguished by the truth of his curse, by the relentless march of years. How strange to discover it within him still, an underground spring that might feed a great river.

Chapter 14

◆

Luzia's new room had no lock, and even if it had she wouldn't have dared to use it. But she put her single chair up against the door, for reasons she couldn't explain. She didn't think Valentina was going to come whip her with a reed in the night, and she had never feared advances from Don Marius. He had beaten her more than once and often at Valentina's request, when she felt her arm too feeble for the discipline required. But Luzia had never worried about him cornering her in a dark hallway. The man's only passion was expensive horseflesh. Besides, she wasn't a stranger in this house. She knew the smell of this room, the linen that she had herself washed in cold water. What would it be like to lie beneath the roof of the De Paredes house? Or at La Casilla? Would a palace have the same smells? Did Guillén Santángel sleep in fine quarters, or was he shoved into some attic, left to roost like a bat?

He was cold and snide, but she couldn't deny his knowledge. She would gladly endure his contempt if he could help her win the torneo and keep her from the Inquisition's notice. She had heard the words in her head, just as he'd instructed, and she'd seen them too, forming in the darkness as if written in golden ink, dancing when they found her tune. Scullions didn't read or write, and she had no interest in inviting more questions about her background. She could work her milagritos and keep the refranes from her aunt's letters all to herself. Here was the chance she had prayed for.

Luzia thought briefly of the hams and the garlic bulbs strung like decorations for a party in the larder. She'd heard of soldiers who returned from long sieges and chose to sleep on hard floors because they couldn't tolerate the luxury of a soft mattress. But maybe Luzia was not of a military bent, or perhaps one dark room is very much like another, because she fell asleep instantly and dreamed of rows of orange trees, the paths between them tidy with white gravel, the sky blue and cloudless overhead. She could hear the splashing of a fountain, music playing somewhere, a song she knew plucked from the strings of an unfamiliar instrument. She was walking hand in hand with someone, but she couldn't tell who.

She woke famished and dressed slowly, unable to shake the pleasure of the dream. The languor of it had seeped into her limbs and made her movements feel like steps in a dance she was still learning. Corset, stockings, skirts. She hummed along to each task, her mind grabbing at that song from the dream, trying to place where she'd heard it before.

Luzia descended to the kitchen to stoke the fire and start the bread. There was still work to be done, no matter where she slept; Valentina was right about that. At the market she dared to spend a little money on an empanadilla stuffed with pork and sweet raisins. Águeda made hers with quince-bud wine and Luzia could admit they were better, but she sat down in the sun and ate it with relish anyway, letting the feeling she'd had in the orange grove overtake her, the peace of it, the delight of that hand in hers. She'd once helped Hualit choose silks for gowns and they'd run like cool water through her fingers. This had been a similar kind of pleasure. She tried humming that song again, felt it spark beneath her tongue. It wanted to be something, if only she could think of the words.

When she returned to Casa Ordoño, she tied on a fresh apron and tucked her hair tightly under her cap. She considered her reflection in the bulge of a tin pitcher. She had tried to make sure there was no dirt left on her neck, but she could do nothing about the sheen of sweat on her brow, the ruddiness of her cheeks acquired in the heat of the kitchen, the freckles that hovered like clouds of pollen on her skin.

Águeda burst out laughing. "Is the fine lady preparing to receive visitors? You can look as long as you like, it won't make you any prettier."

Luzia set down the pitcher with a clang. "Perhaps I should take up bathing nude in the moonlight. Quiteria Escárcega says it works wonders for the complexion."

But Águeda only huffed. "It will take more than that, tonta."

"May you lose two teeth for every one you have," Luzia muttered.

"Who do you hope to impress? Is Don Víctor come to grace us with his presence again? No doubt he'll bring that cursed creature with him."

For a moment Luzia pictured Víctor de Paredes with a bird on his shoulder or a panther at the end of a jeweled leash. She knew who Águeda meant, but she asked anyway. "Creature?"

"El Alacrán." She crossed herself and spat over her shoulder. "Don Víctor's servant, though who's to know what he actually does in that house."

El Alacrán. The scorpion. Her mother had told her that they were more dangerous than snakes because when you chased them off, they didn't have the sense to stay away. They hid until they were ready to strike.

"Why call him that?" Luzia asked.

"It's what he calls himself."

"He dresses like a gentleman and speaks like one too."

"Don't be fooled by his fine manners. And never look directly into his eyes. That's how he steals souls." Águeda lowered her voice. "He made a bargain with the devil for eternal life."

Luzia couldn't help but roll her eyes. "Then he should get his money back. He seems to be on death's door."

"But he never steps through it, does he?" Águeda snatched up a stalk of rosemary, dragging her hand along it to remove the fragrant leaves. "You'd best watch yourself, Luzia Cotado. People who cross paths with that man come to bad ends. Don't think I haven't heard the gossip about your little tricks. That's the devil's work, I'll swear it."

Luzia yanked the rosemary from Águeda's hand and tossed it into the fire. "Say those words again and I'll toss your cap in next."

"You have no—"

Luzia grabbed the cap from Águeda's head and threw it into the flames.

Águeda shrieked. "You've gone mad!"

Maybe she had. But talk of the devil was dangerous. It could take root and grow into a hanging tree. "My *little tricks* are milagritos. They are a gift from God."

"The arrogance—"

"A gift from God." Águeda's knife rested on the table, waiting to be used on the fish Luzia had brought back from the market in her bucket. Luzia didn't pick it up but she tapped her fingers on the handle. "Say it."

"What is wrong with you? I—"

"Say it."

"They're the work of God," Águeda bit out.

"Next time you get it in your head to speak the devil's name in this house, think about what it would mean to have an enemy who has his ear." Luzia stepped back. "Peace, Águeda. Think too of what a godly woman might accomplish for you, if you treated her with kindness."

At that the cook blinked, her indignation and fear giving way to assessment, as if considering for the first time what accidents might befall a lady playwright.

"There," said Luzia. "One must never expect miracles, but one can hope for them all the same."

She expected to find Santángel waiting for her in her room, and she nearly stumbled when she saw Hualit sitting at the writing desk, Doña Valentina hovering at the window. At least she had an excuse to look flustered.

"At last," Hualit said, rising from her seat so gracefully she seemed to simply float upward. She was in her full Catalina de Castro de Oro regalia, swathed in black velvet, her sleeves voluminous and pinked in an elaborate pattern to reveal the cream satin beneath. The corset smashed her breasts into a kind of armor plate so that she looked like a large bell, but somehow it suited her. "I've been so longing to meet you. You're the talk of Madrid."

The words were a near exact echo of what Hualit had said to Luzia in the chapel at San Ginés, and she had a strange sense of doubling. They were Luzia and Hualit, niece and aunt. They were two strangers, scullion and widow.

Valentina's hands fluttered, then settled at her waist. "Señora de Castro de Oro has agreed to help prepare you for La Casilla."

"That is very kind of you, señora," Luzia said, and curtsied.

Hualit's brows shot up. Luzia had practiced her curtsy in her new room the previous night, tucking one foot behind the other. It wasn't so hard, not when your legs and back were strong from servants' work.

"It is, isn't it?" Hualit murmured under her breath. She took a slow turn around Luzia and said, "Well, this won't be easy. She's too short to be imposing, and I could wish for a finer complexion. But Pérez should look at her and see a weapon to be honed. Besides, Gracia de Valera is one of the other hopefuls and it would be foolish to try to place them on even footing."

"I don't know that name," said Valentina.

"No? She is often at court."

Luzia wanted to celebrate her aunt's cruelty, but she couldn't help feeling that in this moment, she and Valentina, ordinary gray birds seldom seen far from their roost, had more in common than she and Hualit.

Hualit clapped her hands and strode toward the door. "Come. There's much to do."

"You're leaving?" Valentina asked.

"*We* are leaving. It will be easiest if we visit Perucho at his warehouse."

"You cannot take her!"

Hualit paused and turned slowly on her heel, the movement exaggerated, almost comical. "We will go together, will we not?"

"Together?"

"Of course. You need new dresses too. Or did I misunderstand?"

How clearly Luzia grasped Valentina's longing, her humiliation.

"We cannot . . ." Valentina's voice was hoarse. "We cannot go unaccompanied."

Widows had greater freedom than most women. Wealthy widows even more. But there were limits.

"My confessor will go with us," Hualit said as if it were obvious. "He is waiting in the coach."

"Your coach?"

Hualit's lips twitched. So Valentina wasn't totally without spine. "The coach belongs to Don Víctor, but he has offered us use of it."

Luzia watched Valentina hesitate. She didn't know which rule she might be violating, which liberty she might be taking. She would have to ask Don Marius for permission to leave. Luzia wondered what Hualit would do if Valentina said no, if she forbade Luzia from going. She probably should. It would put Hualit in her place, and Luzia knew her aunt: such a show of will would impress her. But Luzia didn't want Valentina to refuse this opportunity. The greedy thing inside her was hungry for velvet and fur.

"I will fetch my cloak," Valentina said.

Hualit smiled and Luzia couldn't help smiling too.

Valentina had purchased her two house dresses from a market stall and made the third—the same gown she'd worn for her wedding—herself. There was no pride in this. She knew wealthy women had their own tailors who brought them fabrics or even gowns from Italy or France.

Valentina's confessor, who was much older and sterner and more covered in whiskers than the young man riding beside the widow, had told her that it was a woman's nature to be too concerned with worldly matters and that this was how the devil tempted Eve in the world's first garden. He'd told her the story of a young countess who had pined after a ruby brooch with such fervor that she'd woken with a forked tongue.

So Valentina knew that both her soul and her tongue were in danger as the coach rattled over the streets, and yet she couldn't stop her wayward, venal thoughts. It was unseemly, immoral, but try as she might to tamp it down, she felt as if her delight was oozing from her pores, slicking her skin. It was not just the promise of new clothes. To ride in a coach down the street, to see the world passing by in such colors. She would have happily ridden around the entire city that way, her mind scrambling to recognize streets and monuments, taking in fountains and storefronts and flocks of pale-breasted pigeons. Valentina lifted her wrist to her nose; the sachet of dried herbs tied to her sleeve was stuffed with rosemary and sage and she breathed deeply. It was made to protect the wearer from foul smells, but nothing could be foul about this moment. The stink of the city, even the sludge of garbage and excrement in its streets, was beautiful today.

Marius looked ill at ease in the close quarters of the coach, but he'd been unwilling to let his wife venture out with Catalina de

Castro de Oro, priest in tow or not. Widow she might be, favored for her wit and beauty, and welcomed among the best families. But her allegiance was to Don Víctor, and he didn't want her alone with their Luzia.

Not that Marius had asked, but Valentina thought he was right to worry. There was a peculiar ease between Luzia and the widow. Maybe ease wasn't the right word. It was as if each word they spoke had another meaning tucked beneath it.

When their party emerged onto the street, Valentina felt another jolt of exultation. They hadn't gone far, only to Puerta de Guadalajara, but it felt as if they were an entire ocean away from Casa Ordoño. She wasn't sure what to call the building they entered, part shop and part warehouse. It was not like a butcher's or a bookseller's, but a kind of silo for the storage of luxury, two tall stories full of shelves and racks, connected by walkways and ladders, the stacks of folded fabric and heaps of brocade looming over three cutting tables and a chorus of stuffed dress forms, their torsos pinned with swags of stiff silk and wound with bolts of lace. Two rows of heads bracketed the doors in jeweled caps and veils. Cases full of feathers caught the light from the window, their shelves laden with carefully constructed panaches wound with gold and silver wire, striped pheasant feathers, blue and red parrot, iridescent plumes shimmering green then yellow.

"You're staring," Marius said, pinching her elbow and steering her along.

"Why should I not stare?" she snapped without thinking. "Would a blind man not stare at his first sight of the world?"

Now he goggled at her and she wondered if he might strike her or . . . she didn't know what. She had never attracted Marius's attention *or* his ire.

But the widow looped her arm through Valentina's. "So few pleasures are allowed to women. No wonder we ache for a little silk."

"It is sinful," Valentina said, hating her prim, fussy voice.

The widow only winked. "More sinful to walk around naked."

"This is why there are no tailors in hell," said a short man dressed in heavily embellished layers of plum brocade.

The widow's confessor made a disapproving mew, and Valentina didn't know whether to laugh or beg forgiveness for keeping company with such people.

The tailor bowed to each of them, welcoming them warmly and introducing himself as Perucho with the air of someone who expected his name to be well-known. He wore his hair long and parted in the center, his mustache elaborately oiled. Beside her she felt Marius recoil. While the tailor's accent was pristine, he had the air of the foreign about him.

"You have noted the work of our plumajero," he said, gesturing to the cases. "Second only to the king's. Egret, ostrich, parrot, even night heron. Note the colors. You'll find no alum here. We dye with turmeric and berries from Persia more purple than a bruise." He shepherded them toward one of the tables. "Come. I've just returned from a buying trip that took me over land and sea, and I have such treats prepared for you."

But as he spoke he bobbed his head very subtly toward customers in another corner of the shop, a father and daughter.

The girl was like a tiny doll, her laugh high and sweet, her reddish-gold hair worn pulled back from her face in two jeweled combs.

"Ah," said the widow, her eyes sparkling with interest. "Teoda Halcón. I trust you didn't waste your best wares on that little viper."

"She is a child," Valentina said, scandalized.

Teoda turned as she and her father exited the shop, her gaze roving over their group and landing on Luzia, her lips curling into a smile.

"That is not an ordinary girl," said the widow when they were gone. "That is the Holy Child."

Her confessor crossed himself. "Of the sacred visions."

"She's one of your competitors," the widow said to Luzia. "Take note."

"A little girl?" asked Valentina.

The widow nodded. "That little girl speaks to angels. Her visions are remarkably accurate."

"A pure heart," said the confessor. "The embodiment of innocence."

"We'll see," said the widow.

"What did her father buy for her?" asked Don Marius.

"Fripperies," chortled the merchant. "Gifts for his dear one. His business often takes him to Germany and the Netherlands, so he has little need for my services." He exchanged a look with the widow that Valentina didn't understand. "Now, Luzia, let me see you. I've heard so much about your milagritos. I'm not so crass that I will ask for a demonstration, but perhaps when I transform you, this humble merchant will earn himself an invitation to dine with your benefactors."

Marius stiffened and Valentina felt a sense of sadness. Her husband would never welcome such a man into their house, but what beautiful things might she acquire if he did?

Perucho stepped back and considered Luzia. "How is a scullion to impress a king? She is both performer and servant, so how to show her to best advantage?"

"She should dress as the other competitors in the torneo," said Marius gruffly.

Again the merchant laughed. "That would be a disastrous mistake. The prince is of scant concern to us—"

"Prince?" Valentina squeaked. "Luzia will compete against a prince?"

But Perucho continued on. "The Holy Child will wear pale colors to compliment her hair and eyes. And Señorita Gracia de Valera . . . Well. She has her own tailor, an Italian, and though it pains me to admit it, a genius. But this . . ." He gestured to Luzia. "A challenge. She has a waist. That's something. It's too bad we can't show the bosom. If only she weren't so dark. Like a little nut."

"I know how I should be dressed."

They all stared at Luzia, and Valentina realized that she had nearly forgotten the woman could talk.

"Is that so?" said the widow.

"I cannot compete with beauty. I cannot be winsome like a child. So give me armor. Make it seem as if I have chosen to be humble."

"Intriguing," mused Perucho.

"You have my attention," said the widow.

Luzia's eyes were sullen as she held Catalina de Castro de Oro's gaze and sank into another shockingly graceful curtsy. Valentina wasn't sure if they had just formed a friendship or if she was watching soldiers prepare to face each other in the field. Either way, she would have three new gowns and perhaps a new cap if she budgeted carefully.

Chapter 15

◆

Luzia learned how to comport herself at the banquet table, proper terms of address, how to sit in her new corset, and how to arrange the hoops and buttresses of her verdugado so that she could use a chamber pot without tipping over or soiling her shoes—though she was firmly instructed to wait for a maid to help her, unless the situation was dire. The shoes themselves were leather but the chapines urged on her had quickly been discarded. The wooden sleeves with their corked heels were meant to make her taller, but she didn't have time to master walking in them. She had taken two swaying steps during her second fitting before Perucho had waved his hands and declared, "Not all experiments are a success."

She wasn't expected to know how to dance or play an instrument or to speak on geography or world affairs. She didn't really need to speak at all. Smile and lift your glass when those around you do. Keep your eyes on your shoes or your plate. Safe replies to questions regarding politics or improper advances were the same: "I have lived a sheltered life, señor" or "I hardly know what to think." It wasn't so different from being a scullion.

A girl with orange hair appeared in the kitchen one morning, her full market basket already settled on the table, her arms wet to the elbow as she washed chickpeas for Águeda. Luzia hovered at the foot of the stairs, unsure of what to do until Águeda said, "Does the señorita need something?"

Luzia opened her mouth, shut it. "No," she managed.

Águeda released something between a grunt and a laugh and blew the hair off her sweaty face. "Just think, Juana, if you learn some tricks and wash your neck you may become a fine lady too."

Her tone didn't quite have the vicious snap of her wooden spoon. She was nervous now, unsure of what Luzia might be or become. Luzia wasn't certain either.

But she was more worried about Juana gaping at her over the barley and almonds.

Águeda had warned her the rumors had spread and here was proof of it. Luzia had been trapped in Casa Ordoño, focusing on her lessons, trying to think of new ways to use the words from Hualit's letters. What would happen if I walked to the market now? she wondered. Would heads turn to follow her, a tide of whispers forming in her wake? The thought gave her an embarrassing shiver of pleasure.

Even so, Luzia felt possessive of her dirt floor, her candle kept tucked away in the larder, and had to resist the urge to hiss at poor Juana. Slowly she made her way up the stairs. She'd lost her place, but what was there to grieve? Why this fresh rush of fear? Maybe because none of it had seemed real before this moment. The new bedroom, the clothes, the lessons. She hadn't quite believed in any of it. She'd thought she was rehearsing a play that would never open.

Santángel was waiting outside her room for their lesson. He was so tall she risked a stiff neck if she wanted to observe the angles of his face properly, and he looked different this morning. Still pale and lean, but less like he might expire at any moment.

"You're distracted," he said as he followed her inside, the door left open as it always was.

"I'm questioning where this all ends."

"In victory, of course."

"You're a very poor liar." Across the street, the curtains of the music room were closed, the window shut. Luzia wondered if she would ever hear that harp played. "You and I both know I can't win."

"If I believed that I wouldn't bother."

"You'd do what Don Víctor tells you to do."

He folded his arms. "Tell me more about what I would do."

Luzia was wise enough to hesitate, but she found it hard not to be reckless during these lessons, with no one watching or listening but Santángel. "It's whispered you're an assassin."

"You yourself said I do as I'm bid."

"And does your master bid you do murder?"

Santángel's nod was disinterested. "He has cultivated my skills and they are bloody ones. We do as we're instructed. Is there another way for servants?"

"Not that I've been able to discover," she admitted. Did he care so little about the lives he'd taken? Should she be more afraid that he didn't?

"Why do you think you can't win?" he asked.

"I can see it in your gaze, hear it in your voice. I haven't the manners or the poise. I have a scrap of power and your master has delusions."

"You have more than a scrap of power," he said grudgingly.

Luzia knew that but the sight of orange-haired Juana in the kitchen had tilted her mood. "Enough to win?" she pushed. "Enough to survive life as the king's champion?"

Santángel was unsure how to answer. He had been both thrilled and disturbed by the scullion's progress. Whatever power flowed through Luzia Cotado wanted free rein. That power would belong to Víctor. And Santángel would be free. It was as simple as that. And wouldn't she be happier? More contented than she had been sleeping in the dirt? Víctor's palace might feel like a curse for him, but for a girl with no learning and no prospects, it would be a glorious change in circumstance.

If she could win. Luzia could fill a room with beans. She could make roses bloom in profusion.

"But no talent for prediction?" Víctor had asked only last night. He'd been fussy, irritable, demanding constant updates on the scullion's progress. The closer they drew to the torneo, the worse he became.

"The king has astrologers to make predictions."

"The Holy Child has visions, accurate ones."

"You brought me a girl with a singular talent," said Santángel. "I cannot remake it in the image you would prefer."

"What good are roses and beans to a king?"

Santángel had to marvel at Víctor's lack of imagination. He longed for a girl with visions, but how shortsighted he was.

"What if the beans were ships?" Santángel asked. "What if she could simply make him a new armada? Or a thousand muskets from one?"

"Can she?"

With his help she could. With his luck. But without him? "I don't yet know."

She couldn't multiply gold or precious stones without consequence. He'd learned that to his own detriment when he'd insisted she attempt to turn one piece of silver into many. They'd become tiny hornets and he was still covered in welts. But books she'd made in profusion, multiplying his treasured Petrarch into a stack of perfect copies, each word in its proper place, even if she couldn't read them.

There was advice he should give Víctor. It was dangerous to tie your fate to someone of uncertain talent. A title was one thing, but it was foolish to put yourself in such close proximity to a king's caprice. Had Santángel been a true friend or a true advisor he might have said all these things. But he was a captive, and a captive's only thought could be of freedom.

"She will impress," he promised. "If I have to wring the magic from her myself, she will impress."

Now he watched Luzia go to the desk and sit. She rested her hands in her lap and closed her eyes.

"What are you doing?"

"Sitting."

"And?"

"Sitting is a great pleasure for a servant."

"Doña Valentina was meant to hire another scullion."

"Juana is your doing?"

"My master's. He wants your time and strength devoted to practice and prayer."

Her eyes opened, large and dark, thickly fringed. He understood why she had hidden that gaze, constantly keeping her eyes on her hands or the ground or her clumsy feet. It was too wise, too watchful, and it told him that she knew he was lying.

Santángel had suggested hiring the new scullion when Víctor complained that Luzia stank of the kitchen. "What is the point of dressing her up in velvet if she smells like onions and bacon grease?"

Santángel had been tempted to correct him. He had been close enough to Luzia to know she smelled of orange blossoms and had considered advising her that women of good families didn't wear scent. How was she affording it anyway? Did she have a lover? The thought disturbed him, but only because she could afford no indiscretions. "Then take her out of the kitchen," he'd told Víctor, echoing Luzia's own words. "Pay for a scullion. It will give you another set of ears in the household."

"How eager you are to spend my money," Víctor had grumbled.

"Only because I know how much of it you have."

Santángel considered Luzia, returning her gaze. "You're not pleased to have another pair of hands at work?"

"She's young," Luzia said, "and built like a piece of straw when we need a whole broom."

"That isn't your problem any longer. Your goal is to win. Or to perform well enough that the king will claim more than one champion."

"Is that possible?"

Santángel looked out the window to where El Peñaco leaned against Víctor's coach, awaiting orders. Why would the king settle for a single holy soldier when he could have an army?

"If he can be sure that your power is angelic, it's possible the king will want to hoard milagreros as he hoards relics. But Philip hates court. He is happiest alone with his books or poring over work that should be beneath him. If he chooses more than one champion, he'll only be setting the stage for a grand rivalry. That can be perilous for everyone."

"How do I know . . ." Luzia hesitated, eyes on the heavy crucifix that hung over the door. "How do I know if my power is angelic?"

Santángel sat down on the bed across from her. "That's a dangerous question. More dangerous than being a conversa in the king's court."

When she flinched, Santángel knew his guess had been a good one. The conversos had been the start of the Inquisition, the fear that the Jews who had accepted baptism to save their lives and homes, and then to remain in Spain, were not true believers at all, but frauds who practiced their religion in secret, who might corrupt the very soul of Spain. The priests and their henchmen had done their work well, and these days, there were few secret Jews to hunt, so they'd turned their attention to heretics and fornicators and blasphemers. But any taint of Jewish blood, no matter how many generations old, could not be tied to someone who hoped to rise in status, to join a military order, or to study at university, certainly not to someone who could work miracles.

If Luzia entered the king's service, every element of her life would be scrutinized. Her baptism, the time she spent at mass, when she did or didn't take communion, if she observed feast days or fasted during Lent, or didn't eat from a dish made with pork. She would be challenged to swear faith in the Trinity—easy enough. But then she might have to explain it—something even few viejos could do. Winning the Torneo Secreto would be only the beginning.

"Víctor de Paredes makes no move without understanding the game he is playing," Santángel said. "He has already met with a linajista to attest to the purity of your blood and write up a clean history for you."

"As if I am to be married."

"Into any family of fortune or reputation, yes."

"A scullion doesn't have such concerns."

"No. No one looks too closely at a woman in rags."

"They should," said Luzia. "Who has more power in a house than the woman who stirs the soup and makes the bread and scrubs the floors, who fills the foot warmer with hot coals, and arranges your letters, and nurses your children?"

Her anger radiated from her like heat from a stone left in the sun. She was right, of course. These were the ways women entered the body, through the kitchen, through the nursery, their hands in your bed, your clothes, your hair. There was danger in such trust, and a wise man learned to respect the women who tended to his home and heirs.

"Do *you* not wonder where this power comes from?" she demanded. "Do you not fear it?"

"In the *Ghayāt al-Hakīm* magic was seen as the natural result of a holy life, the mark of a true sage. For a long time, crown and Church shared this belief. It was even translated into Castilian, by royal command."

Luzia laughed. "But I haven't lived a holy life."

"I've seen all manner of power," he said. "Sacred and perverse. I've never been able to locate the lines between science, and faith, and magic, nor have I cared to."

"And you're not afraid . . . of the devil? Of his minions?"

"Fear men, Luzia," he said. "Fear their ambition and the crimes they commit in its service. But don't fear magic or what you may do with it."

It was the closest he could come to honesty.

Chapter 16

✦

With him she wasn't afraid. Here with the scorpion who knew her secrets, with a killer who made Hualit tremble and Águeda cross herself. Perhaps he didn't fear the devil because he was a demon himself. *People who cross paths with that man come to bad ends.* Maybe. But in this room, in the quiet of the morning or the afternoon, there was only the lesson and the pleasure of letting magic take shape, of feeling it expand and grow stronger. It was why she forgot herself so easily with him, why she neglected to curb her tongue or hunch her shoulders.

She could say none of that, so she said, "Tell me about the trials."

"Your lesson first. We've spent too much time philosophizing." He rose and crossed to the desk where he'd set the leather satchel he often carried. Sometimes it held beans or coals or books. Today he removed a small silken bag and emptied the contents into his hand.

"Seeds?" They were tiny and grayish white, stained pink in places. They looked like baby teeth.

"We'll begin with something easy. Your miracle of the vines, to make it bloom." He placed a single seed in his palm.

Simple. The words formed in her head, golden ink spilling onto the page. She didn't know the languages well enough to pull them apart—Spanish, Turkish, Greek, she couldn't be sure. But she felt as if they were gathering momentum, traveling away from Spain to countries she would never see and back again.

A brush of her palm over his and a slender green stalk sprouted where the seed had been, its frail roots grasping at nothing. Another pass of her hand and the stalk thickened, bursting with leaves, the root bulb fattening so that Santángel had to place it on the table beside his bag. A current of heat passed through her, as if the magic had been reflected back against her own hand.

"Pomegranate," she gasped, delighted.

"They take three years to fruit," said Santángel, his gaze like clouds moving over water. "But that's no challenge at all for you."

He reached out with his thumb and forefinger and snapped the stalk. The sapling broke, its green head hanging forlornly over the edge of the desk, and Luzia felt a pang of sadness for the thing she had made.

"It is one thing to repair an object like a glass," he said. "But can you heal a living thing?"

The miracle of the vine, now the miracle of the cup. It should be easy.

Luzia closed her eyes and reached for that simple song she'd used so many times: *a change of scene, a change of fortune.* This time it felt strange, as if the music was being pulled in two directions, hungry to form a new note, a new pattern. The letters wobbled in the dark. She opened her eyes and looked at Santángel, who was watching her closely. How strange his eyes were, and yet she couldn't deny she liked being the focus of his attention. She could feel the shape of him in the room, as if he were a rest in the music, a rock heavy and immovable against its tide. Luzia drew the song back into its proper shape, stronger than before.

The stalk shuddered, some of its leaves shaking free, and then sprang up, like a man woken from a deep sleep bolting upright in his bed. New leaves unfurled from the mended stalk—a trunk now, gray and sturdy. Its roots clambered over the desk, seeking purchase; bright orange flowers burst from its branches. A small smile touched Santángel's lips.

"No soil. No rain. And yet it thrives. Who knows what you may do, Luzia Cotado?"

She blinked, startled by the echo of her own thoughts, thoughts she had told herself to regret since that night she'd felt herself float above Madrid, when she'd first performed for Valentina's guests, when she'd taken her first incautious steps on a path that still remained shrouded in shadow. His belief in her was wine on an empty stomach and it left her light-headed.

The silence was broken by Víctor de Paredes's deep voice. "Meager miracles indeed."

His mouth pulled down at the corners. His high pale brow was flat. He had the discontented look of a man who was afraid he'd just eaten a bad oyster.

"We're making progress," said Santángel. "It's no small thing to restore life when life is interrupted."

"Then let's see what wounds she can really repair. Álvaro, come here."

Luzia recognized the lumbering bodyguard, the one they sometimes called El Peñaco and who accompanied Don Víctor on the days Santángel came for her lessons. He had to duck his head to enter the room. He had pale blue eyes and he wore his yellow hair in a crop around his ears, the texture like straw. His broad face was so pink he looked as if he'd just emerged from a hot bath.

"Now," said Don Víctor. "I want to know where all my money is going. I want to see the great milagrera for whom I've bought gowns and upon whom my entire family has pinned its hopes."

Luzia kept her eyes on her clenched hands. She had never seen Víctor de Paredes in this mood, but she knew it well enough. From Marius. From Valentina. Even from Águeda. A sulky child seeking someone to hit.

"You've been enjoying your lessons?"

"Yes, señor."

"You are fond of your teacher?"

"I am grateful to him and to you, señor."

"I see Catalina's polish has at least put some shine on you. Do you think you're ready to impress Pérez? Do you think your entertainments are fit for a king?"

"I can only pray that is the case, señor."

Don Víctor grabbed her by the chin, forcing her to meet his gaze. "I have no interest in the prayers of a shitty little scullion."

"Víctor." Santángel's voice was cold, an echo heard from deep within a cave. "That's enough."

"You do not use that word with me. *Enough* is forbidden to you."

"Leave the girl alone. Vent your anger elsewhere."

"I'm not angry with her." Víctor gave her head a shake, his gloved fingers pinching. "I'm simply weary of her mediocrity." He turned to Santángel. "It is you who deserves my ire."

"Then beat me. Strike me if you are so sure I cannot find a way to return the blow."

Luzia didn't understand this battle, but she didn't want to be hit and she didn't want to see Santángel beaten.

"He has tried to teach me," Luzia said, hoping to appease Don Víctor. "I am a poor student."

But he didn't care what she had to say.

"How kind of you to volunteer, Santángel. As always, I am grateful for your service." He turned to the bodyguard. "Álvaro, break his fingers. If our student is making such wonderful progress, she will be able to repair them."

"Please," Luzia began. But Álvaro didn't wait. He seized Santángel's hand and wrenched his first finger to the right. The *snap* was like kindling being split. "Don't!" Luzia cried.

"Go on," said Don Víctor. "Fix him as you did the sapling. If you can."

Santángel said nothing. He didn't fight or resist or cry out. His gaze was locked on Víctor, but there was no light in his eyes, only a long cold night.

"Again," commanded Don Víctor.

"Wait!" Luzia pleaded. "Give me a moment to think!"

"She thinks now. Who told you to teach her that?"

Crack. Álvaro bent back another of Santángel's fingers, a branch breaking in winter, an animal's jaws snapping shut. El Peñaco was grinning now. Was he mad? Did this please him?

Luzia's mind scrambled for the words that had come so easily only moments before. *Aboltar cazal, aboltar mazal.* She couldn't find the tune. The sound of Santángel's breaking bones was all she could hear.

"Álvaro will continue until you show me what you are capable of."

Who knows what you might do?

Luzia shut her eyes, shut out the room, shut out the anticipation in Álvaro's eyes, the grim resignation in Santángel's face. There, the melody, the letters forming one after another, but again she felt that pull, that sense of sliding, the song seeking another form.

"Again, Álvaro," Don Víctor commanded.

She had been lulled by this room, by Santángel's patience, by velvet dresses and lessons in comportment. She hated this house and everyone in it. She hated this city too. *Anywhere but here*, she thought. *I would be anywhere but here.* She fought to find the melody and then there, the song, she followed it, humming, the sound blooming from her chest with the strength of a hive, a swarm of bees singing with her, the words taking shape, traveling across the sea, across time, the words of exile, of new beginnings, of survival.

Aboltar cazal, aboltar mazal.

The song emerged in a shout and Luzia screamed as pain tore through her.

Chapter 17

◆

One moment Santángel was staring at Álvaro's satisfied face as he listened to the sound of his own finger bones popping and the next the man was gone. Luzia fell to her knees, blood gushing from her mouth.

The pomegranate tree burst to life beside him, its branches slamming against the ceiling, heavy fruit tumbling from its branches.

Víctor was pressed against the wall, more shaken than Santángel had ever seen him.

He ignored the pain in his fingers and went to Luzia, stumbling over something on the floor. Her eyes were wild and rolling, the noise coming from her throat something between a whine and a growl, an animal sound. Blood covered her chin, her neck, the fabric of her dress. It was on her hands, the rug.

"Luzia," he said, trying to keep his voice calm. "Luzia, your tongue has split and I need you to sing to heal it."

She was shaking now. Soon she would lose too much blood and there would be no way to help her. He didn't have his own magic, and whatever had happened in this room had shattered the protection of his influence with its power.

He heard a sputtering, mewling sound and realized it was coming from Víctor. Valentina was in the hallway screaming.

"Luzia," he said again, her name repeated, an incantation. "Luzia, pay attention to my voice and nothing else. You must find a song.

You are the burnt bread. You are the broken glass. I cannot put you back together, but you can."

She shook her head from side to side and he didn't know if she was rejecting his words or if she was simply too frightened to understand him.

He grasped her hand in his. "I was wrong when I told you to fear men and their ambition," he murmured in her ear. "Fear nothing, Luzia Cotado, and you will become greater than them all. Now sing for me."

He wanted to shout in triumph when she squeezed his hand back.

She couldn't form words, not with her tongue split down the middle. But a tune came anyway, from somewhere in her chest, ragged and faltering at first. Then the melody emerged, became clearer. He knew this song, from long ago. He had heard it in a garden. His nostrils filled with the scent of an orange grove in bloom.

The song rose and fell and rose again and then she was still. Gently, he wiped the blood from her face with his sleeve.

"Open your mouth for me." Her tongue was whole and pink. "It still hurts?"

She nodded.

He looked up at Víctor, who remained pressed against the wall, at Valentina weeping in Don Marius's arms. "Get me ice if you have it, cold milk if you don't. Bring water to get her clean. And stop that sobbing. All is well."

They looked at him as if he were speaking some mysterious language.

It was only then that Santángel understood what he had stumbled over. In the midst of the blood and the cracked bodies of pomegranates, Álvaro, El Peñaco, was lying on the floor. But not all of him. His shoulder, part of a leg shod in the mustard livery of De Paredes, half his head and one staring eye, as if he'd lain down to go to sleep on his side and simply fallen through the floorboards.

"Where is . . . Where is the rest of him?" Víctor panted.

"My study," Don Marius croaked from the hallway where he held his weeping wife. "I was looking at the accounts from our holdings and . . . pieces . . . fell through the ceiling." He pressed his hand to his mouth and Santángel knew they'd find his vomit next to the rest of Álvaro's body.

He understood now what had gone wrong, what Luzia had done, but this wasn't the time for explanations.

Santángel rose with Luzia in his arms, his fingers sending bright bolts of pain up through his shoulders.

"Show me to your room," he commanded Valentina. "Get Juana up here from the kitchen and let the cook go home early. Tell her someone has taken ill. Víctor, send the coach back to the house and have them return with Gonzalo and Celso. They can help us set this mess to rights. Do you understand?"

Víctor closed his mouth and managed a grunt.

"Good," said Santángel. "And if my master would be so kind to send for someone who might set my broken bones so that they heal straight?"

He waited for Víctor to meet his gaze.

"Yes," Víctor rasped.

With his scullion in his arms, Santángel strode past the luckiest man in Madrid.

Chapter 18

◆

Luzia slept in her mistress's room, a silent body around which the rest of the house continued to turn in its new orbits.

Víctor's personal doctor arrived to set Santángel's fingers and offered him something for the pain, which he refused. He needed his mind sharp for all that was to come, and already his body was doing the work of mending itself. The danger was always that he would heal too quickly, before the bones had been properly aligned, and then they would have to be broken again.

The coach returned with two of Víctor's men, who went about scraping Álvaro from the floor of Luzia's room and searching Don Marius's study for body parts. It was as if a butcher's cart had overturned: a leg and groin still in velvet livery beside the heavy desk, half a torso and a limp hand slung over the side of an embroidered chair, and the rest of the bodyguard's head, the skull cleanly severed, the glossy gray mass of his brain exposed like custard in a dish.

The servants said nothing. They hacked away at the pomegranate tree that had already begun to wither without soil and water or Luzia's magic to sustain it. They would take Álvaro's remains to the countryside and bury them somewhere on the grounds of one of Víctor's many estates or find some pigs to feed them to. That was not Santángel's problem to solve.

The widow appeared to look after Luzia since Valentina was

still bursting into tears every few minutes. Juana was summoned from the kitchen to scrub away the archipelago of stains Álvaro's parts had left on the floor. As for the ceiling in Marius's study, it was harder to reach, but its coffers obscured the bloody marks of this disaster.

At the end of the day, when all their grim work had been attended to and Juana had been sent back to the kitchen with an extra coin in her apron and the warning "servicio y silencio," they gathered in the salon.

They picked idly at a plate of cheese and sultanas, and Santángel was surprised to discover he was hungry. He hadn't thought about the strength it had taken to lift Luzia until he'd settled her in Valentina's bed. His health was returning and with it his appetites. Because of her.

The widow looked tired, her face pale. Valentina snuffled gently into a handkerchief. Don Marius still hadn't regained his color and sipped cautiously at a glass of jerez. Víctor had vanished in the hours when work needed doing but now he had returned. His expression was grim, but the arrogance that had briefly abandoned him at the sight of his bodyguard split between the floors of a house had returned as well. He paced, then sat, then paced again.

At last he said, "If something like that happens at the competition we will all be ruined."

"She almost died," murmured the widow.

"I saw no wound."

"Perhaps because of all the blood?" she asked too brightly. Víctor glared at her and she dropped her gaze.

"You saw no wound because she was able to heal herself," Santángel said. "We can resume her lessons when she's had a few days' rest."

"Do you think that's wise?" the widow asked.

Don Marius set down his glass, blinking as if woken from a dream by his own self-interest. "She must continue."

"Yes," agreed Valentina, dabbing at her nose.

If Luzia didn't, there would be no more money, no gowns, no stay at La Casilla. But Santángel was just as bad. Worse. He needed Luzia at the torneo and he would get her there.

Víctor took up his pacing once more. "And what happens when she bleeds all over the grand ballroom? When she slices through a guard or a guest or Pérez himself?"

"What went wrong today?" the widow asked. "What happened in that room?"

Víctor cast Santángel a warning glance. Surely Catalina de Castro de Oro already knew the man's nature, but if Víctor wished for discretion he would have it.

"I don't know," Santángel lied. "I was harsh with her. Her fear may have tainted the miracle."

"That can happen?" Víctor demanded.

Anything could happen, but these were the first lies he'd dared or bothered to tell Víctor in an age. When was the last time? Maybe when Víctor had asked if he felt pain. His master had been younger then, but Santángel had already seen what Víctor de Paredes was becoming, his father's greed seeping into him.

"Not as you do," he'd told Víctor then. Which was less true than he'd wanted it to be. Santángel understood as some did not that pain was fleeting, that very little couldn't be endured. But he remembered too well the torture he'd endured when he'd first entered his immortality. He hadn't trusted Víctor not to test those limits, and Víctor's behavior today was yet another sign that he had been right to show caution.

Yet Santángel was prepared to put an illiterate scullion without protection in his service. Víctor might be ruthless, the widow vain, Marius and Valentina greedy. But Santángel was the only monster in the room. She will have a better life than she had scraping by for the Ordoños, he told himself. Santángel would do what he must. If he was a beast, let him be a beast without a cage.

He lowered his voice, speaking to Víctor alone. "Her mood may impact the efficacy of her gifts. You know how women are. She was afraid and lost her focus."

"Why could we not find a man for a champion?" Víctor growled.

"I've had many occasions to question fate, but fate has yet to answer."

"You must find a way to control her. We're about to place her in a basket of snakes. She can't flinch every time one bites."

"We will find a way, I assure you."

"It's your future at stake here as well as mine, Santángel."

"That is not something I will forget."

That seemed to appease Víctor, and he turned to the Ordoños and the widow to discuss their plans, while Santángel was left to contemplate the truth of what had split Luzia's tongue and the uglier truth of his own nature.

The sun was already setting when Luzia woke. For a moment, she wasn't sure where she was, but then she recognized Valentina's chambers. The bedroom was made blue in the twilight, as if seen underwater. Her tongue still throbbed, a dull ache now, warm in her mouth. She pushed herself up, poured water from the pitcher beside the bed, took a careful sip, felt it slide cool and fresh down her throat. It had been flavored with honey.

She remembered the taste of blood and struggled not to gag. How much of it had she swallowed?

Luzia stood, then had to reach for the bedpost as a wave of dizziness overtook her. She was still in her bloody dress. She would never be able to get the stains out and she had the distressing urge to cry. They can't make you go out in stained clothes, she reminded herself. It would be a shame to the family. But they could make her pay for something new, take the money from her wages. She wasn't thinking clearly.

Slowly, Luzia pushed her feet into her shoes and made her way down the hall to her bedroom. She could hear voices in the chambers below.

There was no sign of the violence that had come before. The floor was clean, the smell of vinegar sharp in the air. She went to the window. Across the street, the music room was dark, the dim shape of the harp like the prow of a ghost ship.

At the basin, Luzia sponged dried blood from her neck, then lit a candle and leaned closer to the mirror. She opened her mouth, examining her tongue in the glass. It looked a little red but there was no sign of what had happened, no horrible scar.

She touched her finger to the wet pink flesh and pressed. There. There was pain. Proof of what had gone so wrong. But why had it? And had she killed a man in this room?

The writing table had been replaced, and here and there she could see scratches on the floor. Santángel's satchel was shoved against the wall, the bag from which he'd produced the pomegranate seeds. She shut her door and knelt down, her hand hovering over the satchel as if she were about to offer a blessing. These were his private things. But when would she have an opportunity like this again?

She slipped the laces free and peered inside. A book in French, which she couldn't decipher, a collection of letters, some with his seal—the scorpion, its tail curled and ready to sting—awaiting a servant to carry them from Madrid. Who did he write to? Princes? Politicians? Spies? Was there a woman somewhere hoping for news from her beloved? There was a letter in Castilian from a scholar at the university in Sevilla, and a letter in Latin too. Her eyes scanned the page. She'd had little cause to use the Latin her mother had taught her, but she hadn't forgotten, and the occasional treatise or manual borrowed from Hualit had helped. Her eyes caught on a name: *Pérez*.

Luzia paused, listening to the murmur of voices in the salon, then read on, trying to glean as much as she could. It all seemed to be about astrology—the sign Pérez had been born under and the meaning he had taken from this reading, a long mention of the king's own stars, and the fact that, when Philip was still a young prince, John Dee himself had read his chart.

John Dee. The protestant queen's sorcerer. He was said to speak to angels as the Holy Child did. But if his God was not Catholic, whose voice did he hear? Was it the same devil who had spoken in this room? Who had moved through Luzia to tear a man in two?

She heard footsteps and hurriedly placed the letters back in the satchel, retied the laces, and lay down on her bed.

"You're awake," Hualit murmured as she entered and closed the door. "You could have remained in Valentina's room."

She sat down and smoothed Luzia's hair back from her face. In the evening gloom she looked like Luzia's mother. Or what Luzia remembered of her mother. She had a sudden memory of Blanca Cotado telling her that scorpion oil could be used to heal all kinds of ailments. *But you have to catch them and fry them up first, mi tesoro. Is the danger worth it?*

Yes, mama, she'd said. *A good remedy is worth some pain.* Blanca had laughed and called her daughter bold.

"I brought rue," Hualit said. "And rosemary. For protection. Does it hurt?"

"Not so much." The words sounded too thick, their shape swollen along with Luzia's tongue. "I have only one dress and it's covered in blood." And she had killed a man.

"I'll give you one of mine."

"I look forward to tripping on the hem."

A smile tugged at Hualit's mouth. "Can you tell me what happened?"

"Are you asking for yourself or your patron?"

"*Your* patron."

"He is a monster, Hualit."

Hualit looked over her shoulder as if she expected to see Don Víctor standing there or the devil in his place. "Not that name. Not in this house."

"He broke Santángel's fingers. Or had Álvaro break them."

"Did you mean to kill Álvaro?"

"No!" Luzia cried. "I . . . I don't think so. I don't know what I meant to do." If she'd had murder in her heart it had been for Víctor de Paredes. "Is he cruel to you? Has he hurt you?"

"He is a man and so the answer must be yes."

"Just speak plainly for once."

"And what will you do if I say yes?" Hualit sighed. "Luzia, he has never struck me, never beaten me. His tastes are not like that. My life is better with him in it, querida, and yours is too."

Luzia turned her head away, but Hualit grabbed her chin just as Don Víctor had. "Listen, Luzia. Do you know where I got the money for the coach I took to the Prado every night to wait for Víctor? For the gowns that so enticed him? For my own linajista to make me a good Christian widow worthy of more than a nobleman's cock? I let a man wash my hair with his piss because it gave him pleasure. I dressed as a milkmaid and let the alguacil fuck me in a field while I pretended to weep. And those were the least of my humiliations. Learning to curtsy, to perform for the king, it is *nothing*. You must seek to please Don Víctor and Pérez or we will both pay for it."

Luzia shoved her aunt's hand away. She sat up and pulled her knees close, wrapping her arms around them. "You know as much as I do about the refranes. Why do they work? Why do they not work? I am lost in the dark."

"What happened here . . . it could be un esticho. Witchcraft. One of the torneo competitors trying to disturb your gifts. I'll write to Mari. She knows all about sheddim and how to deal with angry spirits. Los ke vienen i van."

Those who come and go. Luzia didn't want to believe some vengeful spirit was chasing her, or that she was already in danger from rivals she'd never met.

For a long moment, Hualit was silent. "I'll write Gento Isserlis too, but I have to be more careful with how I phrase things. He's always on guard for idolatry."

"He's a priest?"

"A rabbi."

"You exchange letters with . . . with a rabbi?"

Her aunt closed her eyes. "He leads a congregation in Salonika. I send money for oil, for the lamp in the synagogue. There are many synagogues there. Can you imagine?"

Luzia couldn't make sense of the words her aunt was using.

Hualit looked sad. "Do you really not know what I am? Why I serve olives and figs to you but never ham? Why I have a private confessor to dole out the sacrament and who has his own secrets to keep?"

"But you said . . . my father . . . you said he was a fool. That—"

"Because he is. Because only secrecy can protect us."

"You were baptized!"

"That wasn't my choice. When King Manuel demanded the Jews of Portugal relinquish their children, mothers took knives to their babies' throats rather than see them baptized. Maybe that's what my mother's mother should have done too. Anusim, they called those who chose baptism over death. Forced ones. But what are we, their descendants, who say false prayers and kneel in their murderers' churches?"

Christian. They were Christian, weren't they? But here was her aunt, who had only ever seemed to care for good wine and fine silk, a Judaizer, the embodiment of everything the Inquisition reviled.

"Luzia, I might be the holiest and most pious of Christians and it would not be enough for them. Their great religion can make bread into flesh and wine into blood. But they don't believe that any amount of holy water or prayer can truly make a Jew a Christian."

"Does Ana know?" The housekeeper attended church with Hualit daily. Had it all been performance?

"Of course. We pray together and keep the Sabbath when we can."

Two Judaizers beneath one roof. Luzia leaned back against the wall. "Why tell me this now? Why burden me with such a secret?"

"Is that cruel?" Hualit mused. "Maybe so. Your father wanted you to have a Portuguese name to match his own. But my mother gave me a name full of power. It is not a woman's name or a man's. It is not Hebrew. It is not Spanish. It is not Arabic. It is all of these things. Just like the refranes you use to work your miracles. We don't need to understand where that power comes from, only that it is yours to wield."

"How can you say that? I killed a man today. He died in this room. What if it had been Don Víctor I killed? What then?"

"Don't think he isn't wondering the same thing, Luzia. If he fears you a little, maybe that's a good thing. Show him you can be biddable. Win Pérez, then win the king. Make them shower you in jewels and reales."

"And then?"

"We'll make our escape with our pockets full of gold and silver. We'll join Rabbi Gento in Salonika. We'll bring Ana too. His congregation is full of forced converts. They'll welcome us back. They'll teach us to pray properly. We'll eat mulberries in the summer and brave the winds in the winter. We'll keep the Sabbath holy and fear nothing but old age. But until that day all we have to protect us is the illusion of respectability, and we need Víctor de Paredes to preserve it. Find out what went wrong today and don't let it happen again."

Chapter 19

✦

Luzia was allowed a day of rest, and she used most of it hemming one of Hualit's old gowns. Valentina was better with a needle, but she'd had enough of tending to a servant.

The dress was brown velvet, ill-suited to household chores or work of any kind. It was tight in the waist and across Luzia's breasts, far too long in the sleeves, and finer than anything she'd ever worn. She told herself to be grateful that she wouldn't have to live in bloodstained clothes as they waited for the trunks to arrive from Perucho. But she felt only resentment. Last night her aunt had seemed like a different woman, dreaming and tender. Did she really mean to leave Spain? To take Luzia with her? Luzia couldn't quite reconcile that person with the one who had offered her up to Víctor de Paredes, who had never thought to grant her an extra coin or a discarded gown.

Luzia was dressed and clean and seated at her desk when Santángel arrived. She wasn't sure when he'd come to retrieve his satchel, but she had to assure herself that, should he notice his letters had been tampered with, he would lay the blame at someone else's door. People had been in and out of this room since the incident, and what interest could an ignorant servant have in his correspondence?

But he didn't arrive with suspicion or recriminations. Instead he stood in her doorway and said, "Your dress doesn't fit. I've brought you a pomegranate."

"Is this a new way of saying good morning?"

He set his satchel down on the table and from it drew a square of linen, a small knife sheathed in leather, and a pomegranate.

"It's one of mine?" she asked.

He nodded.

Luzia looked away. She couldn't help but think of the fruit thudding to the ground beside Álvaro's head.

"What am I to do with it?" she asked as he spread the linen on the table and set the fruit upon it. Its deep red skin had the papery thinness that came only when the pomegranate was ripe. "Am I to make it into another tree?"

"Too easy."

"Change its color?"

"Novel."

"Change its flavor?"

"Now, that would be a shame."

There was comfort in this easy exchange and she realized she'd been afraid that what had happened in this room, what she'd done to Álvaro, would alter something between them. It wasn't that she trusted him, but she enjoyed their lessons. She liked the feeling of his concentration on her, the pleasure he seemed to take in her success. And she liked looking at him. Strange as he was, she'd had few occasions to study a man, and he was more beautiful than Don Marius or the farmers and butchers down at the market. He was finely made in the way of a seashell, the silvery gleam of an oyster, the tight, bright-edged spiral of a nautilus.

He used the knife to score the skin of the fruit, making a circle around the crown to remove it.

"Your fingers have healed," she noted.

"They have."

"I thought you might have me sing over them."

"Unnecessary."

How had he endured such pain without ever releasing a cry? How could his long fingers move so nimbly when they'd been broken and useless just two days before?

He dug his fingertips into the skin and pulled the fruit open, revealing its blood-colored seeds, its juice staining the linen. "Eat, Luzia."

Luzia folded her arms even as her mouth watered. She'd had little appetite since Álvaro had died in this room. She had killed a man—and worse, she hadn't intended to. She wasn't sure if it was guilt or fear that plagued her, but she somehow knew that to eat this fruit would compound her sin.

"This feels like a trick," she said. The kind that the devil might play.

"Most good things do." He reached into his bag and handed her another clean cloth. "The time for lessons will soon end and the torneo will begin."

"Don Víctor still thinks I should compete? Even after—"

Santángel gave a single nod. "You must trust me when I say that Álvaro was no great loss."

"But did he deserve to die?"

"Death doesn't come to those who deserve it. I can attest to that."

Her guilt was too great for such platitudes. "You and your master have made me a murderer."

"If you become the king's champion and build him a new armada, you will be responsible for many deaths."

Luzia felt her anger prick. "I can wait to make my peace with that. What happened in this room, Santángel?"

"You tell me, Luzia."

"It was the same song I've always used, the same miracle. 'A change of scene, a change of fortune.' But the melody twisted in my head."

"Into what?"

"I don't know," she snapped, unable to stem her frustration. "I was . . . I couldn't make sense of what I was seeing, the sound . . . your fingers. Who does such a thing? Who commands such cruelty? Who obeys such commands?"

"You know the answer. Servants. Slaves. We do what we must."

"I know," she said hopelessly. "I know. All I wanted was for it to be over, to be anywhere but here."

"Ah," said Santángel.

"Ah?"

He reached for a segment of pomegranate and bit into it as if it were an apple.

"I've never seen someone eat a pomegranate that way." She was annoyed at how tidily he'd done it, not a fleck of juice or pith gone astray.

"It is the best way. Without fuss." He wiped his fingers on the cloth. "Your magic was trying to become bigger. It was trying to offer you escape, to take you from this place."

"Impossible."

"Yes," he said. "Very much so. There are stories in some of the Greek papyri and the *Sepher Ha-Razim* of men who could vanish in one place and reappear miles away—on a mountaintop, in a market square. But who knows if they were true. And they always used a . . ." He hesitated, searching for the right word. "Taewidha. Lapillus. There's a phrase in old Egyptian: aner khesbed wer. But even that isn't accurate. A kind of stone, a talisman. They were rare and used for concentrating a sage's abilities. These spells were of such great power they would crack the stone with a single attempt."

"But they worked?"

"I see your busy mind leaping ahead, but think of your gold coins becoming spiders. This is the same thing. There are limits to the impossible. For every story of a man who managed to fling himself to a distant city or a hilltop, there are a thousand of those who failed, who ended up buried miles beneath the earth, or drowning in an ocean, or split down the middle where they stood."

Luzia touched her hand to her mouth and Santángel's eyes followed.

"You're lucky it was just your tongue," he said.

"Álvaro wasn't so lucky."

"Better him than you." He was being gentle with her today, almost kind, but the hardness in him remained.

She picked up a piece of the pomegranate, admiring its perfect glossy seeds, begging to be eaten. "I've had the same thought," she whispered.

"That's not something to be ashamed of."

"I've spent enough time in churches to know that isn't true."

And if she was honest she could feel the pull of that larger magic. Her greedy, wanting heart longed for it. Not just for the hope of escape from this city and this life. The truth was that she had *liked* being frightening. She had never contemplated what it might mean to be feared by Víctor de Paredes, by people like him. What did it mean for her shriveled soul that she had enjoyed it so much? Men weren't kind to the things they feared.

"I brought you the pomegranate because it means something different to everyone," Santángel said. "When Ferdinand and Isabella conquered Granada, they added it to their coat of arms. You can see it in King Philip's heraldry still. But it doesn't belong to them. The Qur'an says it was a gift from Allah. The Bible says the serpent used it to tempt Eve. Two hundred pomegranates were carved into the walls of King Solomon's temple. San Juan de Dios made it a symbol of healing. A thousand stories. A thousand meanings. But in the end, it belongs to no one, except the woman who holds it in her hand. Eat it or don't. Enter the torneo or turn your back on it. It is your choice."

There were other stories too, about girls stolen from meadows, who had escape within their grasp but whose hunger bested them in the end. A peasant wasn't supposed to know those stories. But she was tired of hiding, of her trembling turnip's life. She was not going to reject the torneo. She was not going to flee on a ship with her aunt.

Luzia had always been a liar and now she was a killer. For it to mean anything, she had to keep going. She had to find a way to win. She would build herself a life of plenty. She would force her world to bloom as she'd made the pomegranate tree grow, and Santángel would help her do it. Even if blood watered the soil.

"I would like three things."

His brows shot up. "Only three?"

"For now," she said. "I want you to tell me about the trials of the torneo, so that we will be ready to face them together."

"I can do that," he said, and his relief was clear.

"I want to eat this pomegranate."

"That's why I brought it to you."

"And I want you to turn your back while I do it, so that I can enjoy it as it was meant to be enjoyed, without worrying what I look like with juice streaming down my chin."

"I can do that too, Luzia Cotado."

For the second time, he turned his back on her.

Chapter 20

✦

The gowns arrived on a Thursday, in trunks marked with Valentina's initials. They were wrapped in muslin, bundles of lavender and rosemary placed between the layers.

Valentina laid them out one by one on her bed. Three gowns, one in lush black velvet trimmed in ermine and pearls, stiff with silver brocade. One in darkest green, the ruff and sleeves edged in lace and silver spangles. One in cream velvet, stitched with birds and scrolls and pansies in ochre and umber and black. There were fresh underskirts, squirrel-lined gloves, and new velvet slippers. A new corset had been sent, of soft quilted silk. She felt a heat pass through her, a liquid pleasure that made her press her thighs together.

What is the true cost? she wondered. Will it be the devil I pay? But she clutched the corset all the tighter.

It was true she had no proper jewels, but did it matter? She would fight not to think on it.

Valentina looked around, unsure of what to feel. She wanted to celebrate, but she didn't dare interrupt Marius. He'd taken to working in the salon rather than his study, and she couldn't blame him. She crossed herself each time she passed the door, and she wondered if some part of Víctor de Paredes's bodyguard might not still be beneath her feet or above her head, wedged between the floorboards, food for boring insects.

She would be practical in this moment. She would make sure that the gowns for Luzia were in order.

She found the scullion in her room, staring at the black lacquered chest as if it might be full of vipers. Valentina entered silently, skirting the spot on the floor where they'd laid a rug, despite the fact that no stains were still visible.

In wordless agreement she and Luzia opened the chest together and lifted the bundles out, setting them neatly on the bed, carefully unwrapping the muslin.

Luzia had also received three gowns. One for day in a kind of rust-colored silk edged in gold lace, one in black velvet, and one in black wool. For performing.

Luzia ran her hand over the rough wool and gave a heavy sigh. "I thought I was being wise."

Valentina frowned. She was glad she hadn't squandered what might be her only chance at luxury on something sensible. "Perhaps it will be less severe on the body?"

"Come," said Catalina de Castro de Oro, bustling in from the hallway. "We will get you dressed."

When had the widow arrived? Had Juana let her in? Why had no one knocked? How had Valentina agreed to grant a stranger such access to her home? She voiced none of these questions. She simply shut the door and they began the process of stripping Luzia and layering her into her new gown. It was silent work, the work of women who had not been tended to their whole lives, who had done the tasks of servants when another pair of hands couldn't be bought or found. That Valentina knew such things was to be expected, but who was this widow who dressed so elegantly, who walked with such natural confidence, and yet whose fingers flew over fastenings and laces with surety?

"Many will bring their own servants to La Casilla," said the widow. "Víctor has arranged for us all to have a girl, but she will have to be shared. Luzia will be her first priority."

And the widow her second, and Valentina would wait and be late for the banquet. *That* was the unspoken part of all of this.

"I will bring my own maid to see to my hair and toilette," the widow continued, but Valentina didn't want to be appeased.

When they finished, they were all pink-cheeked and sheened in sweat. Valentina opened the window as Catalina opened the door to create a breeze. Then they stepped back to examine their work.

Luzia stood in the late morning sunlight. The black wool gown was austere, the sleeves tight instead of belled or flared, the fabric a kind of dull, sturdy material the color of soot. The tailor had built a corset that narrowed and flattened as it should, but the hoop was smaller and more subtle than those Valentina and the widow wore. The white ruff was restrained, simple folds and pleats, a bare wisp of cloud. The effect was eerie. Luzia didn't look like a nun, but she didn't quite look like a woman either. It was as if she had become smaller, a figurine carved from obsidian, a tiny pagan icon one might find in a cave.

Catalina cocked her head to the side and tapped her lips with her finger. "Dare I say it suits you?"

Valentina saw Luzia's posture relax a bit, as if she had sighed in relief. Why should she care so much what the widow thought? And yet did Valentina not hope for her approval too? Did some part of her not long to say, *Come, see what your tailor has made for me?*

The widow circled Luzia slowly. "A compelling idea. It will change the game entirely if she is presented not to appeal to desire but to forbid it. Chaste, pious, unassailable."

Valentina was less sure. "Shouldn't there be . . . *some* enticement?"

"The trick of impressing a man is in letting him believe you find him splendid."

"And if you don't?" Valentina felt her face heating but hurried on. "If you don't find a man splendid?"

"Well, you find something you do find splendid and you think of that when you're with him. Ices, for instance. Ripe figs. A good sunny day."

"Freshly folded linen?"

"Exactly."

"That you didn't have to fold yourself," muttered Luzia.

"Hush," said the widow. "I'm thinking. The dress is good, very good. A fitting costume. A bit of armor. La Hermanita with her milagritos. Lovely theater. The rest . . . needs work. Take your cap off."

Luzia's hands clenched and unclenched in the fabric of her new skirts. "Can I not wear it?"

"No, you may not," said Valentina, surprised at the harshness in her voice. "You'll look a fool."

"A veil, then, or—"

"The king doesn't care for veils," said the widow. "He thinks they make it too easy for whores to pretend to be honest women. Are you not an honest woman?"

Luzia's eyes flashed and Valentina remembered the night she had confronted her over the burnt bread. The feeling she'd had that a wolf had taken the shape of a girl.

"I'm as honest as you, señora," Luzia said to the widow, and for a moment their gazes locked.

Valentina wondered if the widow would strike her. Or if Luzia might strike the widow. But Luzia simply reached for the pins that held her cap in place.

I'll help you," said Hualit.

"I can manage very well by myself," Luzia bit back. "I always have."

Hualit only laughed and whispered, "You started this. Let's see how we finish it."

Luzia didn't know what to make of her aunt's changing moods.

Where was the woman who had sat by her bedside only days before? Who had smoothed her hair and promised escape?

Hualit snatched the cap from Luzia's head and stepped back, tapping her lip once more as if reminding her mouth to stay in place, a gesture she only used in her disguise as the widow.

Every morning, Luzia bound her hair in a tight braid and pinned it in a coil up the back of her head. She knew very well how she looked when she'd just removed her cap, the moist warmth lifting the strands around her face in an exuberant halo. The effect was comical enough that it had made Hualit and even Luzia laugh on more than one occasion.

But it was not her vanity that had her snatching back the cap from Hualit's hands. She had few memories of her mother, but she remembered her hands gently combing oil through her hair when it was wet and pliable, a ritual that had brought her calm and that was the only way to tame the thick mass of black curls.

Desert hair, her mother had called it. Luzia hadn't understood what it meant at the time, but it had pleased her because it felt special.

Even now that she knew better she sometimes took the pins from it and felt the weight of it in her hands. It stayed damp long after washing, held the scent of almond oil in its coils. Hair that had survived the destruction of the temple, the Roman legions, the long road to Morocco, that had endured conquest, and conversion, to be tied up like a secret in her little white cap. Hair of the sands, of sun-washed stones, of a horizon she would never see. Desert hair.

"Is there more of it?" asked Doña Valentina. "She looks like a newborn chick."

Luzia met Hualit's gaze and held it, unsure of the challenge she was making as she pulled the pins from her braid, letting them fall to the floor. A silly gesture. She was the one who would have to pick them up.

Hualit moved behind her and she felt a tug as her aunt pulled her braid free, and now she did want to weep because no one had seen to her hair or touched her with any kind of care in so long. Now again there was a doubling and Luzia was a child, Hualit was the mother whose face she couldn't recall. Her father had never gone mad with grief. He sold leather goods and pieces of tin and they were poor, but they had a home with candles in the window. Her father whispered the hamotzi over the bread, the blessing like a golden cord, one they were all forbidden to grasp but that dangled there above the kitchen table. *What does it mean?* she had asked.

I don't remember, her father admitted. *I'm not sure my own father remembered.*

But her mother had the words, not just the echoes. *Blessed are you, Lord our God* . . . Luzia couldn't remember the Hebrew. Latin had seemed more important at the time.

She had known no real fear then. She had believed she would have a life like that one. She would be married and cook over her own fire and her husband would kiss her cheek at night and call her beloved. Was that why she had helped Valentina? Because she knew what it was to live without love? To believe you would never have it and cling to anything that resembled it—an invitation, a bit of conversation, wine served in a small jade cup?

"Show her," Hualit said.

Luzia turned. That was when she saw Santángel, his eyes glittering in the shadows beyond the doorway, sparks that didn't burn, cold fire. She wasn't sorry he was there. Maybe she wanted him to see something about her that wasn't a dirty neck and a lack of manners.

"There's so much of it!" Valentina exclaimed. "And it's so very thick."

"We could cut it," said Hualit, her hands gripping Luzia's shoulders. "Or shave it so she can wear a wig."

Luzia's gaze snapped to Hualit, who had twined one of Luzia's curls idly around her finger. Why did Luzia care what they did to her hair? Because it looked like her mother's hair? Because her vanity told her it was the one thing about her that might ever be called beautiful even if it couldn't be considered fashionable? Or because she didn't want to be handled this way, talked to this way, moved about like a doll? All she knew was that if they tried to take a razor to her head she would scream and she would not stop screaming. She would fill the house with pomegranate trees. She would cleave them all in two. She could feel the pull of that larger magic, dangerous, impossible. *It was trying to offer you escape, to take you from this place.* She wanted to let it.

"A wig would be easiest," said Doña Valentina. "But—"

"No," said Santángel. His voice was like a sudden change in temperature, the sign of bad weather to come.

Valentina and Hualit both startled.

"You shouldn't be here," said Valentina. "It isn't decent."

"I instruct her every day in this room."

"It's not the same. A man—"

Hualit's laugh was forced. "Santángel is not a man. He doesn't care for women or men or anything at all besides his books."

Santángel's face remained impassive. "A book may disappoint, but it is far easier to be rid of."

"Always the wit," said Hualit merrily, but Luzia didn't miss the tightness of her mouth. She feared Santángel and she knew she was perilously close to overstepping. Was it because he held a position of privilege with her patron? Or did she share the same fears as Águeda in the kitchen? Did she say Santángel was not a man because he was something else entirely?

"Well, Santángel," Hualit mused, "since you seem to have strong opinions on fashion, what do we do with her hair? If she is to look pious we cannot leave it wild this way, and I know nothing that can tame it. The king will take one look at her and seek to set her before his judges or tumble her in his bed."

Valentina gasped.

But Hualit wouldn't stop. "Then again, a man who wants to fuck is a useful thing."

Luzia brought her foot down hard on the floor. "Señora, I beg you."

"Beg her for nothing," said Santángel. He remained in his spot among the shadows, and yet she could see him clearly, as if he were glowing. "No one will touch her hair, or it is my temper you will face."

"This is my home," sputtered Valentina. "Luzia lives under my roof—"

Now he moved forward and Luzia did feel the temperature of the room change, more than a sudden draft, a storm front. Valentina took a step back and Hualit froze, Luzia's dark hair still curled around her finger. They'd felt it too.

"You will not touch her hair," he repeated.

Valentina bobbed her head in a single nod.

Hualit released Luzia's hair and wiped her hand on her skirts as if to forget its feel. "Not a strand of it."

Santángel vanished soundlessly into the hall.

"The impertinence!" chirped Doña Valentina when he was gone, but her voice was too high.

"What was that?" Luzia asked, rubbing her arms.

Hualit seemed to shake free of whatever had kept her rooted to the spot. "Just do as you're bid," she said without looking at Luzia. "We'll find a velvet cap or have Perucho's plumajero concoct something with feathers and jewels. Let's see to the other gowns. I don't want to have to bother with another fitting."

Perhaps they should have cut her hair that day. If Valentina had picked up the razor, or Hualit the shears, if Luzia had bent her head to their ministrations, maybe more than one of them would have returned to the shabby house on Calle de Dos Santos and lived to tell this story.

Chapter 21

✦

Valentina had expected her heart to sing when they reached the gates of La Casilla, when they saw the garden hedges like a march of green soldiers arrayed on a battlefield, the rose trees, the fine white gravel of the drive. It was more grand than she had dreamed, perfect in its symmetry, its windows gleaming, jewels set in stone.

Instead she felt sick and wished for wine to steady her nerves. Across from her, Marius relaxed against the coach's seat, his ruff spangled with silver to match hers, an ornamental sword at his hip. He looked like a well-fed hound. But his family was of higher rank. They had once been more than minor nobility, and even if their lands provided little more than a dusty view these days, there was pride in their name. Somewhere in his blood he carried an ease she could only hope to perform. Beside him, the widow managed to look both poised and mysterious, dressed in perfectly tailored pewter silk banded with black and yellow cording.

Only Luzia, wedged next to Valentina, reflected her own misery. She was wearing her stern black wool gown with its bright white ruff, and she took shallow breaths, still unused to the confines of a proper corset. Her face looked almost green beneath the white lead and violet oil they'd used to try to ameliorate the catastrophe of her freckles.

"Do not faint," Valentina instructed.

Luzia's eyes slid to her with a look of such disdain that Valentina glanced at Marius to see if he'd witnessed it. But he was beaming out the window at the grooms and footmen who swarmed around the coach in their cream livery. The door sprang open. Marius descended first and Valentina made to follow, but the widow had already risen gracefully.

"You forget yourself," Valentina hissed, fear and worry making her brave. "I am to follow my husband, not . . ."

In the confines of the coach Catalina de Castro de Oro looked over her shoulder, a smile playing on her lips. "Not?"

Valentina's tongue felt fat in her mouth but she made herself say the words. "We all know you are Don Víctor's whore."

The widow didn't recoil or reach out to slap her. Her smile deepened and she looked at Valentina as if she were a charming child who hadn't quite learned her letters. "I feel certain your husband would take Don Víctor in his mouth himself for the price of a fine racehorse." She leaned forward. "And I might enjoy watching him do so. Now, let us all remember that we are in a place where even a breath of scandal may doom us and endeavor to have a good time despite the sword above our necks."

She floated out of the coach, alighting soundlessly on the path, her face aglow with easy delight.

"Close your mouth, señora," Luzia said gently as she gathered her skirts. "You look like you're waiting for someone to push a cake into it."

Valentina felt the shameful ache of tears in her throat. "You look like a goblin," she spat, and gave Luzia a shove so that she toppled back into her seat. She descended from the coach and took Marius's arm.

"Are you unwell?" he murmured in her ear. "Your breathing is unsteady."

"Just excited," she lied.

"As we all are." He paused. "You look very well in that new gown. The color suits you."

It was the first time Marius had ever complimented her appearance, and Valentina couldn't even enjoy it. The widow had chosen this green silk from Perucho.

She drew in a breath and then coughed. They were only a mile from home, but the air was so sweet, so clean, so free of the stink of the city. It was like being plunged into cold water, bracing and alarming all at once.

She felt as if she were shrinking in the shadow of La Casilla, as if the great house with its humble name was growing larger. The vast double doors with their golden handles opened like a mouth, and Valentina stumbled as she crossed the threshold, clinging to Marius's arm. This fine carpet is a tongue, she thought. I will put my foot upon it and it will snag me at the ankle, roll me up, and swallow me whole.

There were paintings on every wall and the windows were heavily swagged in cloth of silver.

"It's all so perfect," she whispered.

Marius grunted a laugh. "I bet even his horses shit gold."

Usually she hated when his talk turned coarse, but not today. Antonio Pérez is just a man, she told herself—even a man once second in power to the king is still a man. A man who was nearly a prisoner in his own home since he'd fallen from favor.

Don Víctor's coach had been trailing theirs so that they would all have to wait for him. Now he entered with the awful Santángel close behind. He didn't bother to greet Valentina or Marius but said something to the widow and waved for them to follow.

"Will we not have a chance to refresh ourselves?" Valentina asked.

"They will not grant us rooms until after the first trial," the widow replied. Her sunny expression had dimmed, but she looped her arm through Luzia's and hastened them along after Don Víctor.

There was nothing for Valentina and Marius to do but trail behind them.

"All of the trunks we packed, the new clothes . . . is it all to be for nothing?" Valentina asked. And did some part of her want that to be the case? Why should she long for the miserable familiarity of her drafty, charmless house?

"I suppose . . ." Marius began. "Well," he said as he put his hand over hers. "I suppose that is up to Luzia now."

Chapter 22

◆

The room they entered was large as a cathedral, its ceilings painted with frescoes, its massive chandeliers blazing with candlelight. Luzia couldn't help but do the calculations of how much so many candles must cost and wonder how long it took to light them, to raise and lower the pronged frames, to wipe dust from the crystals. Somewhere in the crowd, musicians played, flute and drum and instruments she didn't know.

"Pay attention," Santángel said. "You are entering the arena and it is time to meet your fellow gladiators."

"I thought I was to perform later tonight. Why did no one tell me the first trial would begin when we arrived?"

"No one knew."

"Pérez is giving us a reminder," said Don Víctor. "It is his game we play."

"Think of it this way," said Hualit. "If you're going to fail miserably, best to get it over with now."

"But the glasses," Luzia objected. "I need—"

"All was arranged on the stage for the trial tonight," Hualit said, gesturing to the raised platform with its golden curtains. A silver medallion hung above the stage, stamped with the image of a centaur at the center of a labyrinth. Luzia remembered the same symbol from the broken wax seal on the invitation to La Casilla.

Santángel had told her that there would be three trials: the demonstration of proof, followed by the proof of purity, and finally, the purity of power.

"Only the first will be easy," he had warned. "We'll use your trick with the goblet but make it more of a performance. This is where you must earn your right to compete in the torneo. Failure is a humiliation Víctor will not forgive. Beyond that I know very little, only that Juan Baptista Neroni will attend the second trial to make sure your milagritos are holy."

The Vicar of Madrid. She supposed she should be grateful she wouldn't face the Inquisitor General.

"And the third trial?" she had asked, thinking of the bribed linajista, of Hualit's letters to the rabbi in Salonika.

"The remaining competitors will be presented to the king at El Escorial."

El Escorial—part mausoleum, part monastery. The king in his palace. The lion in his den. And the kitchen rat freed from the larder and dressed as a fine lady. But she didn't feel like a rat anymore. The costly clothes helped, the first hot bath of her life, but mostly it was the pomegranate, a gift from Santángel, a thing of her own making. She had consumed it ravenously, watching his back in its black velvet cloak, barely recognizing herself as the linen in her hands soaked up red juice and her belly filled. She had made her choice to enter the torneo despite the risks, and whether it was in the choosing or the eating, she was changed now. She looked up at the stage and wondered if either the woman she had been or the woman she was becoming were up to the task.

"So you will perform your miracle a few hours early," Hualit whispered in Luzia's ear. "God will understand." She reached into her sleeve. "I have a gift for you."

She drew a rosary from the gray silk. The heavily carved beads were strung on a braided cord, alternating red and white, and trimmed in silver gilt. Real ivory and garnets? Or maybe just painted boxwood and bone. The string ended in a tassel and a scalloped shell carved with a cross.

"Here," said Hualit. "I will fasten it around your waist."

Again she wondered who her aunt truly was. If the garnets and ivory were real, this gift might be a sliver of safety to clutch in her hands. Money for a house or a voyage or something that could last beyond these gilded walls if she failed. But the warning was also clear: be careful and play your part well, no matter the cost. Luzia needed no reminder. She was a servant. She was Juana scrubbing blood from the floors. Servicio y silencio. For now.

Don Víctor watched them closely. "What does the little scullion think of La Casilla?"

Luzia had never seen so much gold or silver, so many gleaming windows framed by velvet, so many servants in matching livery. She knew nothing of art, but everywhere she looked she saw massive canvases, men waging war, gods making love. It was glorious, magnificent, ridiculous. If you are not the king, she thought, it is dangerous to pretend to be one.

But she said, "I have neither the taste nor the experience to judge my betters."

Don Víctor looked satisfied. "You're finally learning to manage your tongue." He gave a bare nod to Hualit. "Come, I will be introduced to the other patrons, and I would have you there." They moved off together, keeping a respectable distance apart. They hadn't arrived in the same coach, and he wouldn't offer her his arm in public. An agreement like theirs was common enough but not something to be flaunted.

"Are you wondering if she's happy?" Santángel asked, as they moved closer to the stage.

"Does it matter? She is a servant just as we are." She was surprised to hear herself say it. She had never thought of Hualit and herself as anything close to the same. Maybe now that she was in a palace, dressed in lace, sleeping in a bed every night, her vision was less cloudy.

"What do you really think of this place?"

Luzia gave a small snort. "What does a beetle think of the boot that crushes it? It is a very excellent boot with a most impressive sole and made of the finest leather."

A small smile touched Santángel's lips, and it pleased her. "Do you really care nothing for such splendor?"

"Of course I do. When was the last time you took a bath?"

"I . . . Has my person offended you?"

Luzia laughed. "Not lately. But I've never bathed in hot water before today." She closed her eyes. "You cannot imagine such pleasure."

"You should not speak of such things to a man."

Luzia's eyes flew open. She was surprised to see a scowl on his face. "Of the joys of heated bathwater?"

Santángel looked away. "It isn't seemly."

"Well, I am a peasant. Little better than a beast of the field." She was goading him but she didn't want to stop. She couldn't claim that they were friends, but whatever transformation the eating of the pomegranate had worked on her, it had changed something between them as well. "Without morals or manners. And if you want to know what I think of this . . . I think it's a very grim little party. Everyone in black. Sad music, no dancing. The wealthy can afford anything but a good time, it seems."

"What would you do with a fortune in gold?"

Luzia considered. She couldn't say any of the things that entered her head. I would have my mother's name etched in marble. I would find my father's grave. I would buy a great deal of books, and buy myself a house to read them in, and erect a high wall outside of the house, so no one would bother me. I would hire an army to stand atop the walls and guard me from kings and inquisitors and men who tell other men to break fingers. And yet she couldn't quite summon the correct servant's answers she knew she should deploy: I would wish for a comfortable home, alms for the poor, masses to be said for me after my death. When she was with Santángel her mind leapt forward, eager to play, slipped free of the leash of humility she knew might keep her safe.

So she spoke nonsense. "I would build a very large palace."

"Bigger than this?"

"Oh yes. Twice as wide but only half as tall. And in it I would place a very large bed." Again his brows rose and she hurried on before he could tell her not to speak of beds. "I would never leave it except to be rolled into steaming-hot baths."

"And to take your meals?"

"No, I would make my cook lay cakes on my pillow."

"You would grow very fat."

"I certainly hope so."

Santángel laughed then, an odd croaking sound that he silenced quickly, afraid to draw attention. "You are quite mad," he said.

"One has to get through the day somehow."

"Now that you've forgotten to look frightened, let's get closer to the stage. I want you to see the competition."

Had he been distracting her? She had certainly entered the room overwhelmed by splendor and the terror of her first performance, but Santángel had set her mind to the dance of conversation. How annoying that it had worked. How embarrassing that he hadn't been her partner in the dance but her teacher once again.

"What is the meaning of the creature in the labyrinth?" she asked.

"That is Pérez's personal device. The same impresa his father used when he was himself secretary to the king."

Luzia wanted to ask why a centaur would stand at the center of the labyrinth and not a minotaur, but that was too heady a question for a scullion.

Santángel dropped his voice. "It is said Pérez commissioned a new impresa when he fell out of favor with the king. The centaur freed, standing before the ruins of a broken labyrinth. There . . ." he said, his attention shifting. "The Holy Child, Teoda Halcón."

"The girl who speaks to angels."

"One in particular, I've been told."

"Those are her parents?"

"That is her father and one of her nursemaids. They are a wealthy family, so the Holy Child has no need of a patron."

"And her mother?"

"They say her mother's death was her first prediction."

Luzia couldn't banter over such a thought. Would she have felt the loss less keenly, if she had known her mother would die? Or would it have been worse? A death drawn out over weeks or months, the knowledge taking on its own life as if feeding on hers? Would she have wondered if she had brought about her mother's death by dreaming it like Lucrecia with Philip's armada?

"I would think a gift for foresight would give her an advantage in all of this," Luzia said.

"If the gift is real. She is very much the favorite, a direct rebuttal to Lucrecia's dreams of Spain in tatters and Philip being devoured by birds of prey. Now, look to your left. Slowly, please, let's not make a spectacle of ourselves. They are watching you as you are watching them. The young man with all the hair is Fortún Donadei, the Prince of Olives. He comes from a family of farm laborers in Jaén."

The prince. So Luzia would not be competing with anyone of royal blood. The title was meant to mock him. He had a wiry frame and a crown of thick, dark curls.

"He looks terribly sad." And frightened too, his mouth slightly agape as he took in the luxury of the room. That's what I must look like, Luzia thought with sudden shame. A clumsy peasant ill at ease in her finery, gawking at every new thing.

"I don't see why he would be. He has a wealthy patroness who is said to be unabashedly in love with him. The story is that he was tending his olive groves and sat down to play his lute in the shade of a tree when she happened upon him playing."

"So his power is in song too?"

"Yes. He can play any instrument and is said to have materialized a miniature of the marquesa's childhood pony in the olive trees."

"I cannot make something from nothing."

"No one can," Santángel said. "Not even God."

"You think he's a fraud?"

"Fortún Donadei or God?"

Luzia couldn't hide her shock. "You caution me on my tongue," she whispered, "but you could be tortured for such blasphemy."

"I might say this party is torture enough. But you're not wrong. I'll be more cautious."

"You don't fear the Inquisition at all?"

"Why would I?"

Because you aren't natural. Because you know things a good Christian shouldn't. Because there's no sign a man broke three of your fingers only a week ago. His strange eyes studied her, almost amused, daring her to give voice to any of it.

At that moment a hush fell over the room, as if they'd all taken a breath at once. The crowd turned like flowers in a field seeking the sun, necks craning. Luzia didn't even know what she was looking for, but she found herself doing the same.

A woman had entered the ballroom. Her hair was smooth and so black it shone nearly blue. Her milky skin seemed to catch the candlelight so that she glowed like a captured star. Her staid gown was black velvet and covered her completely, but it was so heavily embroidered with diamonds and metallic thread that it no longer looked black, but like quicksilver, sparking beneath the chandeliers.

"Who is that?" asked Luzia.

"That is Gracia de Valera. The Beauty."

"She's something more than beautiful."

"She is said to perform milagritos herself, and I'm told that she can speak to the spirits of the dead. She has asked to perform first."

Luzia watched Gracia drifting through the crowd like a petal borne aloft on a breeze. She had never felt more sturdy, more earthbound, a knob of coal in her dour dress, her coronet of braids with its modest pearls and shells.

"I fear we will all disappoint after such a visitation."

But Santángel's eyes were still on her, not trailing Gracia de Valera through the crowd. "If the king wanted a pretty woman to look at, there are plenty of those in Spain. Do just as we practiced and no one can match you."

A child. A farmer. A scullion. And a young woman who looked like the Virgin herself had stepped from the frame of one of Pérez's many paintings. Luzia could taste the pomegranate in her mouth, the flavor of her own ambition, her appetite for more. She eyed the golden curtains of the stage and knew she would prove Santángel right. She was done going hungry.

Chapter 23

✦

Santángel sensed when Antonio Pérez entered the room. It was like standing in the sea and feeling the tide shift, pulling at your ankles, the sand sliding away as the ocean breathed. Everybody turned as he made his way around the room, acknowledging some, ignoring others.

Beside him Víctor stiffened as Pérez passed without a nod in his direction. The slight pleased Santángel at the same time that it intrigued him. He still didn't fully understand the limits of his own influence. But he did know Pérez had best hope to regain the king's ear. The insult was not one Víctor would soon forgive.

Even in disgrace, Pérez showed no sign of doubt or worry. He was a tidy little man, precise in his gestures, his clothing as lavish as his home, each fold and bit of padding impeccably tailored, as if he were a finely made marionette. He was a man who took pleasure in attention the way only the fearless could.

He raised his glass and the room fell silent.

"There is no greater empire than this one and no greater king than ours. It is Spain that must see to the soul of the world, and this heavy burden rests upon our blessed ruler's shoulders, placed there by God Himself. As the brave Don Juan bested the barbarians at Lepanto, so we take up musket and cross to subdue the Flemish traitors and the heretic wretch Elizabeth. If then our mighty king would have miracles, I will provide them. There is no holier man, no holier country, no holier cause."

The musicians struck a dramatic chord, as if they really were at the theater and someone were about to begin a song.

"Bold to invoke Don Juan's name," murmured Víctor.

"Why?" Luzia whispered.

When Santángel lowered his lips to her ear, the sweet green scent of orange blossoms overwhelmed him. Did she have a lover? And why did the thought make him want to find this mysterious suitor and bury a knife in his heart?

"Bold because the hero of Lepanto was no match for the Dutch," he whispered back to her. "He was trounced and forced to retreat. And Pérez had the man's secretary murdered. It's why he lost the king's favor. You must stop wearing scent if you are to play La Hermanita. No nun is importing perfume from Paris."

Luzia frowned. "I don't wear scent."

He wasn't going to argue the point. "Go take your place in the wings. You will follow the Beauty."

She nodded, jaw set. He almost expected her to roll up her sleeves as if she were about to attack a stubborn stain.

"Why must she march off that way?" grumbled Víctor. "Where has all her training gone?"

"There's a certain charm to it," the widow protested. "Perhaps her determination will distinguish her."

Pérez placed himself at the exact center of the room, where a few chairs had been set. He had no need for a throne or dais. The crowd had opened a path before him, so that his sightline would not be obscured.

Gracia de Valera floated up the stairs and onto the stage, her heavily ornamented gown glittering like a night sky.

"Exquisite," said Víctor sourly. "Have we miscalculated?"

"The dress is not what matters here." And such ornament didn't suit Luzia. Her power would shine more brightly than any bauble or jewel. Though Santángel was beginning to believe her will was the greater gift. She was stubborn as a well-built wall, as decided in her course as an avalanche.

He wondered why the Beauty had chosen to walk to the stage instead of appearing from behind the curtain. She curtsied deeply, as if to the king himself, her movement slow and perfectly controlled, then lifted one delicate hand. The curtain rose, revealing a tower of glass goblets.

Luzia's glasses.

Víctor released a grunt, as if he'd been struck. The widow pressed a hand to her mouth. Marius just looked flummoxed, and Valentina's head bobbed on her neck, up and down, left and right, as if she could adjust the angle on this situation and somehow make it less of a debacle.

Now Santángel understood why Gracia de Valera had asked to perform first.

He searched the crowd for Luzia, but she had already gone. Was she seeing this now from her place in the wings? What would she do? There might be time to fetch candles, but he didn't like the idea of the fire trick. Not so soon, not when they were trying to avoid even a hint of the diabolical. Perhaps the grapevines? He looked around the room, but he could see no arrangements of flowers. He watched in growing fear as Gracia smashed the goblets. She did it coyly, elegantly, drifting past the table and extending a single slender finger to tip each glass off the edge, sharing a shy smile with the audience as she did so.

"Oh, she's very good," said the widow.

She was. Her glance was demure and at the same time mischievous, her walk graceful without seeming practiced. When the goblets lay in a sparkling heap of shards she stepped behind the table, made the sign of the cross, and extended her arms. Her sleeves had been cleverly beaded so that they looked like angel's wings, and she tilted her face upward, the light catching her perfect features.

"Is she experiencing a vision?" asked the woman beside him.

"A visitation?" queried her companion.

"Something certainly," murmured the widow when Gracia released a moan.

The Beauty threw her hands skyward as if conducting an invisible orchestra. A sound like a choir singing filled the room, the voices high and heavenly, nearly inhuman in their purity. Clouds appeared at her slippered feet, billowing up and engulfing her and the stage.

The crowd gasped. The mist cleared.

Gracia de Valera appeared with head humbly bowed as if in prayer.

The goblets stood in a line, all of them perfect.

"Now, that's a performance," said Don Marius.

"Horseshit," said Santángel, and Doña Valentina gasped.

It was all fakery. Very good fakery, no doubt concocted with some of the best set dressers and players from the Corral de la Cruz. But an illusion nonetheless.

If Gracia de Valera had any kind of magic, she hadn't chosen to use it tonight.

So now they knew at least one of the competitors trafficked in fraud. But it might not matter. If Luzia embarrassed herself there would be no coming back from it. Santángel wouldn't be able to spare her Víctor's wrath.

The curtain dropped and the crowd chattered, marveling at Gracia's beauty, her poise, the perfection of her gown. She descended into the crowd to applause, her wealthy patron, Don Eduardo Barril, greeting her with a bow.

Again the musicians struck their chord. Again the curtain rose. The tower of glasses remained and there was Luzia in her plain black dress, La Hermanita, a solemn little penitent with seashells in her tightly braided hair, the rosary Víctor and the widow had gifted her the only sign of ornament.

Santángel couldn't tell what she was thinking. She stared out at the ballroom and he wondered if she was contemplating cracking the table with the song she used to split firewood or if she could make a fig tree grow from the platters at the sideboards. Her mouth was set in what he could only describe as an angry line.

She eyed the tower of goblets, approaching them with none of Gracia's ease. She looked like a frustrated captain surveying her disobedient troops and considering their punishment. She seized one and smashed it to the ground defiantly. Then another. And another. The audience stirred, restless. Someone laughed under his breath. Antonio Pérez was slouched back in his seat, his lips pulled down in a scowl.

She can't be foolish enough to perform the same trick. He felt a sinking disappointment, not that she would be mocked, not even that Víctor would disavow her, but that he had thought better of her, of her wit, of her lively speech that galloped along like a skittish pony, hooves dancing, nothing like the hesitant creature he'd met in the widow's courtyard, a peasant girl who was not at all what she seemed.

As if she could hear his thoughts, she glanced at him, her brow cocking slightly, the look of a woman amused. Well. Enjoy your smiles now. Víctor would chase her from Madrid for the crime of humiliating him. Santángel supposed he should be glad to see his master made a laughingstock, but he remembered Luzia standing in panic before the stalk of a pomegranate tree, trying to find a song to save him. Endure, endure. They both knew that refrain so well.

She closed her eyes. She must be hearing the words to bring the goblets back together. Once she stomped her foot, twice. As if she were furious, as if she wore the boot now and all who watched would be crushed beneath it. When she stomped her foot a third time, her voice rose in a high, eerie wail and the shattered bits of glass rose with it, a gently whirring glimmer of dust in the candles' glow.

The audience went quiet, their attention snared. This was at least different from the mist and artifice of Gracia's performance.

Luzia lifted her arms gently and the cloud of shattered glass rose high above her head, then out over the audience. The pieces hung in the air, some larger, some smaller, shifting slowly this way and that.

Pérez's brow had lowered. He looked perplexed but not pleased.

The cloud separated, lines forming, creating points of brightness. Santángel understood what she was doing a bare breath before the crowd did. They gasped. Pérez's mouth opened with an audible *pop*.

The glass had arranged itself into stars, a glittering constellation that hung above Antonio Pérez's head: the shape was unmistakable, as if a slice of the distant universe had appeared in this ballroom. The Pleiades. The sign under which the king's secretary had been born, the chart that had pleased him so powerfully, the promise that his fate was bound up with kings and queens.

The illiterate peasant girl had read his letter. A letter contemplating Pérez's arrogance, his attachment to this dream of his own greatness. A letter written in Latin.

The crowd burst into thunderous applause, surging toward Pérez, trying to reach up to touch the glass constellation. Pérez himself rose to his feet, his eyes bright and fastened firmly on Luzia.

The scullion had bested Gracia de Valera in stunning fashion. She had taken the Beauty's insult and turned it theatrically to her benefit. Víctor seized his shoulder. "Brilliant," he crowed. "What is the matter with you? Why do you look like you're ready to do murder?"

Santángel mustered a smile. "I am merely thinking of what challenge may come next and how to meet it."

Assuming the liar Luzia Cotado survived the night.

Chapter 24

✦

Still humming, Luzia brought the glass cloud back to the stage and let it fall gently to the surface of the table in a soft heap. She knew she should leave it at that, but when she saw Gracia de Valera staring at her with her perfect lips pressed together like a fresh pleat, she waved her hand over the dust as if she were bored, as if she were swiping crumbs off a table. The glass formed itself into goblets obediently. A petty gesture. They weren't quite as perfect as they might have been if she'd taken her time, but she was interested in defiance, not perfection. She wanted Gracia to know she would not go quietly.

Before she reached the bottom of the stage steps, the crowd had parted and Antonio Pérez glided through. He was so small, so compact, and possessed of a strange, smooth elegance, as if he'd been polished to too high a shine. He smelled of plums and amber. Don Víctor and Don Marius trailed him as best they could, surrounded as he was by courtiers. Hualit and Valentina had been swallowed up by the crowd, and she couldn't find Santángel among them. Pérez waved a hand and a courtier stepped forward—the man with the dyed-red beard and heavy-lidded eyes.

"Luzia Calderón Cotado. Of Casa Ordoño and Casa de Paredes."

Calderón. That was not her name. She was Luzia Cana Cotado. Luzia knew Jews sometimes changed the names of children who were sick. What was she sick with that she needed her name changed? The linajista had scrubbed away her mother's name—Blanca Cana, daughter of scholars, pruned from Luzia's family tree.

Luzia curtsied, keenly aware of the eyes upon her and gladder than ever that she'd practiced.

"How does a simple peasant know the shape of the constellations?" Pérez queried. "Or did your patron plan this little surprise?"

Somehow Don Víctor had made his way closer. "I assure you, Don Antonio, I did not."

"Then how did such knowledge come to you?"

Luzia kept her eyes on her shoes. "It is not for me to know," she said softly, in the humble scullion's mumble she'd spent years perfecting. "And I cannot pretend to answer. God shows me the way and I follow it."

"A good, pious woman," said Pérez, but he sounded like he was sizing up a melon at the market. "Show me your hands."

Luzia felt a pang of fear. Such a command was prelude to a beating with a switch or stick, but if a king, even a man who was only king in his own palace, gave you an order, there was no choice but to oblige.

She offered up her hands. He took hold of them, his rings flashing. His own hands were soft, slick like dumplings when they slid from the soup pot.

He laughed. "Rough and tough as animal hide. They told me you were a scullion, but I did not quite believe."

"I am an honest woman, señor. It is true."

He gave her hands a squeeze, then dropped them. "I have no doubt of that at least." He glanced at Don Víctor for the first time. "The little nun has made a very big impression."

Don Víctor laughed. "I am certain she never took orders."

But Pérez was already gone.

Hualit embraced her. "Well done, querida," she whispered in Luzia's ear. "You showed that bitch what her fancy gowns are worth."

"How *did* you know the sign of the Pleiades?" Don Víctor asked.

Luzia looked at him blankly. "Beg pardon, señor?"

"Be careful," Hualit said. "The Beauty will not be happy with you. Keep your eyes open."

The musicians struck up their cue again, a signal that the next hopeful was to perform now that Pérez had returned to his position at the center of the room.

"Let us learn what we can," said Don Víctor, though his eyes were still on Luzia.

She let herself search the crowd, seeking Santángel. He would know now that she had lied. And that she had read his personal correspondence. She thought of his hands pulling apart the pomegranate, an offering after the nightmare of what she had done to Álvaro, an opportunity for her to renew her faith in herself, and for them to keep faith together. But when she'd stood on that stage, listening to the applause for the Beauty, humiliation flooding through her hot and prickly as a fever, she hadn't been able to think of Santángel or to look any further than the next moment when she would stand on stage and be made a laughingstock. She had felt the pull of the magic that had split her tongue, like a door begging to be opened, escape waiting on the other side.

Then she'd gazed out at those reassembled glasses in their perfect rows, and she'd heard the refrán in her aunt's voice, remembered Hualit leaning back on the cushions in her courtyard, laughing as she read from the letter in her hand. *El hombre es mas sano del fierro, mas nezik del vidro.* Luzia hadn't understood some of the words, and she and Hualit had worked them out together. *A man is stronger than iron and weaker than glass.* She'd never thought of the refrán as something she could use, but standing there, helpless, her anger mixed with the memory and the song leapt to life in her mouth. The words had saved her.

That didn't mean they would spare her Santángel's anger.

Luzia's worry only increased as she watched first the Holy Child and then the Prince of Olives perform. Some part of her had hoped the rest of the competitors might be frauds. But if they were, they were far better at it than Gracia de Valera.

Teoda Halcón began on the stage but descended to the crowd and stood before Pérez, his hand in hers, her small face serene and glowing. She recited the dream she'd had the previous night, which involved an apple orchard, a white horse, and a woman bathed in moonlight, then she gestured for him to come closer, and when he bent down, she whispered in his ear.

Pérez swayed slightly when he stood erect once more, his face pale. He blinked slowly, then said in a quiet, rasping voice, "A secret. Spoken to me by my father on his deathbed." He closed his eyes. "Remarkable."

"Such pride he has in you," said Teoda in her high, sweet voice. She turned to the crowd. "And now I must advise you all that a storm is coming."

"But the skies have been cloudless all day!" someone cried.

His words were lost to a rumble of thunder and the sudden patter of rain against the ballroom windows.

The crowd burst into thrilled applause.

"This will be what the king most desires," grumbled Víctor. "Someone who can see into the hearts and minds of men, into the future itself."

"Just remember," Hualit said. "The king didn't thank Lucrecia de León for the favor."

The musicians leapt into another dramatic chord, and Luzia was grateful for the distraction.

On the stage, Fortún Donadei sat with the curved wooden body of a vihuela braced between his legs. He wore olive green velvet patterned with elaborate cutwork, a falling band of gilded lace at his neck and sparkling at his cuffs, his hose and breeches of the same green. A large golden cross hung at his neck, studded with fat gems. He plucked out a few notes, a tentative melody forming, then took up his bow and bent his head as he drew it across the strings.

The song was cheerful and his booted foot tapped along, the kind of music one might hear in a marketplace or taverna, nothing formal. And yet there was sadness in it too, a kind of longing that seemed to speak through the bow, as if the instrument itself was weary and aching, each pull across the strings a lamentation. He didn't look out of place any longer, not with an instrument in his hands.

Was it Donadei who created this sadness? He looked beautiful in the golden light of the stage, his curls darker, his sun-bronzed skin nearly the same warm hue as the vihuela, as if they'd been carved from the same tree and polished by the same hand. Was it this profound feeling, this trembling ache between joy and misery that had lured his patroness into the olive grove? There was pleasure in this sadness. It was the feeling of remembering great happiness you will never have again, the first flush of desire you know will never be consummated but that you can't help but hope for anyway, the desperate longing to see your beloved even when you know you are not loved in return.

Luzia's eyes caught movement near the ceiling of the room—a bird had somehow gotten into the ballroom. There were two of them, she realized, little black things, chirping and circling the chandeliers. They fluttered toward the stage where they were joined by another, and then another. They were a flock now, moving with the music of Donadei's bow, the flow of their bodies forming shapes that then dissolved with another turn of their wings. Luzia realized she was holding her breath as she watched and that the rest of the guests were too. With a final sad sighing of his bow, the birds rushed from the room in a gust and Donadei's song ended. As one, the crowd sighed too, then exploded into applause that put the Holy Child's thunder to shame.

The Prince of Olives rose, his face still sad, his smile small, and bowed first to the audience and then more deeply to Pérez.

"Well," Hualit said, as Donadei descended the stairs to be greeted by his patroness, who wore matching green and gold. "I think the whole room just fell a bit in love with Fortún Donadei."

"But only one woman has paid for his love in return," replied Don Víctor.

Let them love him, Luzia told herself. It is the miracles that matter.

Chapter 25

◆

L uzia had hoped she might be free to rest and find some
privacy after the performances, but the guests were escorted
to another glorious room, this one nearly as large as the
ballroom and set with long tables blazing with candles.

The feast that followed was less like a meal than a performance
of one, course after course in an endless parade punctuated by
small dishes of water scented with lavender with which to rinse
their hands. Partridge simmered in milk; peacock dressed with bacon and minced almonds; quail stuffed with cinnamon and cloves,
and a mousse of its own livers; boar sauced with bitter oranges, and
toasted bread soaked in broth; pie after pie full of vinegary vegetables and chunks of beef stewed with pomegranate and honey,
their golden crusts washed with saffron. Between each course, the
musicians played, sometimes accompanied by jugglers, or dancers
in costumes of scarlet and gold, and short scenes were performed
on a wooden stage that was wheeled from one end of the room to
the next.

Luzia made certain to eat plentifully from any dish with pork,
but picked at the rest. She wished for wine but drank water flavored
with fennel. She sat wedged between Don Víctor and Hualit, dutifully silent in her convent gown, listening to conversation about
plays she'd never heard of and people she didn't know. If Santángel
was present, she hadn't seen him, but she supposed there was no

reason for servants to dine in such company, not unless they were competitors in the torneo like herself and the Prince of Olives.

Fortún Donadei had been seated beside his patroness, and though he was doing his best to smile and look at ease, Luzia could see he wasn't eating much either.

At last there were plates of ices and sweet cakes with stewed fruit and the ladies were permitted to retire. Footmen led the Ordoños and then Hualit and Luzia to the rooms they'd been assigned.

"We will be in the same wing," said Hualit, "away from Don Víctor and his household, as is proper. The Ordoños are just down the hall. Teoda Halcón is young enough that she is housed with her own family in rooms not far from your own, and the Beauty and her ladies are close by, so be cautious."

Luzia thought she was tired, but when the footman opened the door to her room, fresh elation flooded through her. She had never seen a bed set with linen so white, the coverlet embroidered with the Pérez labyrinth, and heaped with tawny furs. Coals blazed in a silver brazier and thick curtains had been drawn against the rain. Next to the bed, velvet slippers had been set out, and a dressing table was laden with all of the creams and powders Hualit and Valentina had assembled for her, alongside a set of heavy silver brushes and combs.

A maid was waiting and curtsied when they entered. "Don Víctor pays Concha's wages and pays her well," Hualit explained, "so you needn't fear sabotage when she is near. She'll keep your secrets."

"From everyone but Don Víctor."

"Precisely," Hualit said. "Come, let's get you undressed."

She and the maid worked quickly to remove Luzia's bodice and skirts and corset and stockings. When Concha started pulling up her linen smock, Luzia faltered.

"She'll take it to be laundered," Hualit reassured her. "You have others now."

Luzia felt that jab of pleasure and resentment as the smock was removed and a shift of thin white linen was pulled over her head.

The shoes were traded for slippers and a fur-lined dressing gown of persimmon velvet from Perucho's shop.

"You see how it is now," Hualit said gently, removing the shells from Luzia's hair and setting them on the dressing table. "You cannot go back. There is only the path before you. Whether it leads to a palace—"

"Or onto a pyre," Luzia finished. "At least I'll be well dressed when I'm dragged to my cell in Toledo."

"There is that," Hualit said with a smile, and dropped a kiss on Luzia's head before she departed.

When she was gone the maid used tongs to remove the hot brick she'd set between the covers to warm the bed. It was shaped like the round medallion that had hung above the stage and it was patterned with the same labyrinth.

"Is there nothing he has not put his seal to?" Luzia wondered.

"There's a sign above his bed," Concha said with a breathy giggle. "A scroll held up by angels of solid silver. I'm told it reads, 'Antonio Pérez sleeps here.'"

"In case he forgets?"

Concha laughed, then startled when someone scratched at the door.

Luzia assumed Hualit had returned, but Santángel stood in the doorway.

"Go," he commanded the little maid, and with something like a squeak, Concha vanished.

"You cannot be here," Luzia whispered furiously. "Not alone. Not with me."

"No one has seen me arrive and no one will see me go."

"How can you be so certain? Even a breath of impropriety—"

"It is my job to be certain," he said, shutting the door behind Concha. "And yet I have been very wrong about you. Why did you lie to me? And do not think to make a pretty story about what

God has shown you. I know which letters I carried with me the day you nearly killed us both."

"I don't remember your life being in danger. It was my tongue that split."

"And my fingers that broke."

"But how quickly they healed, my honest lord."

"Answer the question," he bit out.

"I never told you I couldn't read."

"You let me believe it."

"It's good to let a man have his illusions," Luzia said, unsure of what to do with herself, too conscious of her state of undress. "No one forced you to assume a servant was stupid."

"I never thought you were stupid."

"I see you are a capable liar too." She folded her arms, trying to stymie the anger rushing through her, as if she could knot it up in her elbows. "Tell me you thought differently that day in the courtyard, when you saw the sad stump of a wax candle that had been brought before you, without charm or beauty, and so of course, without wit. Only a woman who looks like Catalina de Castro de Oro or Gracia de Valera can be presumed to be worth listening to."

"You sell yourself too cheaply, Luzia," he shot back. "That first day when you stumbled into the courtyard and made your miserable curtsy, you did an extraordinary job of humbling yourself, of pretending to be a lump of dirty wax. An actress of your ilk is rare indeed. Can you blame me for not being able to see past your performance?"

Maybe she had wanted him to. *See me. See that I am more than this charade of mumbling humiliation.*

"You may posture and fluff your white feathers if it pleases you," she replied. "But you're like every other man who wishes for a woman who is shapely and kind and pious and only wise enough not to trouble him."

Santángel's laugh was bitter, the sound like dry twigs snapping.

"Why not tell the truth yourself now, Luzia? Admit that the act had gotten so good you yourself had started to believe it."

"I know who I am."

"Do you? I know what it is to lower yourself, to keep your eyes downcast, to seek invisibility. It is a danger to become nothing. You hope no one will look, and so one day when you go to find yourself, only dust remains, ground down to nothing from sheer neglect."

He was right and she hated that he was right. When she was young she'd been fearless—until her mother died, until her father died, until she understood that the world had no place for a conversa who could read and write, who longed to talk and to argue over nothing, who wanted to see enough of the world to have opinions about it. She had learned to hide too well, even from Santángel.

"I know who I am," she repeated, and this time her voice rang with certainty. She was the woman who had eaten the pomegranate, and tonight she had commanded a stage. She had held a room full of nobles in her thrall.

"What other secrets are you keeping, Luzia Cotado?"

She sat down in the chair placed before her dressing table. The woman in the watery glass before her was a stranger, her thick hair free of its braids, her dark eyes wild. She had never seen herself angry before.

"Are we sharing our secrets now?" she asked.

"I have none."

"Another lie."

"Ask me a question and I will answer it truly."

"What are you? Why do people fear you? Did you make a bargain with the devil himself?"

He held up his fingers, enumerating his answers. "In another life, in another world, I would be called a familiar. My gifts are not my own. They exist only to serve others. People fear me because I want them to, because their fear makes my life easier."

"And the bargain with the devil?"

"Depending on your opinion of Víctor de Paredes, there may be some truth to that particular charge. Now it is your turn to answer. What is the nature of the magic you use?"

"I don't know how to answer that."

"Where did you learn it?"

"That is not for me to say."

"Do you think Father Neroni won't ask? Do you think you can mumble and shrug and that will be enough for him?"

She picked up the silver hairbrush. "I will tell them my gift is from God."

"Did He appear to you in a vision? Did He pierce your heart with an arrow of light? Best get your story straight now. Tell me the truth and I can protect you. I can help you. What text did you study? What language do you use?"

She didn't know how to answer. Her refranes were Spanish and Hebrew and Turkish and Greek. They were none of those things. They changed depending on what part of the world the letter came from. They were words battered and blown to all corners of the map, then returned to her, as the people who spoke them could never return.

"No language," she snapped in frustration. "Every language."

She slammed the silver brush down on the table, then hissed as a black shape leapt from its pale bristles.

"Be still," said Santángel.

The scorpion sat poised before Luzia, mere inches from her hand, its shiny black body crooked like a finger.

She thought of the symbol on Santángel's seal. Was this his revenge on her? Had he always intended to see her killed? Had he known the Beauty would sabotage her performance and sent Luzia up there to face ridicule, expecting her to fail only to be thwarted? She hadn't seen him during the banquet. He could have been here, in her rooms, setting a trap for her.

He was moving slowly toward her. She was afraid to look away from the scorpion but she could sense him drawing nearer. He had said he was a killer. Why hadn't she feared him then?

"Don't," she whispered, ashamed of the pleading in her voice.

Her mind sought words of protection, something to keep the monster at bay. Which was the greater danger, the scorpion or Santángel?

"Luzia, do not move." He was behind her now.

She could see him in the mirror, white skin, white hair, a creature carved from ice.

She would scream. She would run.

"Hello, friend," he said softly. "Nen chu mem senuwak." He set his long-fingered hand on the table and the scorpion crept onto it.

He lifted it and stepped away.

"Clever," he said, "to place it in the brush. A sting so near the head or heart could be fatal. If nothing else, you would no longer be a threat."

Luzia watched the scorpion resting on his hand like part of a rosary, her heart beating a jagged rhythm in her chest. If Santángel had set the trap, then why not let it spring shut? Why not let her die? And hadn't he been given countless opportunities to harm her in the past weeks? He could have let her bleed to death when she'd split her tongue.

"How?" she managed. "Who did this?"

"It could have been any of the hopefuls. Bold to act this soon. You should be flattered that you're so worth killing."

"The dream of every young woman." She hesitated. She still couldn't quite catch her breath. "Why doesn't it sting you?"

"We understand each other." He gestured to a jar of powder meant to whiten the teeth. "Empty it."

Luzia shook out the fine dust of coral and alunite, and Santángel took the jar with his free hand. He slid the scorpion inside and closed the lid. Luzia tried not to show her relief.

"It's your symbol, your seal," she said. "El Alacrán." Not the nearly harmless yellow scorpion but the deadlier variety.

"So you must have noted when you were reading my private letters. At least you have the manners to look ashamed."

Luzia was. A bit. "Why choose that for your impresa?"

"I didn't choose it for myself. It was given to me. A little joke by a De Paredes, a warning to others of my true nature." He held the jar up to the candle on her dressing table, and through the murky glass, Luzia saw the shape of the scorpion dance back from the heat of the flame. "But I have come to like it. Scorpions live long lives. And choose when to use their sting. They pick their moment."

Luzia was still thinking of how close she'd come to death. "They meant you to be blamed. If the scorpion was found."

"Yes." He headed for the door.

"You're . . . you're leaving?"

"I need to speak to Don Víctor. We'll arrange for guards and inform Pérez. He'll want to know someone is plotting murder beneath his roof. Besides himself." He turned once more as he slipped past the door, framed by darkness, the jar gleaming in his hand. "Now we know each other. Let's see what we may accomplish with fewer lies between us."

Chapter 26

✦

Morning brought a strange kind of silence to the house. The previous night, Luzia and Concha had looked through every drawer, shaken out every bit of linen, beaten every gown and knocked shoes and slippers and boxes and bottles against the floor. They'd found no other monsters lying in wait and they'd pulled the trundle out from beneath the high bed so Concha could sleep beside her. In the morning, Concha went to empty the chamber pots and heat fresh water, and Luzia sat for a long while by the window, watching clouds of mist move over the hedges and paths like ghostly party guests. She saw gardeners at their work and horses led by their grooms to some distant stable.

Luzia didn't know what to do with herself, if she was meant to go find Valentina or Hualit or Santángel. Or if she was meant to wait in her room until someone came to get her. La Casilla was its own country with its own customs and language and no one had bothered to educate her in this.

It was strange to just sit. She'd been working since she was a child, cleaning the house with her mother, tending to her father's pots and pans and bits of tin, walking the streets by his side, or helping to fix the cart. She had loved that time with him as much as she'd loved quiet hours with her mother spent studying letters and maps, or learning to add and subtract over the household accounts. She had never known a minute or an hour when there

wasn't some task to be done. A dress to be mended, coal to be gathered, bread to be made. Her hands, her feet, her back, always put to
use. Not her mind, though. Not for a long time. Her mother's texts
and lessons had vanished, as if they'd passed into death with her.

When she'd gone to work for the Ordoños, she'd trained her
thoughts to be in two places, to walk the streets and see to her chores
while living in distraction. She had let herself dream of foreign places,
soft beds, and yes, if she was honest, of beautiful men. As a child they
had been slender and smooth-cheeked heroes on horseback, princes
and poets. But she was not a child anymore, and her hopes had been
tempered by time and desire that came upon her suddenly, shamefully. The muscles of the butcher's forearm as he lifted a cleaver, a
fine profile, a long-fingered hand coaxing a scorpion into a jar. She
wanted and longed to be wanted in return. And now it was as if her
working self and her dreaming self were meeting in the quiet of this
place, and they had absolutely nothing to talk about.

So Luzia sat, waiting for interruption, for command. She sat
at *her* window and watched the sun rise fully over the rose trees
pruned into round tufts, the long rows of hedges. She sought the
old dreams of pirate kings and princely courtiers, of unexpected
vistas and foreign towns. But she was writing a new adventure
now. If she won the torneo, she would become a soldier in a war
she didn't understand. And she had no illusion that victory would
mean an end to competition or the danger it presented. Joining
the king's service meant entering a world of politics and rivalries,
of endless scheming and status-seeking. She would never be safe.

Good. Her mind would be challenged, her wits sharpened. She
might not survive, but at last she would be put to the test. *Where
is your own fear, Luzia?* Hualit had asked her. Luzia didn't know.
Maybe she'd eaten it along with the pomegranate.

She let the rosary move through her hands. She'd examined the
beads last night, carved on one side with placid human faces, on
the other with skulls, reminders of the inevitability of death. Real
garnets. Real ivory. The beads cool against her skin. The woman she

was pretending to be should pray, but Luzia knew she was destined for hell because all she could think was that each bead strung together might make a tiny fortune.

Down the hall Don Marius had woken early to take a stroll to the stables and had returned to find chocolate being prepared. He had never had the drink, but his doctor had warned him that it could produce melancholy. He watched it being made with sugar and black pepper and cinnamon and accepted a cup for the sake of appearing cosmopolitan, but then found himself unsure of whether to drink it.

He walked with it untouched back to the rooms that he and Valentina had been given, grand rooms from which he could just see the roofs of the stables if he craned his neck. Valentina was awake but still in bed when he entered, her brownish hair around her shoulders.

"How were the stables?" she asked.

"Remarkable. Pérez's horses live better than we do." He looked down at the cup in his hands. "I have brought chocolate."

To his surprise, she sat up straighter. "Really? What is it like?"

"I . . . I haven't tried it yet," he admitted. "Would you like the first sip?"

He wasn't prepared for the smile that broke across her face. "Yes!"

Marius perched at the edge of the bed and placed the cup in her reaching hands. He waited as she lifted it to her lips and sipped.

A small laugh escaped her. "It's strange," she said, closing her eyes. "Bitter. But . . . I think I like it."

She offered it to him and he took a sip. It *was* strange. He could taste the cinnamon and pepper, and maybe anise too. But he couldn't name what the chocolate itself tasted of and he wasn't certain it was to his liking.

"Would you care for some more?" he offered.

"I don't want to be greedy."

"I brought it for you," he lied.

"You did?" There was something in her disbelief he found shaming.

"I thought my wife might enjoy it."

She smiled again and Marius caught himself preening. It had never occurred to him that his wife could be happy, or that he might be the one to make her happy, or that in doing so he might be made happy in return. Perhaps his doctor was wrong and there was something to this drink of chocolate after all.

In another wing of the house, Quiteria Escárcega was sipping her own cup of chocolate, brought to her by her young lover, Luis Lopez Venegas, and both the drink and the man had begun to bore her. She had hoped the torneo would spark some inspiration, but despite the miraculous feats and feasts, she was struggling, writing a single line, then half a page, then realizing she'd wasted her morning on nothing she could properly use. She glanced at Luis, half-dressed and hoping for attention, and sighed. When she couldn't write, it was almost always a sign that an affair was at an end, and that meant crying and recriminations and many ballads badly sung. She would wait until they left La Casilla to end this romance, and make what use she could of Luis until then. She had begun to imagine a play set in a kitchen, a cook and a scullion at its center, a satire of the empty life their rich employers led.

"My love," she said, and he perked like a dog readying for a run. "Tell me another of your mother's recipes."

"Savory or sweet, my sweet?" he asked, pleased with himself.

Quiteria sighed again. "Sweet," she said, and set her pen to paper.

North of Madrid, in the massive monastery that was also a mausoleum that was also a library that was also a palace, Spain's king woke early as he always did and began a letter to his envoy in Cologne. His fingers and his feet ached, swollen by the gout that filled his veins with fire. But it was essential he manage such communications himself, and he wanted the specifics of this mission to arrive in his own hand. A cache of relics had been spirited away from a Calvinist mob raiding churches in Germany. Teeth and bones and hair, a glorious jumble of saints, rescued from desecration. There was even a femur that belonged to San Lorenzo himself and that was said to have cried out when one of the heretics tried to crush it beneath his boot. He would bring them home to Spain and safety. They would join his collection and the monks would see to the making of the reliquaries under his supervision.

He knew soon he would have to turn his mind to the matter of Pérez. His spies had reported great workings at the torneo, but he would wait to hear what the vicar had to say. He would close no doors that God wanted left open.

Someone was tapping at Luzia's door. Concha entered and mumbled, "The . . . Señor Santángel would have a word." She was pale and shaking.

"He's not so frightening as all that, is he?"

"No, señorita."

"What is it you think he may do?"

The girl's eyes widened and there was something in her look less fearful than thrilled. "Anything at all."

The maid helped her dress in rust-colored silk, since she would not be performing as La Hermanita today. The high-necked bodice ended in a gold lace ruff, and the sleeves were slashed and pinked to show the rose silk beneath. Concha's hands pulled and pinched Luzia's hair into tight braids and tucked two combs of enamel flowers into the strands.

"Do you have no proper jewels, señorita? Your patron is rich, no?"

"I prefer simpler things," Luzia lied.

Her aunt had convinced Don Víctor to place garnets in her hand, but there would be no pearls or diamonds, nothing that would give her too easy a means of escape.

Hualit entered as Concha was placing a fur-lined cape of faun velvet over Luzia's shoulders, the satin bow set at a jaunty angle. Her face had none of the easy merriment Luzia was used to.

"I've come to take you to the gardens."

"I'm to meet Santángel."

"Now, Luzia," Hualit commanded.

She looped her arm through Luzia's and set a brisk pace down the hall, two footmen trailing closely behind.

"I'm glad to see you survived the night. Yes, Víctor told me what happened." She glanced behind her. "Pérez insists it must have been an unfortunate accident but has offered guards to all the competitors."

"Surely this can't be a surprise to you," Luzia murmured. "I took the place of a competitor who—"

"Hush." Hualit halted abruptly. "Stay here," she instructed the footmen. "I would have a private word with Señorita Cotado." She led Luzia to the great window overlooking the gravel drive. "Listen to me, Luzia. Antonio Pérez's position grows more perilous by the day. There are rumors the king will have him arrested if Pérez isn't able to change his mood soon. You must be careful. You can trust no one here."

"Even you?"

"You know exactly who I mean."

"Santángel saved my life." Twice.

"Did he? Or did he create a situation where he would make it seem so?"

"I don't believe that."

"This morning one of Gracia de Valera's guards was found dead in the gardens. He suffocated on his own swollen tongue."

"What does that have to do with Guillén Santángel?"

"Speak plainly, señora." Santángel stood in the hallway where the footmen had been moments before. He wore boots and hunting clothes, and only now, seeing him without his long cloak, did Luzia understand how much he'd changed. It was hard to reconcile the man before her with the sickly creature she'd met in the courtyard of her aunt's home only a few weeks ago. He was still lean, his face set at sharp angles, but now he looked strong and healthy, his back straight, his shoulders broad. It was irritating to realize how handsome he was. They'd been on more equal footing when he looked like he might collapse. "The good widow thinks someone put a scorpion in that poor man's mouth."

Hualit flinched but kept her poise. "I said nothing of the kind."

"Then the mistake is mine. It would be a foolish thing to suggest, after all. Say only that if this guard was the kind of coward who sets traps for young women rather than sullying his own hands with blood, he met the end he should. Say it will be whispered that to act against Luzia Calderón Cotado is to court death itself. Say this tragedy may be for us a happy accident."

"Most felicitous indeed."

"You may go now, señora."

"I am not a servant to be dismissed."

"But you will not want Don Víctor to wait."

Luzia watched Hualit consider her options: stand her ground and risk angering her patron or capitulate and bruise her own pride.

"Remember what I said, querida," she whispered, and with a curtsy of consummate grace, she marched past Santángel.

Santángel stalked toward her—no, Luzia corrected herself, he was not stalking, he was a man who was walking toward her with purpose. Her aunt's warnings had put her on edge.

Her tongue resorted to nonsense. "Did you kill my guards too?" she asked.

"Yes, I stuffed them beneath your bed. Concha is in for a crowded night."

"I'm mostly sure you're joking." She made her nervous hands still. "You're dressed for hunting."

"I will ride out with them. I won't hunt. I know what it is to be shot from the sky."

At least he'd had a chance to use his wings. Perhaps she should leave off talk of death and bloodshed, but he'd told her she could ask him any question she liked. "Did you kill that man? Gracia de Valera's guard?"

"He forfeited his life when he tried to take yours."

She wasn't sure what she had wanted his answer to be, but she knew she shouldn't be pleased by those words. She was worse than Concha with her giggles and gasps.

"Because I belong to Víctor de Paredes," she said.

Santángel hesitated. "I suppose that's a way of looking at it." He joined her by the window, one eye on the corridor, one on the gardens below. "Pérez has ordered the hopefuls to the eastern terrace, where you are to have your portraits sketched."

"For what purpose?"

"That I don't know."

"Perhaps the artist will capture the moment when Gracia tries to stab me."

"At least then we would have proof," he replied. "Go and meet the other competitors."

"And do what with them?"

"Learn from them. Determine their strengths and weaknesses."

Luzia fidgeted with the beads at her waist. "They'll be doing the same."

"Yes, but you have an advantage. We servants are used to watching our betters and to making ourselves invisible while we do. See what you can discover about them and the second trial."

"When will it begin?"

"Tomorrow night. I've been able to learn little else, but we'll run through your collection of miracles."

"Why not begin the trial sooner? Why not today?"

"Are you so eager to compete?"

"Yes," she admitted, wondering if he would chastise her for her pride. "I liked being on that stage."

He studied her. The light shining through the windows made his eyes translucent, shards of gray glass. "It suited you."

Something new had been born between them, something with a shape she couldn't quite determine. Álvaro's death, the pomegranate, now the scorpion, each moment taking on its own alchemy. But was she changing, or was Santángel?

"I want to know what comes next," she said, unsure if she meant the torneo or the wider world or just this hallway. "The anticipation . . . I feel it may unravel me."

"Anticipation," he repeated. His fingers flexed as if testing the weight of the word. "Not fear?"

"That too. The longer this goes on, the greater chance I'll be poisoned or take a mysterious fall down the stairs. And you said the next trial would be a proof of faith. You can't ask me not to dread an audience with the Vicar of Madrid."

"He will be looking for signs of heresy and of treason. You will give him neither."

"Looking for signs in us or in Pérez?"

"How quickly you learn the game. Both, I suspect."

"The widow says his position grows more precarious."

"You remember Don Juan's secretary?" he asked. "The one who was murdered on the streets of Madrid? Escobedo's widow went to see a cleric who read in the stars that her husband had been killed by his best friend."

"That was Pérez?"

"Debatable. But Pérez's role in the murder is not." He kept his voice low when he said, "Pérez had Escobedo killed. It's possible the king ordered the assassination and it's possible he's afraid that fact will come to light. Don Juan resisted Philip's strategies in the Netherlands and Pérez whispered to the king that the great war hero might be trying to take power for himself, that Escobedo was helping him turn traitor." He shook his head. "It was all badly done. Pérez has overstepped too many times, failed too many times. And he knows far too much. His father's motto was 'in silentio,' but when Pérez had his new impresa remade he omitted those words in favor of 'usque adhuc.'"

Luzia touched her tongue to the top of her mouth, then let the translation slip free. She didn't have to hide anymore. Not this at least. "*Until now.* It's a warning, isn't it?"

"It is," said Santángel. "A warning to the king that Pérez knows all of his secrets." His strange eyes looked less so now, their color steady.

Now we know each other. What would it mean to be known?

"Pérez believes he can still repair the rift?" she asked.

"He is the son of a politician. He has been swimming in these waters a long time. Now, go. And try not to be the fish who gets eaten."

Chapter 27

◆

It was still cold on the eastern terrace and Luzia was grateful for her cape and her wool stockings. Gracia de Valera sat upon a golden chair, her luminous face shaded by two servants holding a fringed canopy. She wore a gown of coral velvet, the bodice embroidered with tiny buds and flowers, the sleeves and ruff thick with seed pearls. Her large blue eyes slid once to Luzia, then back at whatever dream of glory lay in the middle distance.

An artist was laboring over an easel, his hands dirty with charcoal, the table beside him piled with sketches. He seemed to be working in a kind of frenzy, as if his hands couldn't move fast enough to capture the perfection of Gracia's features.

Another long table had been laid with platters of fruit and breads baked into the shapes of birds. Teoda Halcón sat on a raised cushion beneath an apple tree, her red-gold hair braided with ribbons, her dress a cascade of white ruffles. Two of her ladies stood at a distance whispering to each other.

Luzia wondered if she should worry about poison, but unless someone had decided to kill them all, it seemed safe to pile her plate with bread and fruit.

Learn from them, Santángel had said. Very well. If she hoped to survive in Philip's court she would need to become a spy for herself.

She made her way to Teoda and sat down on the other tuffet, trying to arrange her skirts.

"We were not introduced last night," the little girl said in her high, sweet chirp.

"No. But I saw you once. At Perucho's warehouse with your father."

"Perucho is the best of tailors. I had hoped he might make me something a little more interesting, but my father says the king prefers traditional styles." She took a sip from her tiny white cup.

"Is that chocolate?"

"Yes, and it's very good. Have you had it before?"

"Only once," Luzia admitted. Hualit had arranged for it at her home. A gift from Víctor. Luzia and her father had met there and they'd watched Ana stir the pot, smelling the cinnamon and cloves, and that strange, bitter, wonderful smell. It was one of the last times she could remember her father being clear in his thoughts. He'd made up silly rhymes for them and told the story of when he'd first met Luzia's mother. Luzia had thought, *If this is what life can be, it is enough.*

Teoda signaled to one of her women. "Bring La Hermanita a cup of chocolate."

"I prefer Luzia."

"Luzia, then." She bobbed her head toward the artist. "My father had a miniature made of me on my sixth birthday. This seems a far more elaborate affair. I've been told only the winner will be painted in oils. The artist is Italian, brought from Venice at great expense. He's been laboring over Gracia's sketches for over an hour."

"You can hardly blame him."

"She *is* very beautiful. Like a lady in a ballad. She should enjoy the attention while she can."

"You don't think she can win?" Luzia asked carefully.

Teoda met Luzia's gaze over her cup. "You're the one who specializes in miracles." She glanced toward the palace, shading her eyes. "Oh good, the farmer has arrived."

Fortún Donadei emerged into the autumn sunshine, pulling at the lace of his collar, the golden cross resting against his chest. He smiled cautiously when he saw them and waved as if from a country road, then dropped his hand, catching himself in the blunder. He had some kind of stringed instrument slung over his back.

"And what do you think of *his* prospects?"

The Holy Child made a humming noise. "Well, his manners need work, but he's certainly not a fraud. We should be so lucky. No, his power is real, but probably not the most valuable of his gifts." She cocked her head to the side. "He is so very beautiful. So many white teeth, such marvelous curls. And funded by Doña Beatriz Hortolano, who will happily have you murdered in your bed should you look at him with too much interest."

It was strange to hear such words from the mouth of a child, but Luzia supposed Teoda Halcón was no ordinary child. She had seen the future, the past, into the hearts and minds of men. One of her ladies arrived with a cup of chocolate set on a delicate saucer.

Luzia took it and thanked her but then paused.

"You do not drink," Teoda observed.

"It's very hot still."

The girl grinned, a dimple appearing in her cheek. "Here," she said, handing Luzia her half-full cup. "Take mine and I will drink from yours."

"I feel foolish."

"Don't. I heard someone slipped a scorpion beneath your pillow. You're right to be cautious."

Luzia shrugged and they traded cups. They lifted them in a toast and drank. She hadn't expected to like the Holy Child, but she did.

Fortún approached and bowed to them. "Señoritas, may I join you?"

"We would be honored," said Teoda. She gestured for him to sit and he settled on a chair a respectful distance away. "Have you come to play for us?"

"Only if you wish it," he said, setting the vihuela at his feet. "I'm more at ease with an instrument in my hands. For a farmer's son, conversation is more frightening than a bit of music."

"We were speaking of Señorita de Valera."

"She was most impressive last night."

Teoda's dimple appeared again. "Was she?"

He ducked his head and stammered out, "Per—perhaps not so much as her patron expected."

"Very diplomatic."

Fortún reached for the neck of his vihuela, then thought better of it. "I . . . May I ask you something, Señorita Halcón?"

Luzia was surprised by the girl's giddy laugh.

"I wondered if you would come right out and ask," Teoda said. "Luzia has not quite worked up the courage. Usually people want to know if they will find true love or make a great fortune, but I think I can guess your question. You wish to know which of us will win the torneo?"

His bronzed cheeks flushed. "Have I made a fool of myself?"

"No, but I can offer no predictions. My angel is silent when my own fate is too bound up in the outcome."

"I suppose that's for the best," he replied, looking around at the gardens, the glorious facade of the house. "That way we can all dream a little longer."

At those words, Teoda's merry grin faltered.

"Is something wrong?" Luzia asked.

Her small shoulders rose and fell. Her gaze was distant. "It's this house. My dreams are troubled here. There's too much silver, too much gold. All of it plunder. All of it stinking of death. At night the walls bleed."

Fortún's hand closed over the gold cross he wore, as if he were afraid she'd try to take it from him. "That treasure is Spain's by right, as God has willed it."

Teoda seemed to wake from her brooding. "Of course," she said with a bright smile. "As God and our great king have willed it. Now, I'm getting restless."

She gestured for one of her ladies to help her rise. Luzia hadn't considered how difficult getting up might be and suddenly missed her stern performance dress with its meager verdugado.

"Signor Rossi," Teoda called, "only God can master perfection. To pretend otherwise is blasphemy."

The artist looked up, flustered, brow shining with sweat.

Gracia rose, a blossom gilded by the morning sun, and joined her own ladies, one of whom offered her a broad-brimmed hat trimmed in pale green ribbon. She drifted into the gardens, trailed by two of Pérez's footmen. As if she were the one who needed protection.

"I don't know what to make of Señorita Halcón," said Fortún, his eyes on the girl as she took Gracia's place in the golden chair, her feet dangling well off the ground. "That was . . . quite terrifying."

Maybe she had wanted to scare them. But Luzia didn't think so. "I suspect it's much more frightening for her."

"I hadn't considered that," he mused. "She's meant to be an answer to the traitor Lucrecia de León. I don't see how we can compete with such a talent."

"You believe in the Holy Child's visions?"

"What I believe doesn't matter. If Pérez and the king believe in her . . . Well." Again he reached for his vihuela and this time he lifted it, let it rest across his knees. "If I may say so, your performance last night was extraordinary. Though . . ."

Luzia waited.

Fortún glanced at the path down which Gracia had disappeared. "I wonder if it was the performance you originally intended?"

As much as Gracia de Valera deserved the blame, Fortún might simply be looking for gossip to repeat. "Opportunity is like porridge. It must be eaten hot."

"And you really are a kitchen scullion?"

"I can't pretend otherwise."

"As a simple farmer's son, I wouldn't wish you to. I'm so glad you're here." Her face must have shown her surprise because he said hurriedly, "Have I said something wrong? I . . . I feel as if everyone here speaks the same language I've known my whole life, and yet I can't understand a word."

Luzia knew that feeling well. It was only that she was fairly sure no one had ever told her they were glad to see her. The closest was Águeda shouting, *Finally! Go fetch more water.*

"You said nothing wrong. I'm pleased to be here."

He smiled, his teeth bright against his sun-browned skin. "What a pleasure to have a few hours of leisure. I feel as if we're children left alone without our mothers."

"We're not alone," Luzia said with a meaningful glance at the guards who stood at every doorway.

"No, I suppose not. I heard of your brush with death last night."

"It wasn't such a near thing, I assure you." Luzia chose her words carefully. "Doña Beatriz is your patroness?"

"Yes." Fortún's hand returned to the gold cross, studded with hefty ovals of jade, a massive emerald at its center, the green dark and cool as a shaded wood. Luzia's rosary looked shabby in comparison, but she suspected its weight was easier to bear.

"Such a generous gift," she ventured.

He gave an uneasy laugh and dropped his hand. "Yes. She is most generous, most kind."

"Is it very important to her that you win?"

A ferocity came into his gaze. "It is important to *me*." He dropped his chin and she wondered if he was going to start apologizing again. But he leaned closer. "You are really, truly a scullion?"

"Must I show you my hands as I did Pérez?"

"Perhaps your callouses are milagritos too."

"I can tell you how to make a lye mixture from grape lees or how to iron a ruff to make a fine curve, if that will help you feel at ease."

Fortún rubbed his forehead with his thumb and forefinger. "Forgive me. This is all . . ."

"I know." Overwhelming, baffling, nothing like the existence that had come before.

"I'm a farmer's son. My days were shaped by sunrise and sunset, by rainfall, fear of blight. When Doña Beatriz found me she gave me music, art, the finest food I've ever eaten. I should tell you I loved the simple life, that I long for home, but . . ." That brilliant smile appeared again, smaller this time, a kept secret. "I don't! I don't want my father's life. I don't want to work until my back breaks. I don't want to clear fields of stones and harvest the fruit and work the presses. I like this easy life."

Luzia couldn't help but smile back. "You think a life at court will be easy?"

"Do I sound like a clay-brain?"

"You sound like someone who would rather sleep on a soft bed than a hard one. There are worse sins."

"Sins," he repeated. He plucked a few notes from the strings at the vihuela's neck. "You must understand I . . . I belong to her. In every way. De Paredes does not . . . He isn't . . . ?"

Luzia knew she should be offended, but the suggestion was so absurd she couldn't be. "Víctor de Paredes would sooner sell his beard than find himself in my bed."

"Ah." Fortún seemed almost disappointed.

"I'm flattered you think a rich man would want me for his mistress."

"Why wouldn't he?"

"Señor Donadei, if we are to be friends, don't flatter me. It makes you look a fool and makes me feel like one."

"I know you're not a city beauty. But . . ." He shrugged. "You look like the girls from my town."

Was this flirtation? Luzia didn't know, but the Holy Child was right—he was charming.

Fortún plucked another series of notes, rising and falling. "You aren't scandalized by my situation?"

Luzia realized she'd made a misstep. She *should* be scandalized, horrified, at a man addressing such things with her, at the idea of a woman violating her marriage vows to take a young musician as her lover. Men and women were brought before the Inquisition for fornication and lewd behavior often enough. But her time with Hualit had made her too ready to accept vice.

"I'm afraid I've revealed myself," she said as lightly as she could. "I'm not one of your good country girls. I was raised in the city, and I've seen things I shouldn't and heard things I never wished to." It was the best excuse she could offer, and it wasn't untrue. "Do you love her? Doña Beatriz."

"I loathe her." The words rumbled in his throat, like a pot brought to boil. "It's why I must win. If the king makes me his champion, I will have money, and silks, and fine food, and I will not have to fuck her to get it. Maybe then I won't hate myself so thoroughly."

Now Luzia knew she should excuse herself with some loud declaration of disgust. A worthy woman would be scandalized at such language. But no one had heard. No one but her.

"You should be careful," she said, her voice low.

"What?"

"I could turn around and tell Doña Beatriz what you've said. It would be that easy to ruin your chances and better mine."

He stared at her, his hazel eyes startled. "But you wouldn't."

"You don't know me."

"We are the only two people here who understand what it is to work until your hands bleed. I knew you as soon as I met you, and I know you won't tell her because you're not a pretty snake like Gracia de Valera."

Maybe Luzia should tell. A clever competitor would steal any advantage.

"I won't," she conceded, neglecting to add *for now*. "But this isn't the country. You can't . . . well, you can't be so honest."

"I can." His bright smile returned, a white sail unfurling. "If I choose my friends wisely."

"Then tell me something useful. Do you know what the next trial will be?"

"Our purity will be tested. I've been told we will face Satan in front of the vicar, but I don't know what that means."

Luzia tried to ignore the chill that overtook her. She supposed the devil himself would come to La Casilla if invited. "I'm not sure I want to guess."

"Luzia!" called Teoda from her perch on the golden chair. "It's time for you to sit for Signor Rossi."

Luzia sighed. "Perhaps I look like the girls from his town too." She started pushing to her feet and was grateful for the hand Fortún offered her, even if it wasn't quite decorous.

"You cautioned me, Señorita Cotado," he said. "I'll give you the same warning: be careful."

"I hardly think I'm in danger of being too honest."

"I saw Don Víctor's servant this morning, riding out for the hunt. El Alacrán."

"Santángel?"

Fortún nodded. "He is not what he seems."

She pulled back, forcing him to release her hand. "What do you mean?"

"Only what I said. Be careful."

Fortún smiled and waved her along, as if he'd merely warned of coming rain.

Chapter 28

✦

The hunt was tiresome and Santángel was grateful to avoid the feast that followed. His appetite for food had returned, but not for the pomp of such meals or the dull conversation that accompanied them. Instead he walked the palace and the grounds, listening to the idle talk of guards and servants, hoping to gather more information on tomorrow's trial. He was not seen or heard. This was the way he'd determined who had placed the scorpion in Luzia's room. The guard had confessed that Gracia de Valera's patron had sent him on his murderous errand and then he had been silenced.

As for the scorpion, Santángel had ridden out to place him in a warm spot by a rocky crag and spoken the same words he'd said when he'd subdued the little creature: "You are not where you belong." The scorpion had crept from his hand, free until death found it.

Luzia had asked him what he was, and *familiar* was the easiest name to put to it. He could have answered, *A servant and a captive.* He could have said, *I am what is needed.* Isidro de Paredes had first dubbed him El Alacrán, a name meant to shame him. But he was a creature without shame.

When he arrived back at La Casilla, he sought out Luzia. He told himself it was to glean what she'd learned from the other hopefuls, but he knew that was not the only reason. He had been without friends or companions for a very long time. The servants

in the De Paredes home came and went, lived and died. The scholars and philosophers he wrote to enlivened his days with their
letters, suggested visits to their laboratories and libraries, places
he would never get to see. He could no longer tell the days or the
years apart. Another business negotiation, another piece of land to
acquire, another ambitious De Paredes to appease. Sometimes he
looked at Víctor and wasn't sure whose face he was staring into.
Víctor's father? His grandfather? The many who had come before?
They all chased power as if it were a great hunt, as if there was
novelty in its pursuit. Their enthusiasm and drive, their constant
burnishing of their name, their flag, their holdings, never wavered,
never changed. Always they spoke to him as if their goals were his,
as if Santángel shared their endless, grasping desire. When all the
while he felt nothing.

Until that cursed day in the widow's courtyard. Now his heart
beat, his stomach growled, his cock hardened. He was a man again,
and he didn't know whether to hate Luzia Cotado for this un-
asked for awakening or fall at her feet in gratitude. It was a kind of
madness, but one that could be cured. When he was free. Then he
would see the world. He would remember what it was to be human
and forget the scullion he had chosen to doom.

Concha opened Luzia's door and scurried away without being
asked.

"At last!" Luzia said when he entered. "I thought you had disappeared entirely."

"If only it were that easy." She sat at her table of powders and
ointments, bundled in her velvet dressing gown, wiping that awful
lead paint from her face. He was sorry to see her remarkable hair
was still in its tight braids, but that was for the best. His grasp of
this tangled situation had begun to slip, maybe in the moment of
Álvaro's death, maybe long before it. He didn't need further temp-
tation. "Tell me what you discovered today."

"I saw little of Gracia de Valera, but the Holy Child and the
Prince of Olives both believe she's a fraud."

"Because they're not fools."

"If it's true, how can she hope to survive the torneo?"

"That's not our concern. What else?"

"Teoda had no kind words for the empire. She spoke of blood and plunder."

Santángel leaned against the wall by the window. "Tell me what she said. As clearly as you can remember."

When Luzia had finished he thought on her words. "So she doesn't just hear voices. She's sensitive to objects as well. Maybe the angel is all invention, a means of tying her power to the Church."

"Fortún didn't like it."

"No doubt he'll repeat every word. That's dangerous. She's been very careful about flattering the king in her predictions. For gold and silver to flow from the New World, blood must too. That's the way of conquest. But Spain's empire is a weak one."

"Now you're the one criticizing the king?" Luzia whispered, perhaps afraid that Concha might be listening through the door. But the girl had gone off to gossip with the other maids.

"All empires are the same empire to the poor and the conquered. But not all empires are the same. The Dutch and the English will build markets for their goods, colonies for their taxes, new routes of trade. They will bleed the world for an age. Spain builds nothing, just spends its stolen wealth on wars that have no end. If the walls of La Casilla are wet with blood, then so are the king's monastery and all of the churches in Madrid, and the houses of every noble. Víctor would drown in it."

"And if I don't want to help Philip or anyone else bleed the world?"

Santángel had no response to that. No matter what power or position Luzia gained, she would never be on sure ground. Even queens must fear their kings, and Víctor de Paredes would control her as he had controlled Santángel. For an eternity.

As if she could read his thoughts, she met his eyes in the mirror. "Fortún Donadei said you are not what you seem."

"What do I seem?"

"Do you want your vanity stroked?"

"I'm a man, so the answer is always yes."

"Are you?"

The question startled him. "A man? Do you doubt it?"

Her cheeks pinked and her gaze shifted away. "Not the particulars. But you are not as other men."

"No," he admitted.

"You are El Alacrán. You don't sleep. You don't eat."

"I do eat. Quite a lot recently."

"You didn't eat."

"Life had no savor."

Luzia turned on the bench and threw up her hands, her frustration clear. "What do you mean when you say these things? You're thriving here. I can see that. So, did Don Víctor keep you in a dungeon?"

He didn't mean to be evasive, but he'd long since lost the habit of honesty. "Not often."

"Then is the cook so much better at La Casilla?"

"Víctor sets a fine table. Are we really going to discuss my appetite?"

"If you would only give me a real answer, there would be no need."

"Does this mean Fortún Donadei succeeded in making you fear me?"

"All of Madrid fears you."

"Not all of Madrid," he corrected with some amusement. "All of Spain."

She clasped her hands and he saw her knuckles were white. "I'm told I'm to face the devil in the second trial."

"It's a metaphor and nothing more."

"Are you so certain?"

"If Padre Juan Baptista Neroni can actually summon the devil, we have greater problems than the torneo. But I'll see if there's anything else I can learn." She had a right to her fear, and he would do his best to appease it. He folded his arms. "You've told me what you discovered about your competition but not what you thought of them."

"I liked Teoda Halcón. She's odd, but I suppose we all are."

"Even Gracia de Valera?"

"No. She's a boil disguised as a blossom."

At that he had to laugh. "Apt. And the farmer's son?"

Luzia turned back to the mirror.

"I see," said Santángel. "The Prince of Olives has made you his friend."

"I wouldn't call him that. He isn't suited to this place any more than I am. But he wants very badly to win."

"And I'm sure he made his case most sympathetically."

"He is in an untenable position."

"More untenable than yours?"

At least she had the sense to pause. "His . . . patroness . . . She . . ."

"She has laid claim to both his body and his soul?" Why was the Prince of Olives sharing such confidences with Luzia? Santángel had to wonder how much of Garavito's gossip might have reached Donadei's ears and what the farmer's son might share with her to earn her trust. "Fortún Donadei is no guileless country boy. He pursued poor loveless Doña Beatriz. He brought his guitar and played outside of her palace for days to get her attention."

"Maybe it was greater attention than he wished for."

"Or he is trying to blunt your appetite for victory, to weaken your resolve. You have as much to lose as he does." Santángel certainly did.

"Maybe."

He pushed off from the wall, unsure of why he felt such irritation. It was like being a green youth again, buffeted by bouts of jealousy and lust. Complications he didn't need. That he had come to respect this woman, even like her, was understandable, if an unwanted burden given what he must do. But that he should desire her, that he should be left addlepated when she mentioned the pleasure of a hot bath? It was unacceptable. Just that morning, when Luzia had said she thought anticipation might unravel her, his mind had been overtaken by the thought of twining a strand of her hair around his finger, of releasing it and watching the curl spring back. *Unravel.* A single word might drive him mad. It stuck in his mind like a thorn, infecting him with a kind of fever, the thought of Luzia Cotado unraveling.

He turned to the window, but there was nothing to see in the darkness excepting a few torches set along the garden paths. He needed occupation. He needed to be gone from here. This sickness would pass, given time and diversion.

"You're done with me then?" she said as he strode to the door.

I haven't even begun. He needed to leave now. For both their sakes.

"We'll practice tomorrow," he said. "Get some rest and dream of how you might destroy a poor farmer's son."

Luzia scowled. "And what will you be doing?"

"I'm going to go learn all I can to help you best the devil."

That much he could offer.

Chapter 29

✦

The second trial was to take place at night, and so Valentina wore her black velvet. Her lack of jewels would be less conspicuous in the dark. Marius had appeared at the door when she was helping Concha finish placing the scalloped cockle-shells in Luzia's braids. He too had worn black and his goose-belly jacket looked a bit snug. The parade of food and wine at La Casilla never stopped. Still, she thought the excess suited him. He loved to hunt and to ride and he'd lost his sullen pallor. His black hair and beard were glossy, his eyes sparkled.

In the past it was as if he'd hoarded the things that brought him pleasure, greeting any question about his day or his interests as a kind of intrusion. But now he seemed eager to share with her, turning to her at meals to suggest she taste an interesting dish, returning from the hunt brimming with stories, even inquiring over her own day.

Last night he'd told of a man being thrown from his horse, a near deadly thing.

"Well," she'd said without thinking, "I had to spend the afternoon with Señora Galves, so I'm lucky I didn't expire from boredom."

When he'd burst out laughing, she'd nearly toppled from her chair in surprise. Had she ever made her husband laugh?

"Isn't she the one with the son who writes poetry?" he asked.

"Yes. She recited some of his verses for us."

"Please tell me you remember them."

"Only the very worst lines," she confessed. They had spent the rest of the night making up awful couplets and getting very drunk, and as the hour grew late, the talking turned to kissing, but still they laughed when they stopped to catch their breath. She hadn't known such a thing was possible or permitted, and though she'd woken with a headache, she felt the price of discovery was well worth it.

Now he said, "Shall we go meet the vicar?" and offered her his arm.

Luzia followed them into the gardens and the blue dusk. Valentina knew this was a holy occasion, a test of purity for the hopefuls, another demonstration of their gifts. She should be solemn in the presence of the vicar and the other church deputies, seated on a raised platform, a blue tent salted with golden stars above them like heaven itself. But the gardens were lit with lanterns and torches, and musicians played from somewhere in the trees. It was hard not to think that she was simply at a party, the most wonderful party she'd ever attended.

Chairs were arranged on one of the lawns and a pretty little stage had been erected, festooned with red and white ribbons, the fabric of the curtain shining gold.

"A puppet show?"

"Yes," said Catalina de Castro de Oro, approaching with a glass in her hand. "Pérez has brought the puppeteer all the way from Umbria."

"Italian painters, Italian puppets," grumbled Marius. "Is nothing Spanish good enough for him?"

The widow lifted a shoulder. "It's the fashion."

"Is that wine?" Valentina asked.

"Wine and lemonade. A mixture from León they drink during Holy Week. They call it matar judíos."

"How clever," said Luzia softly. "I'll have to try it."

The widow lifted her glass in a toast but her smile was sour. The reason soon became clear.

Víctor de Paredes had already taken his seat for the performance. Next to his wife.

Valentina was desperate for a good look at her. She was spoken of as one of Don Víctor's greatest successes, a woman of beauty and fortune from one of Spain's oldest families, a testimony to his luck. Did the widow care because she loved him? Or because her place had been usurped? And why had Don Víctor chosen his mistress to see to Luzia's care rather than his wife? Was such a thing beneath her in a way it was not beneath Valentina?

"All the luminaries of Madrid are here tonight," said the widow. "Poets and singers. Even that lady playwright."

"Quiteria Escárcega?" asked Valentina.

"You know her work?"

Valentina exchanged a look with Luzia, and for once they were the ones who knew more than Catalina. "I've certainly heard talk of her."

"Well, there she is in a very peculiar jacket."

It was odd indeed, rendered in deep crimson velvet and banded with pearls. It made her gown look almost like a military uniform. Her hair was deep brown, her eyes the warm color of the chocolate Valentina had consumed so greedily.

"That woman is a plague," grumbled Marius. "It's said she has an apartment in Toledo where men come and go at all hours."

"Women too," said the widow.

As if sensing her interest, the playwright turned and met Valentina's gaze, then lifted her glass, the gesture curiously bold, as if she were raising a sword at the start of a duel. Valentina felt suddenly warm.

"Are you ready?" she asked Luzia, seeking distraction.

Luzia nodded, but her face was damp with perspiration.

"Something to drink?" Marius offered. "What is all this fretting? Has Santángel failed to prepare you?"

Luzia didn't know how to answer. Santángel had met with her that morning and they'd practiced in the gardens, far from prying eyes. He'd been able to learn of the puppet show and they'd strategized on how she could be most ready. But it was clear he was eager to be gone from her presence. Only last night, he had spoken to her, alone in her room, as if they were lovers, tall and white as a phantom, and yet seeming to grow stronger and more beautiful with every day that passed. He had looked at her in the mirror and again she'd had the sense of rising out of her body. She had remembered the dream of the orange grove and she knew that if she did lose her tether and somehow drifted up into the night sky and over the city, he would find a way to meet her there. She'd been certain of it.

Then he'd snarled at her and left, as if she were just another task to be seen to on his master's behalf.

What else would you be? The trust they'd built between them was a temporary thing, a pact made at Don Víctor's request and nothing more. But she found herself wanting to ask what would happen if she did somehow manage to win. Would her lessons continue? Would his luck remain hers? And which of her secrets had he shared with Víctor de Paredes?

There were other fears she hadn't considered until last night. She'd dreamed of being raised high in the court, of having a position of security and even authority, valued, respected. But she would not just be an advisor or courtier—the king would make her his weapon. It was one thing to be wielded against the English or the Dutch. But would she be used to put down rebellions, to murder heretics and indios and Jews and any other enemy of Philip's God? Would she be covered in the blood Teoda Halcón had seen in her dreams?

As if she had summoned him with her worry, Santángel appeared and said, "You must be led before the vicar. Don Marius, Doña Valentina, you will introduce her."

"I see," said Don Marius with a glance to where Víctor de Paredes was seated.

Santángel gave a single nod of acknowledgment. "I will take Luzia to Don Víctor when the blessing is over."

Luzia let herself be steered toward the dais. More guests had arrived in capes and cloaks, dressed for the cool night. Luzia knew that she should focus on the competition, on the church deputies who sat on the raised platform, three of them in a row, all in their robes and hats, pristine in white and red and black. She couldn't help but think it was like an auto de fe in miniature. The torneo's competitors brought before them as penitents, dressed in fine clothes instead of sanbenitos.

The autumn sun was long gone, and yet she was sweating in her prim gown. Concha had cleaned and starched the collar and cuffs so that they glowed white, and Luzia was grateful that they'd kept her face free of paint, afraid the vicar's sensibilities would be more offended by artifice than by her freckled brown skin.

I have been baptized, she reminded herself. She went dutifully to mass. She knew her Pater Noster, the Ave Maria and Salve Regina, her psalms and commandments. She would happily eat ham and mend a dress after sundown on the Sabbath. And yet she felt her magic like a damning thread, binding her to the past, and to every Jew in every synagogue who still bent their head in prayer. Hualit had slipped away. She might sip from a drink that called for the killing of Jews and do it with a wink, but she would not place herself before the Vicar of Madrid.

Chapter 30

✦

Luzia's fellow competitors had already gathered for the intro-
ductions. The Beauty was dressed in cream velvet tonight,
embellished with pearls and diamonds and braided silver
thread so that she gleamed like the first frost. Fortún Donadei
wore green and gold again, and Teoda Halcón had a cross of silver
embroidered on her red gown, as if she were a tiny soldier.

"La Hermanita has arrived," she said with a smile. "What do
you make of all of this merry show?"

"It's odd, isn't it?" Luzia murmured. "I don't know if we're meant
to behave as if we're at a party or at church."

Teoda's smile curled and she whispered, "Depending on the
church, it can be hard to tell the difference." In a more normal
voice she added, "Gracia, I don't know if you've met Luzia, though
you seem most familiar with her milagritos."

If Gracia was bothered by the jibe she didn't show it. She merely
curtsied. "A pleasure."

"The pleasure is mine," Luzia replied.

"That is Pedro del Valle," said Fortún, bobbing his chin toward
the man to the vicar's right. "It was he who warned Lucrecia de
León to cease her treason."

"Before she was taken to Toledo?" asked Luzia.

Teoda shuddered. "He took her head between his palms and
said, *I have undone many prophets with these hands.*"

"But she didn't stop, did she?" Gracia observed. "Why bring such misery on yourself?"

"Perhaps her dreams demanded it," Teoda said quietly.

Luzia was weary of waiting. She was eager to have these trials done and her future decided. But she suspected she would be sorry when it was all over. She'd had little opportunity to make friends, and even if they were all rivals, they were united in their fears and wants. She liked Teoda and Fortún, and if Gracia hadn't tried to have her murdered, she would probably like her too.

"Who sits to the vicar's left?" Luzia asked.

"Fray Diego de Chaves," Fortún replied, holding tight to his golden cross. "The royal confessor."

Pérez's red-bearded courtier was waving them over, grouping them with their patrons so that they could be brought forward. When they had all made their curtsies and bows and their names had been read aloud, Pérez himself climbed the dais and bowed deeply.

"May this night's work please you and God," he said humbly.

Fray Diego ignored him and leaned forward to address the gathered hopefuls. He had a long face, made longer by drooping jowls, and he gripped the arms of his chair as if he were trying to resist launching himself off the stage.

"Your friend Pérez would have liked Quiroga here to wave his hand over you and assure our king that all is as it should be. But you will have to face our scrutiny instead. True children of God have nothing to fear from our judgment. But be warned: magic may mimic God's power, and the devil may use all his wiles to convince the weak-minded of prophecies and miracles. Our eyes are not so clouded."

His dark gaze traveled over them one by one, and Luzia felt as if he could see every forbidden word she'd spoken scrawled across her forehead. She felt something brush against her fingers. Teoda stood beside her, and though she didn't turn, Luzia was certain it had been her hand that she'd felt.

"We will know whose power is at work this night," Fray Diego continued, "be its source divine or demonic, and we offer you this opportunity now: If you have made a bargain with evil forces, if you have trafficked in witchcraft or heresies, say so. Fall on your knees before almighty and eternal God and beg for His mercy. Confess and be forgiven."

Silence surrounded them like a shroud. The sounds of the guests laughing and drinking seemed far too distant.

These were the men who had damned Lucrecia de León and cursed Piedrola. They had the ear of the king and maybe God Himself. What did they see? What might they already know?

Fear nothing. That was what Santángel had whispered to bring her back from the brink of death. *Fear nothing, and you will become greater than them all.*

They are men and nothing more, she reminded herself, and held her tongue.

A minute passed, another. Would they wait here until someone faltered? Until proof of God's permission appeared or someone sprouted horns?

At last, Fray Diego slumped back in his chair. "Very well. Then do as you will, and may God show you the mercy we will not."

Pérez bowed, smiling, as if the friar had encouraged them all to enjoy a fine meal. "I thank you and our king for this generosity."

Then they were being waved away, herded into the guests milling about their seats, enjoying their wine and lemonade.

"There," said Santángel, appearing at her elbow and steering her toward Don Víctor, "the worst is over."

"Until they round us all up for trial. You abandoned me."

"I did as I was bid."

"Because Don Víctor didn't want you seen with me. Not before the vicar and the royal confessor." She had been right. Víctor de Paredes had never intended to place her beneath his roof. Don Marius and Valentina would be his protection if Luzia failed or if she attracted the Inquisition's attention. "It's why he left me at Casa Ordoño. In case this all goes wrong."

"Yes."

Yes. That was all. She wanted to kick him.

"Did you expect fairness from Víctor de Paredes?" he asked.

"I would sooner expect poetry from a bear."

"Then stop sulking and focus your mind on the trial ahead."

Don Víctor was waiting near the front of the crowd. He rose as they approached and offered his hand to the woman beside him so that she might rise too.

"Come," he said, "my wife longs to meet the famous milagrera. Doña María, this is Luzia Cotado, La Hermanita."

Luzia was surprised by how lovely Don Víctor's wife was. She couldn't have looked more different from Hualit, her skin like a dish of fresh milk, her thick hair the bright gold of newly minted coins. Her gown was blue silk, wrought with a pattern of tiny golden ibises. She looked like a ship about to set sail. She looked like prosperity.

Somehow Luzia had thought his wife would be plain or shy, that he had sought out Hualit for her beauty and polish. But maybe men like Don Víctor didn't need to contemplate what they needed, only what they desired.

Luzia curtsied deeply and Doña María smiled, taking her hand. "What a pleasure to meet such a woman."

For a moment Luzia thought she was being mocked, but Doña María's eyes were warm.

"I am only a humble scullion, señora," Luzia said.

Doña María gripped her hand more tightly. "You are an instrument of God, chosen by Him to help our king and country. I have asked our priest to say masses for your safety and success in this mission."

"Thank you, señora."

"Do not thank me." Doña María pressed a kiss to Luzia's knuckles. Her eyes were too bright. "I gladly serve you as you serve God."

"Come, my love," Don Víctor said, pulling his wife away. "Luzia must prepare." His gaze met Santángel's, who directed Luzia toward where the other hopefuls were reassembling by the puppet stage.

"I've felt frightened of discovery," Luzia whispered. "Angry for the need to dissemble. But this is the first time I've felt ashamed of our lies."

"Doña María is kind and gentle, and being eaten alive by her own longing. An astróloga read her chart and told her that she wouldn't conceive until the Dutch were brought back under Catholic control."

"And that's why she prays so fervently?"

"No, she was always devout. But that charlatan has made her desperate. I've tried to reassure her, but she won't hear me. She thinks God has found her faith wanting."

"But you can't promise her a child."

"Of course I can. It's why Víctor's devotion to her has never wavered. He knows a child will come when it best suits his interests."

"You're so sure of your own influence?"

"Every De Paredes wife has born a son and every son has survived birth, and childhood, and the follies of youth to make my life miserable until he dies contented in his own bed. My confidence is well earned."

"What are you talking about? And why are you snarling at me as if I'd tried to pick your pocket?"

"I did not snarl."

"You might as well have bared your teeth while you did it."

He grabbed her arm and pulled her into a pool of shadow by the stage. "I'm trying to protect us, Luzia. To protect you."

She dipped into a curtsy. "Thank you, señor. Your rudeness is a mighty shield."

"You asked why I'm able to eat, to rest, to ride, why I have regained my health." He glanced back at the crowd and lowered his voice to the barest whisper. "Can you not guess it? It's not the cook who tempts me back to appetite. It is yet another miracle to your credit."

Luzia nearly laughed. "I didn't restore you. I wouldn't know how!"

"Every time you use your gift, every time you use me, you let me take a bit of your power for myself. Just as I make you stronger, you do the same for me. You make the blood flow in my veins once more. You remind my heart to beat."

"A heart cannot forget to beat," she scoffed.

His face shuttered. "All things can be forgotten given enough time. Now cease your complaining and fix your mind on the task ahead."

He strode away and she had to resist the urge not to let a little song slip free and trip him with a tree root. But with or without Santángel she had a real battle to fight. Her rivals were waiting at the front of the stage.

Chapter 31

✦

Santángel had been able to discover that there would be some kind of play about the life of Christ, possibly Satan's effort to tempt him. Each of the competitors would be called upon by the vicar and his companions during the course of the performance, and that was where their practice came in, because Luzia would have to pray aloud, even as she drew upon the words of the refrán in her head. She wasn't worried. This was a skill she'd learned at her mother's knee and practiced her entire life. She had always been two people with two faiths, neither of them whole.

She had prepared a couple of different refranes—one that would allow her to bathe the savior in holy light, another that used the miracle of the vines. Thankfully none of the hopefuls knew the order in which they would be called to perform, so Luzia didn't have to worry about more tricks from Gracia.

"Have you ever seen one of these theatricals?" asked Fortún as Luzia joined the others. "We had a puppeteer come through Jaén. It was marvelous!"

"No," said Teoda. "But don't expect too exciting a performance. The Inquisition tried Federigo Commandino for necromancy when his little wooden men proved too spectacular for sanctity."

"I heard Gaspar del Águila sculpted a statue of the Virgin with two heads," said Fortún. "One happy and smiling, and one for more solemn occasions."

"My father told me that there was a Christ of Burgos made with real hair and eyelashes," said Gracia. "It even had a hidden receptacle for blood. But it's long since been destroyed."

Teoda arched a blond brow. "It's amazing what theatrics may be accomplished with a bit of ingenuity."

Luzia had nothing to add. She had lived in books when she could and in the dark of the kitchen the rest of the time. She had never been to the theater or inside any church grander than San Ginés. She knew Madrid and its crooked streets and the heat of its long summers. *He is in an untenable position*, she'd told Santángel, her heart full of pity for Fortún Donadei and his glorious curls. He might very well loathe his mistress, but he was still a man, free to seek his fortune, free to go see puppet shows and play his songs in the sun.

She was grateful when the drummers flanking the stage found their rhythm. The flutes were next, then a sprightly horn, and the curtain rose.

Luzia was surprised at the scene: a starry night and in the distance, a manger. As they watched, the silhouettes of three magi marionettes appeared atop a hill and descended to give their gifts to the savior. Dawn seemed to rise, glowing golden against the false hills, and around Mary and Joseph and Jesus. A group of animals appeared, the donkey braying, the calf lowing, and even tiny chickens that seemed to hop and peck. Luzia had anticipated fear, even horror, not this dainty enchantment.

Then a new character appeared, dressed in olive green velvet and carrying a tiny vihuela. The guests broke into laughter and applause.

"Fortún," Gracia said with a smile, "you've never looked so well."

"It's me!" he exclaimed.

From the dais, Fray Diego intoned, "Fortún Donadei, how will you greet the Lamb of God?"

Beside Luzia, Fortún picked up his real vihuela. He played a long chord, then plucked the strings carefully, solemnly, the tune nothing like the lively song he'd played at the first trial. Now it almost seemed he held a different instrument, resonant and miraculous, one that had been crafted only to give glory to God. He touched his hand to the golden cross at his chest and lifted his handsome face to the sky. In the dark woods beside the stage, the leaves began to rustle. Then, from between the branches, stepped a small glowing lamb.

The crowd gasped. Someone cried out in astonishment. The lamb made no sound. Its little hooves barely seemed to touch the ground. It offered a tiny bow to the holy men on the dais and then vanished back into the trees. Only then did the guests burst into cheers.

"Look!" a man's voice shouted.

On the stage, a new marionette appeared from behind the mountain, a monstrous dragon that roared with the sound of horns and drums, its gruesome head swaying back and forth on its long neck.

"A tarasca!" Gracia said.

Luzia knew that word, a monster that had been bested by a saint. She had seen them in the Corpus Christi parades, sometimes ridden by a woman her father had told her was meant to symbolize vice.

The dragon reared back and gouts of flame sprayed from its mouth, long cords of red and orange silk.

Atop the hill a beautiful girl appeared in a sparkling white gown. The Beauty.

"Gracia de Valera," Fray Diego demanded, "how will you protect the Christ Child?"

Gracia stepped forward and raised her hands to the heavens, as if beseeching them for help. Her face shone as if she were the very star that had led the magi through the desert. How could anyone refuse such a supplicant? A cold wind began to blow and against the backdrop of the woods, tiny white snowflakes started to fall, glimmering against the dark trees, the air suddenly chill and damp as the torches by the side of the stage were extinguished.

The crowd thundered mighty approval and the dragon sank to its belly.

"It's done with a magic lantern," Teoda whispered, rolling her eyes. "Some ice, a bellows."

"How do you know?" Luzia asked.

"Because we prepared a magic lantern too! Special lenses imported from Sweden. I have no talent for miracles or illusions, only for long sight." She winked. "But that makes me an excellent planner."

Now the dragon reared up again, and this time, it had a woman on its back. She was naked, her pale body wrought from wood, small legs and arms jointed with pegs. She had bright red hair and a miniature crown on her head.

Elizabeth. England's queen.

Below her, a figure in black with a long white beard capered at the monster's feet. This must be her sorcerer, John Dee.

There on the hilltop, a puppet Luzia stood, dressed in black, a sturdy, stern little figure.

"Luzia Calderón Cotado, how will you defend Our Lord?"

Luzia's mind had been racing as she'd watched the others, opting quickly for the second refrán she and Santángel had prepared, seeking the forms of the old, reliable words that felt so right for this moment, the shape of *rosica* blooming in her mind.

Luzia didn't lift her arms or raise her voice. Instead, she fell to her knees, her rosary clutched in her hands. "Ave, Maria, gratia plena, Dominus tecum. Benedicta tu in mulieribus, et benedíctus fructus ventris tui, Iesus." She spoke the words by rote, the way she was meant to have learned them, a peasant making the sounds of prayer, the only Latin she was supposed to know. But in her head, in her ears, another language, a new music. Were the two pleas really so different? Hear me. Save me. Grant me comfort. Let me be held in the arms of a mother once more.

Over the walls of the stage, a flood of roses cascaded, pure white, drawn from the garden, blooming as the grapevines had, as Hualit's iris had so long ago. To the manger the roses turned their glorious faces. But before the heretic queen and her monsters, they formed a wall of long, dangerous thorns.

The applause felt like a benediction. She had survived another trial, and before the prophet killer too.

"Astonishing!" someone shouted.

"Miraculous!"

But they weren't pointing at Luzia or any of the hopefuls. They were gesturing to the stage where the puppets of the sorcerer and the queen on her dragon were cowering before the thorns. Their shadows were not.

The puppet queen raised her tiny fist at the puppet hopefuls. The shadow queen put her hands on her naked hips and stuck out her tongue.

The puppet John Dee tugged at his beard in frustration. The shadow John Dee turned his back to the vicar and lifted his robes, baring the silhouette of his ass cheeks.

The audience's laughter was nervous and Luzia wondered what the king's confessor and the Vicar of Madrid would think of such lewd humor.

"How is it done?" she asked Teoda. "What bit of stagecraft is this?"

Teoda shook her head. She was backing away from the stage. "This is no illusion. Something's wrong."

"Is it part of the trial?" Gracia asked.

The shadows of the puppets were lengthening now, their shapes changing. The queen's head was too long, her arms too thin. They ended in claws. One of them reached out and slashed at the Elizabeth marionette. The body tore and Luzia heard a cry from behind the black batting as the puppeteer dropped the marionette's strings.

The shadow shape behind John Dee was hairy and hunching, two horns protruding from its shadow head, a tail lashing the air, a massive phallus protruding from between its thighs. It leapt onto the Dee puppet's shoulders, strangling it as the crowd shrieked and rose from their chairs, stumbling backward.

"It's a test!" cried Fortún. "It must be a test!"

The shadow queen was on her knees and the shadow dragon was behind her, mounting her. On the dais, the vicar and his holy men rose, seemingly as one, but they didn't take up their crosses or pray; they ran, fleeing down the steps into the gardens.

"The devil is here!" cried Gracia.

"Run," said Luzia, grabbing her arm.

But the demon shadow was the size of a cat on its hind legs now and it leapt off the stage. Gracia screamed and it lunged for her, crawling up her skirts.

Without thinking Luzia grabbed for it. But when her hands brushed its body, she hissed in revulsion. It had no real form and yet it filled her with disgust. She forced herself to reach for it again and seized its wriggling body. It squirmed in her hands, hairy and shrieking, and she hurled it as far as she could, desperate to be rid of the crawling, slippery loathing that filled her.

Luzia lurched away from the stage, searching for some kind of help, but the world around her had dissolved into nightmare. She couldn't see Fortún or Teoda or Santángel. People were screaming and knocking over their chairs, running for the gravel path or back to the palace. The torches had toppled and the tented dais had caught fire. She heard the pounding of hoofbeats and saw guards on horseback streaming into the garden.

"It's real," Gracia said, tears streaming down her face. Her eyes were wide as moons, her whole body shaking. "It's real."

Luzia wiped her hands on her skirts and hauled Gracia to her feet. "Run, Gracia! Come on, you gorgeous lump, I can't carry you!"

They stumbled toward the palace. Surely there had to be safety there. Light. Order. Sense. Everywhere she looked she saw only smoke and fire, people shouting in fear.

"Why did no one tell me?" Gracia wept.

"You thought we were all pretending?" Luzia couldn't quite believe it. "You thought we were all frauds."

"Of course I did!"

"But you couldn't have hoped to win!"

"I didn't come here to win!" Gracia bellowed. "I came here to find a husband!"

If Luzia hadn't been so terrified, she would have laughed. "There!" She pulled Gracia toward the doors that led to the ballroom. Someone had gotten them open.

Luzia lost her footing, her legs tangling in her skirts. Gracia turned to help her, then screamed, her face contorted in alarm. Luzia felt something crawling up her back.

She reached over her shoulder and struggled not to retch as her hands made contact with something shivering and vile. But she couldn't get purchase. Its claws were in her hair, digging into her scalp.

She fell to her knees and then she was on the ground, as the thing on top of her pressed her face into the muck. She could feel the weight of it on her ribs, her neck, impossibly heavy, shoving her down, crushing her ribs.

Hell had come for her, and her mind was too full of fear to find words of salvation. All she could think of was the Ave Maria. *Holy Mary, Mother of God, pray for us sinners now and at the hour of our death.*

She felt herself yanked upward, saw sky and branches, then nothing but the ground racing by beneath her. She let out a grunt as her hip took the brunt of a saddle's pommel.

"Hold on," said Santángel, and then they were galloping through the gardens.

She thought they might just keep riding, past the hedges, past the gates, past Madrid.

But then Santángel wheeled his horse around. "You must stop them or they will only grow larger and stronger. They'll enter the palace."

"I don't know how!" she cried.

"You do. You know you do. What do shadows need to thrive?"

Light. The very light she'd been running toward like a fool.

Santángel's horse thundered toward the stage, and in the flames of the overturned torches, Luzia saw the shadow queen and her dragon, the demon that had been John Dee. They were larger now, taller than men, looming over the guards that tried to skewer them.

Luzia didn't want to speak the words. She knew what would come next.

"You must," said Santángel.

She didn't bother to shape the phrase in her mind or to try to disguise it. She drew in a long breath, and she let the words sing free. "En lo oskuro, es todo uno."

The fires collapsed into ash as if doused by a great wave, the lanterns, every glowing window of the palace. There was only black night.

The words echoed in Luzia's ears. *In the darkness, all is one.*

Chapter 32

◆

For a moment, everything was still, as if the world had been snuffed out like a flame. Then Luzia heard people calling to each other, shouting for help. The shine of candles appeared in the great house's windows. Guards began to light torches.

Luzia slid down off the horse, happy to have her feet on the ground once more. Her dress was wet from the grass and she knew she was bleeding. Her heart still sounded too loud in her chest and she kept her hand on the horse's flank, steadying herself, waiting for something to leap out at her from the flickering shadows.

"The magic is undone," said Santángel.

Sitting on his great black horse, he looked like some kind of wicked spirit, risen from the depths of hell. Perhaps all the stories were wrong and only the devil could best his demons. Except she was the one who had driven them out.

"They said I would face Satan himself," she said. "This can't have been part of the trial?"

"No. This was someone seizing an opportunity."

"You there!" shouted a guard walking toward them, a torch held aloft. "Return to the palace. The hopefuls are to be confined to their quarters."

"You must go," said Santángel.

"Stay," she whispered, terrified, and ashamed of that terror.

"I can't go with you now. I need to learn what I can before

anyone has had a chance to shape a convincing lie. If someone attempts to harm you, use the wall of thorns. They can defend you as easily as they did a wooden Christ."

"It might kill someone."

"Good. I will come to you."

"Swear it."

He looked down at her, his eyes glinting like coins. "This promise I can keep."

Luzia nodded and he nudged the horse's sides with his heels.

The guards had cleared a path to the doors near the eastern terrace. Smoke still rose over remnants of the stage, and the platform where the holy men had been seated had collapsed completely, parts of it smashed to kindling. A horse lay on its side, its big body unmoving, its belly split by deep, bloody furrows that might have been claw marks. On the terrace, a man dressed in the cream livery of La Casilla sat, legs splayed out in front of him, eyes stunned and glassy. He'd lost one of his shoes and his left sleeve had been torn almost completely off. There was a smear of blood across his forehead. From somewhere on the grounds she could hear shouting.

The guard tugged hard on her arm to keep her moving and she felt the words of the refrán tickling the roof of her mouth, but she forced herself to tamp down her fear. Someone was going to be blamed for the disaster of this night, and she had no desire to earn more attention for herself. She let him drag her inside and up the stairs. She was cold now that some of her panic had receded, and her mind was trying to make sense of what she'd seen. Her hands remembered the texture of the shadow on her fingers, how wrong it had felt, the misery and revulsion that had poured through her.

"Do not leave these rooms," the guard said as he shoved her inside her chamber.

"For how long?"

"That is for Don Antonio to decide. Do not think to challenge him or you will enjoy the hospitality of a cell. Guards will be posted in the corridors."

Luzia stood for a long moment staring at the door, wishing it had a lock, wishing she had more than scraps of power that had made their way to her in letters and songs. She wished she had a knife or any kind of weapon. There was the magic that had killed Víctor's bodyguard, but she had no idea how to recreate it, and whose fault was that? *There are limits to the impossible*, Santángel had warned her. But why did there have to be?

"Concha?" she asked quietly, afraid to raise her voice. But she knew the girl wasn't there. The room felt too empty, too silent.

Who had created those shadows? Who had controlled them? Could they slip through doors? Walk through walls? What if the devil really had come to La Casilla, not to be bested, but to brand them all as his creatures?

She was shivering now, her dress damp, her corset chafing beneath her arms. Her skirts were muddy and singed in places. She wanted to change, to be warm and dry, but she had no way out of her gown without another set of hands. Should she go looking for Valentina? For Hualit? What had happened to them? What had happened to the other competitors? A thousand questions, but the only one that mattered was *What comes next?*

She whispered to the coals in the brazier and they sparked to a glow. She could make fire leap. She could crack open a stone. Though she couldn't multiply gold or rubies, she could make a mountain of beans or shoes or muskets.

But always she wanted more. She thought of Álvaro, lying split in two, and what it would have meant if she'd had one of the talismans Santángel had spoken of, if she could have swept herself out of that room and onto a ship or the top of a mountain or anywhere at all. A change of scene, a change of fortune. She had almost died that day and still she wanted more.

The door opened and she nearly screamed. It was Santángel.

She didn't bother to ask how he'd gotten past the guards. That was one of his gifts.

"Where is the maid?" he asked.

"I don't know. Could something have happened to her?"

"Many of the servants went outside to watch the play earlier. Some are sheltering in the stables and outbuildings, but many fled."

Luzia rubbed her hands over the heat of the coals. "I can hardly blame her. If I could run I would."

Santángel walked to the window, though she knew there was little to see on the darkened grounds. "The Holy Child and the Prince of Olives have returned to their quarters with their patrons and attendants. Gracia de Valera has asked to leave the torneo."

A wise choice. A competition plagued by blood and demons was not the place for matchmaking.

"What did I see tonight?" she asked. "Who has such power? Fortún said we were meant to face Satan himself, but—"

Santángel shook his head. "It's shadow magic. I've seen it before. Maybe it's the work of the devil, but if so he had some mortal help."

"Gracia was almost killed."

"I suspect that was the intention. No doubt you would have been blamed."

She knew he was right as soon as he spoke the words. Gracia had tried to ruin Luzia's first performance. Gracia's guard had tried to kill her or at least take her out of the competition. Luzia had every reason to want to harm her.

"I would have to be a fool to attack her so publicly," she protested. "And in front of an inquisitor!"

"Remember, they believe you are a scullion."

"A stupid peasant incapable of scheming." Luzia's laugh was bitter. "Of all the things to doom me."

"Your doom isn't certain yet. Whoever managed this magic had tremendous power, but lacked real skill or control. I highly doubt they had this outcome in mind."

Luzia drew the chair from her dressing table closer to the fire and sat. Her legs could no longer support her. She was tired and cold and she'd never been more scared.

She kept her eyes on the coals and said, "When we were on your horse, I wanted you to keep riding. I wanted you to charge through the gates and onto the road. I didn't want to come back."

For a long moment she thought he would say nothing.

When he finally spoke, his voice was quiet, as if he were confessing. "I thought the same thing," he said. "I wondered how far we might go."

Chapter 33

◆

He shouldn't have said it, but he had no desire to call the words back.

"Why didn't you?" she asked. "Why didn't you keep riding?"

"It would have been as good as an admission of guilt."

"Is that why you stopped?"

"No," he admitted. "I am bound in service to De Paredes."

"Surely there are limits to one's sense of duty?"

He could hear the hope in her voice, that the trust growing between them or his desire for self-preservation might drive him to sever his bond with his master. He didn't owe her an answer. He could simply shake his head. He could leave.

Instead he spoke the truth. "I am bound to Víctor de Paredes as I was bound to his father and his father before him. I have served his family since before the kingdoms were brought together, since before these lands had Christian names."

Luzia didn't say *that is impossible*. He didn't expect her to. By now she knew too many things were possible that she had never contemplated before. Scullions might become soldiers. Little girls could see into the future. Shadows could live and sometimes they had teeth.

All she said was "I'm cold and I'm tired and I need you to help me out of these clothes."

"I'll find you a servant or the widow."

"I don't want them."

The words filled the room, a bell that had been struck, a reverberation that passed through their bodies, through the walls, out into the night.

He should say it wasn't proper. He should go. "If I'm found here, there will be nothing that can save you, Luzia. The cost will not be so high for me."

"If you think I'm letting you leave me alone again, you're mistaken. Clothed or unclothed, if you're found here, I'll be damned, and I might as well be comfortable when I'm cursed to hell."

Refuse her, he told himself. It's not too late to spare her this betrayal. Sparks rose from the heated coals. Outside one soldier called to another.

He held out his hand. "Come here."

Luzia rose and crossed the room. She turned her back to him and he was reminded of the day she'd tried to refuse his training, when she'd said she had to stir the soup. He reached for her laces, and when his fingers brushed the skin of her neck above her collar, he felt a tremor move through her. As if she were the bell that had been struck, that trembled with sound. He wanted to hear her ring out.

His hands were swift.

"This isn't the first time you've done this," she said with a weak laugh.

"I've been alive a long time." His youth had been spent in countless beds, on floors, in fields, once between the rows of a vineyard. There had been times when the only way he'd been able to cope with his own immortality was to fuck himself free, to feel briefly, truly alive in another's pleasure. "I fear the dress is ruined."

"You've lived too long among the wealthy. It can be cut apart and made into something new."

He turned away to offer her privacy and heard the thud of the dress, followed by the corset, and then the shuffle of damp linen being pulled away from her skin.

"I'm going to bathe," she said.

"The water will have gone cold."

"I can heat it."

Of course she could. Desire had turned his mind to jelly.

"I'd like some wine," she said.

"Then I will find it for you."

She had moved behind the screen that protected her bath and he heard her whisper to the water.

He slipped out the door and quickly down the hall. He could hear muffled voices, someone weeping. He knew he shouldn't go back to Luzia's rooms but he knew he would.

When he returned with the bottle, she was already in the bath. The room was soft with the heat of the water, the windows clouded with mist.

"Santángel?" she called, afraid.

"I'm here."

He poured her a glass of wine and set it on the table behind the screen so she could reach for it.

"You'll stay?" she asked.

"I will not leave until you send me away." Or until I'm driven mad by wanting.

He removed his cloak and settled himself against the wall beside the screen.

"Will you talk to me?" she asked. He could hear the sounds of her in the water and imagined her limbs slick with moisture, the glimpse of her bare knees above the surface.

"What would you have me say?"

"I don't wish to speak of the torneo or devils or kings. Tell me what ailed you when we met."

"I was sick because this life has made me so. Because it drains me and bores me, but I still cling to it as a child to his mother's hand. After all these years of sorrow, I want to live."

"You cannot die?"

"I can," he conceded. "But I'm too much of a coward. There's little else to say about it."

"Just talk. Talk to me. As if we were friends. As if there's a future."

"I've forgotten what it is to have a friend, to speak easily and openly."

"All is machination."

"All is scheming."

"Why do you stay with him?" she asked.

How to answer? After so many years of protecting his own secrets the habit was hard to relinquish. "I'll tell you a story. That's all I can grant, a bit of make-believe."

"I'll take it," she said magnanimously, and he found himself smiling, despite the tale he was about to tell.

He tried to think of where to begin. "Long ago, there was a wealthy young man—"

"Was he a prince?"

"Let's say so. It makes for a better story."

"Good. Was he handsome?"

"Some thought so. He was rich. He was well schooled. He was beloved. He was a second son and his father's favorite because he had a gift for learning, which his father valued even above gold. The prince wanted for nothing. He traveled to distant lands and met with scholars and brought back rare manuscripts to add to his father's collection. He spent every day in happy debate over philosophy and science and the moving of the stars. He spent every night pursuing pleasure. He fucked when he wanted to and drank when he wanted to. He knew that he was lucky in the way that lucky people do."

"So not at all."

"Not at all," Santángel agreed. "Everywhere he went he was welcome. When he joined a party they were merry. When he left they fell into despair. He thought his life would always be easy."

"If it had been, there would be no story."

"True. The prince saw many wonders in his travels. Mysteries of the old world that had nearly been forgotten. Miracles, if you want to call them that. He learned to read and write in many languages in the hope that it would open up doorways to the possible, and he had only one true friend through all of it, a young man of no name and no property named Tello."

"A servant?"

"He began that way. But Tello was twice as learned as the prince, and twice as kind, and he quickly became the prince's trusted friend. They drank together, they wooed women together, they spent long nights in study together, and when the prince's father died, it was Tello who kept the prince from hurling himself into the sea. They journeyed home and the prince prayed for his father's soul. He sat with the priest for many hours, thinking it would bring him peace. But when he stood over his father's grave, it was as if he could hear Death calling to him. He tried to go about his business, to return to his travels and his treatises, but always he felt Death beside him. He could sense its patience, how it would wait for him, confident in its inevitability. He could take pleasure in nothing any longer because he knew it would all come to an end."

"He was spoiled, this prince."

"Very. He became obsessed with finding a way to live forever. He and Tello met with sages and healers and seers, with alchemists and astrologers. They went places on maps that had not yet been drawn. But for all the coin they spent and miles they traveled, they had nothing to show for it but foul-smelling elixirs, useless amulets, and sore feet."

Santángel heard a loud splash of water, then smelled sweet almonds. Was she washing her hair? He wanted to ask but didn't quite trust his voice to frame the question.

"He should have stayed home and wept for his father," Luzia said.

"Maybe," said Santángel. "If he had met grief as an honest man, he might not have feared greeting Death on the same road."

"I still meet grief in sudden places, when I least expect it. A familiar song. A smell from the kitchen. Then there it is. An enemy that can't be bested."

"Whom did you lose?"

"My mother quickly. My father slowly. I'm not sure which was worse. But tell me more of the prince and his friend."

"I should warn you, this isn't a happy story."

"I don't recall asking for such a thing."

Though she couldn't see him, Santángel nodded. He wanted to finish, though he knew the ending too well.

"Then let's go on, for this is the moment in the story when a stranger appears. In a marketplace in a southern city, a man approached the prince and Tello, who had been arguing over where to travel next. Tello wished to go north, to go home. But the prince had heard of a nobleman with a text that was rumored to give life eternal if one could manage to read it from beginning to end. The stranger bought them drinks and said he had overheard their conversation. He offered the prince a bargain."

Luzia sighed.

"Yes, I know," said Santángel. "But the young and fortunate believe they will always be so. At first the bargain didn't seem so very terrible. The stranger would ask for payment—"

"Of course."

"Of course. Though it was not such a large amount. The stranger explained the particulars of the ritual he would perform, some words recited, some wine drunk, some blood spilled. The usual stuff. Then he said, 'You will lose the thing you value least, but there's a catch.'"

"Of course."

"Of course. The stranger turned to Tello. 'Your servant will lose the thing he values most.' The prince, and maybe even the stranger, expected Tello to refuse. But they didn't understand how little Tello had. No family, no fortune, no home. Life was not so precious to him, and the prince's obsession with hoarding it mystified him. Tello agreed to the bargain.

"The prince had little faith in this stranger to do anything more than take their money, but he protested anyway. 'It could cost you your life,' he warned Tello. And Tello agreed that it very well could. 'Then why would you do this thing?' the prince asked.

"'Because I love you best in the world,' Tello replied. 'And if this bargain will put an end to this ceaseless travel and we can go home, I will do it.' So the bargain was struck."

Behind the screen, Luzia shifted and he heard water slosh over the edge.

"Come, comb my hair," she said.

"Luzia—"

"Come, comb my hair. I need to know that what I want matters to someone."

He could have refused. He could have left the story unfinished. He fetched her silver comb.

The water was milky with soap, and only the gleam of her breasts and the tops of her knees were visible. Her head leaned back over the edge of the tub, the wet mass of her hair dripping on the linen that had been set on the floor. He knelt behind her, looking down upon her upturned face, her pink cheeks, her parted lips, her many freckles like desert sand. How had he not understood how lovely she was? She opened her dark eyes, her gaze direct.

"Go on," she said. "You won't hurt me."

"I will," he replied. "You have seen what I am. You know it is my nature."

"Go on," she repeated.

He had the sense that the world had shifted, that if he stepped outside, the constellations would be unfamiliar in their shapes. He lifted the comb and set it against her scalp, drew it through her oiled curls. She closed her eyes, and her sigh of pleasure made him wonder, for the first time in many years, if God was real and testing him.

"Is there no more to your tale?" she asked.

He steadied his breath and said, "That night the stranger took them out beyond the city walls and they followed the steps of the ritual he set out. There were no howling winds or flashes of lightning, and the prince felt it was all rather disappointing. But he paid the man his fee and they returned to their rooms.

"The next morning the prince woke late. He felt no different. But when he walked the streets, people didn't smile at him as they had once done. The butcher offered him no fine cut of meat. His landlord demanded payment. Can you guess what he'd lost?"

"What he valued least," she said. "His luck."

"The prince had never understood that there was anything truly special about him. He hadn't grasped that the luck that kept him from shipwrecks and earthquakes and spider bites was a kind of magic, a magic he'd never recognized and so never valued as he should.

"Distressed, he went to find Tello, afraid his friend might have died in the night. But Tello was alive and well and sharing a meal with a group of travelers.

"'My friend,' Tello cried. 'Such news I've had. My uncle has decided to make me his heir, and I must travel to his lands at once.'

"It soon became clear that whatever had happened in the ritual beyond those city walls, the prince had not lost his luck; he'd given it to Tello. *There are worse things*, he told himself, *than to see a friend thrive.* But he couldn't understand what Tello had been forced to give up, and that troubled him."

"It was a trick."

"You are wiser than the prince. In time he understood that the spell really had worked, that it hadn't just deprived him of something but offered him a gift in return. If the prince burned his hand, it healed almost instantly. If he broke a bone, no remedy was necessary but to set it straight and get a good night's sleep. He and Tello tested this newfound power, cautiously at first. A cut here or there. A bit of poison in the prince's cup, then a bit more. He sometimes grew sick, but he always recovered. And as the years passed, they realized that though Tello aged, the prince did not. He was as young and strong as when they'd met the stranger in the marketplace.

"They traveled to Tello's uncle's lands, and soon the uncle passed and Tello inherited. His flocks grew and his harvests were always plentiful. He assembled a group of men and offered them in service to the king. He bought himself a knighthood and more land. He married a young noblewoman and had a son. Tello grew richer and happier, and the prince grew restless, eager to travel and return to his studies once more. He had eternal life and he wanted to use it.

"Tello begged him to stay, but the prince refused. He could remain no longer. He packed his few belongings and set out. He spent the day traveling, his spirits high, and passed the night in a comfortable inn. But when he woke he felt a strange sensation. The rising sun was streaming through his window, and as it did, the prince watched his fingers burn to ash."

A crease appeared between Luzia's brows. "He had been cursed?"

Santángel touched his thumb to the damp skin of her brow and waited for it to unfurrow, then drew the comb through her hair again. "It seemed so. He leapt onto his horse and rode back to Tello's lands, and as he did, his flesh was restored and his strength returned to him.

"'You have come back to me, my friend,' exclaimed Tello. 'Let us never again be parted.'

"'You knew,' said the prince, for Tello showed no surprise.

"'We are bound to each other. So long as you remain in my service, your luck is mine and eternal life is yours. Ah, my friend,

I dreaded this day and the look in your eyes. I'm grateful it didn't come sooner.'

"That was when the prince understood that the stranger in the marketplace had been in Tello's employ. And at last he knew what Tello had given up: the prince's trust, the love of the person he cared for most in the world. It was all he'd had of value then."

Santángel set the comb aside. It was time to tell her the rest.

"Since that day I have been bound to Tello de Paredes and all of his descendants. My luck is theirs. I live, I do not age, but I am bound to them forever. And if I spend a night away from them, I will burn away to ash when morning comes."

"You cannot die?" Luzia asked. She had asked him that before. But for the first time, her voice was less than bold, the truth of his curse and what it meant between them.

"I can. At least I think I can. If you struck the head from my neck or burned me on a pyre."

"How do you know?"

"Because they tried everything else. Tello's son was cruel and wished to test the limits of my immortality. I was beaten with rocks, stabbed, my limbs broken, but still I healed. I was drowned in the river, again and again, but still I rose from the shore. I begged Tello to release me from my bonds, not to leave me to his son's mercy. He wept on his deathbed, he begged for my forgiveness, but he would not free me.

"With every new member of his line, I had hope one of them would see fit to set me free. That their coffers would be full enough, their lands great enough. Víctor promised he would, when he was a young man. But that changed as everything does. Everything but me."

The room was silent. Steam rose from the water. His fingers were damp with almond oil.

She sighed. "Then we are trapped here, you and I. Despite all our gifts." She turned her head to him. "Will you kiss me now, Santángel?"

He should say no. He should rise and go, spend his desire in his hand. For the sake of his heart and her life he should do these things. But in the end, after so many lifetimes, he was only a man.

He leaned forward. Her lips were soft, her mouth sweet, and when he felt the press of her tongue, he knew he could make no more arguments. He lifted her from the bath, soaking his sleeves to the elbows and noticing not at all. He dried her gently and laid her down upon the bed.

"Undress for me," she said. "The only man I've seen without clothes was wrinkled as a walnut."

"If it will please you."

It seemed she had awakened his vanity alongside his desire. He took pleasure in the way she watched him disrobe, in the rapid rise and fall of her breasts, the spreading flush on her cheeks, the shift in her body like the soft swell of a dune.

When she had looked her fill, he lay down beside her and she turned to him. "It's not too late," he said. "If you ask me to go, I will."

"Is that what you want?"

"In all these many years I've never wanted anything less."

She cupped his face, let her hand trace his jaw, his neck, the planes of his chest. His breath hitched when she reached his stomach and moved on, her fingers fastening around him, all hesitancy gone.

"Then kiss me again, Santángel," she said. "It was too late for us before we ever met."

That night Valentina woke bathed in sweat, her head swimming with the memory of a strange and beautiful dream. The air was sweet with oranges and she had been walking with Quiteria Escárcega, who had let her borrow her crimson velvet jacket. But now her room seemed too still, and in the moonlight, she saw the shadows lengthening, long-clawed demons coming for her bitter, grasping soul. She told herself to return to sleep, to drink a little wine to settle her nerves, to stop being foolish. But she felt fretful and uneasy, as if a fire had been lit beneath her skin.

It was less that she rose from her bed than that she was driven from it, and she found herself tapping at the door that connected her bedroom to Marius's chamber. She expected no answer and so she was surprised when he called softly, "I am awake too." She was even more surprised when she opened the door to find him striding across the room to her, and her bafflement only grew when he took her in his arms and tumbled her onto his bed.

"I dreamed of orange groves," he said as he buried his face in her neck.

She had time to think *How strange that he should dream that too*, and then she was so overcome with befuddlement and other unnamable emotions, she couldn't think at all.

In the gardens, one of Pérez's guards turned to the man he'd stood watch with for the better part of two years and said, "Don't you think it's time we stopped pretending?"

They slipped into the shadows of the hedges where the cold ground caught up their whispers and moans, and where the next day the gardener would find a mysterious patch of white blossoms.

Down in the kitchens, the cook and her husband made love on the table beside a regiment of leavening loaves. The morning bread tasted of sweet oranges.

Beneath the scroll of his silver angels, Antonio Pérez wept for his loneliness, his head full of a dream of orange trees, then he rose from his bed and tried to return to his correspondence, but only love poems emerged from his quill.

If any of them had listened closely, they would have heard birds rustling in the branches, and somewhere in the walls, the amorous squeaking of mice. But their ears were too full with whispered words of love.

As dawn broke and Luzia felt for the first time the joy of waking in a lover's arms, she experienced a kind of desperate hope too. "There must be a way to break the curse," she said. "And we will find it together."

Santángel wanted to tell her that Víctor de Paredes had already offered him a way. But he drew her closer and said nothing.

Chapter 34

◆

Luzia woke to the sound of screaming and Santángel shaking her shoulder.

"Get up," he commanded. "I'll help you dress."

"Who is crying out?"

"I don't know," he said, pulling on his clothes. "The Inquisition's alguacil is here with his men. They've come to arrest someone."

Luzia was still trying to climb out of the night's happy haze, but those words were enough to yank her into awareness. The tribunal's constable was here.

She scrambled into her corset and skirts, awkward with Santángel now in a way she hadn't been before, aware of every place on her body he had touched. She should be ashamed, she knew, frightened. But she wasn't sorry for any of it. If she was to die, then she would die with memories worth keeping.

He helped her with her laces, then sat her before the mirror and fixed her hair in a tight braid.

"Where did you learn to braid a woman's hair?" she asked, watching his pale face in the mirror, the concentration there.

"I don't recall," he said. "But I'm happy for the skill. I would spend a lifetime braiding and unbraiding your hair."

Lovers' nonsense. But she would grow fat on nonsense every day if she could. She only wished she had her simple convent dress to wear—as if a shell of black wool could protect her. The velvet would have to do.

There was a harried rapping at the door and Valentina appeared, her face waxen, her hands trembling.

"I was just bringing Luzia to you," Santángel lied.

Luzia watched Valentina take in the rumpled bed, the discarded dress, and the floor wet with bathwater. But all she did was hold out her hand to Luzia. "Come," she insisted. "I don't know where Don Víctor is. Marius wants us to leave, but we have no carriage."

"The alguacil won't let you leave," said Santángel. "They're searching the palace for someone."

The shouts of soldiers rose from below, then the thud of their boots on the stairs.

"I shouldn't have come here," Valentina gasped, as if suddenly realizing that Luzia was the likely target.

Here it is at last, Luzia thought as the soldiers crowded the hallway. No more pretending, no more challenges, her fate finally written. She drew in a breath, as if she were about to plunge underwater. But they thumped right past her, their swords rattling, their boots making the floor shake.

From somewhere down the hall, Luzia heard a new voice, a high pleading wail.

Valentina pressed her fist to her chest. "What is that?"

The answer came quickly. Teoda Halcón's nursemaid was hauled screaming from their rooms.

"Get on your feet!" the cuadrillero demanded, trying to make her stand. But the woman only continued to weep.

"I'm innocent! I didn't know!" Her words came in great gulps between her sobs, rising and falling in gusts of misery. "I didn't know!"

He seized her by the hair, dragging her down the hall. She didn't fight him but clung to his legs, like a limp reed. "Mother of God, help me, I am innocent!"

Teoda's father was next, head hanging, steps measured, as if he were walking in a processional, the cuadrillero's hand on his shoulder. He wore a long linen shirt and a dressing gown, his leather shoes and stockings jutting from the hem. They looked like they belonged to someone else.

Only the Holy Child was fully dressed, as if she had known this moment and this fate were coming. Maybe her angel had whispered in her ear. Or maybe her guilt had done that work. Her face was streaked with tears, but she was calm and she was praying loudly, though the prayers were nothing Luzia had ever heard.

"I reject your priests and accept only the word of God," she said, her small face determined. "I reject your saints and give my faith to Jesus only."

"Be quiet or I will silence you," snapped the cuadrillero, guiding her down the hall. He was slender and round-faced, barely a man.

"Neither you nor your Pope can silence truth. I have seen your king's death, and he will go slowly, drowning in his own filth."

"Be quiet," he growled, and struck her hard across the face.

The girl toppled and slumped against the wall. She looked up at him, spat blood. "I have seen your death too, and it is an ugly one."

The soldier shrank back but one of the others kicked her in the side.

"We'll find a gag for you, demon." He picked her up with one hand and slung her under his arm like a calf, her little heels kicking the air, as he clamped his other hand over her mouth.

As they passed, Teoda's eyes met Luzia's briefly, and she saw no fear there, only rage.

"What is happening here?" Valentina cried.

"Return to your rooms, señora," said the young soldier who had cringed away from Teoda's prediction. "All is well now." But Luzia saw his hands were shaking.

For the rest of the day, they huddled in the Ordoños' rooms. There was no sign of Hualit or Don Víctor. No word was sent.

Santángel came and went, returning with almond cake or a pitcher of wine, or sometimes a bit of information—the grounds had been searched and secured, the puppeteer had a burn on his leg but was well and ready to travel home, the Holy Child's room had been torn apart and Calvinist texts found in her father's belongings. Luzia remembered standing before the church officials, wondering aloud if they were meant to behave as if they were at a party or a church. *Depending on the church, it can be hard to tell the difference.* Had Teoda been preparing to use the performance as an attack on the vicar's holy men? And if she was the one who had created those monsters, what did it mean for Teoda's predictions? Who was whispering in her ear in the guise of an angel? Or was all that invention too, another manufactured miracle?

Luzia's mind could find no place to settle. It alighted on one thought, one feeling, then took flight again, a bird hopping from branch to branch. She would meet Santángel's gaze and her mind flooded with images, his bright head between her thighs, the sound of his breath hitching as he entered her, the press of his thumb urging her desire forward, the grip of his fingers as he lifted her hips. She was a marionette, a collection of limbs, an invisible string connecting her throat, her heart, her lungs, her cleft, and with a mere glance a ghostly set of hands jerked up on those strings, making her catch her breath and clamp her thighs together.

Then right on the heels of that wild, delicious feeling came fear, a cold hand pressed against her mouth, a sinking in her gut. She saw Teoda's ferocious eyes, her father's bowed head, the frightened soldier following as the Holy Child was carried away. Luzia thought of the shadows clutching at her skirts, their claws digging into her skin. She imagined the cell where Teoda would be brought, the tortures she might endure. The inquisitors weren't allowed to spill blood, but they could pop her bones from their sockets, bind her small arms and legs with ropes they cranked tighter and tighter until she screamed out her confession. There were whispers of worse things, of spikes that fornicators were made to sit on, of an iron fork fitted beneath the chin to force your head upright. The Inquisition treated all heretics the same way, and a child sinner was no less dangerous to the soul of Spain.

She was surprised when Valentina set a plate of cheese and olives before her.

"You should eat," she said.

"I have no appetite."

"Even so," said Valentina. "Just a little."

Luzia forced herself to eat a bite of cheese and take a sip of wine.

"Better," said Valentina. She was wearing her cream velvet today and she ran her thumb over a line of the umber embroidery. "It's an impractical gown. The velvet will be so hard to keep clean."

Luzia supposed that would be a problem for Juana or some other servant now. There would be no return to the safety or the drudgery of the larder. "Do you know where Concha went?"

Valentina shook her head. Her finger continued to follow the scroll of embroidered leaves, as if trying to memorize it. "There are whispers about what you did last night. When others ran, it was you who . . . I'm told you were brave."

"I've never been more frightened."

Valentina glanced up at her. "But you didn't run."

"I wanted to."

"But you didn't."

"No."

Valentina nodded. "Eat some more cheese."

Chapter 35

◆

It was long after midday when Luzia heard a light scratch at the door. Marius and Valentina rose. But when Luzia made to open it, Santángel stepped in front of her. In case of what? Monsters? The alguacil? Did she fear demons or the Inquisition more?

Antonio Pérez stood in the hallway, accompanied by the man with the dyed-red beard and a clutch of his liveried guards.

"I've come to see my scullion," he said, looking past Santángel with a warm smile.

He stepped inside and closed the door, leaving his retinue to wait in the hall. Pérez was beautifully dressed in plum velvet, heavily embellished with silver cording, the collar and shoulders plumped with amethysts.

Luzia knew she didn't look as she should. Her gown was rumpled and she wore nothing to cover her freckles. Her hair hadn't been bound up properly and lay in a single damp braid. All she could do was curtsy and keep her eyes on the floor, attempting to look modest and serene.

"Last night was frightening, wasn't it?"

Luzia nodded.

Pérez glanced at the Ordoños. "And you're all a bit frightened of me too, I think."

"No, señor, of course not," Marius protested.

"We are grateful guests," said Valentina.

"And you, Luzia?" Pérez queried.

Luzia knew better than to lie in this moment. "Of course I'm afraid of you."

"Luzia!" Valentina squeaked.

"Do tell me why," said Pérez.

Luzia was confused by the way he addressed her directly when he should put his questions to the Ordoños. They might not be her patrons, but they were her employers and of far higher status.

"Forgive me, señor, but there's no mystery to my answer. You are a man of great power and influence. I am a servant with neither. How could my answer be any different?"

"She is a diplomat, our scullion! And she makes a fair point. I would be sad indeed if people didn't tremble just a little in my presence. Please," he said, gesturing to the wider room. "Let us all be comfortable, if we can. Shall I have refreshment brought? No, I see you are well provided for. Good." He spoke as if enjoying each word in his mouth, stacking another, then another to compound that enjoyment.

Marius took the seat closest to Pérez, while Valentina and Luzia shared a small cushioned bench. Luzia's eyes sought Santángel, and she realized that no one was looking at him or speaking to him. It was as if they'd forgotten he was there, when to her he seemed to be glowing in the murky light of the room. Was this how he slipped past soldiers and outwitted patrols of guards? Had he mastered a kind of invisibility even she couldn't guess at?

Pérez settled in his chair. "I have just come from speaking with Fortún Donadei and his patroness, Doña Beatriz. In a demonstration of wisdom and courage—and I daresay foresight—they have agreed that the torneo should continue."

Marius made a show of nodding sagely. "You feel this is the best course?"

"I fear it is the only course, my friend. The king demands a third trial, and what a king wishes is as good as done."

Valentina glared at Marius and he cleared his throat. "Even in the wake of such violence?"

"Dreadful, I know. But that was the work of Teoda Halcón and her heretic family. Such perfidy, such wickedness. And brought beneath my roof in the guise of holy innocence. They follow a Calvinist sect, and it was Teoda who sabotaged the second trial."

Luzia kept her face expressionless. In Perucho's shop, she had seen the look that Hualit exchanged with the tailor when he mentioned Teoda's father traveling to Germany and the Netherlands. Were there whispers of her heresy even then? Luzia had been standing beside her when the shadows began to move on the stage. The girl might have feigned her fear and surprise, but she didn't have the ability to create such monsters. Like Gracia, she'd prepared a magic lantern to get through the second trial. *I have no talent for miracles or illusions.* Maybe that was a lie too.

"What will become of her?" Luzia asked.

"Luzia," Valentina chastised, "it is not for you to pose such questions."

But Pérez merely leaned back and said, "We needn't stand on protocol after such a night. She's being taken to Toledo to face the tribunal. No doubt she will have interesting neighbors."

He must mean Lucrecia de León. The girl who dreamed and the girl who spoke to angels, both locked away and facing torture.

"As for Gracia de Valera," Pérez continued, "she had quite a lot to say about you."

Marius startled as if someone had poked him with a pin. "About Luzia?"

"She claims you saved her life," said Pérez.

Luzia forced herself not to look to Santángel. This could be a trick. Had Gracia said that Luzia saved her through some strange or demonic means?

"I may have?" she ventured.

"She has left the torneo and is returning to Sevilla. She said she would keep you daily in her prayers and give alms in your name for the rest of her days. She went on like that for quite a while."

Luzia stared at him, then sputtered, "I will do the same for her."

"We all will," added Marius.

"Now, Luzia of the scullion's hands, savior of beautiful maidens, are you prepared for a third trial?"

"Does it matter?" The words slipped out, her defenses eroded by a night spent blissfully without sleep and a morning whiled away in terror.

Pérez only laughed. "Not at all, child. It was a matter of courtesy."

"Don Antonio," said Valentina, her voice thin as broth. "Forgive me. I . . . I hesitate to ask, but even with the heretic under lock and key, can we be certain such a trial will be safe?"

"No," Pérez admitted. "But the king has insisted and offered his own guards as protection. You see, I am just the clockmaker; the king tells us the time."

"Then we will go to El Escorial?" Marius asked.

For the first time Pérez looked uneasy. "A worthy question. And who wouldn't wish to see its splendors? Alas, I do not yet know where the third trial will be held. That is for the king to decide."

Luzia had understood Philip would never come to La Casilla. Not even the prospect of a holy champion with whom to put down Dutch revolts and cow the English queen could lure him to make such a gesture. The world came to the king, and it would be too great an honor for Pérez. But she had thought, maybe hoped, that they would visit the Alcázar or El Escorial. What did it mean that the king would offer them no such invitation?

Marius hurried into the silence. "With Teoda and Gracia gone the king will have few champions among whom to choose."

"Then let us say he'll have less opportunity for distraction." Pérez turned to Luzia and leaned forward. "You must do all you can to show the king what you are capable of, little nun. Then he will decide if you or young Donadei are to be his champion. Or no one at all."

Now Luzia saw. If the king rejected both her and the Prince of Olives, he would be rejecting Pérez as well. Pérez would never return to his ruler's favor or be reinstated as secretary. That was why he was in this room with them, speaking to Luzia as if she mattered. His fate lay with a scullion and a farmer's son.

"I will do all I can," she said, "and pray God does the rest."

"This is all any of us can ask."

"Señor . . ." Luzia attempted, "is there nothing you can tell me of the final trial?"

"That will be dictated by the king's whim. I am as much in the dark as you."

Luzia doubted that, but there was nothing more to say.

Pérez rose and they all followed suit. Before he slipped through the door he said, "Pray tell me, Don Marius, where are Don Víctor and his wife?"

Santángel was most in a position to know, but no one asked him. No one even glanced his way.

"We haven't seen them since before the trial began last night," said Marius.

"I can't say I'm surprised," Pérez replied. "Don Víctor is like a cat. He will be seen when it suits him and not before."

When he felt safe. When he could be certain of the torneo's outcome. Víctor de Paredes was widening the distance between them, creating a path of escape should this all go horribly wrong.

But none of it would matter if she could show the king a true miracle, if she could make him believe in her. The keeping of his favor might prove a greater challenge, but Luzia would solve that riddle when she needed to. For now it was enough to hope.

Faith could be won. Curses could be broken.

Chapter 36

✦

Santángel hadn't been certain Víctor would return to La Casilla, but he sensed when his master was once more on the grounds, the hand on the leash, pulling him to heel. He found Víctor ensconced in his grand rooms overlooking the gardens. He'd timed his return to avoid any visit by Pérez, and long after the Inquisition's dogs had fled. He was, after all, a very lucky man.

"So Teoda Halcón is a heretic," Víctor said as Santángel entered. "What was her plan, do you think?" He'd tossed aside his shoes and was sipping jerez with his stockinged feet propped on a low table.

"Where is Doña Maria?"

"Back in the city. She was badly shaken."

"And you?"

Víctor contemplated the amber liquid in his glass. "I knew no harm would come to me and mine."

"There are limits to my influence, Víctor."

"And yet my wife and I are unharmed, as is my champion."

"I'm surprised to hear you call her that." He didn't want to hear Víctor speak of Luzia at all.

"I have not given up hope that this may all come right for us. The scullion performed well last night and the king's problems haven't changed. Don't tell me you're losing your nerve? Do you fear freedom so much?"

Before Santángel could think, his hand was on his dagger. But anger would do him no good. How many men had Santángel killed in service to this family, silently, easily, as if he were Death's own hand? Yet every action he'd taken against a De Paredes had been thwarted. He had slipped poison into Jorge de Paredes's cup. The man had sickened but then grown stronger, as if the poison were feeding him. He had attempted a more direct approach and simply stabbed Isidro de Paredes in the heart. The dagger had somehow not found purchase, slipping to the side. And the repercussions had been grim.

Isidro had locked him in a box underground, buried alive, left there to waste away. He didn't know for how long. It should have made him angrier, should have made him want to seek revenge. But he had finally broken, as each De Paredes had assured him he would. It was less the punishment than the understanding that he had no recourse, that unless he was willing to take his own life, he was well and truly trapped. Ever after, Isidro had called him El Alacrán for his attempted betrayal, no matter that his sting had proved futile.

His other small rebellions had been equally worthless. He had tried to spoil business deals, deliberately choosing partners he thought most likely to betray his masters. Thieves became honest men without understanding why. He had chosen preposterous ventures that had no hope of success. Gold was struck and silver mined. Santángel could not best his own power.

What tack to take now? If he was wise, he'd tell Víctor of the third trial and nothing more. But he couldn't let Luzia walk into what might be a trap, even if it was one of his own making.

He sat down across from Víctor. "I don't believe Teoda Halcón was responsible for what happened last night."

Víctor's brows rose. "She is the only one calling Pope Gregory the antichrist. Her father has connections in Cologne, and even to the Anabaptists in Poland."

"I don't deny that she's a heretic. But why create such a spectacle at the second trial? Why not wait for an audience with the king? Or entrench herself in his service?"

Víctor shrugged. "Perhaps she never intended to go as far as she did. Maybe she meant for the blame to fall elsewhere. On Luzia or one of the other competitors."

"If that's the case, how was her heresy discovered? Who betrayed her?"

"Why does it matter to us or our cause?"

"Because that accusing finger could just as easily point to Luzia."

"And that would bother you, wouldn't it?"

Santángel wasn't fool enough to snap at that bait. "Teoda Halcón is too convenient a villain. Fortún Donadei is nearly as ambitious as you, and the Inquisition is an excellent way of eliminating competition—whether you're opening a spice shop or trafficking in miracles."

"If your spies had done a better job, Donadei would be my champion and we'd have no cause for concern."

The chance that he might not have met Luzia felt like a fissure in the earth. If fate had chosen that course, Donadei would be the sacrifice that undid his bargain with Víctor. A clean choice, barely a betrayal. He'd be free of this mad desire and the decision to damn Luzia. She would be safe with the Ordoños or competing for some other noble. If he had met her first at La Casilla, would he have recognized her wit, her talent, her beauty? Would he have bothered to look closely enough to discover her? Or would she have been just one more obstacle to destroy in pursuit of Víctor's glory and his own goals? Could he afford to let her be more than that now?

"Luzia is more powerful than the farmer could ever dream of being."

"I certainly hope so," said Don Víctor. "Do you truly suspect Donadei, or do you just not like him?"

"Both things can be true. No one should have so many white teeth." But regardless of his facile charm, it was obvious Donadei had the most to gain. Teoda and Gracia were both gone from the tournament and Luzia had nearly been killed. What tragedy had befallen the Prince of Olives? Had his head of curls been singed?

He refilled Víctor's glass, knowing these little gestures pleased him. "Pérez claims the king is insisting the torneo proceed."

Now Víctor frowned. "But if so . . . why not open El Escorial to the hopefuls? It may mean nothing. Philip has never been one to make a fast decision. He's kept Pérez on a long tether for years now."

"Something is wrong here," said Santángel. "La Casilla could have burned to the ground last night. Someone could have been killed."

"You think Pérez is playing a deeper game." Víctor leaned his head back, as if contemplating the frescoed ceiling. "In the streets and salons the talk against the Austrian is growing louder. Trouble in the Netherlands, raiders in our own ports."

The Austrian. When Spain was strong, its people were happy to claim Philip. But reeling from loss of blood and treasure, he was the Austrian again, a Hapsburg interloper who would never belong on Spanish soil no matter his native tongue, or how many palaces he built.

"Pérez won't act against Philip," said Santángel. "Not directly."

"Perhaps not. But the torneo serves as a kind of advertisement, doesn't it? The king isn't ready to relinquish the opportunities these trials may yield, even if it burnishes Pérez's reputation. But who says Pérez isn't open to other offers? If Philip won't act to seize the power our holy champions offer, maybe someone who wishes to challenge the king will."

Was that what Pérez hoped for? A real rebellion that might lift him even higher than he had been? The king was sick with gout. He grew frailer every day. His son had none of the makings of a ruler. But a weak king was still a king. The comuneros had tried to act against Philip's father and failed. That memory was not so old.

"We could withdraw," he said.

Víctor peered at Santángel as if trying to see through a fogged window. "I can scarcely believe what I'm hearing."

Santángel couldn't quite believe it himself. But he had to say it, had to at least offer up the chance. "It's the prudent choice. Step back, let Luzia hone her skills in private, see whether the king is healthy enough and strong enough to stave off Pérez and his detractors."

"Very sensible. Is that what you really want?"

He no longer knew. Hundreds of years of servitude, of the yoke around his neck keeping him bound to the name of De Paredes. He had endured cruelty, caprice, and relentless boredom. Could he consign Luzia to that? It would be her choice, just as it had been his, but Víctor would find a way to force her decision, and Santángel's luck would help him do it.

Maybe Víctor was right and he did fear freedom. He would be mortal again and he was still the same fool who had run from death so long ago. He would have but one life to squander, to fill with his own mistakes. The first would be leaving Luzia.

As if Víctor could read his thoughts, he said, "You will forget her in time. The world is wide and full of women. The torneo will continue and Luzia will win. Her power will be mine, and you will go live your life and find your death and forget about us all."

And Luzia would go on and on.

Chapter 37

◆

La Casilla felt empty, the quiet hanging in the air like dust. Most of Pérez's guests had gone. There were no hunts or grand feasts, no bursts of noisy conversation filling the halls or peals of laughter from the garden.

Marius and Valentina had spent the rest of the afternoon discussing likelihoods for the third trial, and when Luzia tired of their speculation, she asked for permission to return to her rooms.

"Is that safe?" Valentina asked.

"Are you going to protect me if the alguacil returns?"

"She can go where she likes," Marius said with a wave. "If she's not safe, none of us are."

Luzia had hoped Santángel might come to her if she separated herself from the Ordoños, but she had no visitors and Concha must have returned to Casa de Paredes or run even farther from the nightmares she'd witnessed.

Luzia lay on her bed and made herself think of her refranes and how they might be useful, not the bed, or the way it had creaked last night, or the sounds Santángel had drawn from her, or the wriggling desire that seemed to have turned her body to eels trying to escape from a pot.

Freite en la aceite, y no demandes de la gente. The words she used to heat coals or cooking fires had always pleased her. *Fry in oil before you beg.*

Then the little whispers that had helped with stains and fruit that hadn't yet ripened. Non mi mires la color, mirami la savor. *Judge me by my flavor, not my color.*

Or the words she'd used to open cupboards when they'd lost the keys—*sweet words open iron gates*. Boca dulce abre puertas de hierro.

The familiar song to lighten firewood or heavy buckets of water—el mal viene a quintales, se va a miticales. *Trouble comes in gallons, but goes in droplets.*

They all seemed so meager. Where was the magic that would give her wings? That would transport her to a mountaintop? That would change her into a lion? Where was the magic that would help her master this longing?

At last she could be still no longer. She took her cloak and went down to the garden. The air was cool and the terrace was empty. She wasn't sure if she should go exploring, but she could at least walk through the roses. They'd already been cut back for the fall, and the blooms she'd created the previous night were gone, cleared away with the wreckage of the stage and the dais. There were furrows in the grass, scorch marks where torches had toppled and the stage had caught fire. What had really happened here?

"Luzia."

She nearly jumped at the sound of her name. Hualit's housekeeper stood near the edge of the rose garden, bundled into a shawl, her looped braids curled against her neck.

"Ana?"

"Come with me, please, señorita."

Luzia knew Hualit trusted Ana, but she called up the words she'd used to grow the roses last night. Two competitors had already been eliminated. If she needed thorns they would be ready.

She followed Ana past the hedges to where her aunt waited on a stone bench, enveloped in black velvet, a blue bow tied at her neck, bright sapphires dangling from her ears.

"At last," Hualit said, rising and opening her arms for an embrace. "Ana and I have been waiting for you to step outside all afternoon."

Luzia let herself be held briefly, the sweet scent of bee balm washing over her.

"Where have you been?" she asked as they settled on the bench. "Why didn't you come back to La Casilla?"

"I returned to the city."

"I was nearly killed and you vanished."

"Because Víctor asked me to." As if this were answer enough. "He needed to see to his wife."

"If he didn't banish you, why are you hiding in the gardens?"

"You learn too quickly, Luzia. It isn't ladylike."

Luzia waited.

At last Hualit sighed. "He is afraid I may be questioned."

"About what?"

"About you. About Pérez. About his business here."

"You promised you knew how to play this game."

"Well, savor this moment, because I was wrong. Víctor thinks we can still make a success of this, that Pérez can win back the king, but he's being careful. If he's wrong, too close an association with Pérez could be dangerous for us all."

"Not for Víctor de Paredes."

Hualit studied her. "How well do you understand the familiar's power?"

"I might ask the same."

"Very little," she conceded. "The servants talk, even if Víctor won't. Are you fucking him?"

Luzia rose and paced to the apple trees so her aunt wouldn't see her flush. "Does it matter?"

"Only if you let it. Only if you start imagining you can save him."

"What if I could?"

"Think to your own future, Luzia."

"I am," Luzia said, her anger rising, that flame always ready to catch. "That's all I've been doing. I'm trying to learn to swim while the rest of you wave to me from shore."

"You jumped into the water—"

Luzia held up a hand. "I chose to keep performing my milagritos, the same way I chose to show your patron my power when you ambushed me at your home. So let's say that I jumped and you pushed. Do you know what I intended that day? I had my basketful of food and I thought the Inquisition was at my heels. I was going to run."

"Maybe you should have."

"I'm not sorry I stayed. Or that I demanded something more from this life than scrubbing floors and groveling for Valentina Ordoño. I'm not sorry for any of it." She should leave it at that, but she needed to know. "You had a thousand chances to lift me up, to offer me a little hope, a little comfort, but you never did. Why not? What would it have cost you?"

"I had my own secrets to keep."

"You thought I would inform on you?" Had she really believed Luzia would denounce her as a Judaizer or a fornicator?

"Not intentionally. You were young. Your power . . . You had no control, and I had no idea how to teach you."

"So you left me to sleep on a larder floor?"

"And I was right to do it," Hualit snapped. "You did reveal yourself. You fell into Valentina Ordoño's clumsy trap the moment it was set. I couldn't take the risk."

Luzia thought back to the day when her aunt had first read the words from her letter, when she'd felt the language twist and take on a new shape, heard the melody those words made. She thought of the iris blooming with its hungry yellow mouth. If she had failed that day, if she'd had no gift for miracles, if the words had meant nothing on her lips, would Hualit have taken her in?

Maybe. But then what? She would have been a servant still. She might have had a bed to sleep in, but she would have been as dependent upon her aunt as she had been upon the Ordoños.

"You chose yourself," Luzia said. "I can hardly blame you." And yet she did. It was a petty sentiment, but she'd been so alone. Her mother dead, her father mad. She'd been a child. In some ways she still was one. A woman who had barely had a chance to live.

Hualit held her hand out, beckoning Luzia back to the bench, eager for peace. "Sit, please. Hear me out. It hasn't all been in vain. I'm not quite the selfish wretch you think I am. And I didn't come here to quarrel."

Luzia made herself cross the soft ground and sit beside her aunt.

Hualit grasped her hands. "The life I've dreamed of, the future I've been building, it isn't just for me. Víctor has suggested I travel to Venice until the king and Pérez finish their dance."

A dance that would end with the king's trust restored or Pérez in a cell. "Venice?"

"I'll go. Just as he has instructed. But my journey won't end there. I'll meet another ship to take me on to Salonika. And you'll go with me."

"You want me to travel with you? Don Víctor won't let me go so easily."

"He needn't know. I have the money to get you out of Madrid. We'll meet in Valencia. But we have to go tomorrow night."

Tomorrow. Before the third trial.

"I can win," she said. "I know I can."

"Luzia . . . what do you think will happen if you do? You're clever and determined, but you aren't charming like Fortún Donadei. You don't have his appeal. He is meant for the machinations at court. You—"

Luzia yanked her hands away. "I am meant for what? To go with you to Turkey and take another scullion's job?"

"You could be—"

"Your maid? Could I clean your gowns and see to your jewels and wait for you to find me a husband?"

"Would that be so bad?"

"And will the rabbi welcome a woman who can make miracles?"

Hualit's eyes slid away. "There are healers. Wise women. Prekaduras."

Salonika. Where the winds howled up from the sea and made new music through the alleys, where the Inquisition couldn't reach. Once it would have seemed a beautiful story she couldn't wait to tell. But now she wasn't sure. Women prayed in the balconies in the synagogues of Salonika, separate from the men. They didn't study Torah. They didn't fashion miracles. She would be alone in a city where she didn't speak the language or know the customs, with only Hualit to protect her—and Luzia didn't trust her aunt to do that, not if it harmed her own prospects. She would always choose herself first. Luzia could try not to blame her for that, but it was time she lived by the same rule.

She didn't want to be her aunt's servant. She didn't want a life of quiet and submission. She wanted her audience with the king. She wanted to eat and be full.

And yes, she could admit, she wasn't ready to leave Santángel, who couldn't follow her beyond the borders of Madrid without Víctor de Paredes beside him.

"I'm going to see this through," she said. "I will win. And you'll learn to speak Turkish and keep the Sabbath holy. I'll miss you, Hualit. But I'm done being led by you."

Hualit shook her head, her face full of what might have been wonder or worry, or just disbelief. "You are still the child who thought the city wept for her. Your ambition will destroy you, Luzia."

"Maybe," Luzia admitted. "But let it be my ambition and not my fear that seals my fate."

Hualit cupped Luzia's cheek and sighed. "Even if you win, you can't fight Víctor de Paredes."

"I can if I have the protection of a king."

"Víctor always wins. Always."

Because of Santángel. But if Luzia won the king's favor, if she made herself indispensable to him, she would have the leverage to force Don Víctor to break his hold on Santángel. His luck would be his own again. He would be free. Free to leave. Free to stay with her if he wished it. Víctor de Paredes was used to getting his way and that meant he'd forgotten what it was to be desperate.

"Think on it, querida," Hualit said. "There's still time to decide. All you need do is go to the stables and ask for a horse. I've left money with the groom there. He'll help you. Just consider it. I have failed you enough times. Let me make it right."

"Only I can do that now."

Hualit sighed again and stood. "I don't have magic. I'm not a beata or a bruja or even a good woman. But tonight I'll pray that you join me. And if you don't, if you choose this dangerous path, then I'll pray for you in Salonika. I'll pray for you in Hebrew, so loudly the king and his priests will have to cover their ears all the way back in Madrid. I'll pray that our suffering will be swallowed by the sea."

The sun was just beginning to set, the gardens turning blue in the gathering dusk. Luzia hugged her aunt and bid goodbye to Ana, and made her way back to the lights of La Casilla.

She wondered if she would have to spend the night pining for Santángel, but he was waiting in her rooms.

"Hello," she said. "I was walking in the gardens."

"I know," he said. "I was waiting for you."

Then the door was closed and she was pressed against it, his mouth on hers, his body a dark cloud descending. She had lived too long without rain.

Luzia had a thousand questions about the torneo, the king, Salonika. Instead she said, "Can it be done against a door?"

A kind of growl escaped his throat. "It can."

"Please demonstrate," she managed. Then her skirts were in his hands and she forgot about talking.

Chapter 38

♦

It was dangerous for him to stay, but it had been dangerous for him to come to her room at all, and there was no hiding from this anymore.

Their coupling had been brief and urgent, their bodies wedged against the door, her head buried in his neck, the pinch of her teeth as she bit the skin of his shoulder, stifling her cries. He'd been grateful for the centuries that had given him control.

He should have left then, but he didn't want to. Better to say he couldn't. He had spent so long dreaming of freedom, he had forgotten other wants. The pleasure of warm skin, conversation, the glimmering of connection—tentative at first, then bright and steady, another ship glimpsed on a dark and endless sea.

"What does it mean to be a familiar?" she asked as they lay atop the covers of her bed, her knee hooked over his thigh, her head against his chest.

"To serve."

"To give Víctor your luck and me your strength?"

"Those things are the same. If you win, it will benefit Víctor."

"Then why does only one make you strong in return?"

"Because Víctor has no magic himself. No De Paredes ever has. He has nothing to give back to me."

"But I do."

Gently he pulled one of her thick curls straight, feeling it slide and twist between his fingers as it rediscovered its shape, a living thing. "In abundance."

"Have you ever been drunk?"

He laughed. "Of course. You haven't?"

"I don't think so," she said. "A bit light-headed. It felt like this."

"When I was young—"

"Many, *many* years ago."

This time he was the one to bite her.

"When I was young," he began again, "I did everything to excess. There were nights when I would drink and laugh and sing, but there would be a moment when a kind of misery came over me. When I looked around at my friends making merry and I felt only lonely, and even angry that they could be so happy and light when I was drowning beside them."

"And other nights?"

"Other nights it felt so good to be untethered from my mind that I only wanted to stay drunk, and I would drink more and more, to try to keep that feeling, to stay aloft."

She shifted against him and his cock stirred against her leg. "Águeda once told me that the cure for drunkenness was to drink until you made yourself sick, until you hated the taste."

"And what if you never weary of it?" he asked as she slid atop him. "What if you empty the bottle only to wish for another just like it?"

"Is there such a wine?"

"Yes, but it's very rare," he said. "Put your knee here."

"Sit astride?" she asked skeptically.

"Like that," he managed, feeling the press of her damp flesh, the coils of her curls, wondering where his centuries-old control had gone.

"A rare wine," she said on a sigh, as she guided him inside her.

"One few men get to taste." He slid his hands up the strong

muscles of her thighs, helping her find her balance, then her rhythm.

"Only the very lucky ones," she said. Her words turned to moans and he was borne aloft again.

Santángel left before dawn so as not to be discovered. When he brushed kisses over her cheeks, her lips, her eyelids, she smiled.

"I see you're glad I'm leaving," he said.

"I'm trying to imagine a time when you don't have to."

He made no promises of "someday" but kissed her again and was gone. Luzia fell back asleep, then woke late. She had nothing to do today but fret about the final trial and Hualit's offer.

In the mirror her cheeks were flushed, her skin damp. He'd left her with no bruises or love bites. He was no fool. But she could see him all over her. Her hair was a grand tangle and she knew the brush would do no good, so she worked her fingers through it, again and again, first with water, then with oil, then at last the silver comb.

"I can help," said Valentina when she arrived, and she worked for a while in silence, arranging Luzia's braids in a coronet.

Luzia realized that Valentina must have been without a maid since Concha had gone. Had Marius helped her to dress and undress these past nights? She couldn't quite imagine it, and she really didn't want to, not with another happy evening fresh in her mind.

She knew she was unwise to let that happiness shape her worries for the future. Her focus had to be the torneo and all that might or might not follow. Santángel could speak of an eternity spent braiding her hair, but what did that mean when he was cursed to serve the De Paredes name and she might still become a servant to the king?

If she found a way to force Don Víctor to break the curse, then Santángel would be free to leave and she would never deny him the life he'd longed for. She knew what it was to be pinned in place like a moth. Would she dare to go with him? She might travel the world, visit Hualit in Salonika. They could sleep beneath their own roof in some foreign city. Would he want that? Did she?

"Let's walk in the gardens," Valentina said. "I don't know how many days of good weather we have left."

Luzia was surprised at the invitation but she had no other way to waste these hours. Tomorrow they would see beyond the bend in the road. They would know what lay before them: a world of palaces and power, or a more uncertain fate. If the king didn't select Luzia as his champion, she wondered what choices might remain to her.

Luzia and Valentina made their way down to the terrace. She sensed that Valentina wanted to speak, but she said nothing, only fussed with the lace at her cuffs.

The Prince of Olives was walking in the gardens, trailed by Doña Beatriz, dressed in aubergine silk edged in green and gold, the colors of olive fields in the afternoon hours. She had gray in her hair and her eyebrows had been heavily plucked. They might have been mother and son.

Valentina's sigh was wistful. "She has worn a different gown every time I've seen her."

When Fortún glimpsed Luzia, he raised a hand in greeting. He bowed to his mistress and kissed her hand, and Doña Beatriz bloomed, her eyes bright, alive in his attention. Luzia knew there was a lesson here in the danger of letting someone else make you happy, but she was not in a mood to be taught.

"Is that what happened?" Valentina asked.

It took Luzia a moment to understand what she was asking. She followed Valentina's gaze to the sketch resting on an easel in the shade of the apple tree and drifted closer to get a better look.

Signor Rossi had abandoned his staid portraits of the torneo's competitors in favor of a dramatic rendering of the previous night's horrors, the study wrought in blurred clouds and slashing lines of charcoal. Gracia cowered beautifully, her hands clasped in prayer, while Luzia and Fortún Donadei seemed to float together, side by side, charging in on a divine wind from the right side of the scene, staring down what might have been a large storm cloud, but that, when you squinted, took the form of something more sinister.

"That is less frightening than what we faced," Fortún said as he approached.

Doña Beatriz had been waylaid by Valentina. Was this strategy? Had Valentina asked Luzia to walk in the gardens to encourage a meeting with the Prince of Olives?

"When the trouble started, I don't remember standing side by side with you," Luzia said, too tired and anxious to play diplomat. "I saved Gracia. And myself. And the whole cursed house."

"I was seeing to Doña Beatriz's safety," Fortún protested.

"And your own?"

"I won't apologize for that."

"I didn't ask you to. But this . . ." She gestured to the painting. "This is fiction." Luzia had been drawn in her convent gown, light gleaming around her braided head like a halo, beams of it cascading away from her. Rossi had not made her beautiful, not precisely, but she was all light and shadow, her eyes determined, her mouth set in a forbidding line. This was how she dreamed herself when she was shaping the refranes into song, a woman cut adrift from the earth, her garments billowing around her.

Fortún looked even more handsome in the sketch, holding up his bejeweled golden cross to ward off the evil descending upon them, the hastily rendered gems like eyes.

There was a blur in the crowd, and Luzia realized that was where Teoda Halcón had been erased by Rossi's thumb.

"I think he captured you well," said Fortún, "and it needn't be fiction. This is as it should be. You and I, fighting together, two peasants of unremarkable blood welcomed to the king's court and celebrated."

"You're seeing something that isn't there. Gracia was almost killed, and someone is responsible."

"The Holy Child."

"Do you truly believe that?" She watched his face closely. It might serve Fortún Donadei to blame Teoda for what had happened. Or maybe Luzia was a fool for wanting to absolve Teoda for a crime she had as good as confessed to.

"No," he admitted.

Some honesty at last. "Then what do you believe happened? Who is to blame?"

"That isn't for me to say."

"Then whom?" Luzia glanced over her shoulder, but there was no one to hear. "You tell me we are to be soldiers together, holy servants of the king, but you won't speak the name of someone who may wish us both dead?"

"Not us both." She knew what he would say next, and still the name sounded with a hollow clang. "Santángel."

Luzia turned her back on him and began to stride toward Valentina. Fortún jogged past her and cut off her path.

"Think, Luzia . . . Señorita Cotado, think of what is to be lost and gained."

"That shadow . . . I was almost killed."

"But you weren't. Those demons frightened Gracia out of the competition. Now Teoda is gone too. Santángel murdered Gracia's guard. If he could have dispensed with me as quickly, do you doubt he would have?"

"You're making dangerous accusations."

"But you don't deny them. Because you know what he is. Cursed."

Now Luzia paused. How did Fortún know of the curse? Or was he trying to lure her into revealing Santángel's secrets? "What curse?"

"Surely we're past dissembling. He used magic to obtain immortality and lost his soul in the bargain. My mistress told me so."

"She has proof of this?"

"The proof is in his long life. His demon's eyes."

Luzia made herself laugh. "So no proof at all."

"I didn't think you were such a child. A creature like that can't be trusted."

"And you can?"

"All curses require sacrifice. In the making and the breaking. Have you never wondered what part you might play in it? You are not the first milagrera he and his master have pursued."

He is your rival, she reminded herself. He is a tactician. "Speak plainly. Do you know something real or are you just spinning gossip to scare me?"

"They had spies roaming the cities and countryside, seeking out seers and milagreros. Why do you think I ran so quickly to Doña Beatriz?"

"Doña Beatriz whom you loathe?"

"Yes," he said without hesitating. "I seduced her because I'd heard rumors of Víctor de Paredes and his creature. People who gain their attention do not share in Don Víctor's good fortune."

When Águeda had muttered her warnings in the kitchen of Casa Ordoño, Luzia had dismissed them as rumor, superstition. *People who cross paths with that man come to bad ends.*

She knew she needed to be careful now. Anything she said against Don Víctor could be used by Donadei. "All I hear is speculation."

"The alumbrada Isabel de la Cruz was approached by Santángel. Where did she end up? The Inquisition's cells. Piedrola met the same fate. Santángel was among those who visited Lucrecia de León when Don Alonzo de Mendoza began recording her dreams, and you know how that ended."

Luzia made herself focus on the neat rows of hedges, the branches of the apple tree, bare of fruit. I could make them grow, she thought. I could fill a whole orchard. "Still you offer no proof."

"What proof can I provide but whispers passed from one milagrero to another? Catalina Muñoz was wise enough to avoid Don Víctor and Santángel. The daughter of Maslama al-Majriti vanished from history entirely." He glanced once at Doña Beatriz, still in conversation with Valentina. "I've been told there is a secret chapter from Juan Diánoco where he writes not just of the milagros worked by a farmer named Isidro, but of the devil who appeared to tempt him at his plow. A demon with white hair and silver eyes."

"I see," said Luzia. What else could she say? What was she meant to believe? The sky seemed too close, too heavy, a smothering hand.

"I'm only suggesting there are questions you'd be wise to ask."

"Or you're trying to weaken my resolve and fracture my bond with a powerful ally."

"God wants this for both of us, Luzia. I feel that."

"Do you have visions now too?"

"I don't need a vision to see what we might build together."

"I will think on what you've said." Her voice was steady despite the frantic thud of her heart.

He lowered his voice. "Perhaps I should be ashamed I seduced Doña Beatriz, but I'm not. Despite all her wealth and power, love has made her mine to command. I think you understand me."

Luzia couldn't stop the blood that rushed to her cheeks. Had she and Santángel been so indiscreet?

"I understand you very well," she replied sharply. "You know you can win." She shouldn't say it. Santángel would tell her it was bad strategy to speak so baldly. "You're popular with Pérez's friends and your gift is as great as mine."

"Together we might be greater still." He reached for her hand and Luzia flinched.

"Don't," she whispered furiously. "Your mistress will see. So will mine."

He drew back, ashamed. "I don't . . . I don't know the ways of this place. I never have. I only know I don't want to bear the weight of the king's expectations by myself. What happened to Teoda could happen to any of us."

"She's a heretic," Luzia said because she must.

"Search far enough, dig deep enough, and the Inquisition can find an excuse. I don't want to live in fear."

Luzia considered the sketch on its easel. Was it so easy to rewrite a moment? To change a story she thought she knew? A child erased with the swipe of a thumb. A scullion transformed into a holy warrior. Two rivals made allies.

"I don't want to do this alone, Luzia. I don't think I can."

"But we are alone," she said as she turned away from him. "Always."

A warning to the Prince of Olives. A reminder to herself.

Chapter 39

◆

Luzia stayed in her room the rest of the day, watching the light change, wishing for something to read, hoping Santángel would come to her, afraid of the answers she might demand if he did. *Sacrifice.* She had learned to shape words in her head, to hear the meaning of her refranes and then find a new use for them. But what could she make of the word *sacrifice?* She didn't trust Fortún Donadei, but that didn't mean she should ignore his warnings.

She thought of the Pleiades, the constellation that meant so much to Antonio Pérez. Her mother had told her old stories about the stars, about two angels who had been so besotted with mortal women they'd given up their secrets to them; of Orion the Hunter chasing Atlas's daughters across the sky, and the scorpion that had pursued him in turn. *Pleiades,* she'd said to Luzia. *Khima.*

How can one constellation have two names? Luzia had wondered.

It has many more than that, her mother replied. *Nothing is ever just one thing.*

Luzia's father loved the stories too, but he had never learned to read and took no interest in books or astronomy. *Why name the stars?* he'd said with a laugh, and lifted Luzia onto his shoulders. *Just let them be bright.*

From the moment Santángel had told her the story of the prince and the curse and Tello's betrayal, she had known he was issuing his own kind of warning. Maybe she hadn't understood the particulars of how their fates were entangled, or what she might be asked to give up in such a bargain, but she'd recognized the danger. Yet she couldn't make the figures tally. She was no immortal whose gifts could be passed from one generation to the next. And if Santángel valued freedom most, then how could he bargain it away and break the curse?

It wasn't too late to return to Madrid, to find Hualit's house, to run. She imagined herself walking through the gardens and on to the stable, asking for a horse she could barely ride. It was risky to travel the roads alone, but she wouldn't have far to go. She could even ask a groom to ride with her, offer him some of the beads from her rosary. Luzia wasn't sure how her aunt planned to get her to Valencia without Víctor finding out, but Hualit had never lacked for resourcefulness. She would find a way. Luzia would see the ocean, board a ship, slip away from Spain, from the tribunal, from the king. She would be safe.

"I would rather be powerful," she whispered to no one at all.

When Valentina arrived to help Luzia undress, she asked, "Did you bring me to the gardens to speak to Fortún Donadei?"

Valentina's hands paused on her laces, then she resumed her work. "I did."

"At Don Víctor's suggestion?"

"Doña Beatriz approached me. She suggested that an alliance might serve both our interests."

Did Doña Beatriz believe so little in her champion's skill? And did Valentina believe so little in Luzia's? "You think I'll fail."

"I don't," Valentina said with some surprise. "You don't seem to do that."

Luzia couldn't help but laugh. "There's still time."

They moved to the dressing table so Valentina could take down her hair, and Luzia marveled at how strange it was that her mistress now attended to her, at how easily they had fallen into this new routine.

Valentina began removing the pins. "I thought . . . I thought you might enjoy speaking with him."

The idea that Valentina might be matchmaking had never occurred to her. "I don't think Doña Beatriz would approve."

"That's not an attachment that can last. It's good for neither of them, and she will make herself a laughingstock."

"As I will with Santángel?"

Valentina made a disapproving hum. "Must we speak of him?"

"Why shouldn't we?"

"He is not natural."

"Maybe not. Maybe I'm not either."

Luzia hissed in a breath as Valentina gave a hard yank on her hair. "Don't say such things. Even in jest. A stain on you is a stain on us all."

Luzia met her eyes in the mirror. "Let go. Now."

Valentina sputtered, "If you have his children they will all have tails."

"At least I'll have children."

Luzia regretted the words as soon as they were spoken. Valentina's grip loosened, her eyes suddenly lost, a woman searching the crowd for a daughter she would never find. Luzia turned in her chair and seized her hands. "I shouldn't have said that. That was . . . I shouldn't have said that."

Valentina seemed to sway slightly, a leaf on the branch, waiting for a strong wind to carry her away.

She didn't look at Luzia when she said, "Did you . . . did you prevent me from having children? Because I was cruel to you?"

"You were cruel, señora. But I don't have that kind of power."

Valentina nodded slowly. Luzia couldn't tell if she was agreeing or simply deciding if she believed that Luzia hadn't made her barren.

"Then you can't help me, can you?" she asked.

How long had Valentina been holding this question against her tongue, trying to work up the courage to let it free?

"I'm sorry," Luzia said, and she meant it. "I wouldn't even know where to begin."

Valentina nodded again, lips pressed together, as if considering the taste of her disappointment. Luzia thought she might leave, but she merely drifted backward, moved by an invisible tide, until her hip struck the bed. She leaned against it.

"I sometimes feel I've spent my whole life longing," she said.

"As have I."

Valentina startled, shocked at the thought of Luzia dreaming. "What did you want?"

"Money," Luzia said, and she was relieved when Valentina laughed. "Sometimes they were small wants. A day when there were no floors to scrub or curtains to beat or chickens to pluck. A husband to love me."

"That is not such a small thing."

"No," Luzia allowed. "But I couldn't stop there. I longed for beauty and power and rooms full of people, lively conversation, journeys to mysterious lands. I wanted to be looked at and admired."

"Vanity."

"Vanity, and sloth, and gluttony. Every single sin. I wanted all the time. I still do."

"I thought I desired luxury and plenty. To wear fine clothes, meet fine people. But now I just want to go home, and eat Águeda's cocido, and stop being so afraid. Some part of me hates you for bringing us here."

Luzia raised a brow. "No doubt you hate yourself more."

"Maybe. Ambition is a terrible thing. When I married Marius, my parents were so pleased. Or as pleased as I ever saw them. But I think some part of him will always resent me, the match, my lesser name."

"It's a good name. Romero. It has a good meaning."

"A pilgrimage name?" Valentina scoffed. "There's nothing in it."

"But it's a name for rosemary too," Luzia said, the word *ruda* forming an unsung harmony in her head. Rosemary, rue, hyssop, a little sugar. "For protection."

Valentina looked only skeptical, but she gestured for Luzia to turn so she could finish undoing her coronet. This time, her hands were gentle as they unplaited and smoothed Luzia's hair.

When she was done, she said, "Don Marius, Don Víctor, Pérez, maybe the king himself . . . they're all the same really. They spin in their orbits and we are left to wonder at their movements. You must be careful with . . . with Santángel."

It seemed everyone wanted to warn her today. "Because he made a deal with the devil?"

Valentina winced. She shook her head. "Because he is a man, Luzia."

That night, Luzia kept the lamp by her bed burning a long time, wishing Santángel would come to her, remembering the names Donadei had listed, building his case. She hadn't recognized all of them. She knew of Isidro's miracles, Piedrola's predictions, the mystic Isabel de la Cruz, Lucrecia and her dreams. *All curses require sacrifice.*

Had Don Víctor really sought to become Donadei's patron? What role had Santángel played in all of it? What role was he playing now?

There was a strange mood in the palace that seemed to seep through the walls, a feeling of abandonment, as if the furniture had been packed away, the paintings removed, the windows boarded up. Her mind walked a path to the stables. She saw herself riding a white horse on a moonlit road. Was she a fool to stay, to wager on her own gifts and a cursed prince?

How was she to sort love from desire? It was like planting sage beside foxglove, trying to separate the leaves when the plants were still new. Both were a kind of medicine if only you knew which was which. Santángel was dangerous, but was he dangerous to her?

He had lain with her on this bed. He had whispered her name. A murderer who spoke to scorpions, who appeared places he should not. He was a horizon she didn't yet know. Why seduce a girl of scant beauty or knowledge if not to control her? Why link himself to a peasant if there wasn't some gain in it?

There had to be a path forward through this, a chance at survival if nothing else. And if she'd been witless enough to want more, to long for love instead of crafting plans, then she could put those hopes aside. The rat didn't dream of the ocean, not if it wanted to survive the cat.

Luzia nearly leapt from bed when she heard a tapping at the door.

Don Víctor stood in the dark hallway, his black cloak fading into the shadows so that his long face seemed to float in the gloom.

She recoiled, hiding her body behind the door, conscious of the thin fabric of her nightclothes and what her undress implied.

"I was expecting Doña Valentina," she lied.

He studied her with his cold eyes. "Santángel is running an errand for me. I thought it best you keep your thoughts on the task ahead."

Then he knew, as Donadei had. Had Santángel told his master? Or had it been his master who commanded this seduction in the first place? The thought caught like a hook beneath her ribs. It should have left her in despair, but it only made her angry.

"Be prepared to ride out early tomorrow," he stated.

"Has the location of the third trial been revealed?"

He ignored the question. "Pérez's position with the king is even more precarious than I understood. But this will not all be for nothing. Tomorrow you will be extraordinary, so extraordinary that the king will not care who found this treasure, only that you are a vein of ore so rich you must be mined. Pérez will be of no concern to us."

"Do you forget Fortún Donadei, señor? His gift is as great as mine, maybe greater."

"God's power is all that matters here."

But he didn't mean God. He meant Santángel and the luck that had always served him.

"I will do all that I can."

"Do you understand the sword above your head? It hangs above your aunt's neck too."

Luzia struggled not to show her surprise. Had Don Víctor always known that she and Hualit were kin?

"I can strip her of respectability," he continued. "I can take away everything she's earned with her clever cunt. That is what my money and my influence mean."

He was trying to frighten her. But she wouldn't be goaded into revealing she knew of her aunt's trip to Venice. Soon Hualit would board a ship to Salonika and then she would be beyond Víctor de Paredes's reach.

She kept her head bowed. "I understand, señor."

Silence seemed to stretch between them in the darkened hall. "Santángel has a fondness for you," he said at last. "He has always liked weak and broken creatures."

"I think you will find me very sturdy. Most servants have to be to survive."

"Sturdy like a cooking pot. Perhaps there is some novelty in fucking someone so beneath you, but it's not a perversion that has ever appealed to me."

"How you must hate him." The words slipped free, and they felt so good Luzia let herself go on. "He's stolen any chance for you to know what kind of man you might be without him."

He slapped her, hard enough that she lost her grip on the door and stumbled. Her hand went to her cheek.

"Sturdy, indeed," he said. "I trust you can use your talents to heal any bruise or mark. A wonderful convenience."

I could kill him, she thought. I could impale him on a spike of roses.

Instead she curtsied, no longer worried over the linen of her shift or that he knew she had been anticipating a visit from Santángel.

"Yes, señor," she said softly, humbly, and when she glanced up she saw the unease on his face. Had he thought she would rage? Cower? Crumple from a single slap? There were many ways a servant learned to survive. She had years of experience biding her time, counting up the insults done to her. She wasn't yet sure how badly she'd been wronged, but she could wait until she had allies powerful enough to protect her, for the right moment to let Víctor de Paredes know just what kind of enemy he had made.

"Keep your wits about you tomorrow," he said. "I expect miracles."

Luzia smiled. She knew there was blood on her teeth. "Then I pray God answers both our prayers."

Chapter 40

✦

Valentina arrived early to help her into her black velvet. Luzia had pressed the lace collar herself the previous night, then lain awake, staring into the dark. With every passing hour, she felt the escape Hualit had offered slipping away, until at last dawn came and the chance was truly gone.

"I was scarcely able to sleep," Valentina said as she finished placing the scalloped shells in Luzia's hair. "To think I will meet the king."

For all her talk of Águeda's cooking, a king was still cause for excitement. Valentina had dressed in her green silk today, the sleeves spangled with silver, and she looked surprisingly pretty, her cheeks pink, her eyes bright.

"You look well, señora," Luzia said, and wondered if she'd endure another slap for her impertinence.

But Valentina beamed, flushing even pinker.

The coaches were waiting when they descended the steps of the palace, but some of the party had chosen to ride. Luzia saw Fortún Donadei already mounted, dressed in green and gold, a plumed velvet cap set on his curls. Doña Beatriz was seated on a sleek mare the color of cinnamon. She reached out and adjusted the chain of Donadei's golden cross. It was a fond gesture, and yet Luzia wondered if it felt like the rider's hand upon the reins, a tug to remind her mount that she would set the pace. But if her love was real and his was not, who really held the reins?

And where was Santángel?

Marius waited at the De Paredes coach to help them inside.

"Don Víctor will not ride with us?" Valentina asked, her worry clear.

"Apparently not," said Marius.

They saw it now too: the distance Don Víctor was creating to protect himself. He sat astride a big gray gelding, his tunic ornamented with ropes of gold braid and jewels in every color of Philip's crest. It wasn't subtle, but perhaps the king didn't care for subtlety.

Luzia took one last look at the crowd, then reluctantly settled in the coach. Don Víctor might wish to keep her and Santángel apart, but she didn't think he would prevent his familiar from attending the third trial.

"Do we know where we're going?" she asked, as the coach wheels jolted forward.

"Only the lead coachman knows," said Marius.

Luzia watched the gardens, then the gates of La Casilla slide by, and then they were moving at a faster pace through the countryside, the horses' hooves rumbling over dirt roads. They were heading west, farther away from the city, through dry hills and pastures. Luzia told herself to be grateful she was seeing more of the world beyond her tiny corner of Madrid and the confines of La Casilla. She had never thought the grandeur of a palace could come to feel small.

She wished they could open the windows. Instead she watched her breath fog the glass and made herself think through each of her refranes.

Too soon they turned onto a narrower road and the horses had to slow. Woods crowded in on both sides, slender white-barked trees, their leaves just beginning to turn, the green giving way to sudden exclamations of yellow and orange.

Marius tapped the window. "This is Las Mulas. It's an old hunting ground."

"Will they make her hunt?" asked Valentina. "Or . . . or battle beasts?"

Luzia wanted to tell her she was being absurd, but she had no idea what might be waiting for her or what form the whims of a king might take. What he required, she would find a way to provide. She must. Whatever Santángel might feel or Don Víctor might devise, that much hadn't changed.

"Look!" cried Valentina.

A bright expanse of water had come into view, reflecting the cloudless blue of the autumn sky. It was so flat and calm, Luzia felt as if she might reach out and peel it away from the earth. Some kind of boathouse lay at one end and a herd of sheep grazed in the meadow beyond. The remnants of an old pier lay on the banks, its rotted boards slumping into the high reeds.

"Perhaps the king intends to stage a sea battle?" Valentina suggested.

Luzia doubted it. He hadn't had much luck with those.

As they emerged from the coach, Luzia saw that a grand dais had been erected. The wood was highly polished, the canopy made of red and yellow silk, the chairs upon it cushioned with velvet. It looked sturdier than half the houses in Madrid and twice as imposing.

Long benches had been set just a short distance away and groups of lavishly attired guests had gathered near the shore. She recognized some of them from La Casilla, including Quiteria Escárcega in another of her fanciful quilted jackets—though the young man who usually trailed after her was nowhere in sight. There were new faces too. She wondered if they were friends of the king or Antonio Pérez.

Pérez himself stood surrounded by servants and courtiers. He met her eyes and gave her the briefest nod, a small smile on his lips.

He looked confident and at his ease, but she suspected he'd look the same in a room full of crocodiles.

"Luzia." Santángel emerged from the woods, leading the same black horse he'd ridden the night of the doomed marionette show. His fair hair was ruffled, and the horse bristled and snorted, its hooves stamping the ground.

She glanced at Marius and Valentina, but they were already chatting with the other guests, their attention diverted.

He set his hand on the horse's flank to steady it. "When I realized your coach had left, I rode ahead."

"Where were you?"

"Sleeping off a dose of poison. It's Víctor's way of making sure I don't involve myself in his private business."

Luzia didn't know if she should believe him. "He would deny me your strength in the final trial?"

"He would deny me a chance to see you and trust my influence to do the work of victory. Luzia—"

"He came to see me last night."

Santángel went very still. He wore black velvet as she did, but even he had made some concession to the importance of the third trial: a rope of silver braid spanned his chest, pinned to his shoulder by a heavy brooch, the tower of De Paredes rendered in silver. "For what purpose?"

"To warn me not to fail."

"Luzia—"

But Don Víctor was striding toward them, ignoring Marius's and Valentina's greetings.

"Enough lovers' talk," he said. "The scullion is wanted by the lakeshore."

Santángel gave a sharp nod. "I'll escort her."

"You'll stay with me. She can manage by herself."

"Then you should have used a larger dose."

"Is all . . ." Valentina began. "Is all as it should be?"

"May I beg an introduction?" The lady playwright had stepped away from the swarm of guests, her panache of striped feathers set at a jaunty angle. She looked like a character in one of her own plays.

Don Víctor gave a distracted wave. "The scullion doesn't stand on ceremony, señorita."

"I have so longed to meet the little nun." The words were for Luzia, but her gaze was fastened on Valentina.

"It is an honor," Luzia said with a curtsy, her head too full of Don Víctor's threats, Donadei's warnings, Valentina's fears. "Your work is the talk of our small home."

"Have you been to one of my plays?"

"I have never been to the theater."

"A scandal!" declared Quiteria. "And you, Doña Valentina?"

"My wife and I have attended the Corral del Príncipe," said Marius.

Quiteria eyed him as if he were a fish she suspected had spoiled. "Have you? How traditional. If you're ever in need of real entertainment you must come to one of my salons."

She smiled at Valentina, bobbed her head, and was gone.

"What an unusual woman," Valentina said. She had the bright-eyed look she'd worn the morning they received their invitation to La Casilla.

"Insolent," said Marius. "Wicked, really. Rumor has it she has another conquest in her sights. Some new soul to corrupt. Camila Pimentel had to be sent to Sevilla and married off to a wool merchant to avoid disgrace."

"If she is so very awful, why has the tribunal not taken her for trial?" Valentina asked.

"Who knows? Her father is great friends with Fray Diego. Maybe he has a cache of relics he's promised to the king."

Luzia didn't care about Marius's gossip or the playwright. She needed to think of how the lake might be used in the trial. She needed to speak to Santángel.

The thunder of approaching hoofbeats sounded through the woods and the crowd turned, shifting and arranging their order, jockeying for position, readying themselves for the arrival of the king.

Soldiers poured into the clearing, uniformed servants carrying banners that bore the royal standard. It was grand, but not nearly as grand as Luzia had expected, and a moment later she understood why. She had heard the king had grown frail and sickly, but the man who exited the coach was heavyset and moved like a determined bull plodding across a field.

"A priest?" she asked. Had they sent more holy men to test her and the Prince of Olives?

"Mateo Vázquez de Leca," Don Víctor said, his voice bemused. "The king's secretary. The man who replaced Antonio Pérez."

Luzia risked a glance at Pérez. There was no change in his demeanor, but a new tension had come into the crowd that surrounded him.

"But . . ." Valentina protested, peering down the road into the woods, her hope still alive. "Then the king—"

"The king is not coming," said Don Víctor. His calm baffled her. This was a man who didn't like to be thwarted, but he sounded as though he'd merely lost a game of cards. "Our king has sent Pérez's rival in his stead. The man who banished the Princess of Éboli and who would see Don Antonio banished too, or hung as a traitor."

A stir went through the gathered guests as Vázquez de Leca mounted the stage. With a soft huff, he dropped into the enormous chair that had been placed for the king, bracketed by courtiers and advisors. He slumped to the side and gestured to Pérez as if he were the host here and Pérez little more than a servant slow to fetch the wine.

"Will the trial go on?" Luzia asked.

"Nothing has changed for you," Don Víctor bit out. "Best Donadei. Do it in grand fashion. You will compete and you will perform so spectacularly that Vázquez has no choice but to place you before the king, so brilliantly that he will be itching to present an ugly scab of a scullion and demand she be made this country's holy champion. That is how good you must be. Your life, your aunt's life, your lover's future all hang in the balance. So do your best or I will be forced to do my worst."

Valentina gasped and even Marius looked surprised.

"Are you done being frightening?" asked Santángel.

"I don't know," Don Víctor growled. "Are you sufficiently frightened, little nun?"

Luzia nodded.

"Then go." He turned to Santángel. "And if she fails me, drown her in the lake."

Don Víctor had dropped every pretense of civility, and that worried Luzia—not because the truth of him was any kind of surprise, but because something had changed. Was it the insult from the king? The end of the torneo? Or some new threat she couldn't see coming?

Santángel herded her away from the others. "Tell me what he said to you last night."

She resisted the urge to curl into the shelter of his black cloak. She couldn't afford to be weak now. "He warned me away from you. He isn't the first."

"Has the Prince of Olives renewed his campaign against me?"

"Yes. As has Valentina. She says our children will have tails."

"I can't father children."

"You can't?"

"Luzia, don't be foolish. If I could have given you a child, I never would have spent the night in your bed."

She didn't know what to say. Should she be glad? Grateful?

"Why do you look as if I've insulted you?" he asked. "That's not a risk I would take with your reputation."

Luzia had let herself get distracted. She didn't know how much time she had before the trial began, and she didn't want to think more on children or lost futures that were never meant to be.

"Did Don Víctor want Donadei as his champion?" she asked.

Santángel glanced at her, his expression unreadable. "Víctor had thoughts of building a menagerie, a collection of people like us. The torneo only added urgency to his intentions."

"How many of them ended up in the Inquisition's cells?"

"Too many."

"Because of you?"

Now he stopped and turned to her. "What is it you think I've done?"

"I don't know exactly. I only know I don't want it to happen to me."

"Some were frauds. Some had real power but no sense. Their own heretical talk drew the Inquisition's attention. Víctor understood your potential for greatness well before I did. He believed you could win the torneo and offer him a path to a title."

Luzia could see Donadei and Doña Beatriz waiting by the ruins of the old pier, but she wasn't ready to think on alliances.

"You never finished the story," she said. "Tell me now. Tell me the real ending for the cursed prince."

Santángel watched her with his strange eyes. "For him to be free, a new bargain must be struck."

"Is that why you flattered me and fucked me? So that I would love you? So that I would take your place in Víctor's service?"

His laugh was low and bitter. "I never intended any of this. I didn't want to want you."

"You would bargain me away to him."

"That would be the price."

"Then tell me you haven't considered it." It was a plea, pathetic really. *Lie to me, let me believe in you a little longer.*

But Santángel had promised her truth and he would not relent now. "I have. Every day and every night."

No anguish. No disgust at his own selfishness. And yet, even in her grief, there was some satisfaction too. There had never been shame between them. There never would be.

"I should have told you all of it," he said. "I should have spoken sooner. I didn't understand the trap fate had made until it was too late."

"Víctor has made a fool of you, Santángel. He would never settle for such a trade. I'm no immortal. I can't serve his children or his children's children."

"What is death to a woman who can heal any wound?" he asked gently. "A woman who can cure any sickness—even time?"

Luzia felt the breath go out of her, a door slamming shut. The morning was cool; the sun bright. She saw herself, a woman in black beside an autumn wood, framed with her lover by the mirror of the lake. The stage, the guests in their velvet and feathers, Vázquez brooding beneath a canopy of silk.

Last night, Víctor had been taunting her. He'd said her gift could heal any bruise or mark. *A wonderful convenience.*

Now she recognized the pity on Santángel's face. She had seen it in the courtyard on the day she'd made the vines grow, when she'd first felt his influence on her, when she had first begun to grasp what her power might become. What would it mean to live forever? How was she to know when she had barely lived at all?

"I won't do it," she said at last. "I won't make his bargain. Not for you or for anyone."

"I would not ask you to. But Víctor has a gift for impossible choices. He will connive and maneuver until he is your only protection, until he has your very life in his hands."

Was this why he had sent Hualit away? To close off every avenue of escape? "I can still refuse him."

"You won't. We are too alike. For all the miseries of this world, you don't want to leave it. To survive you'll make the bargain I once made. You'll give up what you value least."

But what was that? The magic that had come so effortlessly, with none of the misery of Latin or arithmetic? The freedom she had never known?

"And you?" she demanded. "You must give up what you value most to break the curse. How can that work when it's freedom you prize most highly?"

"It was, Luzia. For a very long time. But curses are cruel."

She felt as if she'd thrown herself off a cliff. For a moment she had the illusion of flight. His words were wings and she was carried by their meaning, by the elation of being wanted in return. *She* was what he treasured. *She* was what he valued most.

But there were no wings. There was no flight. She was only falling. He had planned to trade her to Víctor de Paredes for his freedom, just as Tello had once betrayed him. Could she not even have the promise of love? Why could this belong to the women in ballads, to poets and playwrights, but never to her?

"What if I killed him?" Luzia muttered. "What if I ended all of this talk of curses and bargains with a knife to Víctor's heart?"

"Even if you had the will for such bloody work, it would be no use. I have seen countless enemies seek to strike down De Paredes. They never succeed. They'd be better served by harming me. But if they can't see a target, they can't take proper aim."

"Then I should kill you?"

"It would be an end to things. If you could manage it. Luzia . . . there is another way."

"Tell me."

"Lose. Fail and fail spectacularly, shamefully. Disgrace yourself so thoroughly that Víctor will want nothing to do with you."

"That's your answer? You would see me humiliated?"

"I would see you free."

Trumpets sounded from the lakeshore and Luzia saw the Prince of Olives press a kiss to Doña Beatriz's hand. Pérez's red-bearded courtier was waving frantically for her to take her place by the water.

On the raised platform, Vázquez pushed reluctantly to his feet to address them.

"Go," said Santángel. "Win or lose. Do what you must."

"You don't yet know what I may do," Luzia said, and strode toward shore.

Chapter 41

◆

Vázquez's speech had none of the pomp of Pérez's introduction the first night at La Casilla or the grim threats of Fray Diego at the second trial. He looked out at the crowd as if unsure what they were all doing there.

"The king has been promised wonders," he said, and sighed heavily. "So let us see how you may best serve your ruler and his empire."

Was that all the guidance they were to be given? Her anger flared anew. Her conversation with Santángel was unfinished, her rage against him and Víctor and the unfairness of it unspent.

Lose, he'd said. *Lose spectacularly.* She had been transformed into La Hermanita, the milagrera in her stern black dress. She could be remade into the bumbling scullion once more, become so wretched that Víctor de Paredes would turn his back on her. She could save her coins, sell off her silk and velvet and the rosary at her waist, find her way to Hualit in Salonika.

Or maybe Víctor would be so angry he'd have her murdered in the night. He was a petty, cruel man, and he had made it clear that she would pay for failing him. He could denounce her to the Inquisition, send one of the king's heretic hunters after Hualit. Why had she not gone to the stables last night? And why did every path before her lead to servitude?

Maybe Santángel loved her more than the promise of freedom.

Maybe he didn't intend to bargain her away. But the grim truth was that love or the lack of it made no difference. A servant did the washing and stoked the fire and scrubbed the floors and carried the water up the stairs. What she felt when she was doing it mattered to no one. There was only the task before her, and the only way forward was what it had always been: win.

But how? Vázquez didn't want to be impressed, and that meant she needed some sort of spectacle to wake him from his contempt. She could make the water boil like a great kitchen pot, but that might too strongly evoke hell. She might make the lilies bloom to fill the lake, or topple the trees on the shore.

"I don't understand," whispered Donadei as she took her place next to him. "Where is the king? Why would he insult us this way? We've done everything asked of us."

His voice was desperate. He was watching his chance at liberty from Doña Beatriz slip away. What was worse, Luzia wondered, to be loved so hungrily that only a king could free you? Or to know the man who wanted you most had contemplated dooming you for an eternity?

"Donadei," she asked, "does your offer of an alliance stand?"

He stood up straighter. "Do you mean it?"

"I am considering it."

He seized her hand. "Stand with me. We both know what it is to be used. Together we might be greater than any noble name or title."

More powerful than Víctor de Paredes or Doña Beatriz. Protected and valued by the king. Maybe it would mean nothing. Maybe it would be enough to defeat all of Don Víctor's machinations and wiles.

"Please, Luzia," he begged. "Surely there is enough room in this glorious future for both of us."

"Then let us show them something beautiful," Luzia said to him. "Something so miraculous neither the king nor Vázquez can deny us."

"Tell me how."

"He's a priest," Luzia said. "So we will build him a cross like no other. A cross to make him believe."

Donadei's smile was triumphant. "Together?"

"Together," she agreed. "Let us make our bows."

She curtsied to Vázquez but did not do the same for Pérez. The game had changed and she would play the rules set before her.

"For God and the glory of our king!" she declared, surprised by the strength in her voice as it rang out over the crowd, as if her anger had built a scaffolding beneath it.

Luzia turned to the water and hummed softly, finding the old healing spell easily. The boards of the pier were rotting, so first they had to be fixed, made new as easily as a goblet could be refashioned or a split tongue made whole. Then she let the song shift. She shaped new words in her mind, the refrán she'd used to fill her basket with more eggs and onions on the way back from the market: *wherever you go, may you find friends.*

If only it were that easy. She let her voice lift, a plea for her aunt on her way to a new future, a prayer for herself. She needed friends now, and if the planks of the pier would be her sturdy allies, she welcomed them.

She began to clap, and to her relief, the crowd joined in. She met Donadei's gaze as she stepped out onto the pier, encouraging him to follow, and he did, vihuela in hand, out onto the lake. He struck a chord, playing the vihuela as if it were a guitar. Fish leapt from the water, in time with the music, arcing along beside them.

Luzia continued to multiply the boards, creating a path that unfurled like a carpet, one plank after the next, until she and Donadei stood at the center of the lake.

But how to assemble the cross? The words leapt into her head, as if they were fish themselves. El Dio es tadrozomas no es olvidadoza. *God acts slowly, but He doesn't forget.*

She saw the shape of the words in her mind. They were a temple, a crescent atop a dome, a hand raised against the evil eye, a cross. The boards spread and increased around her, filling the lake, then stacking one upon the other in a rhythm that matched her clapping hands.

"Make it bigger!" crowed Donadei, his fingers strumming the vihuela as black birds chirped and fluttered above them. "Make it so large they can see it in Madrid!"

The cross rose, towering above them, dripping water from the damp boards as fish leapt at its base and birds sang around it in a circle like a crown.

The crowd on the lakeshore burst into applause. Vázquez was on his feet, leaning forward on the balcony.

"We have them!" cried Luzia.

"Thank you," Donadei said. "I knew you would know how to get their attention." Then he turned to the audience on the shore. "Does the king wish for symbols? Or does he wish for ships?"

He struck his vihuela, the chord jangling, and as it hung in the air, he placed a hand over his golden cross and lifted it. The birds above squawked in response, their wings seeming to lengthen, their bodies shifting from sparrows into seabirds, long-legged and sharp-beaked.

"What are you doing?" Luzia shouted over the chattering of the birds.

"What I must." His fingers played over the neck of the vihuela. The flock multiplied, an army of birds, whirring around the cross. They seized the boards in their talons, tearing them away, assembling a new shape. "My gift is for the living world, not toying with objects and trinkets as you do."

The birds moved faster, swooping and diving, a whirling frenzy, and it was only when they began to pull away, their arcs widening, their wings catching the air and drawing them higher, that Luzia saw what they had done.

The towering cross had been remade into a galleon. Sails of black feathers billowed from its masts, and writhing eels formed black cannon at its railings. Her solid, stately cross transformed into something majestic and terrifying. Something *useful*.

Now Donadei's bright smile was sly. He stood with his hand pressed to the golden cross at his chest as if God Himself sang through the strings of his vihuela. "It is a competition, after all."

"Malparido," Luzia growled. The bastard had set her up. He'd fanned her doubts about Santángel, but worse, he'd made her doubt her own gifts. He'd pretended he was as frightened and as vulnerable as she. He'd gotten her to squander her turn.

She stood helpless on the wooden dock she'd made, and she knew how she must look, her meager boards wobbling in the shadow of Donadei's magnificent warship.

She had lost after all.

Would Santángel think she had done it on purpose? Would he know Donadei had made an ass of her?

Valentina would be disappointed.

Don Víctor would be furious.

And Luzia was furious too.

But there was something in the movement of those eels, the feathers, the long-limbed birds that she recognized.

"You were the one who gave life to the shadows. You attacked Gracia and me at the puppet show."

How? He had played no music, created no song. She would have heard. Luzia realized just how stupid she'd been. He'd used the same trick she had. The music was a mask, a vehicle for the words in his head.

She didn't know which language he was using to work his miracles, but she saw now that his magic was without real substance: birds who could sing but would never breathe, shadow creatures who vanished when the lights were extinguished. Illusions. That was why he had needed her. She had given him all the substance he required, a galleon's worth of lumber with which to build.

She wanted to crack him open like a pomegranate, but she couldn't, not in full view of the crowd.

"I'm sorry we won't be friends any longer," he said, smiling as his birds screeched and swooped overhead, the sails of his warship billowing in an invisible wind. "You really do look like the girls from my town. Sun-baked and solid as a loaf of bread."

Luzia returned his smile. She gestured to the large gold cross with its gleaming green jewels. "Don't give me another thought, Fortún."

Then, in words that had begun as Spanish and been transformed beneath a foreign sun, words made solid by ink and carried over the sea into her aunt's waiting hands, she said, "Onde iras, amigos toparas." *Wherever you go, may you find friends.*

This was the magic that was good for boards and beans and eggs and heads of garlic, but that made spiders out of copper and hornets out of silver. Because magic was never easy; because food was food, but coins were nothing without the greed of men.

The jewels at the four points of Donadei's cross leapt from their settings. Shimmering wings snapped up from their backs as their thick scarab bodies took flight, buzzing around his curly head. The rubies at his shoulders sprouted wriggling legs and giant red ants reared up, clambering toward his collar.

Donadei shrieked, releasing the cross as it dissolved in his hands, a skittering heap of golden spiders. He swatted at the insects, beating his chest and clawing at his hair, trying to drive them away, losing the tune on his precious vihuela. Whatever words he'd held in his mind had been driven out by terror.

The birds and eels and fish vanished around them. The ship began to break apart.

"No!" Donadei screamed, trying to grasp the neck of the vihuela, seeking the song and its secret words once more.

Luzia heard shouts and cries from the crowd.

Donadei turned on her. "You stupid cunt."

Luzia laughed. "Smart enough to learn your name, Fortún. Do

you think Vázquez is thinking of Philip's armada when it was lost to England's queen? Do you think he'll thank you for the demonstration of what a Spanish ship looks like when it sinks?"

Donadei snarled and shoved her. Luzia lost her footing. Her arms pinwheeled and she nearly plunged into the murky water. He swiped at her again and she called up the boards, struggling to keep the refrán in her head as her panic rose and the song tried to split.

No, she wasn't going to lose her tongue or her life to fear today. She sang the boards into being, one after another, a path to take her back to shore. Behind her, she could hear pieces of Donadei's ship plunging into the water, its masts toppling, its feathered sails collapsing into nothing.

She ran, and as soon as her feet made contact with one of the wooden planks, she cast it aside so Donadei couldn't follow, leaving him to the lake. Maybe his fish could carry him to shore.

Had she won? Had he? Would Vázquez curse them both for their petty games? She couldn't think of that now.

But the shore ahead was a scene of confusion. The crowd had broken away from the water and some seemed to be running toward the woods as the king's soldiers followed. Vázquez was bellowing something from the stage.

She stumbled, toppling forward into the shallows.

Then Santángel was before her, hauling her to her feet. "Did you see?" she gasped. "Did you see what he did?"

"It doesn't matter," he said, dragging her to dry land where his horse waited. "Antonio Pérez has fled. He used the trial as a distraction. The king's men are rounding up anyone they can. Can you ride?"

Luzia tried to make sense of what he was saying. Where had Pérez gone? What did the king's men want with them? "Not well."

He helped her into the saddle and then he was behind her and they were riding as she had dreamed they would, away from kings and climbers and curses.

Chapter 42

◆

"Where are we going?" she asked as they plunged into the woods.

"To Madrid. To the widow. She leaves for Valencia tonight. I can bribe Víctor's men to take you too." He didn't know if this was true. He'd tried to act against Víctor before and it had never worked. But perhaps it would be better for his master's fortunes if Luzia wasn't discovered or questioned. If that was the case, then Santángel would be free to help her, as he should have helped her before. "I'll get you to Valencia somehow." He had to believe he could.

He set his mind to the task ahead, trying to plan, sorting through his connections and spies, who would require bribes or favors. He didn't want to think on how badly he had blundered. He'd thought he would have more time to make his choices, to untangle this mess. Would he have told her the truth? Or would he have continued on—selfish, hopeless, made careless by desire until the trap closed around them?

Antonio Pérez had turned all of them into players in his great farce, and Santángel had been too busy falling in love like an untried youth to see it coming. He should have known better when Pérez had claimed the king had demanded a third trial. It was Pérez who must have insisted, and pleaded with his ruler for this last chance. He had known the king wouldn't welcome him to El Escorial and that he would never set foot at La Casilla—the home that had been as good as a prison to Pérez since he'd fallen out of favor. The precise location of the third trial had been of no consequence—so long as he would finally be free to make his escape.

Had Pérez still hoped the king might forgive him, that he might regain the glory he had lost? Had that hope died when his rival had exited the coach? Or had he already known that flight was his only option?

"Keep your head down," he instructed, nudging their mount on as fast as he dared, dodging branches and praying the horse wouldn't put a foot wrong. She is fragile, he reminded himself. No matter her gifts, she is mortal. She does not have a thousand lives to waste.

Luzia and Donadei had provided the perfect distraction as Pérez fled through the cover of the woods. Not just a competition but a battle, a spectacle to snare the attention of Vázquez and his guards. And Luzia might well be blamed for it.

Santángel needed a plan that would benefit Víctor, even if Víctor would punish him for it. If not for his curse, he could ride straight to Valencia with her, see Luzia safely onto a ship. But the port was several days away. He would burn to ash when morning came, and then Luzia would be stranded without allies or protection. He had to find someone he could trust to shelter her, to get her out of the country.

"Ahead!" Luzia cried.

Two soldiers on horseback had emerged from the woods to block their path.

"Hold on tightly," he commanded, ready to charge, but then he heard Luzia whispering, and the woods sprang up in a tangled snarl around the men, forming a barrier, closing them off from the rest of the wood.

He tugged at the reins, urging their mount west toward a clearing, away from the morning sun. They would keep out of sight of the road and make their way back to the city to shelter until nightfall.

He sensed the other soldiers following before he saw them. Santángel's gift for stealth had served Víctor well, his understanding of the way threats moved through the world. He knew instantly that together they would never make it out of the woods, never reach Madrid. But he could create a distraction.

"You'll have to ride without me," he said, wheeling the horse around, so that he could sight the soldiers more easily through the trees. "I need you to make it to the city. Go to the church of San Sebastián. I have friends there. I'll lead the soldiers—"

He had no chance to finish before the arrows flew. He covered her body with his, felt the steel tips pierce his back like bolts of fire. His horse whinnied in distress, rearing up as it was hit too. If it fell it would crush them both.

Santángel forced himself to ignore the pain in his back and leapt free, taking Luzia with him. He hit the ground with her beneath him and struggled to protect her body from any stray hoof, but the horse was already crashing through the trees and away from them, wild in its panic.

He fought to breathe. One of the arrows had pierced his right lung and every attempt to draw air was a jagged stutter. Soon his lungs would start to fill with blood. He needed to remove the arrows before his body tried to heal around them.

"Luzia, close off the clearing," he gritted out, each word an agony.

He heard her whisper, heard men shouting to one another as the woods closed in. His own vision was fading.

He gave his head a shake. He needed to stay awake. "You're not hurt?" he managed.

"I'm fine," she said, though her face was full of fear. "Let me heal you."

"There's no time. You must run. Make a path through the woods and close it off behind you."

"I'm not leaving you."

"I cannot die, but you can. Get to San Sebastián. I'll find you.

Please, if you value your life as I do, go. Trust me to meet you. Trust me to survive as I trust you to do the same."

"Santángel—"

"I have begged for nothing in this life, but I am begging you now, Luzia. Go."

She pressed a kiss to his lips and ran.

Valentina didn't understand what was happening. One moment she was watching the Prince of Olives build a ship of war and cursing herself for encouraging Luzia to court his friendship. The next Vázquez was shouting and the king's soldiers were moving to block the road that led away from the lake.

"Where is the worm Pérez?" Vázquez howled, storming off the stage.

Valentina couldn't see Don Antonio in the crowd, nor his red-bearded courtier, nor his liveried guards.

"What is this?" Marius asked. "Where is he?"

"He has fled," Don Víctor snapped, "and we have all helped him do it."

Valentina wanted to ask a thousand questions. Why would Pérez choose this moment to flee? Had he planned this from the start? How far could he hope to get when the king's authority stretched across Castile, Valencia, Portugal? His forces were every-where.

"Where can he go? Why would he do something so rash?"

"He will go to Aragón," said Don Víctor, "where Philip's author-ity is weakest. Where the hell is my familiar?"

Did he mean Santángel? And where was Luzia? The Prince of Olives was wading through the water as Doña Beatriz stood at the shore, begging the soldiers to help retrieve him from the lake. The surface was cluttered with broken boards; no remnant of Luzia's cross or Donadei's galleon remained.

It all seemed silly now, as people pushed and shoved around

them, some of them fleeing into the woods, others trying to speak to Vázquez or arguing with his soldiers, insisting they be allowed to leave.

"What do we do?" Valentina asked. "Will we be arrested?"

But Don Víctor was already striding toward his coach.

"Will you not help us back to Madrid?" Marius demanded.

"Find your own way," said Don Víctor. "Our partnership is at an end."

"Damn him to hell." Then Marius's eyes alighted on Doña Beatriz's cinnamon mare. "Come along."

"We cannot—"

"Come along."

"We'll be thieves!"

"We'll be free. Look." He bobbed his head to where Santángel was disappearing into the woods, Luzia bundled between his arms. "He will know the way to safety."

He dragged Valentina to where one of Doña Beatriz's men stood watch over her horse.

"Doña Beatriz is returning to the city in Víctor de Paredes's coach," Marius declared. "We are to take her horse."

"I'm not certain—"

Marius seized the reins. "I don't require your certainty." Before the groom could protest, he'd mounted in a single fluid movement and offered Valentina his hand. For all his talk of horses, she had never been with him to ride and it had never really occurred to her that he would be a gifted horseman.

"Help her," Marius demanded, and the groom lifted Valentina up to him, depositing her between his arms like a sack of millet.

She had a bare moment to catch her breath, and then they were moving through the trees. "We're Luzia's patrons," Valentina said as she tried to shift her position to ease the jabbing of her corset. "If they want to question us, they will."

"Then let them come to our home and question us there. I won't be taken to prison while Víctor de Paredes sits comfortably in his palace."

He kicked the horse into a trot, trailing after Luzia and Santángel. But Valentina could hear other hoofbeats, men shouting ahead.

"They're being pursued," she gasped out, her voice trembling. "There are soldiers in the woods."

She heard the high whinny of a horse and then the path before them seemed to vanish, the brambles and branches forming a wall.

Marius yanked on the reins and the mare shinnied backward, feet dancing. But he soothed her easily. He slid from the horse and pressed a finger to his lips. Valentina nodded.

Slowly, he led them around the clearing, following the bramble wall.

"There," Valentina whispered.

They had circled to the far side and through the branches she could see Santángel propped on his elbow, arrows jutting from his back. Luzia was on her knees, tears on her face, her dress covered in blood.

"He is injured!" Valentina cried. But Marius cut his hand through the air, demanding silence.

She could hear Santángel gasping for breath. "Go," he told Luzia. "If you value your life as I do."

She slid down from the saddle, struggling to keep her feet.

"Help them," she whispered furiously. "Luzia won't stand a chance on foot. Give her your horse."

"Have you lost your mind?"

Maybe she had, but she could see the love and fear in Santángel's eyes. He wasn't afraid for himself, but for the woman he loved. Demon he might be but he was trying to save her.

"I'm not leaving you," Luzia wept, her voice raw and red, a new burn. Valentina didn't care anymore that she had lived a life without love. She wanted only to know that it existed in the world and could be saved.

"Help them, Marius. I am begging you. If you ever cared for me at all, help them."

Marius opened his mouth, closed it. "Do not ask this of me."

"What have I ever asked of you?"

She heard men calling to one another, footsteps moving through the brush. Luzia stumbled through a path she'd opened between the trees. Her eyes were frantic, her hair full of leaves, her cheeks laced with narrow cuts where she'd been stung by branches.

"Give her your horse, Marius." Valentina was begging now, and she wasn't sure what she was begging for. For Luzia? For herself? That there was more to Marius than a man who liked fine ponies and good food? Who was only kind when life was easy?

Luzia's gaze focused on Valentina, then Marius.

"Marius," Valentina pleaded.

He gave a single stubborn shake of his head.

Luzia turned her back on them and plunged into the woods, the branches closing behind her.

Maybe she would escape. Maybe she didn't need the horse at all. Maybe her gifts were greater than the king's men or Marius's cowardice.

Valentina held to that hope as they stood silent between the trees, even when she heard the angry shouts of men in pursuit, even when Luzia began to scream.

Chapter 43

◆

On a dark road, the coach Víctor de Paredes had hired rattled along, Hualit safely tucked inside. He'd sent Gonzalo and Celso as outriders because the country was less safe than the city, especially at night. But night it would have to be. Some part of her was sorry she wouldn't get to see much of Venice. When she arrived, she would find a way to separate herself from the hosts Víctor had arranged. She had contacts in Italy and she had already booked passage to Salonika.

Her gown was heavy with jewels and coins she'd sewn into the lining, enough to augment the bit of spending money Víctor had given her and serve for any necessary bribes. She was weighted with every diamond, ruby, and gilded bauble her lovers had given her, but she didn't mind.

Fear made her giddy; it always had. It was less that she loved risk than the thrill of gambling on herself. She only wished Luzia or Ana were here to chatter to. Hualit had always been a social creature. That was her gift, more than her beauty or her limitless will to secure a real future for herself.

Her sister had married a poor peddler and she had died young because of it. Maybe it wasn't fair to lay Blanca's death at Afonso's door, but she had no talent for fairness. Blanca was just and kind and Hualit was greedy and bold. She fell in love a hundred times and out of love a hundred more. As her sister had taken to Latin, she had taken to desire, learning the language of men's needs and the proper responses. She had used this aptitude for translation to will herself into a better life than fate had ever intended for her, one of comfort and pleasure.

But now she would be among strangers. She would have to find a new person to become. Or maybe she could stop pretending, stop pleasing. She would be called by her own name. She would join the other women on the balcony at synagogue. She might even find a husband, one she actually liked. Salonika. Let it be all I've hoped for, she prayed. She'd had enough disappointments to know it was dangerous to long for something, to imagine it for months and years and to find yourself on the cusp of it at last.

She would miss her cheerful house, her courtyard with its grapevine. She wouldn't miss Víctor, but she did wonder if he would miss her. Was it perverse to want to be longed for by a man she didn't love? Still, Víctor was not the type to pine for anything other than more. He would seek out some other woman to entertain him. He would find a new mistress to keep or turn his attention to his beloved wife again.

He hadn't wanted to let her go, but she'd gotten her way in the end. He was always amorous after spending time with sweet, pious María, and she'd gone out of her way to make sure he was well satisfied before she raised the issue. She'd told him the events at the puppet show had scared her, that she was afraid of being questioned, and wouldn't it be better to be free of any hint of scandal should his plans with Pérez go awry?

Again she looked at the empty seat across from her and felt the uneasy sense that she'd done wrong. Ana had gone ahead with her trunks, but this should have been the journey Hualit and Luzia took together. She had never wanted children of her own; the thought had frightened her. She'd had a hard enough time carving out a life without trying to do the same for a helpless creature. Luzia had been too much for her, a burden she couldn't bear. Yes, her magic had been a threat to Hualit's safety. But it was her need that had frightened Hualit the most, her longing for affection, her loneliness. Hualit could not mother her. Would not. It wasn't her fault that Blanca had made the mistake of having a child, then chosen to let poverty kill her in a paupers' hospital.

But if she had been kinder, would Luzia be with her now? She might never see her niece again, the only person in the world who shared her blood. The thread had been cut. Hualit wanted to believe that Luzia would go on to glory. But she knew what court was like. She had moved in Madrid's best circles and there was no way Luzia would survive there. The king was weak. Pérez was dangerous. And the truth was that if Hualit had spirited Luzia out of Madrid, Víctor would have found a way to drag her back.

I should have waited a little longer, she thought. I should have argued with more force. But her fear was greater than her love. That was the truth of it.

The coach slowed, then rolled to a stop. Was someone approaching? She had nothing to fear. Gonzalo and Celso were a match for any brigand or bandit.

The door opened and Celso stood in the moonlight. She could hear the churning of a river. The Tagus? Or had they already reached the Júcar?

"Is there a problem with the bridge?" she asked.

He offered her his hand. "Señora?"

Behind him she could see the soft blue shapes of the hills and Gonzalo watching the road.

"Why have we stopped?"

He said nothing, only waited, his gloved hand outstretched, as if he were asking for a dance.

In a way, she supposed he was. Only she had heard the music too late. The song had been playing all along, if only she hadn't been so distracted by her own cleverness.

"Ana?" she asked.

He shook his head.

So there would be no trip to Venice, no hosts waiting to receive her. She would never slip away to board the ship to Salonika. Mari would never meet her in the harbor. Víctor hadn't capitulated or been swayed by her wiles. He'd used her one last time, laughing at her schemes, knowing as he entered her that he'd sentenced her to death.

A silly part of her wanted to ask why, as if Celso knew or could answer if he did. Had Víctor suspected she meant to slip free of him and decided to punish her? No, it was simpler than that. Víctor de Paredes had decided she would die on this road because it was easier for him. He would never have to fear her testimony or her interference. He would never have to adorn her with another jewel. It was all very tidy, she had to admit. Her death would be blamed on bandits. These roads were dangerous, after all.

"Very well," she said, taking Celso's hand and stepping down from the coach. "If you'd be so kind, I'd like to stretch my legs a bit."

"You cannot run."

"Certainly not. Where would I go?"

She thought of her snug house and its comfortable bed and the fountain burbling in its courtyard. All of it belonged to Víctor. Would he install his next mistress there? She hoped whoever lived there would love it as she had, that she would sit and listen to the birds calling across the rooftops and eat grapes off the vine. On sunny mornings the printer's wife who lived next door sang as she did her housework. She didn't have much of a voice, but Hualit had learned to like the sound.

She had been lonely in that house sometimes. She had wondered what life might have in store for her. She hadn't predicted this.

"I can offer you jewels," she said as she made her way to the edge of the bridge, listening to the sound of the water far below. If she were brave she could jump. "Money."

Gonzalo laughed. "You can't afford us, señora."

"Will you make it quick?" she asked.

"I can offer that," said Celso. He sounded sorry, but his hand was already on the knife at his hip.

"You have other things to bargain with," said Gonzalo.

Now Hualit laughed. "So you can fuck me and then cut my throat and leave me in the bushes?"

"You must prepare yourself," said Celso.

She held her hand out to him. "Pray with me."

"It isn't right," Celso said to Gonzalo. "She doesn't have a priest."

"She's a whore," said Gonzalo. His blade was in his hand.

"I won't fight you," she said, smiling gently, softly.

Hualit hoped they would say prayers for her in Salonika. Shema Yisrael, Adonai Eloheinu, Adonai Echad.

Gonzalo grabbed hold of her shoulder.

"Come," she said, her hands grasping his jacket, her back pressed against the railing. "We'll go together."

He was stronger, but he didn't expect the weight of her, her pockets full of reales, her hems and sleeves sewn full of jewels.

Gonzalo shouted as they toppled from the bridge.

It felt good to take one of them with her.

Hualit's neck snapped when she struck the surface. She died quickly as she'd hoped to, as Celso had promised she would. Gonzalo broke his back but floated along for quite a while, trying to fight the current, until finally, weeping, he slipped beneath the surface.

Months later, a woman brought a fish home from the market and cut it open to find an emerald the size of her thumbnail. She thanked the fish, tucked the jewel into her pocket, and left the house, never to be seen again. Her husband, a drunkard with heavy fists, found only the fish, which he was forced to prepare himself for dinner. He choked on a bone and was buried in a pauper's grave.

His wife walked all the way to Paris, where she opened a parfumerie and lived happily for many years, eating lamb and vegetables and snails, but never fish, who she felt had done enough for her.

Chapter 44

◆

Luzia woke in the larder. It was cold and dark and the air smelled wrong, like iron and urine and damp. I was dreaming, she thought. I dressed in velvet and met an angel. I made miracles on my tongue.

The world returned in an ugly wave of memory. Donadei's warship, the slabs of jade embedded in his cross becoming scarabs, Santángel's arms tight around her as they raced through the woods, his blood on her hands. She tried to sit up.

"Easy," said a familiar voice. "You took a bad blow to the head."

Luzia touched her fingers to her temple. Someone had struck her. She remembered now, soldiers riding her down in the woods, pain splintering through her skull.

The cell was narrow, the ceiling low. The only light came from a candle set on the stone floor. Two low wooden platforms, cots of a sort, had been placed side by side in the room, with a bare scrap of space to maneuver between them. A girl was sitting on one of them, a child, her back settled against the wall, her short legs stretched out before her.

"Teoda?"

"I'm afraid so."

The bundle of rags beside the Holy Child shifted and Luzia realized there was a third person in the cell, an old woman with gray hair pulled tightly back from her lean face.

"This is Neva. She's been here nearly two years."

"Two years? On what charge?"

"Simple fornication," Neva said with a grin that revealed a sparse collection of teeth.

"We are in Toledo," Luzia said. A statement, not a question. Just as Fortún Donadei had warned. A prisoner of the Inquisition like Isabel de la Cruz had once been, and Piedrola, and Lucrecia de León. Fragments of the journey returned to her—the rumble of the wagon, the roar of a river. They would have passed the burning grounds as they entered the city walls through the Puerta de Bisagra.

"We are," said Teoda on a sigh.

"I . . . I need to relieve myself."

"The pot is in the corner," said Teoda. "It's all quite shocking, but maybe you will find it less so."

"Because servants prefer to lift our skirts with an audience?"

"I'm sorry," Teoda said with a laugh. "Neva and I will turn our backs and I will remember that modesty is not just for ladies with rich families."

In truth, modesty was a luxury and Luzia had urinated in alleys and behind market stalls. But she was tired and frightened and her head was aching.

"Our wait for charges will not be so long," Teoda said as Luzia saw to her needs. "There is an auto de fe planned for Todos los Santos. They'll want to sentence us then. If you hadn't been in a prison wagon you would have seen the stages and scaffolding going up in Plaza de Zocodover."

The Feast of All Saints. That couldn't be right. Trials were meant to last months if not years. "That's mere weeks away."

Teoda shrugged. "I have already confessed my heresies. They have no reason to prolong my stay here. Besides, the king will want to make a show of my death."

"Then . . . you are to be burned?"

"Of course. If I repent the executioner will do me the courtesy of strangling me first, but I will not repent."

"She's not as brave as she sounds," said Neva. "Neither am I. You'll hear us crying at night."

Teoda gave a huff that might have been another laugh. "We do each other the courtesy of ignoring it. We have no secrets here. And you should know the inquisitors sleep mere feet away and can hear us unless we whisper. Of course even if we whisper, Neva may denounce us for the sake of earning herself a speedier hearing."

Luzia stretched, paced to the door where there was a small barred opening through which she could see nothing but a dimly lit hallway. A single window showed only the night beyond, and rags had been jammed into its seams to keep out the cold. The air felt too heavy, the damp dragging against her skin. She wished she'd been awake when they'd brought her here. She had no sense of where she was. They could be a mile belowground and she wouldn't know.

"Try to breathe," Teoda said, and Luzia realized she was panting, her hand pressed to her chest. "Or at least sit down so that you won't be injured if you faint."

"I don't understand why I'm here."

"None of us do," said Neva.

"I do," said Teoda.

Luzia sat down on the wooden cot across from Teoda. "Treason is a matter for the civil courts, isn't it? Why am I a prisoner of the tribunal?"

"Count yourself lucky," said Neva. "The city prisons are so crowded they force men and women into the same cells. They die in there and go undiscovered for days."

Teoda gave Neva a meaningful glance. "A song for us?"

Neva beat her fist against her thigh and began to sing about three fountains in her village that ran cold in the summer and hot in the winter.

"A bit of privacy," Teoda explained. "You must be here because of Pérez. He's fled to Aragón, where the king is no match for his popularity. So Philip has sent the Inquisition after his old friend. Only the tribunal's power reaches across every part of Spain."

"How do you know all this?"

"We aren't supposed to be permitted letters, but my brother has found ways to get news from the outside. And gossip is never in short supply here. The guards like to talk as much as we do."

"Have you . . . Has there been word of Víctor de Paredes or his household?"

"I only know none of them are here."

Santángel had promised her he couldn't die. But what if he was wrong? He had lied to her, maybe intended to betray her, but when trouble had come, he'd placed himself between Luzia and the king's soldiers. What if his gifts were mere delusion and she had left him to bleed to death in that clearing without help or defense?

No, Don Víctor wouldn't give up his prize so easily. He may have intended to replace Santángel with her, but now she was tainted by the charge of heresy or witchcraft or some other crime.

"What of Donadei?" she asked.

Teoda's laugh was brittle, the sound strange from her child's mouth. "I hear nothing of him. I only know he isn't sitting in a cell. Wherever he is, he is free."

"I don't see how the Inquisition can pursue Pérez. Has he committed some crime against the Church?"

"They're claiming he has encouraged heresy. The charge is flimsy, but our punishment by the Inquisition will give weight to the claims and remind everyone of the king's strength." She raised her voice. "He can't very well put dear Lucrecia to death, can he?"

"Be silent, demon," said a voice from another cell. "I'm trying to rest. Neva, will you please cease that wailing?"

Teoda rolled her eyes. "Don't rest too well, you may have another dream!"

Then it was true. Lucrecia de León was here, the dreaming prophet, the girl who had predicted the defeat of the armada. "She won't be sentenced alongside us?"

"She is *with child*," Teoda said gleefully. "She fell in love with one of her scribes. It's all very thrilling."

"One of her scribes?" Santángel had claimed he couldn't father children, but that could have been another lie.

"Diego de Vitores. A very nice young man, I'm told. They exchange letters, though that's not supposed to be permitted either."

At least that was one less thing for Luzia to feel miserable about.

"The king won't put her to death," said Teoda. "At least not for a while. She's a good Catholic and everyone knows it."

"And her predictions were accurate," Luzia noted. "That must be inconvenient."

Now Teoda's merriment fell away. "They got her to confess to making up her dreams, but she recanted the next day."

"Then why confess at all?" But Teoda's grim look made the answer obvious. "Torture."

Teoda nodded.

"They've questioned you too?" Luzia asked.

"No." Teoda fiddled with her cuff. The dress was different from the one she'd worn the night of the second trial, and Luzia wondered how she'd gotten fresh clothes. "They brought me to the room where they do their work. They will make you guess at the charge you face."

Heresy, witchcraft, fornication too, she supposed. Maybe Don Víctor would claim he'd been tricked with a false lineage provided by the linajista and she'd be charged with Judaizing too.

"You've been here since the second trial? Since the puppet show?"

"Yes. My brother is moneyed and connected, so he is already filing appeals. He knows the courts well. But it won't matter. My nurse was taken for questioning too. She's trying to deny she knew we are heretics. She thinks it will save her life. And it may. If she's lucky she'll be publicly flogged and banished."

"How do you sound so unafraid?"

"I have God. I know who I am. I fear torture, but I don't fear death. So I will confess to every heresy because it isn't heresy at all, only truth. You see? They needn't torture me at all."

Luzia knew that wasn't true. If they wanted to know the names of other Calvinists and heretics, Teoda would have to name them. But if the thought that she could escape torture made this horror easier, Luzia wasn't going to snatch it away.

"You'll have that same choice," said the Holy Child. "They'll ask if you're in league with the devil."

"I should have such powerful friends."

Teoda's laugh was high and light. "I knew I liked you."

Neva sang on.

Chapter 45

◆

She couldn't forgive him.

The horse had made no difference. Valentina and Marius hadn't found escape in the woods. They'd gotten turned around and wandered aimlessly through the trees for hours, searching for the road. When the king's men had found them, she'd been almost grateful.

They had been taken back to Madrid, where she'd been locked in the women's cells of the city prison. It stank of bodies and excrement, and something more, a misery that clung to her hair and her clothes. It was a sound too, a moan that echoed in her ears. Valentina had the same sense of shrinking she'd had at La Casilla. She would be consumed, but this time she would be swallowed into a wet, toothless mouth. She would rot away in the dark, fruit gone gray with rot, wood turned soft and formless.

She had put her hand to the damp wall and vomited, her body shaking so badly that she thought her bones would fly apart. When the guards led her outside it was night. There were stars above and the air was cool, and to her great shame she wept.

It was only when she'd been brought to the vicar's offices that she understood they'd put her in the prison to terrify her.

The vicar offered her a small glass of wine and a comfortable chair. He told her that she needed to answer his questions truthfully or that he would have no choice but to turn her over to the tribunal in Toledo. She had nodded, still trembling, happy to say anything at all that would keep her from those cells.

He asked countless questions about Antonio Pérez, what he'd said about the king, his comings and goings from La Casilla, how much time he'd spent with Teoda Halcón, which texts he had in his library. She tried to remember what Pérez had told them about the third trial and if he'd shown special favor to the Holy Child, but there was little for her to say. She had existed on the periphery of society in Madrid and nothing had changed at La Casilla. The questions about Luzia were easier to answer but more frightening. Yes, she went regularly to mass. Yes, she took communion. No, Valentina couldn't recall any blasphemous or heretical statements Luzia Cotado had made. No, she had never questioned the Trinity in Valentina's presence.

"She is . . . she's a scullion, señor. These aren't conversations we have ever had. She's a quiet girl."

"Secretive."

"Quiet. Humble. Perhaps a bit stupid." Luzia was none of these things, but Valentina could do her this service.

"That kind of meekness is easily led," said the vicar.

She expected him to ask about Víctor de Paredes, about Guillén Santángel, men of power and influence. Instead he moved on to questions regarding Marius. Did he correspond with anyone in Germany? Flanders? To her knowledge, had he expressed doubts about the Church? Had he taken a hand in hiring Luzia? Did he associate with the followers of Piedrola? Did he speak disparagingly of the king?

When the interview was over she thought they would let her go home.

"Not yet, señora," said the vicar, and she was brought to a convent, where she was allowed to make her confession and then shown to a narrow room that locked from the outside. She spoke no complaint. She had seen the alternative.

Every day, she was brought through the prison and then taken to the vicar, and every day she answered the same questions, described the same scenes and conversations. If anything changed in the telling, the vicar's secretary read back her previous statements and they spent hours poring over the discrepancies.

It went on like that for six days, until Valentina began to question her own memories of Pérez, of Luzia, of Marius.

"You look tired, señora," the vicar said when she was slow to give an answer. "We can find you a cell to rest in if you like?"

"No," said Valentina. "I was only trying to remember accurately."

"You were telling us with whom your husband likes to hunt."

"My husband can't afford to hunt. Not often."

"But when he does."

Valentina couldn't remember. Her mind had been hollowed out by this ceaseless talking, by fear, by the blunt understanding of her lack of consequence. She had been deluded by pretty clothes and fine meals. She was no one, and it would take more than Luzia's miracles to change that. She wasn't even sure she wanted it to change. She was out of words. She was out of thoughts. Her mind could only form one low, long note, a bow drawn across a gut string, back and forth, back and forth, no melody, no rise and fall.

"My husband is a coward," she said, shocked at her own words but too tired to correct her course. "He has no political convictions. He doesn't care about Antonio Pérez. He is loyal to the king because it's easy to be loyal to the king and he likes what's easy. It's why he married me. There was no one to court and no one to impress. No work to be done. He cares about good wine and fast horses. He doesn't have the ambition for conspiracy."

That night, they let her return home. One of the friars deposited her back at Calle de Dos Santos. "I hope you know God has spared you. In future, be more mindful of the company you keep."

Valentina nodded.

"Will you not ask after your husband?"

"No," said Valentina. "I don't think I will."

They had continued to pay Águeda her wages while they were

at La Casilla, but Valentina hadn't had time to send word that she would be back home, so the house was empty. She didn't know where Luzia was or if Juana would return. Maybe she should have asked after Marius, but she found she didn't mind being in the house alone. She went down to the silent kitchen, softened bread in a bowl of wine, made herself eat a little ham and two pickled plums.

She had no water to wash with and no one to help her undress, so she slept atop her covers in her filthy clothes.

The next day she sent for Águeda and asked her to bring someone to help with the house. The cook arrived with a market basket full of food and her ten-year-old niece, who brought water from the plaza and helped Valentina wash and dress.

She was waiting, though she didn't really know what for. For the king's soldiers or the alguacil's men to knock at her door. For word that she was to be arrested or banished. For their property to be seized, though it was hard to imagine who would want a shabby house and fields full of miserly olive trees.

She ate the midday meal in the kitchen, and when she climbed the stairs she was surprised to find Marius in the hall.

He had lost weight and his clothes hung on him. She knew she must look equally haggard. Had she found him more handsome when he was stout? Or had she been taken in by something else, an illusion like those Luzia conjured?

He swept her into his arms. "It's over," he said.

She waited for him to release her. "Where is Luzia?"

His eyelids stuttered, as if he didn't recognize the name. "Toledo. She was given into the Inquisition's custody."

"Then we should go there. She'll need someone to advocate for her and make sure she's receiving proper care."

"The best thing we can do is stay far away. It's a true miracle that we are free."

Valentina shook her head slowly. She was still so tired. "I dragged her into this catastrophe. The least I can do is make sure she's well-fed."

"Have you gone mad?" He looked over his shoulder and whispered furiously, as if the inquisitors might be listening through the walls. "If she's lucky she'll be exiled, but she will not be lucky."

"You should have given her the horse."

"It wouldn't have mattered!"

"It would have," she said. "It does." She couldn't explain why. She only knew she couldn't shake free the memory of Marius standing with the reins in his hand, gripping them as if he were afraid the horse might bolt, unable to meet her eye.

"There's nothing you can do for her," he said.

That was probably true. What could one powerless woman offer another? "I can make sure she doesn't die alone."

He stared at her as if she'd sprouted a horn from her forehead. "You do not want the Inquisition's attention, Valentina. The best thing you can do is wash your hands of that woman. To do otherwise is dangerous, and you are too foolishly sentimental to realize it."

"I recognize the danger," she said. "And I would rather be a fool than a coward."

Marius jolted as if struck. "That is enough. You have forgotten what it is to be a wife."

It was possible she had never known. "I'm going to bed."

"It's the middle of the day."

"And yet I find I am weary."

He stepped in front of her, blocking her path to the stairs.

"You can't save her," he pleaded. "You must know that! What can you hope to achieve?"

"I don't know." She didn't even like Luzia. But she was certain that if she were the one locked in the tribunal's cells, Marius would still be hiding here.

"You brought her into our house! You had her perform those little miracles that could have cost us everything. You brought this disaster upon us, and now I'm the one you blame?"

"Go away, Marius."

"Go . . . Where would you have me go?"

Valentina sighed. She just wanted to crawl into bed. "You're right. I'm stupid and sentimental. When we wed I was a foolish girl who hoped to love you. I grew into a foolish woman who hoped to please you. And now, well, I suppose I'm still a foolish woman who only hopes to be rid of you. Go away, Marius." She turned from him, heading back toward the kitchen. "Go away and be glad I didn't tell the vicar you sleep with a portrait of Martin Luther cradled in your arms."

Valentina descended the kitchen stairs. She couldn't sleep. Not yet. She needed to speak to Águeda.

Chapter 46

◆

Luzia dozed and paced and talked to Teoda and sometimes Neva. They were allowed down to the courtyard to empty their chamber pot and fill jugs with cold water that they heated for washing over a small coal stove. When it was time to eat, they were led down the corridor to the provisioner, who gave them bread, water, and occasionally salted fish. One day a rich, savory smell filled her nostrils.

"Cocido," Neva said. "Some of the prisoners get better food, if their families pay for it."

"Is it good, Lucrecia?" Teoda asked loudly. "Her family is poor, but her followers haven't given up on her just yet."

"Give them time," grumbled Neva.

But it was their door that opened. "Luzia Cotado," said the guard, and set down the steaming bowl. His name was Rudolfo, and when he wasn't picking his nose he was moping about his love life.

"Who is this from?" she asked.

Rudolfo blew his nose into his sleeve. "The money comes, so does the food."

They passed the spoon around, and as soon as Luzia tasted the stew she wanted to weep.

"It came from a playwright," said Lucrecia through the wall. "She has taken up a collection for you at her theater."

Luzia took another bite and then another. It was all impossible.

Maybe she'd died in the woods. Maybe she was asleep at La Casilla. Why would Quiteria Escárcega raise funds on her behalf?

"Pass that bowl to me or I will bite your shins in your sleep," said Teoda, and Luzia obliged.

She had never tasted anything so delicious, but one could grow sick on the impossible.

The mystery of the stew deepened the next morning, when they went down to the courtyard to fetch their jugs of water and empty their chamber pots. Rudolfo handed her a stack of folded clothes—a gown and fresh linen.

"Give me your dirty clothing and it will be sent to your home to be laundered."

What home? Luzia wondered. She had no friends or family in Toledo. She had none in all of Spain now that Hualit had sailed away.

"More gifts from the infamous playwright?" Teoda asked.

When they returned to the cell, Neva whispered, "Feel along the stitching. There may be a note or a message."

Luzia ran her fingers over the seams, and when she pushed her hand through the sleeve, a small green sprig fell to the floor.

Rosemary. Romero. For protection.

Valentina had sent the cocido, the fresh clothing. Luzia rubbed the sprig between her thumb and forefinger and inhaled the scent. She had to fight the hope that bloomed through her. Valentina and Marius had no power or influence with which to help her. But Hualit had sailed across the sea, and Santángel might be dead or captive himself. Maybe it wasn't hope she felt at all, but the comfort of knowing that someone was on the other side of these walls, that they remembered her name, that they might say prayers for her when it had long since ceased to matter.

She did cry at night, and sometimes she screamed into her fist, her rage too big for the confines of her crowded cell. All her striving, the Latin in her head, the refranes she'd bent to her desires, her victory over Gracia at the first trial, over the gruesome shadows in the second, over Donadei in the third, had amounted to nothing. She'd done as she was asked and more. She'd fought her way out of the larder, and despite insults, and treachery, and an attempt on her life, she'd managed to win again and again. But here she was, powerless, and even more wretched than when she'd begun.

The only tonic for Luzia's fear and rage was information. If she was to be tortured, she needed to be prepared, so when Teoda was in the mood to talk, she listened. This was usually in the daytime, after they'd visited the provisioner, when the cells were noisy with conversation and there was less chance of being overheard.

"They will take you to a room and remove your clothes—"

"Everything?"

"They want you to be shamed," said Teoda. "The room is cold, but the worst of it is the devices. The rack. The potro. I don't know the names for some of what I saw. The inquisitors will be there, one of the bishop's representatives, and someone to document everything said and done. My brother says they keep very thorough records."

"Were you frightened?"

Teoda hesitated. "Yes. More scared than I've ever been. I'm lucky though. I knew what I was accused of. They won't tell you the charges, just demand that you confess."

"The trick is that you don't really know what they want to hear," said Neva. "I've fucked my way through half of Castilla–La Mancha. How am I supposed to know who denounced me? I talked and talked, but I wasn't saying what they wanted me to. So they tied me down and they just kept tightening the cords. They didn't care how much I screamed and begged." Neva pushed up her sleeve to display the scars at her wrists and elbows, marks the color of spoiled meat that circled her arm completely, as if she were still bound to the table. "They did send a doctor to see to me when it was over."

"You're scaring her," Teoda said quietly.

"I was already scared," Luzia said. But it was hard not to think of those marks, of what it would mean to cry out and not be heard, and to know all the while that none of it made a difference because she was going to be put to death anyway. There would be no pardon, no gentler punishment.

She thought of poor Lorenzo Botas, sitting by the fishmonger's stall, sliding off to sleep, carried home in his son's arms. Who would carry her? The refranes could heal her. She could put her body back together as she had restored her tongue, but the question twisted and wriggled inside her: Who will carry me?

The answer had to be no one, as it had been for so long.

Hualit was gone, and who else was there? Had she believed Santángel would come to her rescue again? Lift her up on his horse and spirit her away from this place? Some nights she lay awake in the dark, certain he was dead, imagining his blood watering the forest floor. Others she feared that Don Víctor held him captive, punishing him for trying to help Luzia escape. But she knew she was a woman without a soul because the worst nights were not when she contemplated her lover's death or his misery, but when she imagined that he didn't suffer at all, that he hadn't come because she was no longer worth his time or trouble.

A shame. A tragedy. A casualty. He might pity her, even mourn her, but he was a creature who had endured lifetimes of loss. What was one silly, pining woman in the scope of all that? She had known him only a few weeks. He had contemplated sacrificing her to his master even as he'd kissed her mouth and combed her hair, even as she'd lain trusting in his arms. Enough people had warned her to beware of Santángel.

She wanted to ask Lucrecia de León about him. Had he visited her? Courted her for his master? Told her she was brave and powerful and rare? But she wasn't going to shout about Víctor de Paredes or his familiar through the wall, and she never saw Lucrecia out of her cell. The girl who dreamed was never made to fetch her own water, and she had received special permission to visit the courtyard for exercise by herself.

But what real solace could any answers from Lucrecia provide? Santángel had been using her. Santángel had cared for her. Both things could be true and still mean nothing. In the end, she was not worth the risk of the Inquisition's attention or Don Víctor's ire. A cruel calculation, a single efficient blade she could cut herself with every night. You are not worth saving, Luzia Cotado, Luzia Cana, Luzia Calderón. Luzia whose name would vanish in the ashes.

Chapter 47

◆

In the mornings it was easier to be brave. She remembered Santángel telling her that servants were better equipped to be spies. So maybe a lifetime of beatings and humiliation would give her an advantage now too. Mostly she thought about how her refranes might serve her when she was taken to the inquisitors.

Neva and Teoda had advised her there would be no formal trial, and she was ready when she was brought before the tribunal, three men who might have been anyone, priests at San Ginés, bakers at the ovens, farmers at their market stalls. Teoda had told her their names: *Don Pedro, Don Gaspar, Don Francisco.* She wasn't sure which was which, but it didn't seem to be important. Their secretary scribbled away as they questioned her about her family, her life with the Ordoños, her relationship to Víctor de Paredes, his wife, Catalina de Castro de Oro, Teoda Halcón, Antonio Pérez. She stuck to the false family tree the linajista had created, hoping that Don Víctor hadn't revealed her secrets. She never mentioned Santángel or spoke her aunt's true name. She didn't tell them she could read. She did her best to speak the truth, but there were so many lies, she felt as if she were leaping from rock to rock, always in danger of losing her balance.

Three times they warned her to consult her conscience and confess, but she didn't know which crime to claim. She didn't even know enough about Teoda's faith to pretend she had been seduced by it.

When they finally took her down the stairs, she held her re-franes close, all the words she had gathered in her cell, armor forged in exile.

If they used the potro as they had on Neva, the best she could do was to try to heal herself while the damage was done to her.

If they used the garrucha, the nasty trick that had popped Lo-renzo Botas's knees and ankles from their joints, she could lighten the weights they attached to her feet with the same words she'd used to lighten firewood. She would scream and jounce as if she'd been pulled apart so that they thought the torture was working.

"They can only torture you once," Teoda had told her. "That is the law."

"Then it's over?"

Neva cackled. "Oh no, amiguita. They don't stop the session. They just suspend it. It ends when they say it ends."

They took her clothes, stripping her and describing each item to the secretary as it was removed. It was cold, just as Teoda had said, and she had been naked before no man but Santángel. She didn't want to think of him in this room, in this place full of their ugly, awkward machines.

Think of magic, she told herself, think of how it may serve you, remember that secret music—big, dangerous, unwieldy, the song she was meant to ignore, that had swept her up when Don Víctor tortured Santángel, that had torn a man in two. It had nearly killed her, and if the pain got too great, then she would let that song loose to destroy her and maybe leave some damage in her wake. That thought, that she might choose her death, that she could hold the end of it all in her hands, steadied her. It shouldn't. Who knew what torments awaited her in purgatory? But still the knowledge of those words, that bloody song that was bigger than this room and the men who pretended not to watch as she tried to cover herself, that might buy her a little vengeance, gave her comfort.

"It is your guilt that has brought you here, and only your full confession can prevent this. Speak it now."

"Please, señor—"

"Lie down on the table," he told her. Was he Don Gaspar or one of the others?

She lay back and they bound her hands and ankles with ropes, then her hips, her chest.

"Now you will be a bride," said the man whose name she didn't know, and he placed a soft cloth over her face. "You have brought this upon yourself," he said again, "and your confession will end it."

Luzia could only see the shapes of the men, shadows in the room. Don't panic, she told herself. She could sing herself free of the bonds if she had to, if the pain of whatever this was became too great. All she had to do was keep her head as she had at the trials, summon a refrán, and endure.

"Tell us how you created your illusions," said a voice.

"I sing and—"

She didn't have the chance to finish. Her mouth was full of water, her nose, her throat. She coughed but the water kept coming. She was drowning. This was not the potro or the garrucha or any other torture made by man. This was death, pushing into her chest, her lungs. She couldn't sing, couldn't speak, couldn't think. There were no words. There never had been. There was only death, cold and dark.

She was drowning in a bucket, a squirming rat, pink and newborn, looking up at Águeda's face. Her aunt was above her, hands around her throat, choking her slowly, and then her aunt was beneath her, sinking to the bottom of the river. She had no eyes, no lips. The fish had eaten them. Hualit's lipless mouth opened. "I'll pray that our suffering will be swallowed by the sea."

Luzia coughed and sputtered. She vomited water over her face and neck. The cloth was gone. The room had returned. She bucked against the ropes that bound her to the table. The men were talking.

"You used too much."

"I know what I'm doing."

"Another jar?"

Luzia couldn't speak. She knew she was weeping and she hated them for making her weep. She could crack them open. She could set this room ablaze, if only she could find the words. But they were gone. They'd all been drowned, taken out by the tide. She was dead and they were dead too. Where is my mother? she wanted to cry out. Where is God?

"How did you create your illusions?"

"I don't know—" she began.

The cloth was laid back over her face, her bridal veil.

"A magic lantern!" she screamed. "A special mirror!"

"How would a scullion know of such things?"

"The devil whispered to me how to do it!"

"Go on," he said, and she sobbed with relief.

When it was over, she didn't remember what she said. She talked of bellows and curtains and smoke and tricks with special lenses imported from Sweden. She said she was a witch and that the devil met her daily at the market. He told her she would be his bride and put his tongue in her mouth. He had the face of a serpent, of Martin Luther, of Antonio Pérez.

Only when she was back in her cell, her shift soaked, her body still shivering and shaking, did she realize she was bleeding. The ropes had cut into her wrists and ankles and hips when she'd struggled on the table.

"Luzia?" Teoda asked, but Luzia didn't want to speak. She didn't know how anymore.

Sometime in the night she woke, uncertain of how long she'd slept. Teoda brought her water heated over the coals.

"The widow is dead, isn't she? Catalina de Castro de Oro?"

"Your aunt Hualit," Teoda said. "My angel told me her name."

"She drowned, didn't she?"

"Yes," Teoda admitted. "My angel saw her die."

Luzia already knew it was true, just as she knew a shipwreck or some accident hadn't ended her aunt's life. Víctor had struck Hualit from the earth as if she'd never been. Santángel had called her the widow. Maybe he hadn't known.

Did it matter who held the power? Whether it was Pérez or the king or Víctor de Paredes or a man with a funnel in your mouth? What difference did it make if the person with the power wasn't you?

Luzia tumbled back into the dark water, where Hualit was waiting, her lipless mouth whispering in the cold. *The sea is vast and can endure anything*, she said. Her hands were full of jewels.

When Luzia woke, she didn't know what time it was or what day.

Neva was asleep, snoring on her pallet. Luzia gestured for Teoda to come closer.

"Are you hungry?"

"No," Luzia rasped. Her throat hurt. She glanced at Neva's snoring body. "We need to leave this place."

"You want to try to escape?"

"This power must be good for something. I can open the locks. I can kill a guard if I have to. But I have no money, no friends on the outside."

"Valentina—"

"No one I can rely on to help us escape. You haven't considered it? You know what my milagritos can do."

"Of course I have, but there's no point."

"You're so ready to die for your God?"

Teoda hesitated, then whispered. "I asked my angel. He says I will die here. We all will."

"I thought your angel was silent on your own future."

"Always. But he cannot see what lies beyond Toledo. For any of us. It's easy enough to understand. Our story ends here, Luzia. I dreamed you on a pyre."

"Then I'll die on a pyre, but I will not be tortured again."

"They wouldn't take your confession?"

"I don't know what they want to hear. I said everything I could think of, but it won't be enough."

Teoda tugged at the dirty lace of her sleeve. "It's my fault we're here. I was indiscreet."

"I blame the king. I blame Pérez. I blame those bleating toads who tied me down. I don't blame you."

"You don't understand. I . . . Donadei was so beautiful, so charming. I was easy prey. He told me he was in torment, that he couldn't bear to serve a corrupt church."

Luzia studied Teoda in the candlelight. "Prey," she repeated. "Teoda, you don't mean . . . You are a child—"

Teoda laughed softly. "Have you not guessed the truth, Luzia?"

"I fear I'm failing this test you've set for me."

"I'm not a child. I'm thirty-eight years old. Thirty-eight years in this child's body."

Luzia knew how stupid she must look, staring at Teoda, remembering every wise and witty thing she'd said. How arrogant Luzia had been, priding herself on her ability to observe and understand her betters. She shook her head, unable to accept the truth right before her.

"I'm a fool," she marveled. "I convinced myself your visions had made you old beyond your years."

"Everyone does," Teoda said. "It's the voice too."

Luzia nearly jumped. Teoda's high, sweet soprano was gone. Her voice was still youthful, but the effect was startling; her presence reshaped in the space of a few words, a woman in miniature instead of a child.

"Donadei knew?"

"He guessed. Perhaps he sensed that my interest in him wasn't that of a child. Maybe he saw how desperate I was for the kind of attention I've never had. He pretended we shared the same secrets, complained of Doña Beatriz." She hesitated. "I have never been kissed that way before, as a man kisses a woman. I am the fool. And now my brother and I will die because of it."

"Not your father," Luzia said, understanding coming slowly.

"No. He has been protecting me since our parents died. I was given the birth date of a child who died in our parish and we traveled from place to place to hide my true age." She glanced at Neva, who snored on. "I can tell you all of this because there's no more need for secrecy. Because I doomed us both with my stupidity."

Luzia thought of the compliments Donadei had paid her, of the way he'd spoken of Doña Beatriz and his desire to be free. If she hadn't already been besotted with Santángel and his mystery would she have let the Prince of Olives seduce her? Would she have given up all her secrets? A life lived hungry could lead you to eat from anyone's hand. She would have fed greedily and never recognized the taste of poison.

"If you were a fool then we all were," Luzia said. "No doubt Donadei said whatever he could about both of us that would ensure his own freedom. But I will not lie down to die for him. For any of them. Your family has resources, friends in countries beyond Spain. I have milagritos. What is there to lose?"

"It won't work."

"Our choices are death or torture and death, Teoda. I'd rather die skewered by a guard than burned alive."

"Or strangled. If you repent they'll just strangle you."

"In that case, let's definitely stay here."

Teoda barked a laugh. "Very well. The inquisitors have clearly driven you mad, but I'll see if Rudolfo will get word to my brother. He has far more freedom than I have. They even allow him paper sometimes. But Luzia . . . my dreams don't lie. I watched you burn."

"Fate can be changed," Luzia said. "Curses can be broken."

She had to believe that, or she would sink beneath the waves.

Chapter 48

♦

They had little time to act. Luzia was afraid that she could be taken for another interrogation at any time. She didn't want to drown again.

Despite her anger and her fear, some part of her had believed Santángel would come for her, that he would find a way, but she couldn't hope for that any longer. No one would carry her, so she would find a way out herself. And if Teoda's angel was right and they were all meant to end here, so be it. Better to be hunted and brought down than to bare her throat for the slitting. She would die as a wolf did.

Teoda was able to get a note to her brother Ovidio, but only by convincing their guard Rudolfo that Luzia could perform love spells. He was infatuated with a beautiful wool merchant's daughter named Mariposa Baldera.

"But I can't," Luzia had protested.

"You'll suggest killing a guard but you won't lie to one?"

"What do we do when he realizes we've swindled him?"

"We'll be gone by then," said Teoda. "Or dead."

When Rudolfo brought Ovidio's reply, he asked what Luzia needed for the spell.

"First you must prepare yourself," Luzia said, eyeing him up and down. "The . . . incantations won't work if you're not clean of mind and heart."

Rudolfo had nodded as if this made perfect sense and repeated back their instructions to wash his body thoroughly every morning, wear only unstained garments, brush the crumbs from his mustache, and use polish on his teeth.

They had debated whether to include Neva and if she could be trusted not to share their plans, but the question had been answered one night when her snores stopped and she said, "I already know of your schemes and I want no part of them. I am old and my children are here. I want to go home."

Luzia hoped she would get there before life in a cell killed her.

Teoda fretted that they should wait for Ovidio to secure papers for Luzia. But when Luzia thought of the water, her throat filling, her lungs fighting the flood, she shook her head. "No. We go as soon as we can."

Only four days after Luzia had been subjected to the toca, they were ready.

Night came on slowly, as if afraid of what they might do. They needed to look as reputable as they could, so they washed their faces and hands, and Neva braided Luzia's hair. Then they could only wait. They told time by the chiming of the church bells. Luzia couldn't name the parish. In Madrid, she would have known.

"San Vicente," Teoda told her. "It's said he converted his jailer."

Luzia remembered that story and the ravens that had watched over his body.

They counted the chimes, listening to the prison fall asleep, the whispered conversations fading, the sounds of business being attended to in the inquisitors' chambers, the slamming of doors and shuffling of bodies.

"What was your plan?" she asked Teoda, keeping her voice low, trying to pass the time. "If you had won the torneo and the king had made you part of his court?"

"I would have learned all I could and shared it with Spain's enemies. I would have made the king doubt his precious saints and himself. I would have been the greatest spy in all the world." Her dimple appeared. "And the smallest."

Outside, the hoofbeats of horses and the rattle of carriage wheels gave way to the calls of night birds and the gentle hoot of owls from the woods and meadows beyond the city walls. They had only a stub of candle to burn, and soon the darkness of the cell was complete.

At last, a single bell rang out, different from the chimes of the church bells, a clanking sound, like a cow that had strayed away from its herd.

Teoda's hand brushed Luzia's and they held tight to each other, waiting. Again they heard the clanking bell.

Teoda squeezed her hand and they rose as quietly as they could.

Luzia laid her palm against the door and reached for the refrán. She could feel that secret song, that larger magic, eager to be sung, nearer since she'd faced the inquisitors, but she pushed it away. Santángel had been right. She wanted to live.

Boca dulce abre puertas de hierro. Words she'd used to open locked trunks or cupboards rather than go searching for a key. *Sweet words open iron gates.* Help me, she prayed silently to the unknown author of those words, someone sleeping in his bed across the sea, or rising to nurse her child, or laboring away by candlelight somewhere. Help me find my way.

The lock clicked and the door seemed to sigh as the catch released. They waited, listening, but they heard no sound of alarm, no footsteps racing toward them. They slipped out into the dark passage.

They couldn't risk a candle and so they crept slowly down the hall. Teoda led the way, her steps barely a shuffle, Luzia's hand resting on her shoulder.

Luzia tried to picture the map Ovidio had drawn for them, counting off her steps. But she began to doubt herself. Had she already counted fifty? Was her stride too long? Too short? Then

Teoda hissed in a breath and halted. Luzia managed to keep her footing and reached out in the dark. They'd arrived at the door that separated the cells from the entrance to the prison. What was waiting on the other side? Two guards? Ten?

There would be no turning back from what happened next. She and Teoda flattened themselves against the wall and Luzia let new words and a new melody take shape in her whispers. Cada gallo canta en su gallinero. *Every rooster sings in his own chicken coop.*

But she didn't picture a strutting cock. She envisioned the biggest woman she could, thick-necked and bellowing, her face red with blood, her brow sweaty, her fists balled. A mighty giantess, a titan.

The sound that burst from the cells behind them was the thunder of a wave, a dam giving way with a tremendous, shuddering roar. Beside Luzia, Teoda released a startled gasp. But Luzia didn't waver. She kept building the song as the roaring from the cells rose ever higher. The walls and floors trembled with the sound. It was as if the inquisitors had placed a demon on the rack, its screams filling the building. She hoped the sound would haunt the friars in their beds.

Luzia turned her head to the side just in time. The door to the entry slammed inward and struck her ear and the side of her face. She fumbled for the handle and just managed to get her fingers hooked into it as torchlight flooded into the passage and the guards rushed inside, hands on their swords, boots thudding over the stone floor.

Luzia gave the song a last long bellow, and then she and Teoda slid past the door to the unmanned entry. She had little memory of this place, though she knew she must have seen it when they brought her to the prison.

"Teoda." The whisper nearly startled a scream from her, but it was just Ovidio. He looked gaunt compared to the elegant figure he'd cut at La Casilla, and Luzia thought there might be more gray in his hair. "Follow me."

He peered through the small sliding wood casement the guards used to identify arrivals and visitors, then opened the door and waved them through. The courtyard was quiet. If the judges and scribes and servants had woken in their beds at the din coming from the prison, they hadn't roused themselves to investigate. Maybe they were used to the sound of screams.

There was no reason to move slowly now. Ovidio swept Teoda up and they ran, keeping close to the building in case anyone might be watching the courtyard from the windows above.

They reached a niche carved into the stone and hung with the green cross of the Inquisition. Ovidio reached behind it and removed what looked like a rolled-up blanket.

Inside were a uniform for Ovidio, a cloak for Teoda, and a fresh gown for Luzia. Where is your modesty? she wondered as she stripped down to her linen and Ovidio helped to tie her laces. She supposed it had drowned in the inquisitors' chamber.

They looked almost respectable.

Ovidio tucked their filthy prison clothes behind the flag and they hurried toward the gates that would lead them into the city proper.

"Are you prepared?" Ovidio whispered.

But there was only one answer to give. They turned right and passed beneath the arched entry. Ahead were the gates and a pair of guards at their posts.

"Alto!" barked one of them. "What purpose?"

"These ladies need escort to their coach," said Ovidio.

"Talk sense." The guard hadn't drawn his sword, but he had his hand on its hilt. "What are you doing out here at night? Are those prisoners?"

"Who's talking nonsense now? They're visitors for . . . well, that's not for me to tell. But let's say that he hasn't seen his wife or daughter in some time."

The guards exchanged a glance. It was well known that some of the clergy kept secret mistresses and even families.

"Why are they here so late?"

"I can't answer that," said Ovidio, a sly lilt in his voice.

The guards peered at them and Luzia lay a protective hand on Teoda's shoulder, a mother's hand. Outside, she could see the streets that would lead past the city walls and a team of six horses tethered to a coach. Two outriders and a coachman waited in the moonlight.

"I wanted to see Papa," Teoda said in the high sweet voice she'd used at the torneo.

"You know they could be whores," the other guard said.

"Señor!" Luzia exclaimed with all the righteous horror she could muster.

"Where's your sword?" the guard asked Ovidio.

"God's tongue, man. I didn't think I'd need it when Fray ... when I was pulled out of my bed at this shit hour. Can you just let us pass so that I can go back to bed before someone wakes up and starts asking questions none of us want to answer?"

Again the guards exchanged a glance.

The first eyed Ovidio. "If your pocket is being weighted, ours should get heavy too."

Luzia wanted to cheer. A bribe they were prepared for.

"Oh, very well," grumbled Ovidio. "I'm the one who was fast asleep. I'm the one playing nursemaid. But certainly, let me share my hard-earned pay with you."

He dropped silver reales into their hands.

"Come now," protested the guard. "Don't be miserly."

Ovidio scowled. "Fine, but this is the end of it."

The guard grinned and bowed. He unlocked the gates and stepped aside.

Teoda clapped her hands and skipped ahead and Luzia followed. The guard offered her his hand to help her cross the threshold and she took it without thinking.

"Wait," he said, his grip tightening.

"She is not for you to enjoy," said Ovidio. "You've been paid in silver, you don't get to collect her purse too."

"Shut your mouth," snapped the guard, and the other drew his sword, keeping it on Ovidio.

The soldier dragged Luzia toward one of the torches burning in its sconce and yanked her hand close to the firelight.

"Calluses," he said. "But she's dressed like nobility. So is the child."

Ovidio's gaze met hers.

"Go," he growled. Then he drove his dagger into her captor's throat.

"To arms!" shouted the other man.

Luzia stumbled away from the bloody guard, who was still trying to keep his grip even as he crumpled to the ground.

Ovidio snatched his sword away. "Run!" he shouted. "Protect her!"

Luzia lurched toward Teoda, who was halfway to the coach now. The outriders had leapt down and drawn their swords to come to their aid, but it was too late. Guardsmen were pouring into the courtyard and through the arch.

Teoda screamed and Luzia looked behind her. Ovidio was on his knees, a sword through his chest. He clawed at the air as if trying to pull himself to his feet, then toppled.

My angel says I will die here. We all will.

"Not all," she whispered. "Run, Teoda!"

Luzia didn't stop to think. She focused on the cobblestones and let the song roar through her, the words like bursts of fire in her mind, blinding in their light. Onde iras, amigos toparas. *May you find friends. May you find friends. May you find friends.* The stones rose in a heap, a tide of rock that exploded between Teoda and the soldiers, blocking Luzia's path to the coach.

One of the outriders seized Teoda and ran for the coach doors.

"Luzia!" Teoda cried as she was shoved inside.

Luzia thrust the walls of rock outward, trying to give the coach time, closing off the road. But she could feel the song trying to split, her fear pulling her toward escape, *anywhere but here*. If she couldn't keep to the melody she might tear herself in two. So be it. It would be the death she chose.

Something struck her from behind. Luzia fell forward and then they were on her, kicking and punching. Her head struck the stones. The song slipped away.

It has to be enough that one of us got free, she thought as darkness crowded in. Fate was wrong once; maybe it can be again.

Chapter 49

✦

There was a room dug into the earth beneath the home of Víctor de Paredes. It was not quite wide enough to sit in and not quite tall enough to stand in. Its walls were smooth stone and it could only be reached through an iron hatch that latched on the outside. There had been one of these rooms in every De Paredes house for more than four hundred years. It was called the scorpion's den.

Víctor's men had found Santángel on the forest floor where the king's soldiers had left him for dead, the arrows still lodged in his chest. First he had endured the agony of the shafts being pulled from his body and then he had been thrown into his den to heal.

It should have been nothing. He'd endured far worse. He had lived with the futility of his own situation a very long time. He was no different from other men, caught up in the movement of a world that did not care for him, at the whim of a God who did not heed him.

But this time his helplessness drove him mad. He shouted his rage. He pounded on the walls of his cell. He swore bloody revenge. It didn't matter. No one came. No one brought food or water. They knew he wouldn't die. He would wither and shrink to nothing, a living corpse, but he would go on.

Santángel had lived only one life, and it had been both long and remarkably boring. His early years of travel and debauchery, of scholarship and pleasure seeking, seemed like a dream someone else once had and then tried to relate to him. He had forgotten fear, forgotten rage. What had remained was a kind of scholarly curiosity about the world and its workings, a dim hope that one day, in one of his many books, he would discover the secret of the bad bargain he had struck with Tello de Paredes and he would find a way to undo it.

There were no surprises. Everyone reminded him of someone he'd met before; every moment was one he'd already lived. He had thought this unrelenting march of sameness would continue until he found a way to break free or he found the courage to die.

Then Luzia had entered his life, a character in a play who was meant to have a few lines and depart. Instead she had overtaken his story. The plot he knew so well had suddenly confused him, the shape of his narrative bending around her into something new. But a tragedy could not become a comedy. In the end, she had been trapped by his curse, just as he was. The plot's shape returned and his tragedy became hers.

He remembered the pain of the arrows piercing his lung, his side. If she wasn't conscious to heal herself, it would be that easy for her to die. If she'd escaped the woods, could she have made it to Madrid? Was she hiding somewhere or captured? Sometimes he let himself believe that the king had changed his mind, that Luzia was safe in the Alcázar or placed in a convent or even back at Calle de Dos Santos. Sometimes he imagined she was in the house above him. Víctor would enjoy that.

If she was alive, then there was hope, wasn't there? Or was this helplessness some punishment for his selfish youth, his murderous past? If she was in hiding, she would need a way out of Spain. Santángel could get her money. He could even find a way to provide her with documents for safe travel. But how could he predict the way his own influence might ruin any attempt to free her? If her escape was a danger to his master, he would never succeed. He rehearsed arguments for how to persuade Víctor to help her. He would beg for her life as he had never begged for his.

And if his master didn't agree? There was a way to sever his luck from Víctor de Paredes. All he had to do was ride away. He could travel through the night, find a fine horizon to serve as his last sight of the world. He would burn away to ash and his death would break the tether that bound him to this family. Víctor's good fortune would burn to nothing with him. Luzia would have her chance.

He must have been unconscious when Víctor sent Celso to retrieve him from the basement because he had no memory of being transported. He woke in the dining room, to the scent of braised meat and spiced wine. He had no appetite, despite the days of starvation, but he forced himself to eat. If he was to think, if he was to strategize, he needed his strength back.

Víctor watched him and when Santángel pushed away his plate, he said, "Did you enjoy your meal?"

"Did you enjoy your tantrum?" He didn't want to spar with Víctor, didn't want to play these games, but all must seem to be as it had been.

"I hope you had time to think. Free from distraction."

Santángel said nothing.

"Do you not wish to know where the scullion is?"

"You will tell me when it suits you."

"I see your equanimity has returned. I hardly recognized the lovesick fool I found bleeding on the ground in the woods." Víctor tapped his fingers on the arms of his chair. "Your place is with me, Santángel. And your attempt to help Luzia Cotado evade capture did not please Vázquez."

"But my luck kept you from any real danger, didn't it?"

Víctor acknowledged this with a nod.

"Your little friend is making trouble."

His relief must have shown because Víctor smiled.

"Yes, Guillén, she lives. She is in Toledo. A prisoner of the Inquisition."

It took five centuries of patience to keep Santángel in his chair. He wanted to leap up and choke the smug smile from Víctor's face. He wanted to steal a horse and ride through the night to her.

"Why the Inquisition?" he managed, pleased at the steadiness of his voice.

"She was denounced."

"By you?"

"No. I said I was taken in by her illusions but that I knew nothing of heresy or plots against the king."

And he had been believed. He would always be believed. As long as Santángel lived.

Santángel knew he should keep silent, give nothing more away, but the madness of the scorpion's den was still with him, clawing at his good sense. "Has she faced torture?"

Víctor shrugged and Santángel thought, *I will see you suffer. If it takes a thousand years, I will carve that sneer from your mouth.*

"That is the business of the tribunal," Víctor said. "But she attempted an escape last night, with the heretic Teoda Halcón. The child's father died in the attempt, but Teoda is free."

"And Luzia?"

"Back in her cell. She has confessed to everything and she will face sentencing on the Feast of All Saints."

Barely a week away. That left him little time to act.

"The tribunal claims she had help from the guards," Víctor continued. "But my sources say she slipped through the locks of her cell and left the streets outside the Inquisition district in ruins. She is more powerful than I understood and more reckless."

"You still hope to secure her gifts as your own." Of course he did. Víctor saw and wanted, wanted and claimed. He didn't know what it was to be denied.

"She's willful, but she can be broken, as anyone can be in time.

She will have her final audience with the tribunal in three days' time. She will be told of her sentence."

"So she is to die?" Only those slated for death were given their sentences before an auto de fe.

Víctor nodded. "But it is not too late."

"No?" How easy he sounded, how bemused.

"I can use my influence and yours to save her from the pyre."

"There are limits to both. Or you never would have begun this farce to acquire a title."

"But I have been gifted my title. You are speaking to a duke, Santángel."

"I'll make sure to sit a little straighter." Santángel studied him. "You offered your services to the king."

"I didn't have to. The king came to me. The day after the puppet show."

When Santángel's loyalties had altered, when he had given in to his need for Luzia. When he had let himself begin to love her and turn his mind to freeing them both. But while he was free to give his loyalty and even his useless heart to Luzia, his luck belonged to Víctor. The stars had aligned to grant Víctor opportunity even as Santángel had sought to steal it from him. He had felt the world shift but he hadn't understood its direction.

"I have cultivated connections to Philip and the Supreme Council," said the new duke. "I can convince them our scullion was a mere pawn in Pérez's intrigues. That he and the Ordoños contrived to use her for their own ends. She has already confessed that her milagritos were mere illusions."

Santángel saw clearly enough the picture Víctor would paint for the tribunal: a dim-witted girl deluded into believing she had great power, dressed up and made to perform for her betters, manipulated by striving hidalgos desperate for money and social success. She had already confessed. She would repent, face public punishment at the auto de fe, and be placed in Víctor de Paredes's hands. There would be no need for mysterious bargains to bind her. Those who had been tried and reconciled for heresy by the In-quisition received no second chances. If she fled or if Víctor chose to claim she had slid back into irreligious practices, she would be imprisoned and put to death without trial.

"But I don't know what reckless thing she may do next," Víctor continued. "If she's not careful she'll end up in trouble not even I can get her out of."

"You would leash us both to you?"

"Why not? What might I accomplish with a milagrera and a familiar in my home? And won't that be a kind of happiness? An eternity together?"

"She will never agree to it. She has seen what you are."

Víctor laughed. "Guillén, do you think she values her own life any less than you do? Her choices are the pyre or . . ." He gestured to the comfortable room, the coals blazing, the full cups of wine, the heavy stone walls and furs. A life of plenty.

"What is it you want from me, Víctor?"

"Do you love her? I didn't think you had the capacity for it."

"What do you want?" he repeated.

"You will come with me to Toledo. We will attend her sen-tencing before the tribunal, and should she be seized by visions of martyrdom or heroic ideas of dying a free woman, you will be there to convince her that a life beneath this roof, a life with you is preferable."

Santángel doubted such an argument would sway Luzia. "Sen-tencings are not open to the public. Prisoners of the Inquisition are not allowed visitors."

Víctor waved away this protest. "I am not the public. Besides, Lucrecia de León has attended parties with the warden. Ovidio Halcón was allowed correspondence with his business partners to arrange for seizure of his estate. All is permissible where there is money and will."

"She will be a vulnerability to you, Víctor. Forever. People will always wonder if you have a heretic in your household and if that heresy stains you as well."

"You underestimate your own gifts. Besides, Pérez cannot evade the king forever. Once he is in Philip's grasp, the scullion will be of no interest to him. We will make sure she goes to mass as regularly as she pisses and she will be a testimony to the victory of the one true Church. I'll drag her to Rome to take communion if I have to." He leaned back in his chair. "But perhaps I've mistaken your feelings for her. Would you rather her dead than that she belonged to me?"

I would keep her from being buried alive in a future of servitude. But he couldn't save her without Víctor. Every scheme he had would twist to further the De Paredes fortunes. Every move he made would draw the cords tighter around Luzia. He had thought he might buy his own freedom with hers, but now they would both be captives. She would hate him and she would be right to. Maybe she would choose the pyre instead.

"Can my luck not be enough for you?" he asked.

"Your luck brought me Luzia Cotado. If the king will not use her as the instrument she was meant to be, I will."

There was the truth that had choked him in the scorpion's den. He had doomed her before they had ever met.

Chapter 50

◆

The cell was lonely without Teoda and without hope. Neva slept more than anyone Luzia had ever encountered and she listened jealously to the old woman's snores. She would have liked to sleep through these interminable days.

Rudolfo was posted at her door all night long now and he wasn't happy about it, but his bad mood was tempered by anticipation for the love spell he was owed.

"It isn't time yet," Luzia told him. "I need to know more about your beloved."

"She is beautiful," Rudolfo told her. "Smooth skinned, eyes like—"

"Sapphires. Yes, so you told me. But what are her interests? Where is she from?"

Rudolfo faltered.

"Do you want wobbly magic?" she prodded him. "Do you want her to fall in love with some other man named Rudolfo?"

"No!" he cried.

"Everyone knows Mariposa Baldera is beautiful. You must discover her likes and dislikes, find out about her family, learn everything you can about her."

"How am I to do all that?"

"Talk to her."

"I couldn't."

Luzia sighed. "Then there's nothing I can do."

"You will help me or I won't let you out to collect your rations. You will starve!"

"Do as you must," said Luzia. "You will be the one to live without love."

The next day he returned. "Mariposa is from Salamanca. She has a brother who is about to start at the university. She likes fried fish and lilies."

"Then you must bring her lilies."

"It is November!"

"Bring me a bulb."

"I can't afford such things."

"Then dig one up in the monastery gardens."

"That is a crime!"

"You can be an honorable man or you can have love, Rudolfo."

Really, was it any kind of question at all?

He brought her the bulb, and she whispered over it, and Rudolfo had lilies to bring to the girl he loved.

"Can you make me rich?" Rudolfo asked when he returned. "The man courting her is rich."

"Does she love him?"

"I don't know."

"Did you ask her?"

Teoda had promised Rudolfo magic to earn a few favors, and Luzia had kept the charade going to avoid reprisal when he discovered love spells were nonsense. But now she liked the idea of Rudolfo finding favor with his lady. Now that he didn't smell of sweat and his teeth were less stained and he had actually bothered to speak to her rather than gawking at her like all the other dullards, maybe there was hope for them both. Besides, it was the only entertainment she had.

"Are you certain he deserves her?" Neva asked when a glowing Rudolfo told her he had finally stolen a kiss.

"Better a man who works for her love than a man who buys her for a beauty that will fade. He talks to her. He treats her kindly."

"It won't last," Neva scoffed, and rolled onto her side to sleep. "People forget the work it takes to make wine. They drink it down and wonder why the cup is empty."

True enough. But there was only so much within Luzia's power. If she couldn't be happy, if she couldn't live past this week, someone should have the joy she hadn't managed to keep.

The next day, Rudolfo arrived with her water jug. "You're to wash," he said.

"Sentencing," said Neva. "I haven't seen my son in two years, but I guess I need to be a famous beata with money coming out of my ass if I'm to get any answers from the tribunal."

"Be silent," said Rudolfo. It was all he had for an argument.

Luzia took the jug of water from his hands. She could see her face in the surface, a phantom already. Only those who would be sent to die were given their sentences before the pageantry and ritual of the auto de fe.

She heated the water on the stove, then washed as best she could, standing in the basin. She didn't care what the judges thought of her appearance, but she didn't know if she'd have a chance to clean herself again.

She was led downstairs and out into the large, empty courtyard, and on into the sala dorada, the gilded coffers of its ceiling floating above her, the tiles patterned in undulating ribbons beneath her feet. She remembered the water choking her, filling her throat, the darkness crowding in, Hualit's lipless, eyeless face. There should be no beauty here, she thought. There should be no lie to offer visitors or dignitaries. There should be no pleasure for the men who tied me down.

Two big windows looked out into the courtyard and the walls of the prison beyond. Why didn't she know words for flight? Or was that another form of magic too big to contain, another spell that would crack her in two? Maybe real miracles did belong to saints. She thought of Teoda's angel. Did he see a future now?

Was he watching over the child who wasn't a child? If nothing else, Luzia had that proof of her defiance. If Teoda lived, someone would remember.

The inquisitors were seated in their three chairs behind the table, a notary at their side. There would be no torture today, and pain had taught her to be less afraid of death. They wanted her to fear the pyre and being burned alive, but she would never let that happen. She'd repent and let the executioner strangle her. Or maybe she'd let them light the fire, then heal her skin and her lungs until she was too tired and had to let the flames consume her. What would they think when the heat didn't blacken her skin? When her hair burned away but her body didn't turn to ash? Would they set upon her with knives? Pull her apart? Or would they wonder if they'd made a new martyr? She supposed she could just give in to the wild magic and let herself split. Maybe she'd take some of the crowd with her. Or if the king came to watch, she could try to cut him in half before she died. Let Spain fall into chaos. She wouldn't be here to punish for the crime.

But Luzia's steps faltered when she saw the judges weren't alone. Víctor de Paredes stood in a relaxed pose before a row of chairs to the right of the tribunal. He wore black silk corded with black velvet and trimmed in silver braid, his hand resting on the jeweled hilt of the sword at his hip. Behind Víctor, the shadows seeming to cling to him like cobwebs, was Santángel.

He was alive, and there was no visible sign of a wound that should have been mortal. She knew that if she unhooked his jacket and pushed aside his tunic, she would find no scar or mark on his smooth skin. He'd lost some of the strength he'd gained at La Casilla, but still he seemed to glow.

Who was he, this man she knew more intimately than any other? She wanted to believe that he'd only stayed away from her because Víctor had prevented him from coming, but that faith felt out of reach. His gaze stayed on her, but she didn't know how to read it. Was he there to advocate for her? To denounce her? How long had he and Víctor been here, in conversation with the tribunal?

Don Pedro—or at least the man Luzia thought was Don Pedro since she still struggled to tell them apart—addressed the room at large. "The accused, Luzia Calderón Cotado, has been brought here because Don Víctor de Paredes, a good and wise friend to the Church, has offered to speak on her behalf. If she will answer her conscience and the will of God with true and honest confession, her sentence will be decided by this consulta de fe, her punishment and penance to be performed tomorrow in full sight of the people of Spain in the Plaza de Zocodover."

So Víctor had come to claim her after all. Despite the failed torneo and the specter of the Inquisition, she had somehow held her value. But what price would his protection demand?

Now Don Pedro turned to Luzia. "Luzia Calderón Cotado, you have been charged with heresy and for contriving to collaborate with other heretics to pervert the teachings of the Church and mock God Himself. If you speak now and tell us who led you so astray, you may not save your life, but you will save your soul."

Luzia wasn't sure what game they were playing. She might still face a death sentence. Were there words that could keep her from the pyre, even if they landed her forever in Víctor's debt? Who was she meant to accuse? And if she said the wrong words, spoke the incorrect incantation, would they drag her back down those stairs and under the water?

Luzia cleared her throat, swallowing her fear. "Ovidio Halcón," she ventured. The tribunal could do nothing to him or his sister now. "He introduced me to strange new teachings. He said that I had been misled by my parents and my priests."

Don Pedro made a dissatisfied grunt. "We are well aware of the Halcóns' perfidies and your association with them. Ovidio Halcón is beyond our reach but not the reach of God, and when his daughter is apprehended, she will face her own retribution."

Then Teoda was still alive and free. Luzia hoped she was far from Spain's borders and that her nights were dreamless.

The man to Don Pedro's right shifted in his seat. *His* name Luzia knew now: Don Francisco, the man who had placed the bridal veil so lovingly upon her face.

"If this is all the prisoner can offer, there is nothing we can do for her. It's clear she isn't prepared to unburden her conscience fully."

They wanted new people to blame, new prisoners to fill their cells. But who was she meant to doom?

"Señores," said Víctor, his wet green eyes fixed on Luzia. "Did I not tell you she is slow-witted? She will need more guidance."

Don Pedro steepled his fingers. "Tell us what happened beneath the Ordoños' roof."

"I already have," Luzia replied.

"You told us of when you went to mass and when you fasted, but what of your masters?"

Then she was meant to denounce Marius and Valentina. They were the sacrifice Don Víctor wanted her to offer. Luzia thought of the smell of cocido, of Valentina unbraiding her hair, of the sprig of rosemary tucked into her sleeve, the barest scrap of protection, the barest scrap of kindness after years of slaps and punches and disdain.

"They prayed as good people do," Luzia said.

"They met with Antonio Pérez," Víctor prodded.

Luzia allowed herself a small, embarrassed laugh. "Oh no, señor. They did not keep such company as that. They were not fashionable people."

Don Víctor's hand flexed on the hilt of his ornamental sword. He gestured to Santángel. "This is my servant. He helped her prepare for the torneo and can attest to how stupid she is, how easily led. He can encourage truth from her."

Luzia saw the men of the tribunal blink. The notary frowned and sorted through his pages, his face confused. Luzia knew they would say nothing, but that each of them would wonder how they had failed to notice the stranger in their midst.

"State your name that it may be entered into our record," said Don Pedro.

"Guillén Barcelo Villalbas de Canales y Santángel."

"And what role did you play at Casa Ordoño?"

"I acted as a kind of tutor to Señorita Cotado."

"So you had cause to spend time with Don Marius and Doña Valentina."

"No."

Víctor pressed his lips together.

"Then what good are you to this tribunal?" asked Don Pedro.

"In the years I have served my master, I've done all I can to protect his good name. I have seen many people attempt to harm and defame him, and I have learned that the most dangerous attacks are never direct. It is the arrows shot from the flanks or from behind that find their targets."

"I fail to see what—" Don Pedro began.

But Santángel wasn't looking at Don Pedro. His opal eyes were trained on Luzia when he said, "Sometimes his critics have even attempted to aim at me in their attempts to do him harm."

Luzia remembered standing by the lake's shore before the third trial, full of rage and love, threatening to kill Víctor de Paredes. Santángel had warned her that his luck would ensure her failure. *I have seen countless enemies seek to strike down De Paredes*, he'd told her. *They'd be better served by harming me. But if they can't see a target, they can't take proper aim.*

Luzia saw him clearly. She always had. And now he was telling her to attack him, but why? What was his plan?

Don Pedro said, "That's all very well, but how does it relate to the prisoner?"

"I have testimony to offer," said Luzia. All she could do was pray Santángel knew what he was doing.

Don Pedro waved his hand impatiently. "Then we will hear it."

"The man called Santángel did witness my time with the Ordoños. He visited me there nearly every day. I didn't understand
what I was being asked to do. I was told I would be given money,
and food, and pretty gowns. So many pretty gowns." Let them
believe she was a fool so long as they believed her. "I was seduced away from the Church and to the devil's side. By Guillén
Santángel."

Víctor released a surprised croak.

Don Gaspar pushed his chair back and even the notary couldn't
hide his surprise.

"The girl has had her wits muddled," Víctor attempted.

"Ask my maid from La Casilla," Luzia continued. "She is in
Don Víctor's employ. Ask her who came to my rooms late at night.
It wasn't Marius Ordoño who took my virtue and invited me to
consort with the devil. Santángel admitted to being a demon himself."

Víctor's laugh was unconvincing. "The girl is more deluded than
I realized."

"He said Christ was no more than a magician," Luzia continued, enjoying the anger in Víctor's eyes. Santángel had pointed
the way, and even if she didn't understand the destination she was
choosing, she at least saw the road before her. "He said that resurrection was a trick that anyone could master. Cut him and see how
he heals. Stab him through the heart and he will rise up, living and
unharmed."

Santángel smiled. Their path was chosen. The crossroads long
past.

The judges didn't look scandalized, only uncomfortable. The Inquisition considered witchcraft a delusion. The devil was real, but
he didn't visit the kitchens of Madrid. Don Pedro shook his head
and Don Francisco sighed.

"It's clear she's gone mad," said Don Víctor, "and would repay
my kindness with cruelty. Best to put an end to this pathetic display."

"You're right," said Santángel slowly, testing the words in his mouth. He stepped forward, and the judges recoiled. The scribe made a little mewl. It was as if they were truly seeing him for the first time, a creature of light and shadow, his bright hair, his glittering eyes. "It is time to end this deception. The scullion speaks the truth. I am the devil's own man."

Chapter 51

◆

Santángel felt the room tilt, the planets shift, as if a new alignment had been reached. It was the same sensation he'd experienced his first night with Luzia. As if the sky above had rearranged itself and night would show new constellations—the shape of a pomegranate, a path through an orange grove.

Luzia had been the dagger in his hand. She had taken the only aim she could, at his reputation, not his master's. She had turned Santángel into a liability. But was he irredeemable enough? Tainted enough by the threat of dark magic? So dangerous to Víctor that the preservation of his good fortune would demand they be separated?

"You think you will save her this way?" Víctor whispered furiously.

"Are you going to claim me now?" Santángel asked, unable to keep the smile from his face. "I will die on a pyre and she will go free. They may beat her or banish her, but she will live. She won't need your money or your influence when no charge of heresy hangs over her."

"I will find her and bind her to me. She will be a gift I give my sons and their sons."

"She is powerful enough to thwart you, and she knows all about the bargain I made with Tello. You cannot use me to bend her fate once I am in my grave. The trap will not spring. Go on, tell them

I'm mad too. Call me a liar. You know what I can show them. You know what will happen if they torture me."

"You are making a confession?" asked Don Pedro. "You understand that every word will be documented, that you are confessing to demonic possession and witchcraft. There are no punishments for this crime. No means to recant. You will be handed over to the civil authority for execution."

"I understand."

"What of the Ordoños? And Víctor de Paredes? Did they know what abomination they were host to?"

Santángel would have liked to see Víctor thrown into a cell, but he couldn't risk it. If he denounced and incriminated Víctor, he had no doubt the judges wouldn't find him credible. He'd be deemed a lunatic or blame would swing back to Luzia to preserve Víctor's reputation. The influence of Santángel's luck wouldn't allow for Víctor to suffer real pain or humiliation.

"No," he said. "I assure you, the Ordoños were mere dupes, and Víctor de Paredes would never countenance such blasphemy beneath his roof."

Don Francisco signaled to the warden. "You will be taken into custody. The warden will find you a cell and . . . We will meet in private to consider trial."

That worried Santángel; it could take years to face sentencing. Víctor might find a way to bring him back into his household in that time. But of course, if Víctor left Toledo, Santángel would burn to ash the first morning he was gone.

"You are still bound to me," Víctor whispered. "You will speak no word against me."

"I should have stolen this from you long ago."

"Señores," said Víctor, "I would beg a little more patience from you—"

Don Pedro interrupted him. "It's hard for me to fathom that a man of your intellect and knowledge of the world has had two people in his service—"

"Luzia Cotado did not serve in my home."

"But you are her patron, are you not? And you plan to make her a member of your household after she is publicly sentenced and punished?"

Santángel waited, wondering which way the room would tilt now.

"I do," said Víctor, though he didn't sound sure of himself.

"You will be responsible for her spiritual well-being and her education. She cannot be led into such delusion again."

"I understand."

For a few moments the judges turned to each other, whispering, but Santángel couldn't hear what they had to say. He was about to be deposited in a dark cell for an unknown time to wait for death, and yet he felt freer than he had in hundreds of years. Because Luzia would live. Because Víctor might stay rich and happy, but he would always know what Santángel had taken from him.

He watched Luzia now, paler than she'd been, her skin sallow beneath her freckles. Her dress was mostly clean but gaped at the waist and her expression was troubled as she watched him too. He knew she was waiting for him to reveal some trick that would free them both. But he had no fresh hand to play. He would die and she would live. A tragic bargain but a clean one. She would be angry with him, maybe she would weep for him, but once he was dead, she would find her way free of Víctor. He would no longer have Santángel's luck to protect him. She would have a chance.

He wished he could tell her all of it, but instead they stood in silence.

The warden vanished through the eastern doors, and Santángel expected him to come back with chains or more guards to escort him to the cells. But when he returned he had the Prince of Olives in tow. Doña Beatriz trailed in their wake, gowned in golden lace, her hands clasped tightly.

Donadei wore an expression of respectful humility but he looked as healthy and bronzed as ever, dressed in velvet, his curls gleaming. Only his cross was different. The massive emerald sat at its center still, but the jade stones that had surrounded it had been replaced with what looked like diamonds.

He bowed to the judges.

"Fortún Donadei, we commanded your presence today because you are a true and loyal servant of the Church and because you were at the torneo. You witnessed the strange goings-on there. You saw the illusions created by the fraud Luzia Cotado. Did you see her in the company of this man, Santángel?"

Donadei's eyes darted around the room. He was trying to get his bearings, to find some indication of what the tribunal wanted. "They are fornicators. I know that."

"How?"

"They flaunted it. I saw them embracing in the gardens."

How easily he lied. Santángel wondered what might come next.

"Who else knew of this relationship?" asked Don Pedro.

Again Donadei paused and Santángel watched him calculate. "The Ordoños. Valentina Ordoño even offered Señorita Cotado to me. She wanted us to form an attachment. I think she hoped to sway the results of the torneo."

"That cursed tournament is of no interest to us," said Don Pedro. "Consult your conscience and speak truly."

He was silent.

"Who else?" urged Doña Beatriz, her gaze angled purposefully toward Víctor.

Even before Donadei spoke, Santángel felt it again, that shift, the sense that luck was taking hold.

"No one else. It was not commonly known. I did not spread any gossip." He paused, then said, "I know that Don Víctor believed his champion was nothing but pure and holy. He spoke of her often as a good and pious woman. I fear the creature Santángel and Luzia Cotado conspired to deceive him."

There it was. Donadei was making his bid for a new patron to free himself of Doña Beatriz. There had been a time when he'd sought to avoid association with Víctor de Paredes. But he was too arrogant to fear curses, and his worries had been banished by his own ambition now that service to the king wasn't an option. Santángel's good fortune had moved the pieces on the board to save Víctor's reputation and place two milagreros beneath his roof—Luzia and the Prince of Olives. Fortunate Víctor de Paredes, the luckiest man in Madrid.

Don Pedro leaned forward. "Then do you mean to say Luzia Cotado was party to these schemes?"

Now Santángel tensed. His gambit could not be undone so quickly. Donadei must say no.

Donadei's gaze shifted from Luzia to Víctor de Paredes. What forces moved upon him beyond his own greed? Which way would the influence that preserved Víctor's benefit move him?

At last he said, "She is coarse and immoral, but not so ill-educated as she seems. I saw her many times whispering with Antonio Pérez and the heretic Teoda Halcón."

That easily the stars had found their new alignment.

Deny it, Santángel pleaded with Luzia silently. Tell the court Donadei tried to woo you to an alliance against Pérez, that he demeaned Doña Beatriz and Jesus and all his apostles in your presence.

But Luzia only shrugged. "All he says is true. I lie as easily as I breathe. The devil whispers and I answer. I would see the Pope hung by his ankles and King Philip nailed up beside him."

The men at the table gasped. Doña Beatriz made the sign of the cross. Santángel wanted to roar his frustration. What was she doing? Why concede so easily? Why indict herself so thoroughly? Could the force of his cursed influence be so strong? Had all of this been for nothing?

The guards took hold of Luzia as the warden strode toward Santángel.

"I will watch you and that useless whore burn," Víctor muttered. It was over. Santángel had done nothing but doom them both.

"That you may be better entertained, I will attempt to die slowly." As the warden led him away he murmured, loud enough that his master would be sure to hear, "Good luck to you, Víctor."

Chapter 52

✦

Back in the darkness of her cell, as Neva mumbled in her sleep, Luzia contemplated the road that she and Santángel had chosen. She knew he had intended to free her by damning himself and she had almost let him do it. She wondered if the Prince of Olives knew just how ruthless his new master was.

Donadei had approached her in the audience chamber as she waited to be taken to her cell.

"I will pray for your soul," he said loudly, then whispered. "You see, little nun? I did win in the end."

"Are you so certain?"

"My miracles will work wonders for him and I won't have to listen to him moan beneath me every night to earn my keep."

"What happened to the whispers of milagreros and your fear of Víctor de Paredes? You should listen to your own warnings."

"Do you really still take me for an honest country rube? Don Víctor has the king's favor and soon I will have a place at court. I will be the king's champion yet."

"Your ambition will bury you."

"Give me more advice before you're clapped in chains."

"Then call it victory, Fortún. Over me. Teoda. Pérez. I ask only one thing: Do not come to witness my humiliation. Do not attend the auto de fe and what is bound to come after. I beg you, grant me this consideration."

Donadei's face split in a radiant smile. "You even beg badly. I will be there to watch you and your lover burn. Then Don Víctor will have one milagrero, and I will be on my path back to the palace." He bowed and declared, "May God have mercy on you, Luzia Cotado."

His ugliness should have shown on his countenance, she thought. But only stories and plays worked that way, and maybe she should be grateful for it. If this were a tale told to children, she'd sprout horns and fangs for what she intended to attempt.

"Did you mean those things?" Rudolfo asked when he took up his post outside her cell for the night. "That you fucked the devil's man?"

"If I can get Mariposa Baldera to love you, do you care how wicked I may be?"

He hesitated. "No. But she is already fond of me."

"Fond. That's nice. It's good that fond is enough for you."

Rudolfo pressed his face against the grating of the door. "But it is not enough for me!"

"Then you must do as I bid, for I die tomorrow."

When she had told him her demands, he said, "Impossible! No, I cannot."

"At least she's fond of you."

"I want her to love me completely," he pleaded. "Without sense. Without reason."

What a curse to place upon someone. "Then what happens when the prize is won? When you tire of her?"

"I will never tire of her," he said fervently.

He meant it, and maybe it would prove true. But Luzia was glad she didn't really have the power to alter hearts, and she prayed Mariposa would make her choices wisely.

"I can tell you how to make a nuska," Luzia said, "and where to place it. Then it will be done, but first you must do as I have asked."

He refused. He argued. He seemed about to cry. And then, of course, he relented. Because he believed that love was within his grasp. Was there anything more dangerous than a man full of hope?

When the bells struck ten, he brought her to Santángel's cell.

"You have an hour," he whispered. "Do not make . . . noise."

Santángel rose. He glowed in the dim light, unexpected treasure.

"Why?" he said. "Why sentence yourself to death?"

"Do you want to argue or do you want to kiss me?"

He closed the space between them in two strides and took her in his arms. "I assure you I am capable of both."

Why had she wasted time doubting him? He was a killer. He was a liar. He was not a good man. But it was possible she didn't want a good man.

"I was trying to save you," he said as he cupped her face, traced the curves of her neck with his fingertips.

"I know," she said. "It was very grand of you. Very romantic."

"And yet we die together tomorrow. Why would you not let me save your life?"

"You have lived centuries in Don Víctor's service. Would you really consign me to that?"

"You wouldn't be bound by my curse! You would know better than to make his bargain."

"Despite his gift for cruel choices?"

"You would have found a way to best him as I never did."

"You believe I could?"

"I know it."

"Then trust in me now, Santángel. As you once asked me to trust you. Our deaths will not be in vain. If nothing else, I can make it painless." She drew closer, grateful for his warmth, for the pleasure of leaning into him, as lovers did, as they might never do again. "I saw you once, before we met in the courtyard. You were in Víctor's coach. When I looked at you, I felt as if I were lifting out of my shoes."

"I know," he murmured against her hair. "It wasn't spring, but the almond trees bloomed, and I wondered what chance had passed."

"That was me?"

"That was your power recognizing mine. I didn't want to wake to the world. But you forced me to."

"Are you sorry?"

"Let me unbraid your hair and I will have no regrets at all."

She laughed, the sound strange in the damp misery of the cells. "You aren't afraid to die?"

"Will you think less of me if I am?"

"No. I'm terrified."

"I wish I could have died a free man, not bound to a post. But I've earned my place on the pyre. You did nothing but try to live."

"Don't deny me credit for all my immoderate striving. I worked hard for my place in this prison."

It was strange to know at last that she would disappear as her mother had, as her father had. Perhaps that was always meant to be her fate.

Her father had been difficult to predict, prone to sudden storms and bouts of merriment. Her mother had known how to weather his changes, letting the rain pass with little more than a shrug. Luzia tried to follow her example. She learned to endure the deep sadness that fell over him, when all he wanted was to sleep and to be left alone in silence. She'd even made peace with the bursts of anger that seemed to arrive without provocation. But his sudden enthusiasms were harder to bear, his chattering excitement. She would smile and nod along with him, even as she felt herself closing up like a fist. Someone had to be wary, to be practical. Someone had to be ready when it all fell apart.

When he had tipped too far in either direction, Luzia's mother had been there to reach out a hand and steady him. But when Blanca died, he lost his balance. He swayed from moment to moment, mood to mood, chased from one day to the next by loss.

Sometimes he worked and came home for his meals, but more often he would wander from his route and simply stand in the street, talking or weeping, face raised to the clouds, looking for some sign Luzia didn't know. A neighbor brought him home one evening and whispered, "I found him speaking Hebrew outside of San Ginés. I don't know who else heard, but he must be careful."

Luzia had waited, frantic, sure that someone less kind had overheard and would denounce him, that the Inquisition would come for them both.

"If only he had been able to wash her body," she said to Hualit. "If he'd been able to pray for her, to mourn her properly—"

But Hualit had no patience for such talk. "It wouldn't matter if he'd been allowed to plead for her to find menuchah nechonah at the top of his lungs." She tapped her temple. "His mind is unsettled."

Then how do I settle it? Luzia wanted to know. She was twelve years old and she missed her mother and she didn't know how to live with a man who wept and tore his garments, then vanished for days and came back bright-eyed and full of promises and plans.

One morning Luzia realized her father had returned home in the night, but without his cart. She wandered the streets looking for it, as if searching for a lost dog, whispering prayers that it would be around the next corner, the next, that some good and honest person would say, "Oh, not to worry. I knew it shouldn't sit out on the street where just anyone could take it." She had walked until her feet bled, and when she'd finally made herself return home, her father had been whistling as he sat at the table, scrawling notes on the paper they used to wrap the bread. The cart didn't matter, he told her. They would open up a shop.

Eventually he stopped coming home at all. They lost their apartment. Luzia went to work for the Ordoños. Her father would appear sometimes at Hualit's house or in the alley behind Calle de Dos Santos. Luzia would try to feed him, try to get him to stay and talk. He would only take bread if it had been burnt, vegetables if she told him they were starting to rot. If she offered him money, he gave it away.

"He thinks he's atoning," Hualit said. "He can't forgive himself for not burying your mother properly."

One winter Luzia used her wages to buy him a new coat and boots. She had saved for months so that she could know he would at least be warm when he was out wandering. He'd donned the coat proudly, beaming with pride. He'd done a joyful dance in his new boots and told her that a daughter was a blessing.

Two days later, she was walking near the Prado when she saw a group of people gathered by one of the bridges. The cuadrilleros were trying to fish a corpse from the river.

She told herself not to look, to go home, that it was none of her concern. But her feet were already carrying her through the crowd. Her father knelt beneath the bridge, his hands clasped, his face tilted to the sky, exultant. He was barefoot and dressed in rags. He'd frozen to death in the night.

Hualit warned her not to claim his body. He might be a beggar, but he was also a rumored Judaizer. "It's too dangerous, querida," she'd said. "There's nothing you can do for him now. We all end up in the same place anyway."

"I killed him," she had whispered. The new coat and boots had been too fine, too precious. Of course he had given them away. If she had simply left him to his threadbare clothes and worn-down boots, he would have been cold, but he would have lived.

Hualit sighed. "At least he died happy. That's more than most of us can hope for."

Now Hualit was dead too.

Days later Luzia had gone to the bridge. She'd recited what she could remember of El Maleh Rachamim. She prayed that the coat would keep someone warm. She prayed she wouldn't end in the cold on her knees.

All curses require sacrifice, Donadei had once warned her. How she had fretted over those words, over the meaning of sacrifice, when so little ever came from loss. She had killed her father with her love, her fine intentions. Now her love would kill Santángel too. She would destroy him and herself. This would be her offering.

She rested her head on Santángel's chest. "Do you know any real magic? Grand magic? The kind in stories?"

He took her hand, pressed his lips to her knuckles, then he rested their clasped palms against his heart. "Only this," he said as morning drew near. "Only this."

Chapter 53

✦

On the day of the auto de fe, Marius Ordoño chose to stay in his bed. It was a feast day, so he would have to rise and go to mass later. But for now, he would just sleep a while longer. He knew if he rose and requested food, Águeda would prepare something for him but she would do it grudgingly. The meat would be tough. The soup would have no salt. He couldn't help but feel the cook was judging him for Valentina's absence. Besides, the kitchen seemed very far away and the morning was a cold one.

When he rose to relieve himself he heard the sound of some stringed instrument being played, and he wandered through the house in his nightclothes, trying to discover the source. At last he arrived in the empty nursery where a window had been left open. In the house across the way, he could see a woman seated at a harp, her hands moving slowly over the strings. He sat down and listened and after a time he wept.

Across the street the woman at the harp played on, unsure of why she'd chosen to return to the music room that morning when it had been so long since she'd sought pleasure in it. She didn't know whom she was playing for or why she'd chosen such a sad piece. She'd never given much thought to the residents of Casa Ordoño, and so she didn't wonder where the women had gone. She played and played, without thought for the way her fingers stung, or for the scullion who had gazed out the window and longed for music, and who would never hear her song.

In the kitchen below, Águeda and her niece played cards, since there was nothing else to do. Her son sat at the table, fiddling with a spoon and brooding. She had gone to mass that morning and prayed for Luzia's soul. No doubt the scullion had gotten what she deserved for her wickedness, but Águeda could be generous. She made sure to offer prayers of thanks too, that the Ordoños hadn't been imprisoned or had their property taken, that she still had a job and could pay her rent, since her husband was long dead and her son did nothing but mope over Quiteria Escárcega now that the playwright had left for Toledo. Another gift from God. She set a bowl of sweet porridge made with cinnamon and honey before him, commanded him to eat, and said another prayer that it would cure him of his sighing.

The king had arrived in Toledo the previous night. His gout had made the travel unpleasant, along with the news that Pérez had escaped him once again. There were rumors the traitor was sailing for England to find a buyer for his secrets. He cursed himself for his indecision, for letting Pérez proceed with his torneo, for the mad speculation and rumors it had fostered. Today would be the first step in setting all to rights. He would pray with his people. They would be reminded of the cost of heresy and that one might run from Spain but not from God. And when the traitor was caught and La Casilla seized, Philip would make it a holy place. He would let his ministers sell off Pérez's paintings and his heaps of silver cloth. He would have every image of his labyrinth impresa smashed.

When he entered the Inquisition district, Philip saw the elaborate scaffolding and amphitheater that had been raised in the month since the auto de fe had been announced, and he noted that the stage with the rostrum for the Inquisitor General sat higher than the balcony set aside for the king and his children. Perhaps it troubled him or maybe it pleased him, for Philip was a devout man. Who is to know what thoughts fill the head of a king?

Quiteria Escárcega woke at dawn, ate a boiled egg sprinkled with chopped thyme, and wrote furiously for two hours. She had been surprised to receive Valentina's letter asking for help and requesting an invitation to Toledo. In fact, she hadn't quite believed the woman would really make an appearance. But one day a knock sounded at the door and there she was in a surprisingly fashionable cobalt traveling cape, a single sad trunk beside her.

They took up a collection for Luzia among Quiteria's friends, sent letters and requests for provisions to the warden, and consulted priests and astrologers on what more could be done. Quiteria had no housekeeper and she'd thought Valentina might complain, but she'd only set to work, washing clothes, scrubbing floors, and arranging Quiteria's pages in neat stacks that were invariably in the wrong order. She seemed to need occupation and Quiteria didn't mind the help. Neither of them could cook, so they muddled through meals of burnt bread and sardines, subsisting mostly on plates of cheese and olives, and plenty of wine.

One evening over glasses of jerez, Valentina had turned to her and said, "Am I not appealing enough to corrupt?"

When Quiteria had met Valentina at La Casilla, she had sensed that beneath the sour expression and the meager jewels was a woman waiting for a chance to live. From the first kiss, she was proven right. Valentina had a glutton's heart and had spent too many years surviving on scraps. Quiteria was shocked to discover that, after years of infamy and seeking every kind of pleasure, she had finally found a lover who could keep pace with her.

Now Quiteria read back over the pages she'd written, setting them aside carefully so that Valentina couldn't helpfully tidy them into confusion. Her new play was more complicated and more ambitious than anything she'd attempted before. She just hadn't quite settled on an ending. When she was satisfied with the scene she'd written for the character of the lovesick prison guard, she went to find Valentina.

Valentina had woken when Quiteria left their bed to work. She took the time to make herself a cup of chocolate that she hoped would restore her energy after a sleepless night and ease the guilt she felt for enjoying such happiness when Luzia was about to die. She was still somehow surprised this day had come. She wasn't sure what she had believed would stop it, only that she hadn't thought such a thing could really come to pass.

She knew Luzia would have no more need of fresh dresses or linen, but she did the laundry anyway, pressing the cuffs and collars carefully. Then she and Quiteria walked to the Plaza de Zocodover. The streets were thronged with people, the churches bursting with penitents. They prayed with particular fervor this morning, grateful that they were safe from the Inquisition's reach and, for this moment at least, purgatory and its punishments.

The parade that snaked from the prison to San Vicente to the plaza began with the carpenters and masons who had erected the amphitheater, the scaffolds, and the balconies. Among them were the coal provisioners and woodsmen who had supplied kindling for the pyres that would burn at midnight beyond the city walls. Hidalgos arrived on horseback, council members and ambassadors, persons of great renown, in gilded coaches.

"Come," said Quiteria as they approached the plaza. "I can get us good seats. The inquisitors want us all to behold their might."

The auto de fe had really begun the night before when the friars and chaplains and priests gathered to sing psalms and celebrate. In the morning, they said mass, and then breakfast was served to anyone who had a part to play in the ceremony, even those condemned to die. Valentina wondered if Luzia would eat or if she was too frightened.

When the king appeared high above them with Prince Philip

and Princess Isabella, she felt a strange sense of disappointment. After all Valentina's effort and hope, there he was with his children, far more frail than she had imagined.

"He's just a man," she said.

"What did you expect him to be?" Quiteria asked.

Valentina wasn't sure. He wasn't a saint or even a priest. But somehow she had believed that to be in his presence, to be gazed upon by him would change her, give her value, turn her from common lead into something worth keeping.

Quiteria had warned her that the day would be long. First came the horrible spectacle of the parade, the crowd shouting at the penitents in their sanbenitos and pointed pasteboard hats, their feet bare. They carried candles or rosaries, and ropes were tied around their necks, the knots indicating how many lashes they were to receive. Most wore yellow banded with red, but those condemned to die wore black sanbenitos painted with dragons and flames. There were only three of them. From a distance it was hard to see their features, but she recognized Santángel by his height and Luzia by her lack of it. How small she seemed standing on that stage as the crowd jeered and spat at her.

Valentina clutched the sachet of rosemary at her sleeve. For protection.

I'm here, she wanted to shout. I'm sorry. I only wanted a little warmth. I didn't know what kind of fire I would start.

Another mass followed, and then a sermon delivered from the rostrum. Only then did they begin to read out the charges and punishments for lesser crimes like fornication or blasphemy. Valentina had to look away when the floggings began.

They paused for the midday meal, and the inquisitors and king retired while the rest of the friars and chaplains ate at long tables.

Valentina and Quiteria bought pies from the stalls. She'd thought she would have no appetite, but the cold and the boredom had left her eager for comfort. She couldn't reconcile this performance of piety, this purging of sin, with the Spain she knew.

Even in her sheltered time on this earth, she had seen enough drunkenness, swearing, fornication, and corruption to know that life was sinning. It happened all around them, a constant tide of iniquity.

If she herself had ever been truly pious, she certainly wasn't now. She hadn't known what she was reaching for when she'd set out on the road to Toledo, only that she couldn't spend another day with Marius, angry and ashamed, and more lonely than she'd ever been.

"Did you ever wish for children?" she asked Quiteria.

"I have a son. He lives with my husband in Calahorra."

"You have a husband?" Valentina exclaimed. What man could manage such a woman?

"It was a necessity. He's a sweet fellow. He's good with the boy and he leaves me to my own devices, so long as I return every few years to tell him I love him. I think I've always been lacking that thing that would make me a good mother."

"I would have liked to have children," Valentina said. At least she had thought so. Knowing how quickly the world could change, how cruel it could be, she was less sure now.

"It's not too late."

"I am barren."

"Is Marius the only man you've ever fucked?"

"Of course!"

"Then take a lover. Do it quickly, and if you conceive, tell your husband the child is his."

Valentina laughed, then stifled the sound. Despite the tumult around her it felt wrong to laugh, to eat, to think on a future in the shadow of the tribunal. "I wouldn't know where to start."

"I can help with that," Quiteria said, and Valentina turned to hide her flush.

Was it really possible for her to have a child? It would tie her to Marius in a way she wasn't at all sure she wanted to be bound. When she thought of going back to Madrid, she felt only dismay.

After hundreds of years, if there were so many sinners left, what had the Inquisition accomplished? They might root out Jews and Muslims and Erasmists and alumbrados, but then what was left? The machine had been built to consume heresy and impiety, so would it simply keep finding heresy and impiety to feed on? Valentina's soul certainly hadn't been saved. The vicar's threats hadn't made her good, only scared—and not of purgatory. All this spectacle, all this misery, and she didn't fear hell more than being shut up in a house with her lawful husband.

"It's time to return," Quiteria said. "They're going to read the rest of the sentences."

Even those prisoners who had escaped the Inquisition's grasp or died in prison had their charges read. Small pasteboard figures were brought forward and placed in cages where children threw rocks at them. Trunks painted with flames and devils were placed beside them, full of the bones of those who had been sentenced after death and exhumed from their graves. They would be burned at midnight too.

"It used to be worse," Quiteria said. "There was a time when the condemned were whipped through the streets. I don't like to see things suffer."

There are different kinds of suffering, Valentina thought. The kind that takes you by surprise and the kind you live with so long, you stop noticing it.

The day wore on, sentence after sentence, people beaten or sent off to galley service or confinement in prisons or monasteries. They confessed, they repented. Some were banished. Eventually, it was time for the heretics and secret Muslims and Jews who would be banished or exiled. Light ebbed away, as if the sun, like the audience, had grown bored and wished to abandon this wretched sight for happier entertainments.

"The world is a lonely place," Valentina said.

"I have always found it to be a rather cheerful place," said Quiteria. "Though on days like this that can be hard to remember."

Because you are beautiful and charming and talented, Valentina thought but didn't say.

Maybe this was why she'd come, why she'd washed Luzia's linen, why she'd sold off Marius's books to pay for better rations in the prison, why when this was all over, she would join the crowd beyond the city walls, why she wouldn't turn away when the pyres were lit. It had taken years and strange circumstances but she understood now that she and Luzia were lonely in a way that only the overlooked could be.

She was sorry she had made her scullion perform milagritos. She was sorry she'd struck her and called her stupid. Mostly she was sorry that when midnight came and the fires burned, Luzia would be gone, and the world would be lonelier still.

Chapter 54

◆

After so many years of refusing to die, Santángel had been sure he would be afraid to face the hour of his mortality. But he had no urge to weep or wail. He had seen plenty of the world. Without Luzia at his side, he had no wish to see more of it.

The humiliations were over, the floggings and recriminations. Ordinarily the male and female prisoners were kept separate, but there were too few facing the pyre this night for it to matter: only Luzia and Santángel, an old Flemish pirate who had been gagged to keep him from spewing Anabaptist calumnies, some trunks full of bones, and a heap of paper effigies to burn in place of prisoners who had died in prison or fled to countries where the tribunal couldn't reach.

Their candles had been taken, their ropes removed, along with their absurd hats. The tribunal could spill no blood, and execution was forbidden on sacred ground, so they would be turned over to the city authorities to be murdered. Santángel thought they might be forced to ride asses—another gesture of humiliation the Inquisition liked to employ. Instead he, and Luzia, and the pirate were led barefoot beneath the Puerta de Bisagra, past the city walls, and on to the quemadero. Much of the crowd went with them. Some walked in silence. Some prayed. Some were drunk and laughed and heckled.

Last night, when Luzia had come to him in his cell, he'd told her he wasn't sorry to die. He would have gladly taken a few hundred more years, but he regretted how little life she'd gotten to claim for herself.

"I'm sorry for all the things you will never see."

Luzia had laughed. "I feel sorry for all the people who will never get to meet me."

"How can you be so merry?"

"I make no promises, Santángel. I only know that when we were in that audience chamber before the tribunal, I saw a path before me. I don't know if it leads to heaven or to hell, but there's only one way to find out."

"What is it you intend?"

"If I'm to die, I plan to tear a hole in the world as I leave it."

Wild magic. True magic. The kind that had almost killed her. What was there to fear now?

"There's still time to run," he murmured as they climbed the stage. She could sing her bonds away easily, create a cover of darkness.

"Wherever I go they will follow. And I have work to do here still. Pray for me," she said. "Pray for both of us."

He wasn't sure he remembered how.

Coal and kindling had been piled high beneath the platform and atop it. Their sanbenitos were stripped away to be hung in churches, reminders to the parishioners of the Inquisition's power. He made himself watch as she was bound to a post. One of the alguacil's men tied a gag around her mouth.

"What are you doing?" Santángel demanded.

The cuadrillero ignored him. Had Víctor suggested this? Was he afraid of what miracle she might work in her final moments? He could see fear in Luzia's eyes, but he didn't know how to reassure her.

Santángel was next to be bound to the post.

Each moment felt too quick, as if he'd already lost his hold on the world. So many years, so much life lived, and he would leave no one to mourn him.

In the crowd he saw Víctor, and beside him Fortún Donadei. Doña Beatriz was nowhere to be found. Perhaps she'd gone back to her husband. Would Víctor grieve when Santángel was gone? Not yet. Not until his businesses faltered or he stepped on a nail. Not until he felt the lack of what he had so long taken for granted.

Valentina Ordoño was there but not her husband. She stood with that playwright in her crimson velvet jacket. In the light of the flames, she seemed to be weeping.

The executioner passed his torch before their faces one by one.

"In what law do you die?" he asked, giving them a chance to repent and be rewarded with a quick death by strangulation. But Luzia had told him she wouldn't take this route and that he must not either. So he would die as she did.

The executioner set his torch to each of the four corners of the stage. There was no great ceremony. The time for sermons was over. All that remained was the fire.

He could hear the crackle of the flames, feel the smoke already burning his eyes. He turned his head and saw Luzia naked on the pyre, her chin held high. She met his eyes and he had the strange sensation that he was lifting up off the pyre. As the smoke filled his lungs, he could swear he smelled orange blossoms.

Luzia knew Santángel was afraid. She was too. But soon it would be over and either way she would be dead. There would be no grave or any sign she had ever walked this earth, only a sanbenito hanging in San Ginés and one more name in the Inquisition's records.

She searched the crowd and felt a twist in her chest when she saw Valentina. She clutched the dry sprig of rosemary in her hand. She'd kept it with her through this long, awful day.

She could damp the fire rising around her. She could heal herself and even Santángel. She could make the trees that bordered this cursed place shake, or crush the crowd gathered to watch them die.

There was Víctor de Paredes, who had killed Hualit, who had kept Santángel like a tame animal, who had meant to do the same to her.

And there, just as he'd promised, was Fortún Donadei, his golden cross shining on his chest like a holy beacon.

Luzia had known he wouldn't be able to resist appearing here, to share his triumph and her defeat. She had counted on him for the violence of this moment, and she would give him a gift as she passed from one world into the next. He was not the worst of the men here, though he might well suffer the most. But life couldn't offer fairness and neither could she.

Nothing might happen. Or blood might be spilled. Or maybe there would be a miracle for no one to witness.

The flames sounded like they were whispering. The smoke smelled sweet like a cooking fire.

Breathe deeply, Teoda had said. *If you take enough smoke into your lungs you may die before the flames reach you.* She hoped Teoda was safe. She hoped she found happiness and that her angel spoke only glad tidings. She hoped she might see her friend again.

Luzia turned to look at Santángel through the rising smoke. He was watching her with his peculiar eyes. The heat was nearly unbearable. She could feel beads of sweat sliding over her thighs and between her breasts. She should wait, but her panic was growing and she needed to be strong enough to manage this feat.

She sought the words that had begun this journey: Aboltar cazal, aboltar mazal. First the bread made new, then the gown, then the glass. Destroyed and then restored.

She could feel her terror pulling at the song inside her, trying to change its shape. The power wanted to follow. This time she let it. If it wished to be dangerous, to be unwieldy, to grow bigger and more awful than it should, who was she to stand in the way of its ambition?

Luzia trained her eyes on Donadei, on his smug face, and on the fat green emerald at the center of his golden cross, the cross he put his hand to whenever he sought great magic. The only gem that hadn't been altered by her refrán in the third trial, that hadn't become a scarab or a spider or any other crawling thing. When he'd appeared in the audience chamber to denounce her, when she'd seen that emerald just as large and perfect as it had been on the lake, she'd heard Santángel's voice in her head. *A kind of stone, a talisman. They were rare and used for concentrating a sage's abilities. These spells were of such great power they would crack the stone with a single attempt.*

She had heard her mother's voice too, naming the constellations. *Nothing is ever just one thing.*

The scent of orange blossoms filled her nostrils. She could feel Santángel's strength, the power that had met hers that day on her aunt's street, and his influence, the luck that might protect Víctor de Paredes in this moment, that might help to save them too.

Víctor's brow was furrowed, his mouth set in a petulant line. She had no doubt he was the reason for the gag she wore. Or maybe Donadei had suggested it. But they should have known she didn't need her voice, only the words Hualit had given her, Spanish reshaped with the hammer of exile. She'd sung around her own bleeding tongue to heal herself, and she sang again now, finding the letters, just as Santángel had taught her, golden in the dark.

Aboltar cazal, aboltar mazal.

The song spilled through her one last time, splitting, changing, tearing open the world.

A change of scene. A change of fortune.

Chapter 55

◆

That night, in the shadow of the Puerta de Bisagra, not far from the rush of the Tagus river, the traitors Guillén Santángel and Luzia Cotado died by order of the Inquisition, alongside a Flemish pirate known only as Pleunis. They were consumed by earthly flames and passed onward to eternal damnation to burn again and again in the fires of hell.

At least those were the words spoken by Fray Diego, the royal confessor, to his king. If there were whispers that no remains were found in the ashes, then it was deemed further proof they had been creatures of the devil, not mortal at all, but illusions in corrupted bodies.

Those whispers never reached the king, who lay dying behind the walls of El Escorial, his gout burning through him. He was unable to find a comfortable position in which to rest.

Philip had heard what the gargoyle Teoda Halcón had predicted, but he was determined his death would be a good one. He would not plead with God or give in to his suffering. He would show the world how a great man passed on to paradise. He called to his confessor and his brothers and had them bring his precious reliquaries to him, pressing the bones of his saints to his lips. He sought comfort and found little, though he marveled at the scent of orange blossoms that each holy relic seemed to emit. Surely, he told himself, as he wept for Spain and for a loneliness he couldn't name, that meant something.

Doña Valentina returned to Madrid after the execution, but she refused to welcome Marius back into her bed. Instead she invited Quiteria Escárcega to stay along with her loud artist friends. The cook quit, but Valentina didn't seem to care. She hired a new one from the orphanage, who Quiteria taught to read and write, and who had a great talent with sauces. They filled the rooms with singers and actors, artists and poets. They held a ceremony in Luzia's old room over the place where the bodyguard had died. They washed the floor with sugar and drank water boiled with rue. They claimed the spirits had been appeased and great art would be created in the house. They laughed constantly over jokes Marius didn't understand.

When he could bear it no longer, he decamped to the countryside, where he could ride his horses and bemoan his paltry olive groves, which still failed to fruit. Valentina never did bear a child, but she had many daughters, who came from all over Spain to the house on Calle de Dos Santos, seeking sanctuary.

Fortún Donadei did not sleep well that night or any night after. After the execution, his great powers seemed to desert him. He could still sing beautifully and raise a mournful or merry tune on the vihuela. He could even summon the occasional illusion to entertain. But there would be no galleons or singing birds or shadows that did his bidding. His new patron demanded explanations but he had little to offer.

"Why do you never wear your golden cross, Fortún?" Víctor asked him. "Have you had a crisis of faith?"

"I gifted it to the poor," he lied.

He couldn't tell Don Víctor that the great emerald at the cross's center had cracked and why this was so disastrous. The stone that had collected and magnified his gifts, that had made so many milagritos possible, had split in the heat of the flames. He couldn't explain it and yet he felt sure that somehow Luzia Cotado was to blame.

So he told his patron he was feeling poorly, that he was certain his abilities would return. Don Víctor had assured him that he knew a wise man who could restore his talents, who could give him strength and power beyond all he'd imagined. They'd have to travel far to see him, but at the end of their journey, beyond the gates of a southern city, they would strike a bargain.

Víctor had told his disappointing milagrero that they had a trip to take. He had the map and the instructions Tello de Paredes had written in his own hand, and that had been passed from one De Paredes to the next for nearly five hundred years. He told Donadei they would leave soon, any day now. And yet every morning he found new cause to delay.

He was afraid to leave his wife.

He was afraid to travel.

He was afraid of what news the next letter would bring.

When his wife became pregnant, he experienced a dread so vast he had no way to contain it. Fear was too new to him, too fresh, too limitless.

I'll be different when my child is born, he told himself. But when he saw his newborn son lying in his cradle, his fear only grew larger. He could think of nothing but the perils this world held for anything small or helpless. He feared drafts. He feared heat. He called doctors and consulted with astrologers. His holdings dwindled to nothing because he was afraid to make a choice, lest it be an unlucky one.

Eventually his wife left him. "Find me when you're able. I will wait for you," she promised, and went home to her wealthy parents with the baby in her arms.

I will go to her, Víctor vowed. Tomorrow.

We will journey to the southern city and I will regain my vigor, he told Donadei. Tomorrow.

He died that way, alone in his bed, afraid to leave, afraid to stay, afraid to whisper anything but "tomorrow."

In the early hours of the morning, in a cheap room, in a shabby inn, in a disreputable neighborhood in Valencia, a young couple waited for the sun to rise.

Sometime around midnight, three people had appeared on a street near the harbor, naked and streaked with soot. One of them, a Flemish pirate who had somehow been granted a second life, didn't question his good fortune. He pulled the gag from his mouth and, without a word, ran off into the night.

The other two bathed themselves with salt water and dressed in laundry off the line that the woman multiplied with a few whispered words. They had no money, but the man with the ice-colored hair had connections among the outlaws and thieves in every port town.

Now they lay together atop the covers, the door locked, their hands clasped, forehead to forehead.

"If you are the last thing I see," he whispered, "it will all have been worth it."

Perhaps he would have said more, but as the first rays of sun shone through the window, he burned away to ash. Luzia had known her love would destroy him.

She closed her eyes and prayed in Castilian, in Latin, and in the scant Hebrew she remembered. And then she spoke in a language that was all of these things and none of them, the words she'd used to free them. The only real magic she knew.

She breathed in, breathed out, watched the ash gust away from her across the bed, and then his pale body was stretched out beside her once more, made whole as a broken glass had once been made whole.

"Perfect," she whispered as he returned to her in the soft light of dawn.

No one was pursuing them. No one knew they were alive. Luzia had waited until the last second to throw her words into the flames. They had to die, so that they would never be hunted again.

He booked their passage on a boat bound for Holland.

They did not age. They did not change. They traveled the world a thousand times over. They may be traveling still.

Each city is new to them, each shore a strange one. Time has that effect on places, when enough of it has passed. One day they open the gate to a garden in an unfamiliar village. They walk between the orange trees hand in hand. They both think, *So, this place is real*, never knowing they have both dreamed this moment.

Every night she shuts the windows tight to guard against drafts, and every morning he dies and is reborn beside her. She reminds his heart to beat again, as she did so long ago. He kisses her fingers, and combs her hair, and he treasures her, as only a man who has lost his luck and found it once more ever can.

Author's Note

Refranes are essential to Ladino and a vital way the language lives on. It's difficult to know precisely where and when such sayings originated, but the chance that these refranes existed in this particular form, in this particular era, is unlikely. They cross oceans and miles to find Luzia, and I found it acceptable to let them cross time as well.

For the sake of dramatic urgency, I've altered the dates and some of the circumstances of Lucrecia de León's imprisonment by the Inquisition, as well as Antonio Pérez's fall from grace and subsequent flight from Spain. He did escape captivity multiple times—and believed his ability to do so was foretold in his stars. He ended up in England, where he is believed to have inspired the character (and caricature) of Don Adriano de Armado in Shakespeare's *Love's Labour's Lost*. His property was seized by the Spanish crown, and La Casilla became a convent.

Acknowledgments

At Flatiron Books and Macmillan: Many thanks to my editor, Megan Lynch, who helped to guide me through this new territory with kindness and insight. Thanks also to Bob Miller for giving this book a home, Kukuwa Ashun, Keith Hayes, Kelly Gatesman, Katherine Turro, Maris Tasaka, Erin Gordon, Nancy Trypuc, Cat Kenney, Marlena Bittner, Emily Walters, Morgan Mitchell, Vincent Stanley, Peter Richardson, Donna Noetzel, Elizabeth Hubbard, Malati Chavali, Louis Grilli, Meaghan Leahy, Patricia Doherty, Brad Wood, Jenn Gonzalez, and all of our incredible sales team who have done so much for my books and me. As always, thank you to Jon Yaged for the very real magic of this gig.

In the UK: Huge thanks to my team at Viking-PRH, and to Harriet Burton and Vikki Moynes for taking this leap with me.

At New Leaf: I am deeply grateful to Lindsay Howard, Keifer Ludwig, Tracy Williams, Jenniea Carter, Goddezz Figueroa, Hilary Pecheone, Eileen Lalley, Joe Volpe, Alaina Mauro, Kim Rogers, Donna Yee, Gabby Benjamin, the tough and gracious Jordan Hill for repeatedly preventing me from falling over, and Joanna Volpe—my rue and my rosemary warding off the evil eye. Thank you for keeping the faith.

Many people helped me to build Luzia and Santángel's world. I'd like to thank my research assistant, Robin Kello, who fielded so many peculiar inquiries with patience and creativity; Javier

Castro-Ibaseta, who was kind enough to read this manuscript in an earlier form; Robin Wasserman, who helped me to get my head around the Renaissance view of magic and science; David Peterson, who assisted me with Middle Egyptian; the Stroum Center for Jewish Studies at University of Washington and their Sephardic Studies digital collection, Professor Canan Bolel for her translation of this book's dedication to Ladino, and the many people who seek to preserve Ladino and its refranes, including Lela Abravanel, Ladino Uprising/Living in Ladino, Sefardiweb, eSefarad.com, and Michael Castro.

Some of the books and articles that most aided my research include *From Madrid to Purgatory: The Art & Craft of Dying in Sixteenth-Century Spain* by Carlos M. N. Eire; *Power and Gender in Renaissance Spain: Eight Women of the Mendoza Family, 1490–1650*, edited by Helen Nader; *The Jews of Spain: A History of the Sephardic Experience* by Jane S. Gerber; *The Spanish Inquisition: A Historical Revision* by Henry Kamen; *Secret Jews: The Complex Identity of Crypto-Jews and Crypto-Judaism* by Juan Marcos Bejarano Gutierrez; *To Embody the Marvelous: The Making of Illusions in Early Modern Spain* by Esther Fernández; *Speaking of Spain: The Evolution of Race and Nation in the Hispanic World* by Antonio Feros; *Imprudent King: A New Life of Philip II* by Geoffrey Parker; *Daily Life in Spain in the Golden Age* by Marcelin Defourneaux; *Daily Life During the Spanish Inquisition* by James M. Anderson; *Inquisition and Society in the Kingdom of Valencia, 1478–1834* by Stephen Haliczer; *In Spanish Prisons: The Inquisition at Home and Abroad* by Arthur Griffiths; *At the First Table: Food and Social Identity in Early Modern Spain* by Jodi Campbell; *Picatrix: A Medieval Treatise on Astral Magic*, translated and with an introduction by Dan Attrell and David Porreca; *Trezoro Sefaradi: Folklor de la Famiya Djudiya* by Beki Bardavid and Fani Ender; *Ritual Medical Lore of Sephardic Women: Sweetening the Spirits, Healing the Sick* by Isaac Jack Lévy and Rosemary Lévy Zumwalt; "A Conversation in Proverbs: Judeo-Spanish *Refranes* in Context" by Isaac Jack Lévy and

Rosemary Lévy Zumwalt, as published in *New Horizons in Sephardic Studies*; *Lucrecia's Dreams: Politics and Prophecy in Sixteenth-Century Spain* by Richard L. Kagan; *Lucrecia the Dreamer: Prophecy, Cognitive Science, and the Spanish Inquisition* by Kelly Bulkeley; *The Inquisition Trial of Jerónimo de Rojas, a Morisco of Toledo (1601–1603)* by Mercedes García-Arenal and Rafael Benítez Sánchez-Blanco, published as part of Heterodoxia Iberica; "Lelio Orsi, Antonio Pérez and 'The Minotaur Before a Broken Labyrinth'" by Rhoda Eitel-Porter, as published in *Print Quarterly*; and "The Collection of Antonio Pérez, Secretary of State to Philip II" by Angela Delaforce, as published in *The Burlington Magazine*.

In Los Angeles: Morgan Fahey (who helped me to find my way to Robin Kello), James Freeman, Adrienne Erickson, Gretchen McNeil, Michelle Chihara, Sarah Mesle, Kristen Kittscher, Robin Benway, Rachael Martin, Robyn Bacon, and Ziggy, who will tell his own marvelous tales one day. Many thanks to Christine, Sam, Emily, and Ryan Alameddine for being the very best and for the assistance on Arabic. Love and thanks to my mother, who was easily the most excited to hear this story told; to Freddy for snoozing beside me as I worked; and to E, who always knows the right words to put me back together.

Everywhere: Thank you to Zoraida Cordova, Susan Dennard, Alex Bracken, Rainbow Rowell, Gamynne Guillotte, Michael Fernandez, and Ludovico Einaudi, whose music guides every draft. Endless thanks to Kelly Link, Holly Black, and Sarah Rees Brennan for reading the earliest drafts of this book.

Some of my own ancestors fled Spain during the 1492 expulsion. Some remained for a time but were eventually forced into exile. My final thank-you is to the ghosts who kept me company throughout this book's writing.

About the Author

Leigh Bardugo is the #1 *New York Times* bestselling author of *Ninth House* and *Hell Bent* and the creator of the Grishaverse (now a Netflix original series), which spans the Shadow and Bone trilogy, the Six of Crows duology, the King of Scars duology—and much more. Her short fiction has appeared in multiple anthologies, including the Best American Science Fiction and Fantasy. She lives in Los Angeles and is an associate fellow of Pauli Murray College at Yale University.